KAR

Steve Tesich was a screenwriter whose credits include *The World According to Garp*, *Eleni*, *Four Friends* and an Academy Award for the screenplay of *Breaking Away*. He died in 1996, aged 53, just after finishing this novel.

ALSO BY STEVE TESICH

*Summer Crossing*

Steve Tesich

# KAROO

V

VINTAGE

Published by Vintage 1999

2 4 6 8 10 9 7 5 3 1

Copyright © Bambino Productions 1998

The right of Steve Tesich to be identified as the author of this
work has been asserted by him in accordance with the Copyright, Designs and Patents Act, 1988

First published in Great Britain by
Chatto & Windus 1998

Vintage
Random House, 20 Vauxhall Bridge Road,
London SW1V 2SA

Random House Australia (Pty) Limited
20 Alfred Street, Milsons Point, Sydney
New South Wales 2061, Australia

Random House New Zealand Limited
18 Poland Road, Glenfield, Auckland 10, New Zealand

Random House South Africa (Pty) Limited
Endulini, 5A Jubilee Road, Parktown 2193, South Africa

Random House UK Limited Reg. No. 954009

A CIP catalogue record for this book
is available from the British Library

ISBN 0 09 977791 6

Papers used by Random House UK Ltd are natural,
recyclable products made from wood grown in sustain-
able forests. The manufacturing processes conform to the
environmental regulations of the country of origin

Printed and bound in Great Britain by
Guernsey Press Co. Limited
Guernsey, C.I.

# KAROO

# PART ONE

# New York

# CHAPTER ONE

I

It was the night after Christmas and we were all chatting merrily about the fall of Nicolae Ceausescu. His name was like a new song that everybody was singing. The *New York Times* carried a daily box listing the names of all the major players in the current crisis in Romania along with a phonetic guide to their authoritative pronunciation, so everybody at the party made it a point of honor to pronounce all the names properly and as often as possible.

## Pronouncing the Names

SILVIU BRUCAN, an opposition leader: SEEL-vyoo broo-KAHN

NICOLAE CEAUSESCU, the ousted leader: nee-koh-LAH-yeh chow-SHESS-koo

ELENA CEAUSESCU, his wife and second in command: eh-LEH-nah

NICU CEAUSESCU, their eldest son and leader in the city of Sibiu: NEE-koo

Lieut. Gen. ILIE CEAU-SESCU, the leader's brother: ill-EE-yeh

Lieut. Gen. NICOLAE AN-DRUTA CEAUSESCU, another brother: ahn-DROO-tsah

CONSTANTIN DASCALES-CU, the Prime Minister: cohn-stahn-TEEN dass-kah-LESS-koo

ION DINCA, arrested Deputy Prime Minister: YAHN DINK-ah

Lieut. Gen. NICOLAE EFTI-MESCU: nee-koh-LAH-yeh ehf-tee-MESS-coo

GHEORGHE GHEOR-GHIU-DEJ, Mr. Ceausescu's predecessor: GYOR-gyeh gyor-GYOO-dehzh, with hard g's

Maj. Gen. STEFAN GUSA, the Chief of Staff: Shtay-FAN GOO-sah.

ION ILIESCU, an opposition leader: YAHN ill-ee-YES-koo

CORNELIU MANESCU, a former Foreign Minister: kor-NEHL-yoo mah-NESS-koo

VASILE MILEA, the Defense Minister, who reportedly committed suicide: vah-SEE-leh MEEL-lah

Col. Gen. NICOLAE MILI-TARU: nee-koh-LAH-yeh mee-lee-TAH-roo

SORIN OPREA, an opposition leader in Timisoara: soh-REEN OHP-prah

TUDOR POSTELNICU, arrested Interior Minister: TOO-dor post-EL-nee-coo

FEREND RARPATI, Defense Minister: FEHR-end rahr-PAHTS-ih

Col. Gen. IULIAN VLAD: yool-lee-AHN VLAHD.

There was a quality to these names that made them delicious, almost irresistible to pronounce, and made speaking as pleasant as eating canapes.

"nee-koh-LAY-yeh chow-SHESS-koo," somebody shouted his name to my left.

"eh-LEH-nah chow-SHESS-koo," somebody else pitched in to my right.

I drained another glass of champagne and, picking up a glass of vodka, added my own voice to the din.

"The man to watch now," I shouted, "is YAHN ill-ee-YES-koo. I don't think that cohn-stahn-TEEN dass-kah-LESS-koo has much to say anymore about the situation in Romania, I really don't."

"Everything is still in a state of flux," somebody cautioned me.

"Flux or no flux," I insisted, "the man to watch now is YAHN! YAHN ill-ee-YES-koo."

I downed my glass of vodka and poured myself another, Polish vodka this time, with a sprig of buffalo grass or something floating at the bottom of the bottle. It was all totally hopeless but I kept drinking, moving from tray to tray and group to group.

## 2

It was a tradition with the McNabs, George and Pat, to have a day-after-Christmas party but never before had the events of the world conspired to make the party so lively and appropriate. There was so much to celebrate and talk about. There was Havel, the Berlin Wall, the end of the Cold War, the collapse of Communism, Gorbachev, and, for the next few days at least, there were all those Romanians with their delicious-sounding names.

I was now drinking red wine again, which I drank when I first came to the party. In between, I had drunk every form of alcoholic beverage available on the premises. White wine. Bourbon. Scotch. Three different kinds of vodka. Two different kinds of brandy. Champagne. Various liqueurs. Grappa. Rakija. Two bottles of Mexican beer and several goblets full of rum-spiked eggnog. All of this on an empty stomach and yet, alas, I was stone-cold sober.

Nothing.

Not only was I not drunk, I wasn't even high.

Nothing.

Absolutely nothing.

By all rights I should have been strapped to a stretcher inside a speeding ambulance on my way to some emergency detox center where I would be treated for alcohol poisoning and yet I was sober. Completely sober. Lucid. Totally unimpaired. Nothing.

My drinking problem began a little over three months ago.

I had never heard of anyone having this disease before. I didn't know where or how I had contracted it or its cause.

All I knew was that something was wrong with me. Something had snapped off or screwed off or come undone inside of me. It was something physiological or psychological or neurological, some little blood vessel somewhere had burst or clogged, some brain synapse had blown, some major chemical change had occurred in the dark interior of my body or my mind, I really didn't have a clue. All I knew for sure was that getting drunk was gone from my life.

An odd side effect of my drunk disease, probably caused by denial, was that ever since I discovered that I couldn't get drunk no matter how much I drank, I wound up drinking more than ever. I might have become immune to alcohol but not to hope, and no matter how hopeless things seemed I kept right on drinking and hoping that one evening, when I least expected it, I'd get intoxicated again as in the good old days and become my old self.

The music stopped. The record changed but not the composer and, after a brief interlude filled with the din of unaccompanied human voices, it was back to Beethoven. It was, as always with the McNabs, an all-Beethoven day-after-Christmas party.

I poured myself a glass of tequila, a nice tall glass meant for mineral water, and drank it down.

I couldn't understand it. I just couldn't. Blood, after all, was blood and if you put your mind to it and made sure that the alcohol content in your blood exceeded fivefold, all known standards for drunkenness, then you should be able to get drunk. Anybody should. It was a matter of biology. And not just human biology either. Dogs could get drunk. I had read about a plastered pit bull attacking a homeless man in the Bronx and then passing out a few blocks away. Some local kids were later apprehended and charged with intoxicating the animal. Horses could get drunk. Cattle. Pigs. There were wino rats who got pissed on Ripple wine. Bull elephants, I was sure, could get drunk. Rhinos. Walruses. Hammerhead sharks. No living creature, man or beast, was immune to alcohol. Except me.

It was this biological exclusion, the unnatural nature of my affliction, that made me feel ashamed and stigmatized, as if I had contracted a strain of AIDS in reverse and was rendered immune to everything. It was the fear of becoming a pariah in public should my disease become known that made me pretend to act drunk. I also couldn't bear to disappoint those who knew me. They expected me to be drunk. I was the contrast by which their sobriety was measured.

But my immunity to alcohol, as disturbing as it was, was not the only disease I had. I had others. Many, many others. I was a sick man.

Unheard-of diseases with bizarre symptoms were making a home for themselves in my body and my mind. It was as if I were on some cosmic mailing list of maladies or had within me a fatal gravitational field that attracted strange new diseases.

### 3

The McNabs, George and Pat, our hosts, lived in a labyrinthine apartment on the seventh floor of the Dakota. Plants and lamps were everywhere. Quartz lamps. Table lamps. Italian floor lamps with marble bases. Antique lamps with cut-glass Tiffany shades purchased at auctions at Sotheby's. There was a huge crystal chandelier in the huge living room and another huge crystal chandelier in the huge adjoining drawing room. But despite this delirium of illumination, there was something about the McNabs' apartment that devoured light the way Venus flytraps devoured bugs. The atmosphere, far from being sunny and bright, was one of dimness and dusk.

To be drunk in that din of human voices and music and in that twilight was one thing. To be in the merciless grip of involuntary sobriety was something else.

"To freedom!" George and Pat McNab shouted and raised their glasses of champagne in the air. "To freedom everywhere!" Pat McNab added, her voice breaking with emotion.

"To freedom!" Everyone, myself included, replied. We all drank up whatever it was we were all drinking. Mine was another tequila.

The huge Christmas tree—it was at least nine feet tall—was a chandelier in itself. Its countless little bulbs of several colors blinked on and off in time, it seemed, to the music of Beethoven.

For some reason, that Christmas tree, the well-dressed crowd, the toast to freedom, and the chandeliers brought to mind a cruise ship sailing on the high seas.

We would soon be leaving the whole decade of the eighties and cruising into the "new gay nineties," as somebody had dubbed the coming decade. In our wake lay the collapse of Communism, the fall of various tyrants, and ahead of us lay some new New World. Some new New Frontier. A magnificent recording of Beethoven's Fifth was blasting out of the huge Bose speakers as we sailed on. You had to shout to be heard, but the mood of the party was so merry that you felt like shouting.

Despite my array of diseases, or because of them, I shouted along with the rest.

Even my divorce was turning into a divorce disease. My wife Dianah was at the party. I didn't see her arrive, but I caught a glint of her platinum hair under the chandelier in the drawing room before she vanished in the crowd.

We had been officially separated for over two years but saw each other regularly in order to discuss our divorce. These far-ranging discussions at a French restaurant where we always went became, in the course of time, the basis for another form of marriage instead of divorce. We even celebrated the two anniversaries of our mutually agreed-upon separation. Apparently, it was easier for Eastern European countries to topple their totalitarian governments than it was for me to topple my marriage.

Although independently wealthy, she had gone into business for herself since our separation. She owned a boutique on Third Avenue called Paradise Lost. She didn't run the place, she just owned it. Some second-generation Pakistani woman managed the store and its all-women sales force. The store carried dresses, designer T-shirts, and fashionable scarves of various fabrics, all of them bearing images of various endangered species: wolves, birds, bears, the Bengal tiger, the snow leopard, a snail. I could tell, before she vanished in the crowd, that she was wearing one of those dresses herself this evening, but I couldn't tell which doomed creature adorned it.

We made a point of showing up at events we had attended before our separation. Her public position regarding our separation was this: No hard feelings. It was important to her that position be widely perceived, and everybody we knew did in fact perceive it and thought it admirable.

Our adopted son, Billy, had come with her. He was a freshman at Harvard and home for the holidays. Home, in this case, meant our old apartment on Central Park West where Dianah still lived. When I moved out, I got a place on Riverside Drive, going as far west from Central Park West as I could without moving to New Jersey.

No problem spotting Billy in the crowd. He was at least a full foot taller than anyone around him. He was six foot six, or something like that, and still growing. Surrounded presently by older women, meticulously made-up and lavishly begowned. Unlike most boys his age, he seemed at ease in their company.

His face was white, almost snow white, but on each cheek he had a silver-dollar circle of rosy pink so that, despite that strange whiteness of his complexion, it was easy to think of him as rosy-cheeked.

Deepest eyes. So deep-set and dark that from a distance he seemed to have no eyes at all.

His long black hair came down almost to his shoulders, but there was something about Billy which made long hair endearing rather than rebellious.

He saw me and waved. His hand, raised high above his head, almost grazed the chandelier. I waved back. He smiled. The older women around him turned to see who it was he was greeting.

I had an empty glass in my hand and headed for the bar again. I disappeared in the thick throng which obstructed my progress, but I couldn't rid myself of the sensation that Billy, towering above everyone there, could see every move I made.

He wanted something from me. I knew what it was and it was very simple. He wanted to go home with me tonight. To my apartment. Just the two of us. To wake up in the morning and resume something we had begun the night before. Simply to be there with me without anyone else around for once. Just the two of us.

I knew this because it was nothing new. But I also knew, because I knew myself, that I would find a way to keep him from coming home with me tonight.

It had nothing to do with love. I loved Billy, but I was absolutely incapable of loving him in private where it was just the two of us.

That was another disease I had. I didn't know what exactly to call it. Evasion of privacy. Evasion at all cost of privacy of any kind. With anyone.

## 4

I stumbled around, lurching and weaving, bumping into people, apologizing in a slurred voice if I caused their drinks to spill, and then moving on, did my best to appear drunk and therefore normal. It was no fun being an impostor. It was bad enough having been an irresponsible boring alcoholic who was getting on in years, without the necessity now of assuming that identity in order to hide some other, far more calamitous problem.

So I stumbled along from lamp to lamp, from plant to plant and group to group, mingling, engaging, disengaging, drinking whatever came my way and then moving on. I bumped into people I knew who introduced me to others I had only heard about. Some of them had heard of me as well. I met a woman who had gone to school with Corazon Aquino. Before I left her to move on again, I felt that in some genuine and profound way I now knew more about Corazon Aquino in Manila than I did about my own mother in Chicago.

Beethoven's Sixth was blasting away now. Nobody was really sure if the McNabs played all nine symphonies on that day, as they claimed they did, because to play all nine they would have had to start playing them long before the party actually got going. All I knew was that I normally showed up during the Fourth. In the years past, I was pleasantly high by the time I heard the pom-pom-pom-pa-a opening of the Fifth and completely plastered by the time the "Pastorale" rolled around. Not tonight.

Suddenly, I felt ravenously hungry. In preparation for the party I hadn't eaten all day. In the hope against hope that if I had a perfectly empty stomach on which to drink, I would manage to get, if not nicely blotto, at least a little high. It seemed self-evident now, even to a self like myself, that neither would occur tonight. So I began eating, grabbing things off stationary and passing trays, the latter carried by an all-women catering crew dressed in black-and-white uniforms like some New Age order of catering nuns.

I ate whatever I saw, whatever came my way. They were mostly little things stuffed with things. Phyllo dough stuffed with feta cheese and spinach. Stuffed vine leaves. Stuffed cabbage leaves. In between portions of meat, vegetable, and cheese, I stuffed myself with baklava.

Dr. Jerome Bickerstaff, my family physician from the days when I was still a family man and had a family, came up to me while I fed and he just stood there, looking on in disapproval as I devoured desserts and canapés in no particular order. Some of the things I ate had toothpicks stuck in them and I tossed these away, like bones, on the floor.

"Are you all right, Saul?" Dr. Bickerstaff finally asked me.

"No," I gave my standard reply. "Why? Do I look all right?"

I laughed, encouraging Bickerstaff to laugh along with me.

He wouldn't.

"You don't look well, Saul. I haven't seen you in a while, and you look a lot worse since the last time I saw you."

"I do?"

"You do, indeed. You should see yourself."

Because we were at a party, because Beethoven's Sixth was blasting away through Bose speakers, each the size of an imported subcompact car, and because the people around us were shouting almost at the top of their lungs so they could be heard above the din of music and conversation, Dr. Bickerstaff and I were not merely chatting about my unhealthy appearance, we were shouting for all we were worth.

"Your hair," Bickerstaff said.

"What about my hair?"

"A doctor can tell a lot about a person from the look of his hair. Your hair looks dead, Saul. I've seen medium-priced dolls at F.A.O. Schwartz with healthier-looking hair. Your hair looks sick. Dead."

"What were you doing at F.A.O. Schwartz, Doc?"

He disregarded my comment as if he didn't hear it. To be fair to the man, perhaps he didn't hear it. It almost required risking a distended testicle to be heard in that atmosphere.

"And you're putting on weight," he continued, alluding with his chin to my stomach.

"Am I?" I looked down at it.

"Aren't you?"

"I didn't think I was," I said.

"Think again," he said.

Being perceived as overweight hurt. It hurt more than actually being overweight, which I knew I was.

"But I'm not fat, am I?" I pleaded. "I'm not what you'd call a fat man! There is no history of fat people in my family."

"There was no history of money in the Kennedy family either, till Joe came along," he said, a little sorry to be wasting such a gem of a reply on somebody like me. I could tell, because such things are easy to tell, that he was filing it away for future use.

"I saw Dianah a couple of weeks ago," he told me, giving me a grave stare meant to imply that he had more to tell.

"Oh, really." I ignored the import of his stare. "I just saw her myself about half an hour ago."

"Professionally," Bickerstaff explained. "I saw her professionally."

"How is she professionally?" I asked and laughed, encouraging him again to laugh along with me. He wouldn't.

"Is it true what she says?"

"I don't know, Doc. What did she say?"

"She told me, I can't really believe it's true, that you no longer have any health insurance."

"What's to insure," I screamed hysterically. "I no longer have any health."

It was a waste of time trying to be funny around Bickerstaff, but it was a waste of time talking to him at all, so I thought I might as well waste my time in a lively endeavor.

"So it is true," he said and looked away from me as if needing a moment to compose his next remark.

"Listen to me, Saul," he then said and put his hand on my shoulder. Unlike most New Yorkers, Dr. Bickerstaff never touched anyone in public. It was an indication of the gravity of the situation that he did so now. "Please listen to me and listen well. I know you're drunk but . . ."

"I'm not," I interrupted him. "I'm not drunk at all. I'm sober. Cold stone sober." I almost burst into tears at the memory of using these very words not that long ago and actually being drunk when I said them. My overemotional delivery confirmed to Bickerstaff that I was drunk.

"When you sober up in the morning," he went on, "take a good look at yourself in the mirror. What you'll see is an overweight man past fifty who's an alcoholic with a history of cancer and madness in his family. You'll see a sallow man with dead-looking hair. You'll see a man, Saul, who not only needs health insurance, but who needs the most extensive coverage available. If you can, I would advise you to join plans from several carriers."

I took all this in and replied: "But other than that, how do I look to you?"

My flippancy no longer amused anyone. It had never amused Bickerstaff. He shook his head once, like a pitcher shaking off a sign from the catcher and, squinting at me, turned to go. I grabbed his arm.

"Listen to this, Doc. I quit smoking!" The trumpet of the Annunciation could not have been more jubilant than my voice. A point arrives in every man's life when he desperately wants to please his doctor, even if the doctor isn't his anymore.

I couldn't actually hear the groan for all the din around us, but Bickerstaff's face assumed a groanlike expression. It was clear that he didn't believe me.

"I did, Doc, I swear. I quit. Yesterday. Not a puff since then. Not one."

I was telling the truth, but for some reason Bickerstaff's conviction that I was lying seemed far more substantial and authoritative than my truth.

He pulled his arm loose from my hand and his parting look informed me that I had become officially boring. Then he left. The mouth of a medium-sized congregation of people parted and swallowed him whole.

5

The McNabs' apartment had more vegetation per square foot than any other I had ever seen. There were plants around my ankles, waist-high plants, there were veritable groves of trees scattered around the premises. Sections of it could have served as a set for the old *Ramar of the Jungle* TV series. It was one of the most photographed apartments in North America. It had been featured in *Architectural Digest, New York Times Magazine, Vanity Fair, Ms.,* and at least a dozen other publications. From what I'd read of the devastation caused by acid rain, I was sure that this apartment had more greenery than did whole communities in the Ruhr Valley.

To the accompaniment of the "Pastorale" I stumbled around from grove to grove until I found one to my liking. There I sat down underneath a canopy of leaves and resumed drinking.

People came and went as they tend to do at parties. Singles, couples, trios. They lingered in my grove a while and then moved on. We talked about the chow-SHESS-koos, Bucharest, Broadway, and the Berlin Wall.

People I barely knew and who barely knew me seemed to know all about me and I all about them. In the Information Revolution the world really had become a global village and, as in the villages of old, gossip was once again the dominant form of communication.

George Bush had a mistress.

Dan Quayle was gay.

One of the most dispiriting side effects of my inability to get drunk was not just that I was sober while this global village gossip went on but that I would remember it the next day.

Loss of memory was one of the true pleasures of getting drunk and when I was my old healthy self and drunk every night, I would wake the next morning feeling refreshed and completely oblivious of the night before. Every day was a brand-new day with no strings attached. Every morning was a new beginning. I was in synch with nature. Death at night, birth and renewal in the morning.

It all changed when I contracted my drunk disease. Ever since then whatever I did or said or heard the night before greeted me the morning after. A new, merciless continuity entered my life which I was not equipped to handle.

In the Tuesday Science section of the *New York Times* I had read an article on physics that described the theoretical possibility of the existence of antimatter in outer space, antiworlds, entire antigalaxies composed of subatomic antiparticles.

It made me wonder while I sat in my grove and gossiped along with the rest if, in this yin-and-yang scheme of things, an anti–Betty Ford clinic existed where diseased ex-alcoholics like myself could get help. Where my immunity to alcohol would be reversed and my system, after a two-week stay, would be completely retoxified by trained professionals.

My grove began to fill up with people. Some stood. Some sat. All of them talked and when they talked they had to shout if they wanted to be heard and all of them wanted to be heard. I was neither included nor excluded from various conversations. It was up to me. They babbled. I babbled back every now and then. It was therapeutic. The booze was having absolutely no effect on me, but the meaningless babble was almost intoxicating.

A horrific possibility suddenly presented itself to me. I wondered, what if my immunity to alcohol extended to other chemicals and drugs? Pain. Horrible pain. Unbearable pain. What if I came down with unbearable pain that no chemical substance could alleviate?

I saw my wife coming toward me. Serene, smiling, with a glass of champagne held away from her body, she looked like somebody crossing the grand ballroom of the *QE2* to invite me to dance.

She stopped and just stood there, looking down at me.

"Would you like to sit down?" I offered and motioned to get up.

She shook her head and said, "No, thank you."

I slumped back in my chair and took in the dress she was wearing. The endangered beast du jour was an owl. There were little endangered owls all over her dress. A flock of little owls with those big, round eyes stared at me from her bosom and her belly. If I didn't mend my ways, their eyes seemed to be warning me, I too would end up on an endangered-species list someday. Maybe even on a dress like this.

"Nice dress you're wearing. What kind of an owl is that?"

"Anjouan scops owl," she answered, sighing, as if she was wasting her breath even talking to me.

"I thought so." I nodded. "Delightful-looking birds. They look like a jury of insomniacs."

I laughed, inviting her to laugh along with me, knowing ahead of time she wouldn't. She didn't. She didn't even acknowledge the invitation. She just looked at me.

My wife. She was still my wife. My married life was over, but my marriage went on.

Dianah's face had all the features of this year's beautiful women. Everything about it was prominent. Eyes. Cheekbones. Lips. Teeth. Her platinum-blond hair extended at least six inches away from her ears, like some flung-open raincoat. The effect of that coiffure seemed to be that she was flashing me with her face.

"I don't suppose you noticed that your son was here," she said as her gaze wandered past me to the people in my grove whom she was summoning as witnesses to our conversation.

"Billy? Sure I noticed. He's hard not to notice. There he is." I pointed across the room where, in the distance, his head dominated the horizon.

"He needs to talk to you, Saul. He really does. What's that on your shirt?"

I looked down at my crumpled blue shirt. Some stuffing from one of those canapes I had devoured had fallen and landed there. Some reddish stuff. I tried to brush it off, but it smeared. The resulting stain made it seem that I had been gored.

She sighed, rolled her eyes, and looked away.

"You're drunk."

"No," I shook my head. "Not even close. I'm completely lucid and, sad to say, all my faculties are intact."

Some moral perversity made it pleasant for me to speak the truth in the complete assurance that it would be rejected by Dianah. The more sober I claimed to be, the drunker I appeared. Her conviction that I was drunk was so strong that for a moment at least I felt myself getting high on her conviction.

"Please, Saul. Enough. I'm tired of these games. Everyone here—" again she swept the grove with her gaze, summoning witnesses "—can tell you're drunk. You're not fooling anyone." She stopped, heaved a huge sigh, and resumed. "We were talking about Billy, if you don't remember."

"I remember. He wants to talk to me."

"Not wants. Needs. He needs to talk to you."

"Fine, have it your way. He needs to talk to me. What does he need to talk to me about?"

I had to look away from her dress. All those large, unblinking owl eyes were making me nervous.

"He's your son, Saul."

"I know that."

"What does any son want from his father?" she addressed the gallery in my grove.

"Beats me," I replied.

"He wants to be with you. He *needs* to be with you. I can't remember the last time you spent any time alone with him."

"I can't either, but it doesn't mean it didn't happen."

She raised her eyebrows, disgusted by my flippancy, and then proceeded again, slowly, patiently.

"He wants to go home with you tonight. He needs to spend a couple of days with you before he goes back to school. This is very important to him, Saul. Very, very important, and if you have any feelings for him . . ." She went on.

She had managed, in the short time she was there, to silence all the other conversations in the grove and now, as she went on, she had the full attention of all those people sitting or standing on either side of us. I was grateful for the presence of this audience. If marriages, like parades and parties, were strictly public affairs, Dianah and I would still be living together and I would probably consider myself happily married. It was the privacy, our time alone, that ruined my marriage. Not public privacy as we were having now, but private privacy. Just the two of us. In this regard, at least, I was totally blameless. I had done all I could to avoid all private moments between us.

"Fine, fine," I gave in. "You're right. You're absolutely right. I'll take him home with me tonight."

"You will?" She regarded me with suspicion of rare vintage. "You won't try to get out of it as you always do, will you?"

Of course I would. I knew I would. But I lied.

"I promise I won't," I said.

"You promise!" She laughed. The owls on her belly and breasts fluttered as if in preparation for takeoff. "You could pave all the potholes in Manhattan with your broken promises, darling. You know that. You do know that, don't you?"

I did indeed and so did probably all those people in the grove who were listening to us.

"Do you think I'm putting on weight?" I asked her, patting the stain on my shirt and the stomach underneath the stain.

She winced and sighed.

"Surely, darling, a fat monster like you has more important shortcomings to consider than the weight you've gained."

To be called a monster was one thing. To be called a fat monster hurt.

"Really? Do you think I'm getting fat?"

"You're falling apart, sweetheart. Physically, emotionally, spiritually, and psychologically."

"So then, you think that at least intellectually I'm still . . ."

"You," she cut me off. "You're like the last days of the Ottoman Empire. You're the sick old man of Manhattan."

An attentive audience always brought out the best in her.

"Don't you think, then, that it would be a bad idea to have somebody like me spending time alone with Billy?"

"I certainly do. He deserves a better father, but unfortunately for him you're the only father he has. You're spilling your drink, darling."

I was. I tried foolishly to brush the spilled bourbon off my thigh.

The "Pastorale" concluded. In the short hiatus without music, Dianah just stood there looking down at me and then gazing to her right and then to her left at the people in the grove. I was, she soulfully conveyed to them all, a cross she had to bear. And then Beethoven's Seventh began.

She asked me, in that bearing-the-cross voice she now assumed, if I had done anything about my health insurance.

"Yes," I lied. "I did."

"You're lying," she said.

"No, I'm not," I lied. "I'm covered. Completely covered."

Lying was nothing new for me. What was new was the ease with which I lied now.

"You haven't even noticed." I switched from lies to truth the way liars like to do. "I've quit smoking. Not a puff since yesterday. Not one puff. Cold turkey. Just like that." I snapped my fingers. "I think I've done it this time. I really do."

"Oh, Saul," she sighed.

I heard myself circumscribed by her sigh. She knew me, and everybody who knew me seemed to know me, better than I knew myself. Our audience in the grove had no doubts that either A, I was lying, or B, I would start smoking again very soon.

"The only thing you've quit cold turkey, my darling, is telling the truth and taking responsibility for your actions. You have become a menace to us all."

She turned to go and then stopped.

"By the way," she said. "This is the last time I'm going to ask you to come and take your father's clothes out of my apartment, or I'm going to give them away."

My father died three years ago. Cancer of the spine. The cancer worked its way up his spinal column to his brain. It took a while for him to die and for the last months of his life he was completely mad.

In his madness, he came to believe that he had two sons. The good son, Paul, whom he loved madly. And the worthless son, Saul, whom he hated, just as madly. I had no idea, whenever I visited him, which son he would see in me. It varied from visit to visit, from day to day, from hour to hour. Sometimes in mid-moment, in a blink of an eye, he switched from one to the other. All I could do was play along.

As his good son, I conspired with him and castigated the behavior of my worthless brother. As the worthless son, I sat in silence and contrition while he raved and condemned me to various forms of capital punishment. "I sentence you to death," he told me over and over again. He was, before his premature retirement, a judge in the criminal court system in Chicago and when he sentenced me to death it was in his capacity as a judge, not father. Before he died, he left an insane will behind.

In that will he commuted my sentence of death to life imprisonment without parole. To his good son Paul he left all his clothes. My mother, for reasons of her own, could not bring herself to throw his clothes away. She prevailed upon me to take them and, as the good son, I took them back to New York. When I left Dianah, I couldn't bring myself to throw away his clothes either, but I certainly didn't want to take them to my new apartment.

"Fine, fine," I now told her. "I'll come and get them in a few days."

"You've said that before."

"I promise," I lied.

"This is the last time I'm going to ask you, Saul."

"This is the last time I'm going to promise, Dianah."

She turned to go again and stopped. Arrested for a moment in mid-flight, she bestowed upon me one of her famous forgiving looks. Forgiveness not just for the many, many wrongs I'd done up to now but, being the kind of man I was, forgiveness for the many, many wrongs I was bound to commit in the future. It was a look of daunting forgiveness. Were I to live two hundred years, I couldn't imagine how I could possibly commit enough wrongs to warrant a forgiveness of that size.

And then she left, turning this way and that as she worked her way through the crowd, leading with her champagne glass. Her platinum hair brightened and dimmed as she walked past various lamps. In the distance, at the far end of the room, towering above the throng, I saw my son. His head was bowed as it always was when he conversed with normal-sized people.

He brought to mind a sunflower.

## 6

A short time later, I left the grove myself. I moved around the rooms, mingled, drank, and babbled about the realignment of the nations of the world. I could babble about anything. The less I knew about the subject, the more convincing I sounded to others. To myself as well.

I loved parties at other people's apartments. I had developed a home disease of some kind and felt at home only at other people's homes. Almost always I was the first to arrive and the last to leave. The ambiance where music thundered and men and women screamed banalities at each other appealed to me.

It appealed to me as well (in an on-again, off-again kind of way) to think of myself as The Uninsured Man. I was positive that I was the only uninsured man there. This knowledge filled me with a reckless bravado. How bold of me! How independent. I not only took my uninsured status in stride, I made it a part of my stride as I journeyed from plant to plant and lamp to lamp and group to group. The Uninsured Man.

A European gentleman at the party did the European thing and offered me a cigarette before lighting one himself. No, I told him, no thank you. I quit. Not a puff since yesterday. Those around me who knew me laughed as if I were either telling a joke or lying. Strangely enough I really was beginning to feel that I was lying. That I hadn't quit at all. Telling the truth was one thing, but feeling in touch with the truth after telling it was something that no longer seemed to depend on me. It was granted me or denied me by the response of others. It was a disease, a truth disease, and one of its symptoms was that I felt much more at home in other people's truths than I did in mine. Even when their truths were the exact opposite of mine.

Wherever I went, I could see Billy in the crowd, keeping his eye on me lest I slip away and leave without him. Fleeing from my son's eyes as if from an assassin, I moved on.

I had to pee and, doing my best imitation of a drunk who had to vomit, I stumbled into the McNabs' men's room and locked the door behind me.

One of the many decorative touches of the McNabs' apartment was that they had a clearly marked men's room and ladies' room. The signs on the door were antiques that their fabled interior decorator Franklin had found for them.

The men's room, in addition to a toilet, had a large antique public urinal. Another Franklin touch. The urinal rose from the floor half up to my chest. Its old porcelain was marbled with cracks and its overall color was the color of unhealthy old teeth of smokers like myself.

I unzipped my fly and fished out my prick and leaned toward the urinal.

There were plants in the men's room as well. So many plants that I felt I was taking a piss outdoors, in the park.

Used to be, whenever I peed all I had to do was point and shoot and wherever I pointed that's where I shot. It was one of those activities I could do, and enjoyed doing, with my eyes closed.

No more.

My prostate was putting the squeeze on me. Like a pistol firing bullets out of the side of the barrel, my piss went wide left or wide right, or suddenly dried up to a dribble. Looking down, I observed a whole new development. Instead of a single stream, there were two streams shooting out of my prick like a V-sign. And all the time there was the burning sensation as if I were pissing ReaLemon.

There. I was done. I shook my prick and flushed. I sucked in my gut and zipped up my fly. The song of the ages sang in my ear: You can shake and you can dance, but the last drop always goes down your pants.

On top of the marble sink was an ashtray from the Plaza Athénée Hotel in Paris. Inside the ashtray was an extinguished cigarette, two-thirds unsmoked. I glanced at it and looked away. I washed my hands.

My latest attempt to stop smoking had been motivated primarily by my inability to get drunk. Lung cancer seemed like a terrible way to go, but what really terrified me was the thought of not even being able to get drunk on the day I got the news.

Years ago, I was completely cured of smoking and didn't have a cigarette for almost three months. I was cured by a procedure I had been positive was a hoax. Hypnosis. The hypnotist was a Hungarian named Dr. Manny Horvath.

I took the treatment just to prove to a friend who had recommended it that the whole thing was a hoax. I went to Dr. Manny Horvath's office positive that I couldn't be hypnotized in the first place, not to mention be cured of smoking.

How wrong I was. Dr. Manny Horvath hypnotized me in record time. When I came out of the trance, the mere thought of a cigarette filled me with nausea. For several weeks, I chastised other smokers and proselytized the virtues of hypnosis.

But the cure, good for my cigarette habit, proved disastrous to the rest of my life.

I discovered that I loved being hypnotized and that the hypnotic trance into which Dr. Manny Horvath had put me never really left my mind. It was like plutonium or strontium 90. Once inside of you, it was inside of you for good. I learned, much to my surprise, that I could put myself in a hypnotic trance without any help from Manny Horvath. And so whenever I encountered some crisis in my life that I found too difficult or painful to handle, I simply drifted off into my self-induced trance and cured myself, so to speak, of the need to deal with it. The mere thought of dealing with crisis filled me with nausea.

This caused chaos in my life. Personal. Interpersonal. Professional. Everything.

In the end, in order to cure myself of this nausea for dealing with life's problems, I had to cure myself of my newfound belief in hypnotism. I had to unhypnotize myself. And in order to do that, I had to prove to myself that Horvath was a charlatan who had never really cured me of smoking. And to do that, I had to start smoking again. It was very unpleasant at first, but eventually I was back to two packs a day and bad-mouthing Horvath all over town.

In the mirror above the sink, I saw my face. Instead of waiting until tomorrow morning, as Dr. Bickerstaff had suggested, I decided to take a real good look at myself now.

Everything he told me seemed true. My complexion was sallow. My hair did look dead.

Was I fat? Or was I a burly six-footer, as I had come to think of myself?

The face of The Uninsured Man in the mirror did not seem sure of anything, nor was there even a hint now of that bravado of being uninsured.

I took a couple of steps back in order to see more of myself. I pulled the shirt out of my trousers and lifted it up to look at my gut in the mirror. It was not a pleasant sight. I was still a six-footer, but burly was too kind a description for the six feet of flesh I saw.

No doubt about it. I was at the age when things break down. The probability of somebody my age developing prostate cancer was high. Other cancers as well. Spleen. Pancreas. Lungs, of course. Lungs, by all means. All those years of smoking. But cancer wasn't the only threat. The number one killers of white males in my bracket were the diseases of the cardiovascular system. All those years of smoking, and drinking, and eating suicidal orders of lamb chops and cottage fries. Clogged arteries. Like jammed telephone lines. And all the time, even if I was doing everything right, my brain cells were dying by the tens of thousands, so even if I managed to avoid crippling heart attacks and cancers of various kinds, I had senility to look forward to as my reward.

But, for the moment at least, the prospect of these catastrophic illnesses, the prospect of succumbing to them in my uninsured state, seemed of far less consequence than something else. Something else was wrong with me, which made the threat of these known and documented diseases of no more concern than the common cold. Something was drastically wrong with me and whatever it was, it was wrong through and through. I didn't know what it was. I didn't know if it was something I was getting or something I was losing, but I knew, the way animals know that an earthquake is coming, that something huge was coming or going in my life. It hadn't come yet fully, if it was coming. It hadn't gone yet fully, if it was going.

So instead of it being a cause of concern, my unhealthy, flabby body, with its numerous disease-prone organs inside, was a sight, so to speak, for sore eyes. The hardening of my arteries while everything else went soft, the deterioration and the devaluation of my body, the shortness of breath, the pounding in my temples after the slightest exertion, the painful burning sensation when I peed—all these were blessings almost, welcome reminders all of them, that I was not totally abnormal and that my condition was something that I had in common with other people at the party and the rest of my fellow men. To be sick in this way made me feel healthy almost.

I sucked in my gut and tucked in my shirt, huffing and puffing as if I were setting up a circus tent.

Drawing close to the mirror, I took one last look at my face, and the face that looked back could have been anybody. Who was I to claim that I had stopped smoking when all those good people out there were positive that I hadn't? They knew me better, all of them, than I knew myself, and basking in their knowledge and conviction and wanting so much to belong to a community of some kind, I plucked the cigarette from the ashtray and put it in my mouth. I then rejoined the party, looking for a light.

I smoked the rest of the night, borrowing cigarette after cigarette from the few smokers at the party. Everyone seemed pleased and relieved to see me smoking again. People like to be right about other people and I enjoyed having their view of me confirmed. Even Dianah and Dr. Bickerstaff, despite the almost operatic show of disapproval, seemed gratified to see smoke coming out of my mouth again.

7

Beethoven's Ninth began to play. This was the McNabs' polite, musical way of announcing that the party was winding down. Some, like Dianah and Dr. Bickerstaff, had already left. Others were leaving now. The huge rooms were becoming depopulated even before the first movement was over. The catering nuns were cleaning up, their friendly smiles no longer in evidence. Like scattered outposts, little groups of people were all that remained of the once mighty throng.

My son Billy was waiting patiently for me, chatting with some older women he had met during the evening. They were now leaving but had sought him out for a few final pleasantries. He obliged them all.

It had become a trait of his, this ease he had around women who were old enough to be his mother. He was far more comfortable around them than around girls his age. The women, in turn, were enchanted by him, as was the woman he was talking to now. Billy's presence, his proximity, was making her act a little silly. She kept touching him and throwing back her head to laugh.

Listening to the last symphony that Beethoven wrote, I was reminded of Billy's childhood. He was born with a little hearing problem which an operation corrected, but his habit of leaning toward the speaker in rapt attention, his head turned ever so slightly to favor his good ear, remained. It now gave him a quality of being eager to hear what somebody had to say, and that made an already beautiful young man positively irresistible.

I had habits of my own and one of them was to get overly sentimental about Billy prior to hurting him. The party was winding down and I had to dump him, get rid of him somehow. The question was not if I would do it but how.

The best way out of taking him home with me tonight was to take somebody else. Some woman. Any woman. Drink in one hand, a cigarette I had bummed in the other, I stumbled off on a hunt for an unescorted female. I scanned the horizon for signs of smoke, like a tourist lost in a wilderness and looking for civilization. In the various adjoining rooms, there were tight little clumps of people still left, but only one wisp of smoke other than mine.

Three men were there and five women and one of the women was smoking. But she wasn't the one for me. She was far too vital-looking. The kind of woman who carried Mace in her purse and Mace in her eyes. As a hunter of women I was long past my prime, like some aging predator. A successful hunt was now not so much a function of my masculinity as of the chance encounter with a lame or sickly prey, which the rest of the healthy herd would want culled from their ranks. I sidled up to the group and took in the chatter. The chatter was about Gorbachev.

I smoked, listened, nodded significantly, and inspected the females for signs of weakness, low self-esteem, and general lack of group dominance. Everybody had something to say about Gorbachev, but I quickly noticed that when this one young woman spoke, nobody seemed to be listening. The only beta there. Neither the men nor the other women, alphas every one of them, seemed to have much use for her.

"He's so different," the young woman was saying of Gorbachev. "There isn't a politician in this country who would dare run for the highest office in the land with that big blemish on his head and yet it's that very blemish that makes him look so . . . so . . ."

"So human," I jumped in.

"Yes." She turned her squinty eyes toward me. "That's what it is. So human. It makes him look so very, very human."

It didn't take the others long to perceive the purpose of my interest in the squinty-eyed woman. They exchanged little looks and little smiles which she failed to observe and then, amused by the whole thing, the game, if you will, they withdrew, letting me know in a mocking kind of way that she was mine for the taking. I bummed a couple of very long cigarettes from the Mace-eyed woman before she left and then turned all my attention on the abandoned young woman before me.

We exchanged names. Hers was Margaret. Margaret Mandel. Peggy, I started calling her.

"Only my daddy still calls me Peggy," she said, swaying as if the floor were rocking.

"Well, since I'm old enough to be your father, I will too," I told her.

Her eyes got all misty. She was dead drunk but trying hard to appear sober. I was the other way around. With a little token maneuvering on my part, I knew that I could get her to come home with me tonight.

She was not totally unattractive. I like squinty-eyed women, and she was almost pretty in that squinty-eyed way of hers. The fact was that I had no real or virtual desire to take her home and sleep with her. I would do my best to seduce her as I was seducing her now, but it was a seduction with an ulterior motive. To keep my son away. She was somebody else's child and if I had to be alone with somebody tonight, it was easier with a total stranger, somebody else's child rather than my own.

We talked politics, perestroika, glasnost, the fall of the house of chow-SHESS-koo. The quality of banalities we exchanged never slipped below the acceptable level. By and by, I steered the conversation back to fathers. When trying to seduce women under thirty, I always zero in on their fathers. When they're over thirty, I've learned that it's much more productive to inquire about their former husbands or lovers, or in some cases siblings.

"Are you close to your dad?"

"We were. We were very close at one time."

"And now?"

Her eyes welled with drunken tears.

"Now—" she shrugged and shook her head "—now, I don't know. Something's changed, but I don't know what it is. He just seems to . . ."

She went on. I lit another cigarette and listened. I had a talent for inspiring strangers to open up to me. It was not so much a talent, actually, as a knack, the same kind of knack I had in the profession I pursued. I asked questions about my colleagues' lives and then I listened. They mistook, just as Peggy was doing, the affection they felt for the sound of their own voices, the closeness they felt to their own stories and memories, for a closeness to me.

This technique was not always as cold-blooded as it was tonight. It was something that had evolved during my drunken days when I was simply too far gone to do much talking myself, when in fact I had no idea what I was doing and was innocent of using any technique at all. The unfortunate consequence of my disease was that the technique remained even though I could no longer get drunk. To be perfectly sober and completely conscious of using this technique was not pleasant. But it wasn't unpleasant enough to stop me.

It was getting late. The last little group of people was heading toward the door.

"Shall we?" I asked Peggy. The question was pitched perfectly to cover the next ten to twelve hours of her life. Although drunk, she understood its implications. She took a deep breath, drained her glass, and said: "Yes, let's go."

Billy was waiting for me in the foyer, by the coat rack. He was already wearing his long, down-filled jacket. He was ready to go and seemed to have no doubts about where he was going. His innocence was maddening. It both infuriated me and made me love him all the more. Made me all the more determined that someday, somehow, I would make it up to him. For the harm I'd caused him over the years and for the hurt I would inflict upon him tonight. In one fell swoop. That's how I envisioned myself doing it. In one magnificent fell swoop.

"Peggy, this is my son Billy. Billy, Peggy."

He nodded easily, smiling, gazing down at us like a streetlamp.

Peggy seemed stunned either by the beauty of Billy's face or by this sudden and puzzling appearance of my son. Were we all going to my place together? And what would we do when we got there? After all, the boy she saw was much closer to her in age than I was. Something bothered her. A hint of reluctance appeared in her eyes, but she was too drunk and too committed to do anything about it now. Her face assumed a blank expression of somebody awaiting further instructions.

Out we all went, into the corridor, to the choral accompaniment of Beethoven's "Ode to Joy."

The ancient, hydraulic elevator of the Dakota descended at the speed of radioactive decay. The decline and fall of Rome, it seemed to me, probably occurred faster. I had no idea how these hydraulic elevators worked, but if this elevator used water then judging by the speed it probably needed to have water evaporate to go down, and condense to go up.

There were seven of us crammed into the small car which was paneled with dark stained wood. We were in the back. Peggy was on my right, Billy on my left. The other two couples stood in front of us. They were reassuring each other in a lighthearted way that the elevator was in fact moving.

"How can you tell? I can't feel anything."

"It's moving."

We all looked up at the panel of numbers and saw number 6 light up. The McNabs lived on the seventh floor. Here, then, was conclusive proof that we had traversed one whole floor.

"Only five to go," a man in front of me said, and we all chuckled. Sensing a receptive audience, he added, "Who knows, maybe by the time we land, the Democrats will be back in power."

"I think the Democrats built this elevator," a woman next to him said.

We all chuckled again. And then, as so often happens after jokes, good or bad, things got silent.

I desperately wanted a cigarette. I was fully readdicted to tobacco. In addition to this craving, I was feeling a mounting hostility toward Billy for being so goddamned blind to the situation. What should have been settled upstairs was not. I dreaded the thought of actually having to tell him when we got out into the street that he was going one way and I another. I felt victimized by his innocence. And then there was Peggy. I could see out of the corner of my right eye that she was staring up at Billy. Transfixed. If I could have found an easy, graceful way for the two of them to go home together to her apartment and let me go home alone to mine, I would have.

It was bitter cold outside and no cabs were in sight. Two waiting limos took our foursome away. The liveried Dakota doorman left his little guardhouse and stood out in the street, looking up and down for a taxi.

I smoked. The three of us shivered.

The cold front, which had killed a dozen homeless in Chicago, frozen citrus crops in the South, and stranded barge traffic in the ice of the Mississippi, was now blowing through Manhattan along Seventy-second Street.

Billy, being Billy, seemed to have no doubts that he and I were doing the gentlemanly thing and getting a cab for this Peggy in a fur coat, after which we would get one for ourselves or, if need be, walk together to my apartment. He even seemed to be shivering in a recreational way, going along with the bitter cold Peggy and I felt rather than feeling any himself.

What the hell was I going to do with him?

I smoked and babbled. I asked him about life at school. I gave him credit, in that macho way I sometimes assumed when I was around him, for having a lot of girlfriends at Harvard. I asked him if he had seen his old high school flame, Laurie, while in town. No, no he hadn't. But they did talk on the phone. Did he remember, I asked him, how her mother used to bring her over to our apartment to watch me shave?

"She's a wonderful girl, Laurie. Wonderful. I'll never forget that time when she . . ." I babbled on.

A bright yellow cab, almost like an apparition, shot out of Central Park, and the Dakota doorman raised his mittened hands in the air and began waving. The cab stopped. The doorman opened the door. I slipped a five-dollar bill into his mitten. Peggy got in. And as I followed her inside the cab, I gestured to Billy to come along.

In the snow-white whiteness of his face I saw his deepest dark eyes take in the momentarily puzzling situation and with computer speed come up with the wrong solution. The scarcity of cabs was such that we would drop off this Peggy in the fur coat first, and then the two of us would continue to my apartment on Eighty-sixth and Riverside Drive.

Tripodlike, he tucked in his long limbs and sat down next to me in the cab. He shut the car door with a flourish as if, with a combination of magnanimity and innocence, he was slamming shut once and for all the book in which was recorded the history of all my past misdeeds.

His height was all legs. Mine was all torso. Sitting next to each other, we were of equal size. I waited until the cab was in motion and said, putting my arm around his shoulder, "We'll drop you off first."

My tone could not have been more loving and caring, but the trouble with language is that it sometimes has a content in addition to the tone, and the content of my words caught him totally off guard. The wind and the cold, to which he had appeared youthfully immune when we were standing outside, fell upon him in an instant. His body stiffened under my arm, I could feel him shivering.

I told the driver Dianah's address. He could have made a U-turn but he didn't. We went straight across Seventy-second and then took a left on Columbus Avenue. The heater in the cab was on full blast. It was, if anything, too hot inside, but Billy couldn't stop shivering.

And I couldn't stop babbling. It was a short ride, but I made it long by babbling the whole way.

Not only did I not want to take my son home with me, I didn't want to take the memory of his disappointment and hurt home with me either, I wanted to be free of both son and memory, if possible. I had to disarm him somehow and dilute the pain that he was feeling, so I wouldn't have to think about it the next day. If only I were drunk, I wouldn't have this problem.

The Berlin Wall was going down, but I brought it up again. I resurrected the ghosts of the dead chow-SHESS-koo and interposed the executed tyrant and his wife between myself and Billy.

What did he think, I asked him, of chow-SHESS-koo's execution. Was it, in his opinion, the correct thing to do under the circumstances or was it an ominous precedent for the future of Romania? I argued both sides and gave him credit for being profoundly concerned about the recent developments in Eastern Europe. The credit of concern I extended to him was almost impossible for a boy like Billy to refuse, impossible for him to be selfish enough to say out loud that his own personal concerns were of such a high order that they overrode those of an entire nation. He had no choice but to identify himself with people who cared, as I was pretending to, about the larger issues in the world. I knew this. I knew my son. And so I babbled on. About the poor, unwashed orphans found living in cages like animals. About the endemic reliance of the people of Eastern Europe on paternalistic tyrants for political order. On and on.

When the cab finally stopped in front of Dianah's apartment building on Central Park West, my former home, I dropped Europe like a piece of junk mail.

"It was good to see you, big guy," I told him. I stepped out of the cab with him and, while Peggy and the driver looked on, because they were looking on, because I had an audience, I gave him a kiss on each cheek.

"Good night, Billy. Good night."

"Goodbye, Dad."

"I'll call you," I shouted and waved from the cab.

The cab made a loop and a few minutes later we were driving once again past the Dakota, as if the detour with Billy had never occurred. The driver didn't mind if I smoked, so I smoked. I had him stop on Broadway so I could pick up a carton of cigarettes and then we went on.

When Billy left, some part of Peggy, however small, left with him. It was as if we had dropped off some daydream of hers and she was now sitting in the backseat of the cab with reality itself.

I smoked and talked about Billy the rest of the way. I told Peggy, and spoke loudly enough so the driver could hear me as well, what a wonderful boy he was. How much I loved him. How proud I was of him. What a priceless privilege it was to be a father. The further away we got from the actual Billy, the closer I felt to him.

There was certainly no need for me to tell Peggy and the cab driver that Billy was adopted, but one of the symptoms of my truth disease was to flaunt unsolicited truths to total strangers.

"Adopted. Really?" Peggy's whole face squinted at me.

"Yes. He was just a baby when we got him."

"He's so beautiful," Peggy said. "So very, very beautiful." And then she started crying, sobbing like a sentimental drunk in a manner much older than her years.

"But who," she cried, "who in the world would give away such a beautiful boy?"

We stopped at a red light and the cab driver turned his head, as if waiting for me to answer.

# CHAPTER TWO

I

The unseasonably cold weather didn't last long. It was replaced by unseasonably warm weather, and the first week of the new year, 1990, and the last decade of the twentieth century began on the note of unseasonableness.

My friend Guido (my very last friend) and I were pausing before parting outside the Russian Tea Room, where we had had lunch. Both of us took turns commenting on the un-Januarylike January we were having.

"It's like spring."

"It's like Indian summer."

"I had to turn on my air conditioner."

"Me too."

Glancing at the enormous wristwatch on his big wrist, Guido sighed. "I better get going," he said. "Damn nuisance, this Maria mess."

"You'll find somebody," I reassured him.

I waved. He waved. We parted, he heading east and I west.

The Maria mess had to do with Guido's cleaning woman. His former maid, Maria, had suddenly quit to return to her country of origin and he needed to find another maid to clean his apartment.

Almost every cleaning woman of the people I knew in Manhattan was named Maria. Dianah and I had a Maria when we lived together. She stayed with Dianah when I moved out, and I got an apartment and a Maria of my own. The McNabs, George and Pat, had a Maria. The name Maria was no longer a name to me, it was a job description. I never saw my Maria after I hired her. She came to clean on Fridays, and even when I had absolutely nothing to do at my office I made sure not to be home when she came.

Something is called for when you have another human being in your apartment. Some minimal human transaction is required, which I prefer to avoid when it's just me and one other human being. This evasion of privacy extended even to somebody like my Maria.

I paid her in cash, leaving the money on the dining room table under a heavy glass ashtray. When I returned in the evening, the apartment was clean and the money was gone.

My memory of this woman, who worked for me for almost two years though I never saw her again after hiring her, was of a woman between thirty and fifty. She was dressed in black for our interview, as if she were in mourning. Short arms. Short legs. A sturdy-looking body with no discernible waist. Indian features. Her neck was tucked in the whole time we talked, as if her people had been taught by history, by the Spanish conquistadors and the Catholic church, always to keep their necks tucked in.

My phone was ringing when I entered my office, but it stopped before I could get to it.

## 2

The telephone rings.

I light a cigarette and pick up.

"Hello."

"Mr. Karoo?"

It's a woman's voice, and although I haven't heard it in a long time, I know who it is.

Some people specialize in remembering faces, others remember names, with me it's the sound of the voice. Once I've heard somebody's voice, I never forget it.

"Hello, Bobbie," I say.

Her name is Roberta but everyone calls her Bobbie, and not just Bobbie but, for reasons unknown to me, "that Bobbie woman."

She works for Jay Cromwell, though her little cubicle of an office in Burbank (which I saw once) isn't even attached to Cromwell's office. It's off by itself down the corridor.

I have never actually seen her. I only know her voice, and her little throwaway laughter which brings to mind the sound of a cigarette lighter being struck.

"It's that time of year again," Bobbie tells me. "I just want to make sure my Rolodex is up-to-date."

She rattles off my two telephone numbers, home and office, and my two addresses, home and office, and I confirm that yes, that is me all right. No, I still don't have a fax, I tell her. Yes, I lie, I'm thinking of getting one next year.

Shifting gears, she inquires, "Do you plan to be in town, in New York, I mean, on the twenty-second and twenty-third of February?"

"Yes," I tell her, "I think I will be in town on both of those days."

"Mr. Cromwell is planning to come to New York for the presentation of the Spirit of Freedom Award to Vaclav Havel, and he wants to know if he could see you while he's in town. At first he didn't think that he could attend the ceremony, but a change in his schedule . . ."

She goes on, telling me what a very busy man Mr. Cromwell is and how he is really looking forward to seeing me.

She is sure, she tells me, that Brad will be calling me soon to verify the dates and the particulars.

"I'd rather have you verify my particulars, Bobbie," I tell her.

She laughs her little laughter into my ear and then, wishing me a good day, and I wishing her the same, we hang up on each other.

3

Perhaps it's ironic but, despite my many diseases, my nickname in the business is Doc.

Doc Karoo.

I'm a small but comfortable cog in the entertainment industry. I doctor screenplays written by somebody else. I rewrite. I cut and polish. Cut the fat. Polish what's left. I'm a professional hack with a knack that's come to be regarded as a talent. People who live in LA and do my kind of work are called "Hollywood hacks." The term "New York hack," for some reason, does not exist. A hack in New York is called Doc.

I have never written anything of my own. A long, long time ago, I tried, but after several attempts I gave up. I may be a hack, but I do know what talent is and I knew I didn't have it. It was not a devastating realization. It was more in the nature of a verification of what I had suspected all along. I had a PhD in comparative lit, I was a Doc to begin with, but I didn't want to teach. Thanks to some contacts I made, I segued quite painlessly into my true calling, where for the most part I rewrite screenplays written by men and women who don't have any talent either.

Every now and then, very rarely, of course, I'm given a screenplay to fix that doesn't need any fixing. It's just fine the way it is. All it really needs is to be made properly into a film. But the studio executives, or the producers, or the stars, or the directors, have other ideas. I am confronted with a moral dilemma. I am capable of having a moral dilemma because I have this mascot within me called the moral man, and the moral man within me wants to stand up for what's right. He wants to defend the script that doesn't need fixing from being fixed or, if nothing else, he wants to refuse to be personally involved in any way in its evisceration.

But he does neither.

The moral man within me feels uncomfortable and pretentious at these times. He feels, as I do, the burden of precedents we have set for ourselves. Why should we stand up now for what's right when we remained comfortably seated on other, much more crucial occasions? In this way, the moral dilemma becomes diluted and rationalized, and I accept the assignment and the money that comes with it, enormous sums of money, knowing ahead of time that my contribution, my rewriting, my cutting and polishing, can only cause harm or ruin to the work in question.

These occasions, when I'm given something I admire to ruin, are fortunately very rare. In the last twenty years or so, I have eviscerated no more than half a dozen screenplays and of those only one still haunts me.

The young man who had written the original screenplay for Cromwell showed up uninvited at the sneak preview of the film in Pittsburgh. I now remember only two things about Pittsburgh. I remember the beautiful view from my hotel suite of the confluence of the Allegheny and Monongahela Rivers and the painful scene that the young (he was so young) writer caused in the lobby of the theater after the film was over.

Like some clean-shaven Jeremiah, he shrieked at us, trembling with rage. The director was a pimp. The producer, Jay Cromwell, was a fucking monster. The studio executives were castrated piranhas. I was a worthless slut. Personally, I had no quarrel with any of these terms. They seemed quite accurate to me. What hurt me was seeing how hurt he was. He wept while he tried to insult us, not realizing, because of his youth, that we could not be insulted. He was too young and he had loved what he had written all too much. He never wrote again. Perhaps it was unrelated, it's hard to know for sure with these things, but a year or so later he committed suicide. I still remember the sound of his voice. The film, like all films produced by Cromwell, did well at the box office and my reputation as a man who can fix troublesome screenplays received yet another boost.

Most of the time, however, I work on screenplays that are so bad I could have written them myself.

My job for the most part involves cutting the fat and adding jokes. I'm handy at both. I get rid of subsidiary characters, dreams, and flashbacks. I cut the scenes in which our hero or heroine visits his or her mother or his or her favorite high school teacher. I get rid of aunts and uncles, brothers and sisters. I have cut entire childhood sequences from the lives of characters and have left them up there on the screen without a mother or a father or a past of any kind.

I keep my eye on the story line, the plot, and I eliminate everyone and everything that doesn't contribute to it. I simplify the human condition of the characters and complicate the world in which they live. I'm aware at times that this approach has been put into practice in real life, that men like Adolf Hitler, Joseph Stalin, Pol Pot, Nicolae Ceausescu, and others have incorporated some of the techniques of fixing screenplays into their endeavors. Sometimes I think of all tyrants as being glorified hacks, rewrite men like myself.

In addition to working on screenplays that were taken away from their original writers, I have also been employed, thanks to what somebody called my "facility with celluloid," in fixing completed films that were taken away from their directors.

The work is essentially the same. I sit in the screening room with a producer or studio executives and watch the film. I do what I always do. I follow the story line. I suggest cuts, reversal in the order of scenes. I look at the outtakes and rummage through them for bits and pieces that could be put back. I recommend pieces of music with which to underscore certain scenes and, in extreme situations, when no other means of giving a film cohesion are available, I recommend voice-over narration, which I then write. Sometimes the powers that be follow my advice and make the changes I suggest. Sometimes they don't. Sometimes they hire another fixer. Sometimes they hire a whole team of fixers. If the film I've worked on succeeds commercially, I get a lot of credit in the so-called film community, and my reputation grows. If the film I've worked on does not succeed commercially, even if it fails completely, I'm never the one who is blamed. That film joins the ranks of those films that "even Doc Karoo could not fix."

I am paid extremely well for what I do. Thanks to Arnold, my former accountant, who now manages Dianah's financial affairs, thanks to him and his conservative but relentless management of my money, I am a wealthy man. If I'm not independent in any other way, I am financially independent. I don't have to worry about paying the outrageous rent for my office on West Fifty-seventh Street. I only have to worry about what I do when I get there.

One other worry has emerged recently. It seems to me at times that all the so-called fat that I cut from all those screenplays and films is beginning to wreak its revenge on me. There is mounting evidence that my personal life is now composed almost exclusively of those very fat, unnecessary scenes that I so skillfully eliminated from the films and screenplays of other people.

# CHAPTER THREE

## I

*Dear Dad,*

*Even before I begin this letter, I'm afraid of what might happen to it. I have observed you over the years and seen how you make little distinction between what's private and personal and what's not. I have watched you repeatedly betray the confidence of your former friends over dinner in some restaurant by converting their sometimes painful affairs into witty stories with which you entertain others. I don't know why you do this, but I do know, because I have seen it happen over and over again, that when the energy drops at one of those dinners, and the chatter starts to fade, you will dredge up and say anything just to pick things up again. I beg you to make an exception this one time with this letter: Don't tell others about it, not even Mom. Don't quote me, don't paraphrase me to others. Please. If we can have nothing else that's strictly private, just between the two of us, then let this letter serve as our one and only private event. I will continue this letter as an act of faith that you will respect my wish and not betray me as you have done so often in the past. So, with that out of the way, let me begin again:*

*Dear Dad,*

*I have not been keeping track of time, but both of us are aware, I'm sure, that for years now, a paralysis of some kind has set in between us. I'm not sure when it started, because it's taken me this long just to accept the fact of its existence. No, we're not drifting apart, to use a phrase my friends use when talking about their own parents. It would be better if we were, because then the* possibility would exist that eventually I would drift far enough from you to no longer feel the pain of proximity without contact.

But we're not drifting, Dad. There is no motion of any kind. There is only the sad spectacle of a father and a son frozen in time.

I have thought about this a lot and in my opinion it has nothing to do with the fact that, biologically speaking, you're not my real father. The issue here, Dad, is not blood and biology. What's missing between us is something that should exist between any two human beings who have known each other as long as we have. There either was, or I chose to believe there was, an unspoken promise which I took to heart when I was very young. It was a promise of wonderful things to come. Some test awaited me, or a series of tests, and if I successfully negotiated them, that would eventually lead to a loving relationship between us. In a way, I've had a very happy childhood because I believed so blindly in the promise of things to come.

I am now neither young enough anymore to go on believing blindly, nor old and cynical enough to dismiss the possibility of your love and move on to other things.

Tell me the truth, Dad. Please, if you know the truth, tell it to me.

To learn the truth, that I can never have what I want from you, would probably be very painful, but not nearly as debilitating as this wondering and waiting. I'm held in check, Dad. While I wait for your love, close ties with others are held in abeyance. Lovely girls come and go, friends come and go, love comes and goes and I never ask it to stay because I'm waiting for you.

At the risk of oversimplifying the situation, let me remind you that what I need from you is not all that much. You need not fear that I want to take over your life, or that I have some dark, forbidding agenda.

Until you sensed that I had no use for it anymore, you were always willing to be with me in public. To take me to a play or premiere or sneak preview or some other public event, and then afterwards, with others, to dine in some restaurant where the event we had just attended became the event again. I die in public as if upon a stage. I play the part of a public son badly.

Let me, not always, but every now and then, let me be the event. Please understand that I have no specific scene in mind that I want to play with you. It's the very absence of a scene I yearn for. My daydreams of being alone with you are all of an inconsequential sharing of time, of basking in ease and inadvertence.

I know I'm taking a chance by writing this letter. I don't know you well, Dad, but I do know you well enough to know that you might find it easier to sever all ties with me rather than address the issues in this letter. If you must *do that, then you must. It will be better than the position in which the two of us find ourselves in now, where we languish like two chess pieces of an abandoned game.*

*Your loving son,*
*Billy.*

*PS. I hope you don't find this postscript patronizing but please, if nothing else, get yourself some health insurance. For my peace of mind, if not yours.*

## 2

It was neither warm nor cold. The sun was shining, but something in the air prevented it from being a sunny day.

Folded *New York Times* under my arm, my son's letter in the inside pocket of my sport coat, I waited on the corner of Eighty-sixth and Broadway for a cab.

A brand-new yellow cab lunged to pick me up. It could not have been newer or yellower. I put out my cigarette, got in, and we headed downtown.

The interior of the cab was overheated. There were two large, dangling car deodorizers in the back, one on my left and one on my right. They were green and shaped like Christmas trees, dispensing a sickening pine scent.

I rolled down the window.

The traffic moved slowly but steadily. I loved motion. I loved the feeling that I was getting somewhere.

I crossed my legs and thought once again about Billy's letter. I had already thought about it Monday, and yesterday, but in the fatherly mood that I was in, nothing was too good for my son. Not even putting in overtime and thinking about his letter three days in a row.

His letter truly moved me when I received it on Monday. I was moved by it off and on for almost the entire day. On Tuesday, I decided to do something about it, and the issue I chose to address in his letter was in his postscript to me.

He was worried about my having no health insurance. If I got health insurance, I reasoned, I could then call him and tell him not to worry. I could tell him that I had become insured again because he had advised me to do it. The way I saw it, he would feel flattered that I had taken his advice. The two of us could then have a nice chat on the phone about the whole thing and, in the process, disregard everything in his letter that had preceded it.

Therefore, yesterday, first thing in the morning, I called my new accountant, Jerry Fry, and told him to get me reinstated with Fidelity Health, my former carrier. Jerry congratulated me on coming to my senses finally. I told him I was doing it for my son, whom, as he knew, I loved very much. He congratulated me on my fatherly feelings and told me to leave it all to him.

"Leave it to me, Saul," he said, "You'll be all set by tomorrow."

Today, I would call Jerry from my office or he would call me from his office, and another one of life's little problems would be resolved. I considered several opening lines to Billy when I called him tonight and opted for "Billy? It's Dad. Guess what, Big Guy? I'm covered again . . ."

I lit a cigarette.

"No smoking," the driver said. There was an edge to his voice, as if he had warned me once before not to smoke. "I have asthma," he added with authority.

I took one last, quick puff and put out the cigarette in the shiny new ashtray.

Judging by the number of cab drivers who suddenly claimed to have asthma or some other respiratory disease, one might easily assume that the large cab companies had made it company policy to hire only the hard of breathing. Even Afghan and Pakistani drivers, who spoke not a word of English and had no idea where Lincoln Center was located, knew how to say, "No smoking. I have asthma."

My driver looked like a combination lumberjack and linebacker for the Chicago Bears. He took up three-quarters of the space in the front of the brand-new Peugeot he was driving. The windshield, had it been just a little smaller and just a little bit more curved, could have been a pair of goggles he was wearing.

There was something festive about this cab ride. It was my farewell tour as The Uninsured Man. In honor of which, I decided to befriend the hulk who was driving me.

"What kind of asthma do you have?" I asked him. I knew he was lying, by the sound of his voice. There was always a melody to the sound of lies, which I recognized as a tune I sang myself.

He pondered the question.

"What do you mean, what kind?" He checked me out in the rearview mirror. "What kind of asthmas are there?"

"I don't know. You're the one who's got it."

"It's just asthma," he said, rolling his big shoulders. "Regular asthma. Haven't you ever heard of people with asthma?"

"Yes, I have."

"Well, that's what I've got. Asthma. I smell smoke and bingo!" He snapped his fingers. "I get an attack just like that."

"Really?"

"Yeah, and it's no joke, believe you me."

I nodded as if I did.

"What's it like?" I couldn't resist asking him.

"What's what like?"

"To have an attack."

"Of asthma?"

"Yes."

"It's terrible. Positively terrible," he said, wagging his head slowly.

He had a neck like a Sunday pot roast. When he wagged his head, a nature show on PBS flashed through my mind. The grizzly bear from the wilds of Montana, wearing a radio collar. Now relocated and re-trained and driving a cab in Manhattan.

It was a pleasure to be driven by him. I couldn't smoke in the cab, but I much preferred to be deprived of my cigarette by an out-and-out liar like himself than by an impersonal city ordinance sign. I was pre-disposed toward liars. Being a congenital liar myself, I took to others with the same affliction. There were no longer any truths I had in com-mon with others. Lies were my last link to my fellow man. In lies, at least, all men were brothers.

"It's terrible, huh?" I asked. I didn't want the subject to die, the lying to end.

"To have an attack of asthma?"

"Yes."

"It's more than terrible. Believe you me, mister, you don't want to know."

"That bad, huh?"

He looked at me again in the rearview mirror and asked, a little sus-piciously, "You ever have asthma yourself?"

"No."

My answer reassured him.

"It's terrible. Horrible. Positively horrible." He was getting expan-sive, feeling his oats. "It's like . . . like being held underwater in a pub-lic swimming pool. That's what it's like. You ever been held underwater in a public swimming pool?"

"A long time ago," I lied.

"That's what it's like. Only worse."

"Worse?"

"Yes, worse. Because with asthma you can't come up for air. See. Because when you come up for air, there's no air. There's only more asthma."

"Sounds pretty bad, all right."

"Bad, nothing. It's positively horrible."

"How long have you been an asthmatic?"

"Been what?" He sounded suspicious again.

"Asthma. How long have you had asthma?"

"Oh," he nodded. "Since birth."

"That long?"

"Yes. Runs in the family."

He changed lanes constantly, but his bulk obscured the steering wheel from my view. From where I sat, he looked like he was steering with his shoulders, lurching left, lurching right, throwing the Peugeot around like a toy.

"Do you have any other diseases?"

"No, just asthma. I thought I had something else, but it turned out I didn't. Why do you ask? You a doctor or something?"

"Of sorts."

"Oh, yeah?" He got suspicious again. "What kind of a doctor are you?"

"A movie doctor," I told him, and I tapped my temple with a finger when I saw him looking at me again in the mirror. "If you have bad movies in your head, I fix them up."

He thought about this for a bit and then came up with the answer.

"A shrink? Is that what you are, a shrink?"

"Yes," I lied, out of courtesy for all the lies he had shared with me.

"You're in the right city, that's for sure. No shortage of sick individuals in this burg. I see all kinds."

"I bet you do."

"People walking around the city with cornflakes for brains. You make eye contact with the wrong guy and you're dead."

He stopped the cab in front of the building where I had my office.

"Nice talking to you," I told him and gave him a big tip.

"Thanks a lot, Doc."

3

I sit at my desk and smoke, reading the *New York Times*. An old floor lamp with an enormous shade, reminiscent of hats worn by Edwardian ladies, is my primary source of light. There is track lighting overhead, but I never use it.

On my desk is a typewriter, a large black Remington, a screenplay I'm supposed to be rewriting, a telephone, an answering machine, and a large ashtray.

To my left, facing south, is a window with venetian blinds looking out on West Fifty-seventh Street. There is a large air conditioner in the window. It's on "high" at the moment. I like the sound it makes. I chose this particular model for the sound it made. At the height of our marriage, Dianah and I used to rent a house in Easthampton for the summer. It was close to the ocean and at night, through the open window, I could hear the ocean waves attacking the beach. It's not quite the same thing but close to the sound my air conditioner is making now.

To my right is a bookcase, with books I've kept since my college days. My comp lit collection.

In the southeast corner of my office is a pyramid of cardboard boxes. Inside the boxes are my word processor, printer, and two years' supply of printing paper.

In a sudden fit of passion to keep up with the times, I purchased the word processor a little over five years ago. While I waited for it to arrive, I proselytized the virtues of having a word processor to one and all. I convinced Guido that he simply had to get one himself. And he did. When mine finally arrived, the accompanying owner's manual in three languages filled me with despair. The more I read it, the more I despaired. A few days later, I put everything, including the owner's manual, back into the cardboard boxes and moved them to the southeast corner of my office, where they still reside. At the time of my purchase, the equipment was on the cutting edge of technology. It is now, for both me and its manufacturer, a relic from the past.

I light another cigarette and turn another page of the *Times*.

## 4

The rent on my office is exorbitant. The trade-off is that my office is located at an exorbitant address. I recently renewed my lease for two more years. When the new lease goes into effect, my rent will almost double to keep up with the rising exorbitance of the location. Money's not the problem. I can afford it. My problem is that I no longer need an office. I have more than enough empty rooms in my apartment where I can do my rewriting.

A nostalgia for my rotten marriage comes over me. I don't so much miss living with Dianah as miss having a Dianah to leave five days a week in the morning. To have a Dianah for a wife not only made going to the office in the morning a matter of some urgency, it made being in the office itself a constantly pleasant reminder that I was not at home.

When I left Dianah, I no longer had a motive for being in my office. It was no longer a refuge, it was just an office.

More about Romania in the *Times*. The students who made the revolution and toppled the old regime don't know how to make a new government. The people who know how to make a new government are the people from the old regime who were overthrown by the students. Those very people are now coming back to power in Romania. The students feel betrayed.

I feel for them. I find many analogies in the turmoil in Romania to my own life. Poor students. If they think they feel betrayed now, wait until they grow up and start betraying themselves. It gets bad when you have only yourself left to topple for life to get better.

I turn a page.

## 5

The homeless are becoming a nuisance. There are more and more of them. It's a new decade and there is a new impatience with this old problem.

Racism is on the rise on college campuses. Hate crimes are on the rise. I read the story carefully and make a mental note to remember it as a useful topic to interpose between myself and my son when I call him tonight. Should things get tense in our conversation after I tell him the good news about my health insurance, I could go right to it.

"Oh, by the way, Billy, I've been meaning to ask you something. There are all these stories in the paper about the rise of racism on college campuses. What, in your opinion, is causing this to happen? Do you have any idea?"

## 6

I take a short break from the *Times* and regard the screenplay I'm supposed to be rewriting. It's almost an historic occasion. I have rewriter's block. I've never had it before, but this particular screenplay has given it to me.

The problem with the screenplay I'm supposed to be rewriting is that I rewrote it once already. That was three years ago. It had another title then, and it was with another studio. At that time, the problem with it was that it had no plot. It had a cast of characters larger than a high school graduation class but no story. So I got rid of all kinds of people and gave it a story line. It then moved on to be rewritten several more times by other rewriters. Now it's back on my desk with a whole new set of problems. Now it's all plot and no characters. In the intervening years, its plot has not only thickened, it has congealed. It has become the La Brea Tar Pits of plots. Our hero, his friends, his enemies, his love interest are all trapped in the tar pits, but you can't tell one from the other. My job is to fix the problem and give our hero and his love interest a sense of humor.

I consider the possibility, as I regard the 118-page screenplay on my desk, that in the near future rewriting one screenplay will provide a lifetime of work for a team of rewriters like myself, the way the building of a single Gothic cathedral did for generations of medieval craftsmen.

## 7

The telephone rings. I snap out of my trance. I rub my hands, anticipating a call from Jerry Fry, who will inform me that Fidelity Health has taken me back into its family of insured Americans.

I pick up the phone.

It's Guido. Calling to tell me that he will have to cancel our lunch at the Tea Room this Friday. He's going to LA on business. Guido Ventura, my last friend, is a talent agent.

We chat. He tells me about the clients he has lost and the clients he has gained and the new client he hopes to snare in LA, and implies that the arithmetic is in his favor. I could remind him that the clients he has lost he once considered irreplaceable and that the clients he has gained, including this client he hopes to snare in LA, he once found beneath contempt. But I don't. He is my very last friend and I don't want to lose him. And besides, since I tend to balance my books using the same moral arithmetic he employs, who am I to talk? So I concur with his results and wish him happy hunting in LA.

I light another cigarette and, while waiting for Jerry to call, continue my journey through the *New York Times*.

## 8

The Arts and Leisure section. Theater reviews. Movie reviews. Music reviews. Book reviews. TV reviews. I read them all. There's a tone that emerges, the tone of Arts in review, which is like a wonderful gin and tonic to me, or what a gin and tonic used to be. I can no longer get drunk, but this tone makes me high.

I think about Billy's letter while I read the paper, but my thoughts are now in tune with the tone in the *Times*.

I now appreciate his letter on a whole other level. His command of the English language. His mature style for one so young. His ability to explore emotional territory without becoming overly sentimental. His easy alliteration. His vivid imagery.

The more I praise his letter to myself, the more the point and the purpose of it fade.

This is a new disease I have picked up. I don't know what to call it. It could either be called an objectivity disease or a subjectivity disease, depending upon how you look at it.

The symptoms are always the same.

Despite my nauseating preoccupation with myself, that self seems to slip away rather easily. Try as I might, I am unable to remain subjective about anything for very long. An hour or so, a day or so, a couple of days at best, and my subjectivity leaves me and I move on to begin observing the event in question from some other point of view.

I don't do it on purpose. My mind simply moves on and starts to orbit the event.

The event can be a person, an idea, an issue, a heartbreaking letter from my son. It doesn't matter what it is, the fact is, it's only mine, truly mine, subjectively mine, for a little while. And then I start to orbit. I circle the issue, the idea, the letter, the telephone call. I see it from many different angles, various points of view. I do this until I become almost totally objective. Meaning that I can no longer experience how I felt about the letter, the telephone call, the idea, the issue, in the first place. Meaning that I can no longer summon any subjective emotions about the event one way or another. Meaning that it no longer has any meaning for me.

I turn a page.

## 9

The telephone rings.

Jerry, I think.

"Hello, sweetheart."

It's Dianah.

I tell her that I can't talk to her now because I'm expecting an important phone call. She laughs and sighs. She laughs and sighs all in one sound. The only woman, the only man, woman, or child I know who can do that.

"Oh, Saul," she laughs and sighs.

I have never heard the sound of my own name used against me so effectively.

"I'm not kidding, Dianah," I say, trying to be firm but friendly, "I have an important business call I'm expecting, so if you wouldn't mind . . ."

She cuts me off.

"Maybe this is it, sweetheart. Maybe I'm the call you've been waiting for."

"I hate to be rude, Dianah, but . . ."

She cuts me off again.

"Oh, I *know*," she says. She is speaking in italics now. "It's pure *hell* for you to have to be *rude*."

Her words, if printed on a page, would require several fonts to do it justice. The months of painstaking labor that it took for the monks in the Middle Ages to create a single illuminated letter, Dianah can conjure into existence in an instant with the sound of her voice.

We go on in our adversarial way. Me telling her that I can't talk, she telling me in sounds more than words what she thinks of me. I try to resist, but eventually I become enraptured by the brilliance of her performance. She's in wonderful voice today. I could be listening to Hildegard Behrens doing Wagner and not my wife, Dianah, doing me in on the telephone.

Finally, she tells me what it was she wanted to tell me when she called.

"I've given away all your father's clothes to this church group that was making a collection for the homeless. I warned you I would do it if you didn't come to pick them up and so I've done it. Somebody around here has to keep their word and we both know, don't we, darling, that it's not going to be you. Ciao, darling. You have yourself a wonderful day, all right?"

She hangs up.

## 10

While I smoke and wait for Jerry to call me, I grow more and more certain that it was a disastrous mistake on my part to have ever left Arnold, my former accountant.

I was very fond of Arnold. An accountant from the old, almost Dickensian school. He even looked like an accountant. His father, I was sure, had been an accountant. Gaunt, pale, overworked, nearsighted. Unlike Jerry Fry, with his tan. There is something suspicious about an accountant with a year-round tan, who keeps a tennis racquet in his office.

I could have kept Arnold and told Dianah to get a new accountant but, as a way of easing the strain of separation and providing some continuity in her life, I decided to be generous and get a new accountant myself. So she kept Arnold and continuity, and I got Jerry. With his tennis racquet.

I've only had Jerry for a little over a year and already I'm uninsured.

Somewhere along the way, a fuckup occurred with my health insurance carrier, Fidelity Health. According to Jerry, although his office informed them of my change of billing address, some dippy secretary at Fidelity kept sending my premium-due notices to Arnold's office, just as they had been doing for the last twenty years or so. And, according to Jerry, some dippy secretary at Arnold's office kept sending them back to Fidelity, with a note saying that I was no longer with Arnold but without telling them who it was I was with now.

By the time the fuckup was discovered, my health insurance policy was canceled.

In all fairness to Jerry, as soon as the fuckup was discovered, he wanted to institute reinstatement procedures on the spot. The fault from then on was mine. It struck me as a novelty, an almost pleasant change of pace, to find myself uninsured. So I told Jerry to do nothing until he heard from me. I wanted, I told him, to consider my options.

"What're you talking about?" Jerry wanted to know. "What options? Being uninsured is not an option."

But the longer I remained uninsured, the better it felt. I had so many personal problems and diseases that were, I suspected, insoluble and incurable, that it was genuinely refreshing to have a problem that I could resolve whenever I felt like it. The quicker I resolved it, the quicker I would be back to having only problems that could not be resolved.

My problem also provided me with a temporary persona I enjoyed playing. The bravado, the overly sentimental fatalism of being the only uninsured man I knew. The cachet of not caring that I was. The opportunity it offered me to say things like: "So what if I'm not? Neither Alexander the Great, nor Alexander Hamilton, nor Thomas Jefferson, had health insurance."

And there was something else as well. It seemed fitting and honest to be uninsured. In moments of rare clarity and blinding insight, which I usually had while taking a long shower, I saw that there was no insurance policy on earth for what was wrong with me. I didn't know what was wrong with me, but I knew it wasn't covered.

Had Billy not brought up the issue in the postscript to his letter, I might have let the whole thing slide indefinitely.

I light another cigarette and turn to the Business section in the *Times*. The power of the labor unions is weakening.

The telephone rings.

I I

"Saul."

It's Jerry.

"Jerry," I say.

"Got a minute?" says he.

"Sure," say I.

There's something about this opening that's not to my liking, but I withhold judgment and listen.

Jerry starts by reviewing, once again, my whole insurance fuckup with Fidelity. It's back to dippy secretaries doing dippy things. I try to stop him because I know the whole history, but Jerry insists on the review "as a matter of record," as he calls it.

Serves me right, I think, for leaving Arnold. Jerry is just not a proper name for an accountant. Jerry is a name for an office boy who makes Xerox copies and runs out for sandwiches.

The gist of Jerry's review "as a matter of record" is that his firm is not to blame for anything.

"Fine, fine," I tell him. "Your firm is not to blame. I'm not interested in blaming anyone. I just want to be reinstated by Fidelity, that's all."

There is a pause and out of the pause comes Jerry's voice.

"It's too late now," says he.

"What's too late?" I almost scream.

"You waited too long," he says and goes on. "Your grace period is over. You see, there was an administrative grace period for members in good standing during which time you could have been reinstated easily. During that time, although your policy was canceled, it was only canceled in an administrative way."

"And now?" I ask.

"Now you have been canceled in a corporate way."

I start to sweat. I reach for another cigarette and as I light it, I see that my hand is shaking. I don't know what it means to be canceled in a corporate way, but the word "canceled" suddenly sounds different. I don't know why, but it does. My whole cavalier attitude to having no insurance, my whole Byronic persona of being The Uninsured Man, my whole reason for wanting to be insured again as a way of reestablishing contact with my son—it all goes out the window. I am canceled! My God, I am canceled in a corporate way. Not my insurance policy. It somehow seems that it's me, personally, who is being canceled. Me. Saul Karoo. The word "canceled" acquires an existential quality of being cast out, beyond the pale. What excommunication means to a lifelong Catholic, this canceled in a corporate way now means to me.

I am sweating like a horse.

"What?" I stammer. "What does that mean, Jerry?"

"It means that you can't be reinstated with Fidelity without having a complete physical examination. And I know how you feel about that. And then, depending on the results of your physical, they'll either take you back or reject you as being medically unqualified. You see, you're starting from scratch with them."

"But I've been with them for over twenty years!"

"Not anymore you haven't," he tells me. "You've been purged. Canceled in a corporate way."

There is a ringing in my ears and a pounding in my chest.

"But did you talk to them? Did you talk to Fidelity? Did you tell them it was just a fuckup by some dippy secretaries?"

"You can't talk to Fidelity," Jerry tells me as if he's telling me one of the great truths of our time.

My breathing is now so loud it's drowning out the sound of the air conditioner in my office. Jerry can hear me breathing and tries to calm me down.

"Saul, Saul," he says, "listen to me. Nothing to worry about. This whole thing is a blessing in disguise. In my opinion, you never should have been with Fidelity in the first place. I don't want to say anything against Arnold, but had I been advising you, I would have had you leave Fidelity a long time ago. I think we can do a lot better with some other insurance carrier. Wider coverage. Psychiatric and organ transplant included. Lower premiums even. We're now in a position to shop around for the best deal. See what I mean?"

"Tell me, Jerry. What should I do?"

"I think you should forget about Fidelity and go with GenMed."

"GenMed," I scream. "What's GenMed?"

"What's GenMed?" Jerry can't believe that I've never heard of GenMed. They're only one of the top Fortune 500 companies, that's all, he tells me. Have I seen what their stock has been doing lately, he wants to know.

I remember using his tone of incredulity myself. I was stunned to discover that a girl I was taking out on a date in college had never heard of Tolstoy. Never heard of Tolstoy, I lambasted the poor girl. Leo Tolstoy! Count Leo Tolstoy? GenMed was Jerry's Tolstoy.

"So let's say," I say to Jerry while sweat is pouring down my face, "let's say I do as you suggest and go with GenMed. What then? Do I have to have a complete physical for them, too?"

I'm positive that I can't pass a complete physical. I can't even pass water properly, not to mention a thorough physical exam.

"You do, yes," Jerry tells me, "but it's a lot more relaxed."

"Relaxed," I scream. "How so, Jerry?"

"You see," says he, "with Fidelity, they have this list of doctors. You have to be checked out by a doctor who's on their list, and these guys on their list have no flexibility. No sense of humor, if you know what I mean. With GenMed, on the other hand, we get to pick our own doctor. I know this great guy, Dr. Kolodny. Ever hear of him?"

"Kolodny?" I just can't stop screaming. "No! What's he, Hungarian or something?"

"He is, but that's the least of his charms," Jerry laughs. "The guy's great. Very flexible. I use him all the time for cases like this. You see, with Kolodny you go in knowing ahead of time that he's not going to find anything wrong with you. He does all the tests that they all do. He checks out your blood pressure. He takes a blood sample and a urine sample. He attaches you to an electrocardiogram, but with Kolodny, you might as well be attached to a toaster oven for all the problems he'll find. Know what I mean? If they hoisted Lenin out of his tomb in Red Square and shipped him to Kolodny for a physical, Lenin would pass with flying colors. It's all very relaxed. You go in, you're fine. Kolodny signs the forms. We send the forms to GenMed, along with your premium, and you're back on cruise control. Covered from head to foot, psychiatric and organ transplant included. What do you say?"

"Can I think about it?" I scream.

"What's there to think about?" Jerry wants to know.

He has me there. I suddenly can't think of anything to think about. So I agree.

"Great," Jerry says. "I'll have Janice make an appointment for you and we'll get back to you. Or better yet, I'll put you on hold and have Janice take care of it now. No sense in wasting time. Janice!" I hear him call his secretary and then I'm suddenly put on hold.

## 12

It was as if there were a vacuum in my head. Not just a vacuum in my mind, but a vacuum inside my head. As if there were no mind inside my head. A void. Nothing.

This wasn't the first time that I'd been put on hold, but it was the first time that I'd sat there holding without having something to think about while on hold. I just couldn't think of anything to think about. Or, more to the point, I seemed to have nothing with which to think.

I was canceled.

Canceled in a corporate way.

Everything was on hold. My thoughts. My plans. My memories. My breathing. I was holding my breath. There is no way of saying what I want to say without having it sound grandiose, so I might as well be grandiose and say it: My whole life seemed to be suddenly on hold.

I sat there, sweating and holding, and my sweat seemed to be pine-scented, as if my body had absorbed the sickening pine scent from those dangling dispensers in the cab and was now dispensing it on its own.

I had the earpiece of the telephone pressed so hard against my ear that the receiver, as if held there by a suction cup, could have stuck on its own without me holding on to it, but I held on. I was not connected to anyone, nor was I, strictly speaking, disconnected. I was on hold. I was on some whole new kind of hold. The telephone receiver I was holding and which, in turn, was holding me felt like a component of some elaborate life-support system to which I was connected. Circuits and cables and fiber optics extended from my office into offices and homes and dormitory rooms of everyone I had ever known. Into homes of people I was yet to know. I was on hold with Janice from Jerry's office, but there was a growing dread that the next voice I heard would not necessarily be hers. It could be someone else. Anyone.

Some moment was upon me, whose nature and purpose I did not know, but it was mysterious and huge and approaching. Some moment containing something incontrovertible. Like the first moment or the last moment of conscious existence.

And this moment, or something within it, like the ghost of Hamlet's father, would speak to me.

Until now, the danger of something real occurring, a thing I dreaded and avoided at all cost, had always been the danger of the real from without. The danger of something real happening to myself and my son, my friends, my father, my mother, my wife, the women I took to bed, anyone and everyone, but always someone on the outside. Now, however, it seemed that the danger of something real occurring was a danger from within.

It would speak to me from within myself. From a depth I never suspected I possessed. From some mind within my mind.

There was not a second to lose. If I heard that voice, my dread informed me, I would be lost. If I allowed the contact to be made with that thing deep within me, it would be a contact from which there would be no return.

In desperation and self-defense, I reached out for my *New York Times* and pulled it toward me. I opened it at random and started to read. I reread what I had already read, but that was fine. The spell, the stupor, if that's what it was, was broken. My terror subsided. The empty ballast of my mind filled up with whatever fluids of information I needed to once again regain my equilibrium and lose contact with myself.

I lit a cigarette. I was no longer merely holding, I was smoking, I was reading the paper.

I turned the page.

## 13

In the Metro section of the *Times*, I found a little article I had somehow managed to miss the first time around. A teenage mother in the Bronx, carrying a baby in her arms. Both of them killed by stray bullets. Another case of random violence.

Freed to think again, I sat there at my desk, smoking and thinking about this strange new phenomenon of stray bullets and randomness.

More and more people were becoming random victims. Randomness was acquiring epidemic proportions. It was becoming a statistical category.

There was nothing in the article about the death of the teenage mother and her child to suggest any doubt that the cause of death was total randomness. For all I knew, there were now forensic experts who could examine the extracted bullets and scientifically prove that those bullets were genuine strays. Bullets without a motive.

Surely, I thought, if bullets can be included in this category, why not people. I myself, I thought, have probably played the role of a stray bullet and will probably play the role of a stray bullet again in somebody's life. And they in mine. It seemed inevitable. The laws of probability were quite meticulous, but improbability obeyed no laws and was left to wander lawlessly through the world.

The telephone suddenly came to life. It was Janice from Jerry's office. She mispronounced my name, as she always did. For some reason, she just couldn't remember to include the "a" in Karoo and always called me Mr. Kroo.

"Mr. Kroo?"

"Yes, Janice."

"Dr. Kolodny can see you next week. Is Tuesday all right with you?"

I told her that Tuesday was fine.

"How's eleven fifteen for you?" she wanted to know.

Eleven fifteen was not just fine for me, it was perfect. It suggested a doctor who went through patients on an assembly-line basis. Complete physicals every fifteen minutes. This Kolodny, I thought, is my kind of guy.

# CHAPTER FOUR

I

Going to the cleaners on Saturdays was as close as I came to having a religion. It was a chore I cherished. It gave me a sense of spiritual renewal to go to the cleaners. My place of worship was Kwik Kleaners on Eighty-fourth Street, just west of Broadway.

They knew me by name there.

"Hello, Mr. Karoo." The woman behind the counter smiled at me.

I gave her my dirty clothes and left, carrying over my shoulder two sport coats, three pairs of slacks, and half a dozen shirts. All on wire hangers. And all of it encased in a thin, transparent plastic bag.

Instead of turning north and going home, I turned south, down Broadway. I always took a little Saturday stroll after I picked up my clothes from the cleaners. It felt good, almost athletic, to be carrying that plastic bag of clothes over my shoulder.

It was another unseasonable day. February and winter in name only.

Brought out by the mild weather, the homeless were everywhere, sitting, standing, lying down, talking to each other and to themselves, panhandling, selling junk.

Some had shaved heads like the inmates of Buchenwald. Others had more hair than biblical prophets and seemed to consider themselves as such.

A phone freak, totally involved in the bogus telephone conversation he was having, shouted at the top of his lungs into the receiver of the pay phone: "What can I tell you? I don't know what to tell you. I just don't know what to tell you anymore. I mean, what do you want me to say?"

The would-be merchants among the homeless sat on crates, surrounded by rubbish they were trying to sell and which nobody in his right mind would buy. Old *Newsweek* magazines. One with a picture of Nicolae Ceausescu on the cover. Last Sunday's *New York Times* Arts and Leisure section. Unstrung tennis racquets, cracked frames. Dented bicycle wheels. Mismatched pairs of shoes. Decapitated dolls. Aluminum pots and pans, blackened with oxide. Old bathroom scales. Old toilet seats. Baby bottles with hardened, discolored nipples.

The sight of these homeless had at one time evoked a profound feeling of compassion within me. But there was no holding on to it. My subjectivity, or my objectivity, disease, I still didn't know which to call it, but this disease of mine made me see the plight of the homeless from so many different points of view that in the end the sight of them became simply a view like any other view.

What the sight of these people evoked in me now were feelings of a different kind.

Nothing, I now thought, could be discarded anymore. Not the rubbish that had been thrown away and that they had reclaimed from garbage cans to put back into circulation on the sidewalks of Broadway. Nor the rubbish of these people themselves, human rubbish, officially discarded but without an official dumping place to keep them out of sight. The public and the private sewers were full, backing up and overflowing, disgorging into circulation again what had been discarded.

## 2

The southwesterly wind, blowing uptown as I strolled downtown, caused the thin, transparent plastic of my dry-cleaning bag to flutter in the breeze. The sound it made brought many images to mind.

A letter falling down a mail chute.

A moth beating its wings against a windowpane.

A sail in need of trimming.

It was the sail image that caught my fancy on this day.

A year or so ago I had read a story in the Tuesday Science section of the *New York Times* about what space travel might be like in the not so distant future. Men would sail through space, according to this story, in schooners rigged with enormous solar sails more than a mile high. The artist's rendition of one of these solar schooners was so lovely it took my breath away.

Something in me responded to that image. I couldn't stop thinking about it. The solar schooner, and the mile-high Mylar sail rising above it, became an image that frequented my dreams.

Finally, one night, while I was taking a long hot shower, an idea occurred to me. My one and only so-called original idea for a movie.

Ulysses. Homer's *Odyssey*, but set in the future.

There would still be a battle of Troy, but it would be set somewhere in space, and after the battle Ulysses and his crew would head back home in their solar schooner, back to Ithaca.

Solar winds blow them off course. They encounter great cosmic currents called the Rivers of Time, which sweep them away into unexplored and unheard-of regions of space and time. Trials and tribulations follow. Cosmic maidens and cosmic warriors. But through it all, my Ulysses remains a family man at heart, yearning only for his home, his faithful wife Penelope, and his beloved son Telemachus.

Nothing came of my idea. I approached several studios with it, but none were interested in pursuing it.

Although nothing came of it, it still made me happy to think about it from time to time and from time to time I added further plot complications and incidents to my story line. There were even times when I felt certain that I would sit down and write it someday.

## 3

The panhandlers, the homeless, the drunks, derelicts, and phone freaks thinned out after Seventy-ninth Street and were replaced by Saturday afternoon shoppers and other productive members of society.

My reflection in the shimmering sea of shopwindows I sailed past did not look all that bad, so long as I kept moving.

I was putting on weight, that much was indisputable, but I could still pass for a strapping six-footer who was a bit on the burly side. The plastic bag of dry cleaning slung over my shoulder gave me the appearance of some vital businessman on the go.

In keeping with the image, I gave myself over to the calendar in my head of appointments and upcoming events.

There was my Tuesday appointment with Dr. Kolodny at eleven fifteen A.M.

According to Jerry, I would be fully insured with GenMed by the end of the week.

Give Billy a call at Harvard. Tell him the happy news.

Lunch with Guido on Friday.

Another divorce dinner with Dianah. When?

Jay Cromwell was coming to town and according to that Bobbie woman he wanted to see me. February twenty-second and twenty-third.

It wasn't like me to remember dates, but these I remembered.

Cromwell's arrival loomed as the most anxiety-provoking feature on the landscape of my mental calendar.

## 4

Jay Cromwell was a film producer by profession, but he could have been a head of state or some charismatic religious figure with messianic powers.

It was in his voice. In his eyes. His teeth. In that oversized horrific forehead of his.

(When you sat across a table from him, it was like confronting a warhead with human features.)

He was the only man I knew personally who was truly evil.

He was evil the way the grass was green. He was a monolith of such fathomless treachery that at times I actually enjoyed his company, for the simple reason that, in comparison to him, I was the moral force of my time.

The inclination to feel this way in his presence was, of course, a symptom of yet another disease I had.

My Cromwell disease.

I had collaborated with him in my capacity as a rewriter on three different screenplays. The third one belonged to that young man who showed up uninvited to the sneak preview of his film in Pittsburgh.

The image of that young man in the lobby of the theater after the screening, trembling with rage and lambasting us until he broke down and started crying, was transformed by Cromwell over dinner that very evening into an incident of broad comedy.

The way Cromwell laughed while retelling the story of the young man's histrionics. The way he threw back his head and laughed so that all his teeth showed. The way I laughed along. The way Cromwell scrutinized me while I laughed.

I resolved after that dinner, long before I learned of the young man's suicide, never to have anything to do with Cromwell again.

That was almost two years ago.

But although I had had no contact with Cromwell since then, I was still made to feel that I was on hold with him. That he had me on hold.

The problem with my resolution never to see Cromwell again was that it was a private resolution.

My resolution, as far as Cromwell was concerned, was nonexistent. He was free to think that the only reason there had been no contact between us was that he had not initiated any, making no offers or overtures in my direction.

My resolution, therefore, although still intact, was completely untested.

The prospect of his arrival and his desire to see me presented me with an opportunity to set the record straight and break all relations with him in public.

He had risen considerably in the eyes of the world since our Pittsburgh preview. He had become, in a business full of superstars of one kind or another, the first acknowledged superproducer. There had been lengthy profiles of him in *Time* and *Newsweek*, in which the writers had praised his genius for knowing what the public wanted, his unbroken series of huge commercial hits, and "his zest for life, not just his own life but his zest for the lives of others."

All the better, as far as I was concerned. The bigger he was in his own eyes and in the eyes of the world, the more heroic would be my harangue.

"Listen to me, Cromwell, and listen well," I could hear myself telling him to his face. "I may not be a superproducer or super anything, I may just be a human being, but in the immortal words of e. e. cummings, 'there is some shit I will not eat.' And furthermore . . ."

My private harangue was cut short. I was about to step off the curb and cross the street when I saw, shuffling toward me from the other side of the intersection, my dead father.

5

I froze, one foot still on the curb, one off.

He shuffled toward me slowly, like an old sea turtle walking upright. He looked neither left nor right as he crept across the intersection.

The shock of seeing him made me almost drop my Kwik Kleaners bag. Even the dead can't be discarded anymore, I thought to myself.

He was so slow of foot that by the time he finally reached the other side where I stood, I had plenty of time to get my bearings again, to come to my senses, and to realize the silly but understandable mistake I had made.

It was the wrong old geezer in the right camel-hair overcoat. Dianah, true to her word, had given away my dead father's clothes to some Upper West Side church group to distribute to the homeless. There, a little old man had come, and this overcoat fit him as it had fit another little old man in Chicago, a former judge, my father.

I knew the coat well. As well as an art student might know the work of a master. The straight, rectangular outside pockets with flaps. The buttons that were still all there. The wide collar and the ragged tip of the right lapel, which my dad, in his madness, had chewed in one of his fits. In another fit, he had taken an indelible china marker and drawn a large, crude facsimile of a human heart on the outside of the coat. In his mad ignorance of the human anatomy, or in his mad rejection of it, my father had placed the heart on the right side. My mother had the coat dry-cleaned after his death, but a black china marker stain remained.

It was one of those unbearably hot summers in Chicago the summer that my father died, but toward the end he complained constantly of being cold. We had to turn on the furnace for him. The thermostat was set at eighty-five and there he sat, wearing that camel overcoat, his teeth chattering from the cold, his little body shivering while I, wearing only my sleeveless T-shirt, dripped sweat in his company.

It is not that his hair fell out that summer, rather it became finer and finer, like thistledown, like cobwebs. When the furnace kicked in and the air from the registers blew, it made his hair move in various directions. At those times, he was like someone already dead, sitting on the bottom of the sea, invisible currents playing with his hair.

"Where is your heart?" He demanded to know from me that summer. "Where is it? Show it to me. Here is mine. Right here!" And with his tight little fist he pounded that facsimile he had drawn on his chest.

At times I was tempted to tell him that the heart was on the wrong side but, as if in concurrence with his accusation, I didn't have the heart to do so. The few times I tried to object to something he said, the judge in him roared into life.

"Objection denied! Clear the courtroom!"

During my visit that summer, his favorite form of capital punishment for me, when he saw me as the bad son Saul, was beheading.

"Tomorrow at dawn," he roared. "Since you have no heart, off with your head. Off with your head, you miserable dog!"

When he saw me as the good son Paul, I sometimes tried to plead insanity as the cause of my brother's many transgressions. But my father wouldn't hear of it. His long career as a judge had inured him to that defense.

"Insanity's no excuse. The sentence stands. Off with his head!"

There were times that summer when I lay in bed at night feeling as if the sentence had already been carried out and that I now existed solely as a head upon a pillow, completely separated from my body.

I moved aside to let the little old man in my father's overcoat shuffle past me. A close-up of his face revealed that the only resemblance between him and my father was the resemblance of one shriveled-up old man to another. Nothing more.

6

Why, then, did I turn around and follow him? I asked myself that very question, but could think of no satisfactory answer. But follow him I did. Citarella fish store, La Caridad restaurant, all the places I had passed heading south I passed again heading north, walking at a turtle's pace.

The old geezer stopped at the next intersection and just stood there, despite the green light, as if trying to remember what chore had prompted him on this Saturday to set himself in motion.

Finally, gingerly, he stepped off the curb, and we crossed in the fullness of time to the north side of Seventy-eighth Street. The Apthorp Pharmacy was just ahead, on our left. Ah, I decided. That's where he's going. To get his prescription filled. Like fifties teens around a soda fountain, the old men and women hung out at the Apthorp Pharmacy, waiting for their prescriptions.

But, no. Once on the other side of the intersection, he turned right, as if intending to cross to the east side of Broadway.

He stopped at the traffic island separating the uptown Broadway from the downtown. There, as slowly as he had walked, he slowly sat down upon the westernmost part of a long park bench, his destination.

I sat down myself, neither too close to him nor too far away. I took down my sail, my plastic bag, and folded it across my lap. I lit a cigarette.

There we sat.

7

And there we continued to sit.

From time to time, I took in the old man. He seemed to be taking nothing in except the sunshine. He had come to this bench for the sun. His spa.

Whose father, if anybody's, was he, I wondered. If nothing else, he had been at one time somebody's son. Their darling, maybe. Their sweet baby boy.

Cheap sentiment made me feel a little high. In a blubbering mood. People who knew me well, friends I once had, used to admonish me that I tended to get sentimental when drunk. Embarrassingly so. My problem now was that this tendency remained despite my inability to get drunk. All my drunken tendencies remained, except drunkenness.

My father had brought his camel-hair overcoat at Marshall Field's on State Street, when that store was *the* store in Chicago. The coat had fit him well when it was new and he was healthy. The sicker he got, the more his head seemed to shrink, dehydrate, so that when I last saw him wearing it, the coat overwhelmed his head.

The old man next to me had a similar problem. A dry little turtle head sticking out of the formidable shell of the overcoat.

His scrawny neck was more wristlike than necklike.

The feet of his short legs barely touched the ground. The shoes he wore were brown and far too large for his feet. His thin ankles stuck out of them like rake handles. A bit of hairless shinbone showed above his sagging socks. On the shinbone, a grayish scab of some kind.

It was the used shoes he wore, those big brown brogans, that gave him away as indigent, homeless. If you didn't look at his shoes, you might have mistaken him for a retired civil servant living in a rent-controlled apartment, on an adequate pension. But not with those shoes.

My father, perverse to the very end, despite his advanced cancer and total insanity, died of a heart attack. My mother, as she later informed me, found him collapsed on the living room floor.

Whose father was he, once again I wondered, smoking, looking at the old guy, who didn't seem to be looking anywhere. He could have been anybody, anybody's father, and in that sense he could have been mine as well.

8

So we sat there, as clouds of various shapes sailed across the sky and the earth sailed on around the sun.

A syrupy nostalgia for my unhappy marriage returned, as it always did.

If nothing else, my marriage had provided me with a sense of home, and since home for me by definition was a place from which I wanted to flee, my unhappy marriage had given me hope that escape was possible. Without a home of one's own—not an apartment, not even a wonderfully spacious apartment like mine, but a home, a sense of home—without it, there was no hope of escape.

The advantages of an unhappy marriage were not easily dismissed. My many, many diseases.

All Billy wanted from me was to spend some time alone with me, but what he wanted I could not give him. I had no idea what to properly call this disease. Middleman disease? Third-party disease? Observer disease? Whatever its name, the disease precluded my ever feeling at ease with somebody without an audience to observe us.

It wasn't just Billy. I hoped he knew. I hoped he knew it wasn't just him. All my relationships with people had, in one way or another, become public spectacles.

Guido was my best friend, my last remaining friend, we had been friends for years and years but in all those years I had never been alone with him. The few times I went to his apartment during the tenure of his two marriages, it was to attend a party he gave. When he came to my apartment, while I was still living with Dianah, it was to attend a party we gave.

As mad and vindictive as my father was before he died, his madness did not keep me from visiting my parents in Chicago. His death, and the prospect of being alone with my mother, did. The last time I saw her was at his funeral.

If I never had to be alone with a woman, truly alone, if the sex act, for which I sometimes desperately yearned, could be performed in public, right there in some restaurant, before coffee and dessert, or in the lobby of a theater during intermission, my love affairs with women would last a lot longer.

It was not the fear of intimacy. I was ready and willing to be indiscriminately intimate in public. To open up myself and to embrace the openness of another in turn. But being alone in an apartment with a woman, or my son, or my wife, or my mother, always made me feel that we were waiting for somebody else to come. Somebody who was far more capable of appreciating what we were doing than the two of us were. Some middleman. Some third party. Some monitor who could make sense of it all and allow us, through his eyes, to make sense of it ourselves.

Even a simple phone call to Billy was an endeavor that was much easier to bring off when I had somebody listening to my conversation with him.

I've called Billy from Guido's office and, although he insisted on leaving while I talked, I made sure the door to his office remained open, so that the secretaries outside could overhear what I was saying.

I've called Billy from my apartment when I had a woman there. By talking to my son on the telephone, I avoided being alone with that woman, and by having her in my apartment, listening to me, I avoided being alone with my son on the telephone. It was a perfection of sorts, in which nothing, absolutely nothing real could occur while the phone call lasted.

These phone calls, of course, were never of the kind that did anything to satisfy my son's hunger for contact with me. That was because I wasn't really talking to him, I was playing to some third party. My son was merely the medium through whom I talked to others about my fatherhood.

I knew this was wrong. I knew the harm it was causing us both. The problem was not one of lack of insight on my part.

My insights were many. I was full of penetrating insights. But they led to nothing except an ever-growing private collection.

What I needed was more than just an insight. What I needed was some super insight that could go to the very source of all my diseases.

This recurring notion, however, was tempered by a recurring dread. Super insights did not necessarily lead to the kind of clarity we could bear seeing. The first thing Oedipus, King of Thebes, did when he at last saw clearly was to gouge out his eyes.

I sat there, thinking my thoughts. The old man in my father's overcoat, I assumed, thought his. Buses, cabs, cars, delivery vans roared past us in both directions. Subways thundered beneath our little traffic island. People walked past us to get to the east side of Broadway. Others, to get to the west side. Clouds sailed by overhead. So did a Fuji blimp. Nobody else sat down on the bench. The two of us sat there, the old man and I, "like two chess pieces of an abandoned game."

# CHAPTER FIVE

## I

Monday, the wind began to blow. It began in the early morning and picked up in intensity as the day went on. By the time I left for the office, it was blowing so hard the maintenance man was taking down the canopy outside the entrance to my building to keep it from shredding.

The wind pushed me up Eighty-sixth, toward Broadway. Seagulls from the Hudson River, blown off course, screeched overhead. The newspaper vending machines, chained to utility poles, rattled and shook in the wind as if they contained some pandemic trying to get out.

I skipped lunch, as an athletic gesture to my physical exam the next day, and stayed in my office and listened to the wind blow.

Through my window, I saw sheets of newspaper swept out of trash cans and become airborne. Some flew low and away toward Fifth Avenue. Others, caught in updrafts, wheeled and spiraled high above Fifty-seventh Street. People walking east lurched like drunks being given the bum's rush by the wind, hurrying against their will. Those walking west, into the wind, struggled, shielding their eyes. Individuals and little groups walking backwards, like members of some strange religious sect. People getting into cabs. Cab doors flying out of their hands when they opened them. And then the struggle to close them again.

Despite Jerry's assurance about the kind of doctor this Kolodny guy was, I had some anxiety about my exam. But it was just a trace. It could have been induced by the drop in the barometric pressure that was causing the wind to blow.

I couldn't even remember the last time I had had a complete physical.

The telephone rang.

2

It was from Cromwell's office in California, but it didn't feel like a long-distance call. Ever since the breakup of AT&T and the subsequent rush of other companies into the long-distance field, the quality of the long distance "sound" has gradually lost all sense of distance. The fiber optics that some of the new companies use has produced a reception so disturbingly clear, it destroys any sense of separation between you and the person at the other end of the line. The sound of their voice is like something implanted in your brain, or like a tiny CD playing in the earpiece of your telephone. I consider the loss of that sense of distance in long-distance calls a tragedy.

The person calling me was Cromwell's assistant. His name was Brad. But it wasn't the Brad I once knew who had been Cromwell's assistant at that time. It was another Brad.

This Brad told me how the Bobbie woman had told him that she and I had had a wonderful chat. Brad, speaking for himself, wanted to make sure I understood what a thrill it was for him personally to speak to me. I was, as far as he was concerned, one of the true pros of the entertainment industry.

He sounded very young. Early to mid-twenties.

I pondered the mystery of his name while he showered me with praise. Almost every studio executive or producer I ever knew had a young man named Brad for an assistant. Brads were the Marias of the movie industry.

This Brad, like the others I had known, had a very easy, mellifluous voice, as if he had been trained from childhood in some music conservatory to talk on the telephone.

"As a student of film . . ." he went on.

There was something touching about all the Brads I had ever known. They were all partial to certain phrases like "brainstorming." They not only used them, but they actually seemed to believe that such storms took place on a daily basis in their line of work.

I had no idea what happened to these young men when they got older. Nobody wanted an old Brad for an assistant. Cromwell went through Brads almost as fast as he went through young girls. And none of the Brads that I had ever known managed to climb up the ladder of the movie industry hierarchy. I didn't know a single movie executive or producer named Brad.

Cromwell, according to Brad, was definitely coming to New York and wanted to see me about a project while he was in town. Was I free to have dinner with him on the twenty-second?

"I'm available," I told Brad, "but I'm not free."

Brad laughed. When he laughed, he bleated like a sheep, or a young lamb. But a sheep or a young lamb with its throat slit. Gurgling and bleating, but laughing, as if he were happy to have his throat slit.

Would ten o'clock at Cafe Luxembourg be all right with me?

Yes, it would.

Would I mind leaving my afternoon free the next day, just in case?

No, I wouldn't.

Mr. Cromwell, Brad informed me, wanted to make sure I knew that he would have called me himself were it not for his hectic schedule. In addition to everything else he was doing at the moment, Mr. Cromwell was asked, and he accepted despite his hectic schedule, to serve as one of the organizing forces of the Vaclav Havel thing.

"And you know how he is when he gets going on a project," Brad said, and laughed. Because of the fiber optics, and the static-free, distance-free reception on the line, his laughter had the verisimilitude of a hallucination.

### 3

I lay in bed, unable to sleep. I could hear the wind blowing outside and the sound of my heart beating.

I spent some time embroidering the harangue I would loosen upon Jay Cromwell.

I wondered what kind of a girl would accompany him when I saw him. He always showed up with some very beautiful, very young girl. Some were almost children. Most of them tended to be refugees from a devastated country in vogue at the moment. Vietnamese girls. Russian Jews. A Christian girl from Beirut. A beautiful black girl from Soweto.

Police sirens outside. First one. Then another. Then, a minute or so later, the sound of an ambulance siren heading in the same direction.

Suddenly, I remembered a nursery rhyme that Billy used to get wrong as a little boy and I smiled at the memory.

> *Baa, baa, black sheep,*
> *Have you any wolves,*
> *Yes sir; yes sir,*
> *Three bags full . . .*

It struck me (I was a man of countless insights) that my relationship to my son was that of a father, a loving father, but a father who cherished the memory of a son long dead, and not a father with a living son.

I moved on to other thoughts.

My heart continued to beat audibly. Like the sound of a little, lonely drum beating on itself.

## 4

My appointment with Dr. Kolodny was at eleven fifteen, but my lifelong mania for punctuality made me arrive at his office ten minutes early. His office was located on Fifth Avenue, a few blocks south of the Metropolitan Museum. The large waiting room could have been furnished by the same interior decorator who had done the McNabs' Dakota apartment. Italian lamps. Chrome, wood, leather, and plants everywhere.

"Can I help you, please?" The receptionist was young and very professional-looking.

"Yes, I have an appointment," I told her, and then I thought it best to inform her about the kind of shyster service I expected. I leaned toward her and lowered my voice. "I'm here for one of those insurance physicals." I gave her a little wink and added, just to make sure, "Jerry sent me. Jerry Fry."

"What is your name, please?"

"Saul Karoo."

She checked her ledger and found me.

"Yes, Mr. Karoo. You're a little early and we're running just a bit late. It'll be twenty minutes to half an hour before Dr. Kolodny can see you."

She gave me, since I was a new patient, a white clipboard with a questionnaire to fill out.

I sat down and started filling it out. Cigarettes were invented for doing just such chores as this and I was keenly aware of nicotine deprivation while I wrote. Name. Address. Telephone number. Height. Weight. Date of birth. Place of birth.

Halfway through the questionnaire, I got weary of my own life and the factual information that constituted it. So I started lying and filling in the blanks with invented details. Normally, I needed no excuse to lie, I just did it, but this time I even had an excuse. I didn't come here to have a real physical, so why should I need to provide real answers to these questions?

Under occupation, I wrote: commodities broker.

I checked off that I was a nonsmoker.

I had two grown sons.

Both of my parents were still alive.

No history of cancer or diabetes or anything in my family. I had a family with no medical history whatsoever.

As for me, I said that I had regular medical checkups, every six months.

There was a question marked "optional" inquiring about my religious denomination. I lied and said I was Jewish.

The character that emerged from my lies seemed in many ways a lot more substantial and considerably more comprehensible to me than I was to myself.

## 5

Dr. Kolodny's office was a complex of offices shared by three other doctors. The waiting room was three-quarters full.

There was a pile of magazines and newspapers on the long, low glass-top table in front of my chair. I picked up the *New York Times* and went right to my favorite section of the week, Tuesday Science.

The illustration on the front page was an artist's rendering of a human chromosome, enlarged thousands of times to focus upon a single gene.

The accompanying article, which I devoured, had to do with a potentially revolutionary reappraisal of psychosis. According to the spokesman for a team of scientists responsible for the study in question, there seemed to be strong evidence to support the thesis that the vast majority of patients suffering from various forms of neurological disorders had a certain gene (see the illustration on the front page) in common. This gene had peculiar nodules around its oblong shape, giving it a vague similarity to the letter S. Hence its name: the S-gene.

Its very shape, the scientists speculated, seemed to determine its function. Each nodule seemed to trigger a set of responses over which the patient had no control. They were still a long way from a cure, but the discovery of this S-gene was a major breakthrough.

It seemed to me, as an avid follower of the Tuesday Science section of the *Times*, that some of the most exciting scientific research of the past few years had been in the field of biochemistry and biogenetics. In the last half a year alone there had been articles linking diabetes and genes, dyslexia and genes, alcoholism and various other forms of addiction and genes. Studies conducted in penal institutions found almost conclusive evidence that psychopaths, murderers, and rapists were victims of genetic triggers over which they had no control. Evidence that crime itself, instead of being a social problem, or a personal problem, was instead a problem of biology and genetic disorders.

Although I was not a scientist myself, as a diseased layman I applauded these findings.

The story of the S-gene rekindled my hope that my many diseases had a common, genetic source.

Even if a cure was never to be found for my genetic disorder, merely knowing the true cause of my many diseases would almost be a cure in itself. Armed with this information, I could warn others, my son, for example, not to expect certain things from me, because I had scientific proof that they were not mine to give.

I turned the page.

An article about the lemurs on the island of Madagascar caught my eye, when I heard the receptionist call my name:

"Mr. Karoo."

I went up to her desk.

"Room three." She pointed down the corridor.

## 6

The corridor was lit by overhead fluorescent lights hidden behind a lowered ceiling.

I had no reason to question Jerry's reassuring description about the kind of perfunctory physical exam I would have, but even so, I felt this tiny bit of anxiety in the pit of my stomach.

When I opened the door and stepped into room three, it was so bright inside that I had to shield my eyes.

Everything was white. The walls, the floor, the cabinets, the two white chairs, the venetian blinds in the windows, even that adjustable contraption on which you lay down to be examined was white and had a white disposable paper cover on top of it.

In the midst of this whiteness stood a young woman wearing a white nurse's smock and white pantyhose, holding that clipboard with my filled-out questionnaire in her hand.

She had big blue eyes and a fluffy pillow of thick, shiny, blond hair. She was in her early twenties, a little overweight, and had enormous breasts.

I knew, of course, that I shouldn't be gaping at her breasts, but I couldn't help myself. Mesmerized, like a rabbit in a python cage, I had not a single thought in my head other than: My God! Would you look at those things.

She wore a little name tag on her left breast, which read: E. Höhlen-rauch. The name tag looked as lost on her bosom as a lifeboat in the Pacific Ocean.

When at last I managed to pry my eyes away and look up at her face, I saw no hint of displeasure in her big blue eyes for my having gaped like a fool at her breasts.

She understood. With a contented smile, she looked down at her breasts and then up at me again, and the expression on her face was one of lazy sympathy. Who can blame you, her smile seemed to say. They really are magnificent, aren't they?

"Hello, my name is Elke. Dr. Kolodny will be with you shortly. But first there's a few little things we have to take care of. Strictly routine."

She spoke slowly, as if she were on drugs, or recovering from a very gratifying orgasm.

I detected what to my ear sounded like a trace of Austrian or German accent in her voice. Completely rattled by the size of her breasts, I seized upon her accent and her name as the opening gambit with which to launch my attack. I saw it all in a twinkling of an eye. I would seduce this Elke Höhlenrauch with my sense of humor and I would bring her with me to my dinner with Cromwell at Cafe Luxembourg. He might show up with a younger girl, but it was inconceivable that he could find one with bigger breasts. Elke's breasts would put me in a position of power even before I went into my harangue.

"Elke Höhlenrauch," I said. "What is that, French?"

Without so much as a smile, Elke answered, "No, I am German." And then, while my humorous opening lay there on the floor like a piece of lox, and before I could think of another opening with which to replace it, she told me: "Would you like to strip down to your under-wear, please?"

"Yes, I would. Very much so. Would you?" I laughed.

Elke either didn't hear my reply or chose to ignore it. It was hard to tell.

I began taking off my clothes, trying to undress in a manner of some sophisticated elder statesman who was, despite the shambles of his body, still sexy in his own, worldly way.

The more clothes I took off and the more times I glanced at Elke's magnificent breasts, the more a breast-induced hysteria within me threatened to explode. It was all I could do, as I hopped on one foot, trying to get out of my trousers, to keep from screaming out loud, or laughing out loud, or strumming on my lower lip with my index finger like an imbecile. I could think of no other banter with which to engage her, humorous or otherwise. Only names of movie stars I had met over the years, in my role as a rewriter, came to mind. It was hard to keep myself from ululating their names, rending the air with movie stars, as a way of making an impression on Elke Höhlenrauch.

Dustin Hoffman, Elke. I've met Dustin. Meryl Streep. Robert Redford. Yes! Robert Redford. Three meetings, Elke. I've had three meetings with him. Paul Newman. Dinner with Paul Newman. Lunch with Richard Gere. Bill Hurt. Robin Williams. Sigourney Weaver. Kevin Costner. Kevin Kline. You want stars, Elke? I'm a rewriter for the stars. Jay Cromwell, the superproducer? Friend of mine. He knows Vaclav Havel. You want to meet Vaclav, Elke? I can arrange it.

I was down to my boxer shorts, socks, and a sleeveless T-shirt.

"Please," Elke said, and gestured with her soft, plump hand, each finger a French dessert, toward a stainless-steel doctor's scale standing against the wall.

She walked on ahead. I followed. The inside of her thighs rubbed as she walked, and the material of which her white pantyhose were made caused static electricity to be heard underneath her smock. Like the sound of one of those electric bug zappers, killing bugs in the night.

Ever so gingerly, I stepped on the scale, as if stepping on the gallows. I hated being weighed. I hated weighing myself, but I especially hated having somebody else weigh me. It always made me feel as if I had been suddenly abducted from a country with a constitutional democracy and dumped into some totalitarian state.

Elke's hand moved the gleaming stainless-steel tumblers inexorably toward my right.

To my complete horror, I saw that I weighed two hundred and twenty-five pounds.

My mouth dropped open.

What!

I have never, in all my life, weighed two hundred and twenty-five pounds. Even fully dressed and wearing heavy shoes, with a lot of loose change in my pockets, I had never, ever, gone beyond two hundred and five pounds.

Dumbfounded, I stared at the total. It was like staring at some trumped-up charge of crimes I never committed.

I wanted to protest, but before I could get over the shock, Elke Höhlenrauch chuckled.

"You're a bad boy, Mr. Karoo." She wagged her cream-filled index finger at me. "It's not nice to fib."

Breasts or no breasts, I suddenly felt grim and in no mood for games. "Fib? What fib?"

She pointed with her ballpoint pen to the spot on the questionnaire where I had entered my weight. Then, as if in a nightmare of some Stalinist or Third Reich show trial, she crossed out the figure I had entered there, 198 lbs., and before I could stop her, wrote over it, in large lurid figures, 225 lbs.

Her presumption, without even knowing me, that I could lie about something as petty as my weight, infuriated me. I knew, of course, that I was quite capable of lying about anything, and had in fact lied about all kinds of things on this very questionnaire. But not about my weight! That she would single out one of the few truths I had stated and attack it as a lie, while ignoring all my other lies, allowed my indignation to assume a self-righteous character.

"Look, Ms. Höhlenrauch," I said, putting a heavy and semi-sarcastic stress on Ms., and an equally heavy and slightly derogatory emphasis on the umlaut in her last name, "I'll have you know that I have never in my life weighed over two hundred and five pounds and the one time that I did, I was fully dressed and wearing Timberland boots because it was winter."

In her lazy, detached manner, she cut me off and said: "These things happen."

"These things? What is that supposed to mean? These things happen. What things?" I started to get off the scale, but with a firm little push on my chest with her soft little hand, she gestured for me to stay where I was but turn around and face out. She walked behind me, her smock rustling, the bug zapper of her thighs sizzling.

"Erect, please," she said.

"What!"

"Erect. Stand erect, please."

I thought I was standing erect, but I tried to comply with her request and invent some new supererect posture for myself. I heard a sound behind me, like the sound of a ceremonial sword being pulled out of its scabbard, and then felt a flat metallic object land on the top of my head.

She was measuring my height.

Never had I tried to stand so erect before. I was barely breathing. It felt like I was in a gulag or a Nazi concentration camp.

"You're such a bad boy," Elke chuckled behind me. "You really are."

"What!" I shrieked. "What now!"

She came around to my side and showed me my questionnaire, pointing with that infernal ballpoint pen of hers to where I had entered my height. Before I could so much as squawk, the nightmare repeated itself. She crossed out what I had written, 6 ft., and over it wrote 5'10½".

Whatever composure I had, if any, vanished. I began screaming at her.

"Just hold on, Elke! Just hold on a goddamn minute! What the hell do you think you're doing, anyway?"

"I'm just bringing you up to date," she smiled, her dimples deepening.

I felt like punching her in the mouth. Right in her sensual little mouth.

"Oh, yeah!" I shrieked. "We'll see about that."

I jumped off the scale and ran to my trousers, which were draped over the back of one of those white chairs. I whipped out my wallet, and then I whipped my driver's license out of my wallet. I stormed back and shook the license in her face.

"Do you see this, Elke? Do you know what this is? This is an official document of the State of New York. And here"—I pointed—"if you can spare the time to observe, you'll notice that it states that I am six feet tall! I have been six feet tall since I graduated from high school."

"I'm sure you have, Mr. Karoo. It's just that you're not six feet tall now and never will be again. You're five foot ten and a half now. These things happen."

"These *things* again, Elke. These goddamn *things* you keep on about. What are these *things*?"

"People, they shrink," Elke said.

"People, they shrink!"

"Yes. The spine, it contracts."

"The spine, it contracts!"

"Oh, yes. By all means. It's like an accordion, Mr. Karoo, the spine is." She demonstrated, as if playing one.

"First you grow and grow"—her arms went out—"and then the little vertebrae in your spinal column start to press closer and closer together and you shrink and shrink."

She seemed delighted with her little demonstration. I was either hyperventilating or not ventilating at all, it was hard to know which. To have this double-breasted Brunhilde standing there in front of me and cheerfully playing an accordion with my spine was like having an image out of Dante's Inferno come to life.

But, to be still transfixed by her breasts, to be still erotically aroused by the same white-smocked mädchen who was so blithely annihilating me, surely deserved a special little circle of its own in the Inferno.

I felt a harangue coming on.

"This is all a little too Teutonic for me, Ms. Höhlenrauch," I barked at her. "This is America, not Germany. We don't reclassify people in this country just like that. Actually, Elke, we don't classify people period, not according to their physio-racial traits at least. I mean, why don't you measure the size of my cranium while you're at it, like your ancestors did to my people? I mean, just because I'm a Jew . . ."

I wasn't, of course, but having a blond Elke in front of me made me feel that I was. And not just a Jew, but a self-loathing anti-Semitic Jew who still yearned to take Aryan Elke out to dinner.

My harangue ("Germany is the vampire of Europe, etc., etc.") went on for a bit more. Elke listened, blinking occasionally, secure in her awareness that I adored every cubic inch of her breasts and that, my harangue notwithstanding, I was still trying to sell myself to her. Her crime, her great crime, her unforgivable crime, was that she wasn't interested.

"Dr. Kolodny will be with you in a minute," she told me when I paused to catch my breath.

Her smock rustling, her thighs rubbing, her pantyhose making that sizzling sound, she then left the room, breasts and all.

I stood there in my boxer shorts, socks, and sleeveless T-shirt, still holding my driver's license, feeling in a state of shock.

According to Elke, I had not only expanded horizontally, I had contracted vertically as well.

The spine, it contracts.

These things happen.

It wasn't so much the weight; although two hundred and twenty-five pounds was quite a blow, I could always lose the weight. But the one and a half inches I had lost could not be regained.

I was five foot ten and a half inches again. The last time I was five foot ten and a half, I was a sophomore in high school. Smoking Lucky Strikes.

When, I wondered, was the last time I was six feet tall? And how was it that I could lose a whole inch and a half without being aware of it? What was I doing that was so engrossing at the time that prevented me from realizing that I was shrinking?

I sat down on the white chair with my trousers across my lap, to wait for Dr. Kolodny.

It was too late for a complete physical. I wasn't complete anymore. There was an inch and a half missing.

On the other hand, there were twenty-five extra pounds.

Down and out, the two simultaneous directions of the journey of my body.

And to think, I thought, that all this was caused by losing my health insurance and wanting to be insured again.

Insured against what?

I had been insured all my life and what were the results? The results were that I was riddled with diseases. I had lost a full inch and a half while being fully insured. And yet here I was, slumped pathetically in my chair, with my trousers in my lap, petitioning to be insured again.

Only this time, in addition to the premiums, there was another price to pay. A terrible price. I had walked into this room, this goddamned gulag number three, as a strapping six-footer, and if I wanted to walk out as an insured man, I would have to accept my new classification as that of a fat man of medium height.

The choice, it suddenly seemed to me, was mine. There were no armed guards outside the door. If I was confined to this room, it was a voluntary confinement. Voluntary submission. Voluntary compliance with being reclassified.

But if I didn't want to be insured by GenMed, I didn't have to accept the results of my reclassification. I didn't necessarily dispute Elke's figures. As a free man, I simply didn't have to accept them.

To be free, I thought, and felt my blood heating up, to be free is better than to be insured. To be truly free is to be uninsured!

I rose—that's how I saw it, I didn't just stand up, I rose—and got dressed as quickly as possible. Already I felt better. Taller. Defiant. Free. Free in the Dostoyevsky and Hannah Arendt meaning of the word. Rebellious. A rebel in the Camus meaning of the word.

I stormed out of the room, not walked, I stormed out of there, and as I stormed through the waiting room where some of those poor, helpless souls were still sitting and waiting, I could not help but think of myself in the third person.

He was a man who would not give an inch. He had walked in as a strapping six-footer and by damn he was walking out as a strapping six-footer.

# CHAPTER SIX

## I

Three days later, Friday, I have lunch with Guido in the Russian Tea Room.

I am early, as always. I sit in his booth (it's the third booth to your right as you enter), smoking my cigarette and drinking my Bloody Mary and waiting for him to show up. Neither the drink I'm drinking nor the drinks which, I know, will follow will have any effect on me, but it will please Guido, my last friend and a confirmed alcoholic, to see when he arrives that I've started drinking already.

It's a strange thing to be down to one last friend. It's hard to decide while I sit there if this predicament is something I enjoy or not. It's hard even to find the basis for deciding. My mind oscillates between two polar opposites. I enjoy it. I don't enjoy it. It keeps on oscillating like a metronome, the oscillation precluding any need to decide one way or the other.

But something about the phrase, "my last friend," something about the very sound of those words, is compelling. It's as if I had a whole, ever-growing list of lasts, and the last remaining measure of my personal growth as a human being is to be found in this ever more bountiful list of my depletions.

I light another cigarette and turn to more pressing questions. Where in the world am I going to get a date for my dinner with Cromwell? I need to come armed with a beautiful woman when I have my dinner with him.

2

Every restaurant I frequent in New York has its own sound which, were I blindfolded and led inside, I could recognize. The musical pitch of the plates and the silverware is different in each, and so is the tempo, the tone, the din of the crowd. I think I could distinguish the din of the Russian Tea Room from the din at Orso's the way more discerning ears could distinguish if a piece of music was recorded live at Carnegie or Avery Fisher Hall.

I see Guido coming toward me.

He's a big man, almost as tall as my Billy, but beefy. A jock with a strong pitching arm, he was drafted out of high school by the Chicago White Sox and ruined his arm on their farm team. The rotator cuff, or something like that. A snappy overdresser, the way former jocks tend to be when they become successful in another line of work, he still retains, despite the booze and the years and the excess weight, an easy athletic grace and lightness of foot, which makes it seem he's dancing through the Tea Room toward me. He knows a lot of people and touches a lot of shoulders on the way, never once stopping, scattering remarks over his shoulders like New Year's confetti. He is wearing a huge grin. It wraps around his head like the grin of a porpoise.

"Good to see you, you sonovabitch," he says and drops a big paw on my shoulder. He shakes me with it. Shakes me hard.

3

We're now both smoking and drinking. Guido is telling me about some movie screenings he saw in LA.

Ever since we've known each other, we've both been active alcoholics and heavy smokers. From time to time, we used to take turns counseling each other about the need for changing our ways and ridding ourselves of our addictions. Nothing, of course, was further from our minds. Our friendship was cemented by the unspoken vow that neither one of us would ever change. To talk of change was admirable. To try to change was heroic. But for either of us actually to change would have been construed by the other as nothing short of betrayal. It was during Guido's short-lived attempt to move to LA that I dared to try and stop smoking and, thanks to that Hungarian hypnotist, actually managed to succeed for a number of weeks. By the time Guido came back, I was smoking again and my flirtation with quitting was a story I told him. He loved the story. He told it to others. Attempts at change, so long as they resulted in complete failure, made the bonds of our friendship even stronger.

That's what made it so difficult to get together with Guido since the onset of my drunk disease. Guido was not just an active alcoholic, he was, in his own way, a brilliant alcoholic.

I do the best I can, I sham the symptoms of an intoxication I don't feel, but it feels treacherous to be fooling a man I consider to be my best, last friend.

Were I to tell him that I have been rendered permanently sober by some mysterious disease, I fear that our friendship would end. And I fear that it would suffer before it ended. He would feel constrained by my revelation, aware of every word he said, overly eager to demonstrate, but now in an artificial way, that he was still fond of me and that we were still the best of friends. In short, he would feel just as I am feeling now. But there's a big difference between the two of us. Guido has many other friends. I have none left but Guido. So I keep my disease a secret and play drunk.

### 4

We met years ago, when I was still an up-and-coming rewriter. We met at a party where we were both drunk out of our minds and terribly delighted with ourselves and each other. As a result, I dropped the agent I had at the time and Guido became my agent.

This proved disastrous.

Either because he truly believed in me, or because he felt obliged to make me think he did, he kept telling me over and over again that I was too talented to be a rewriter and that I should write something of my own. An original screenplay. An original adaptation, if nothing else.

I tried explaining to him that I was a hack, a happy hack, a rewriter who was only capable of rewriting. That I had no coherent point of view and that a point of view was the minimum requirement of someone who would put an empty page into a typewriter to write something of his own.

But Guido persisted. He continued to press the issue until finally, worn out by having to defend myself against his faith in me, I decided to call it quits. I left him and his agency and never got another agent. It turned out that I didn't really need an agent for the kind of work I did. My reputation preceded me. The demand for my services, if anything, only grew after I left Guido.

The fact that we remained friends despite the breakup of our professional relationship convinced both of us, I think, that we were much better friends than we thought we were. It raised what had up to then been a pretty good friendship to a whole new level. For a while, we became inseparable. We went out together every night. We got drunk together. We cheated on our wives together. We went on vacations to strange places with strange women together. I did things with Guido that I have not done with any other man. I even went bowling with him once, in the middle of the night.

Out of that togetherness, and inspired, perhaps, by visions only drunks can behold, a new faith was born between us, which we embraced with a passion of two besotted souls clinging to a common dream. Our faith had no name as such, but the object of our worship did. It was the Family.

We became, or rather came to think we were, family men extraordinaire. Fathers who not only loved their children, but lived for their children. If there was such a thing as a Fundamentalist Family Man religion, then Guido and I were its founding fathers.

True faiths, as everyone knows, are immune to reason and empirical evidence. Those are things reserved for cynics and unbelievers. So even though Guido and I seldom saw our own families, even though our families were never the beneficiaries of our newfound religious fervor, our faith in ourselves and in each other as Family Men was impervious to such piffles of reality. And when we found ourselves separated from our wives and estranged in more ways than one from our children, our faith in the Family was stronger than ever. Freed from the everyday burden and petty details of our earthly families, our faith was allowed to soar, to become totally spiritual, as all great religions are.

So it wasn't mere friendship that made me cling to Guido, my last friend. We had founded a faith together.

## 5

He's rip-roaring drunk now, and roaring with laughter. Tears stream down his face.

The two stories I told him, in the order in which they occurred, were both big hits. Guido's response to them was so contagious that even I laughed while finishing the second.

I began with the story of the old man in my father's overcoat. Even to tell a story, you need a point of view. I chose a poignant point of view, intent on telling a poignant story. But as soon as I got to the part where I thought the old man was my dead father, Guido started laughing. The explanation for my mistake, the overcoat, only intensified his laughter. And when I said it was a camel-hair overcoat, Guido for some reason found that so funny that he started gagging and banging on the table.

"Camel hair!" he roared. "It was camel hair!"

Seeing how things were going, I dropped my poignant point of view and went with Guido's hilarity for the rest of the story.

The story of my physical examination was an even bigger hit. Just the mention of GenMed made Guido laugh. The name of the doctor was even funnier.

"Kolodny, his name was Kolodny!"

By now I knew that I had a real winner in the wings by the name of Elke Höhlenrauch. And sure enough, when I got around to her, Guido exploded.

"Elke what?"

The more authoritatively I pronounced her last name, umlaut and all, the more he laughed.

Even the denouement was funny, even the fact that I sat there now completely uninsured was hilarious.

"No GenMed for you," Guido, drunk as a skunk, advises me. "It's too late, pal. It's too late for insurance for you, my friend."

6

Our lunch arrives. Two salads. Caesar's for Guido, chef's for me. And a flashing V sign from Guido to our waiter for another round of drinks for us both.

"I knew I had something to tell you." Guido bangs the table with his hand, irritated that it had almost slipped his mind. "I must be getting old," he says, and he says it in precisely the tone of someone who thinks that by admitting to something he automatically escapes the consequences of the admission.

"You'll like this," he assures me, then pushes away his salad and lights a cigarette.

I do likewise.

"I don't suppose you've heard what that scumbag pal of yours did recently?"

"Scumbag pal" is Guido's official designation for Jay Cromwell. He knew, of course, that I had worked for Jay, and he knew as well, because I like to advertise such things, that I would never work for him again.

Guido is a discerning disseminator of Hollywood dirt. He is aware, I'm sure, that examples of Cromwell's treachery are so commonplace that nobody bothers mentioning them anymore unless it's something truly satanic.

We're both smoking. Guido's talking. I'm listening. Listening also are the three men and one woman at the table across from us.

Cromwell, it turns out, didn't do anything out of the ordinary in itself. It was his choice of victim that made the gossip sickening.

Using a fine-print clause in a contract, Cromwell, as a producer, had taken away a completed film from its director. But the director in this case wasn't just any director. He was part of the history of American films. Arthur Houseman. The grand old man of movies was so respected and loved that everyone simply called him the Old Man.

He had retired some years ago and then, I remember reading, he had decided to come out of retirement to make one last film so that, as he put it, he could go out "on a note of grace, God willing."

That was the last I had heard of him until now. According to Guido, not only was his film taken away from him but the Old Man was very ill as well.

Guido is outraged. "I mean, to even think, to even contemplate doing such a thing would be criminal, but to actually do it when it's the Old Man's last movie and he's sick and possibly dying, it's . . . it's . . ." He paws the air with his hand in quest of some damning word.

"It's monstrous," I say.

"That's what it is." Guido bangs the table several times in rapid succession. "That's exactly what it is. It's monstrous. It's fucking monstrous what he did."

"He's evil," I tell him, "he's out-and-out evil. I've met other people in my life who had an evil streak in them, but Cromwell . . ."

I go on.

Then Guido pitches in.

Then it's my turn again.

Then our table becomes a free-fire zone, where the two of us alternate firing away at Cromwell at will, like a couple of freedom fighters with Uzis. We berate the scumbag sonovabitch.

I say, or Guido says—it's hard to say after a while who's saying what— but one of us says: "Somebody should put a bullet through his head."

I don't tell Guido that I'm planning to have dinner with this very Jay Cromwell we're tearing to shreds. The timing is all wrong for such a piece of information. It would put a damper on our outrage, and our outrage is so animated and freewheeling that it seems a shame to undermine it when it's going so well. It seems to me much better to wait. It will make a much better story that way. The story of my harangue delivered in that monster's face.

We're on a roll. So we just roll on with our outrage, feeling ever more invigorated, rejuvenated, refreshed, remoralized by our indignation at this evil man.

## 7

My lunches with Guido in the Tea Room, and over the years there have been many of them, are as bound by tradition as a three-act play. Over drinks, he tells stories or I tell stories; jokes are allowed. We laugh and smoke and make disparaging, male-type remarks about each other's appearance, and that roughly is Act I. Over the lunch itself, which varies but tends to be a salad of some kind, we try to become concerned citizens of our city, state, country, the world, and find an issue that can trigger our sense of public outrage or moral indignation, and that's Act II. Act III, ever since we cofounded our religion, is reserved for the glorification of family and family life.

The waiter clears away the lunch debris and sweeps the cracker crumbs off our tablecloth. We have said all that we could say about Cromwell. We have divested ourselves fully of our outrage, and our mood is reflective now.

Our waiter knows us well and because he does, and because he knows what pleasure it gives us to refuse, he asks:

"Some dessert for the two of you today?"

We dismiss the offer out of hand. Dessert? For us? We don't even dignify his offer with a verbal rejection. We just shake our heads in the austere, preoccupied manner of two men on a mission. Just coffee.

The waiter nods and departs.

Over coffee, decaf for Guido, regular for me, we light our cigarettes and begin.

Sometimes I begin. Sometimes he does. For all I know, there is a definite pattern here, whereby we take turns from lunch to lunch, invoking the topic so close to our hearts.

This time Guido begins.

"How's Billy doing?" he asks.

"Ah." I leave the cigarette in my mouth, because I need both hands for the gesture I make. Arms half raised, hands spread out, my shoulders shrugging in delight. "He's wonderful. He's just wonderful. I think he's really found himself at Harvard. While you were in LA, I drove up there to see him," I lie, "but I didn't tell him I was coming. You know. Didn't want him altering his schedule. And the damnedest thing happened. I knock on his door and he shouts, 'Come in, it's open.' So I come in, and there he is with a telephone in his hands. 'Dad,' he shouts, as if he can't believe it's me. And do you know what he was doing?"

"What?" Guido smiles, anticipating something wonderful.

"He was on the phone, calling me. Can you believe that? I mean, there he was on the phone, calling me in New York, and the door opens and there I am."

Guido claps his hands, basking in the warmth of my story.

"Some people don't believe in this," I go on, "but I just had this feeling that he wanted to see me. It was just a feeling, but when it's your own child, you somehow just know."

"Of course you do, are you kidding? It's the parental instinct in you," Guido tells me.

"Maybe that's what it is."

"No maybe about it, pal. The parental instinct is older than the pyramids. It's older than civilization. It's older than history. It's prehistoric." He points drunkenly toward the back of the Tea Room, as if that's where prehistory is to be found, and goes on:

"It's nature's way." He's beginning to shout, to bellow. He's feeling inspired. "Every living thing on this planet of ours which we call the Earth, every living, breathing thing on it, cleaves to its own." His big arms wrap around himself in a vivid demonstration of what he's talking about. Cradling himself in his own arms, he goes on. "Dogs cleave to their own. Cats do. Kangaroos in Australia. Wolves in the tundra. Polar bears in Alaska. Squirrels in Central Park. They all have this need inside of them. This family need. Even trees! Even goddamn trees grow in groves and what's a grove but a family?"

"What, indeed," I reply.

"They say that no man is an island, but I say, what's an island? That's what I say, Saul. What is an island? Think about it, pal. Even an island, an inanimate object, when you think about it, but even this inanimate island isn't just an island. It doesn't just float on top of the water like a bunch of scum. It's connected, right? It's anchored to the rest of the earth. It cleaves, is what it does. It cleaves to the earth in the midst of the turbulent sea the way you and I cleave to our darling children, our families."

What all those Bloody Marys I drank have failed to accomplish, I now come close to achieving in another way. I begin to feel the symptoms of virtual intoxication. I get high on our own fiction of family and fatherhood. My faith soars, taking me along with it.

What does it matter that Guido and I are living alone, that he sees his daughter Francesca almost as rarely as I see my son, and even then, following my lead, never alone. Those are mere facts and faith is not sustained by facts.

"My daughter Francesca called me on the phone last night," Guido tells me. He reaches across the table and places the full weight of his left hand on top of mine. "It was late when she called. I was in bed, but not asleep. Do you know what she said?"

"No, I don't."

"Papa," she told me, "I'm just calling to see how you are and to tell you that I love you."

His big chin begins to tremble. Tears well up in his drunken eyes. A sob escapes.

"How about that, Saul? What a girl, right? My angel. My sweet angel. My Franny." He squeezes my hand, weeping.

I know, because I know Guido, that no such telephone call took place, but knowing that does not prevent me from being moved by his lie. I find his need to fabricate that phone call probably far more moving than if it had actually occurred as described. Truth, it seems to me yet again, has lost its power, or the power it once had, to describe the human condition. It is the lies we tell now that alone can reveal who we are.

"Oh, Saul," Guido cries out, "how lucky we are to have the children we do. How lucky we are to be smart enough to know what really matters in life."

"Yes, my friend," I pick up the chant, "how lucky indeed! How fortunate beyond words we are to be loving fathers of loving children. Because when you come right down to it, what is life without love, and what is love without children and family? What would be the point of even getting up in the morning if it weren't for . . ."

I'm on a roll.

# CHAPTER SEVEN

### I

Getting a date for my dinner with Cromwell, an idea that had sprung to my mind at the sight of Elke Höhlenrauch's breasts, became a full-time job as the day of Cromwell's arrival drew near.

I was determined to have it out with him in public, to tell him to his face and in front of witnesses what I thought of him and that I never wanted to see him again.

My moral man monologue was coming along fine. "Listen to me, Cromwell, and listen well," it began, and went from there to denounce in detail the evil in him.

But to show up alone for my dinner with him when he, I knew, would be accompanied by some beautiful young woman would be to undermine my position in an instant. Implicit in anything I said would be the damning fact that I was alone. That despite weeks of advance warning I had been unable to come up with a suitable dinner companion.

My moral man monologue, my whole harangue under those circumstances, no matter how withering and devastating it was, could be easily dismissed by Cromwell as the ravings of a lonely, envious loser with a fat gut and a limp dick. The episode, after my departure, would be turned into broad comedy. I would be a story Cromwell told others, instead of a story I told others.

Getting a date, therefore, was not merely a social convention this time, but something attached to a high-minded moral purpose. A crusade against evil.

But the women I called didn't seem to care what my purpose was. Most of them didn't even listen long enough to learn that I was inviting them out to dinner. Some hung up as soon as I identified myself. Others laughed and said, "No, thank you." A few seemed to be on a crusade of their own against me and men like me. They told me to go fuck myself instead of fucking with them. What did I take them for, they wanted to know. Did I think they had forgotten the kind of man I was?

What astounded me about these women was not that they had unpleasant, or hostile, or even sickening memories of me. That I could understand. Their attitude was, in almost every instance, perfectly justified. What astonished me was how vivid their memories of me were in comparison to my own dim memories of them and the even dimmer memories of myself.

Even that squinty-eyed Peggy turned me down when I called her.

"Why should I go out with you," she wanted to know, "when I already went out with you once?"

She had me there. I could think of no convincing rebuttal.

## 2

Further complicating my life, and distracting me from the focus I was trying to maintain on getting a date for my dinner with Cromwell, was the unexpected behavior of my accountant, Jerry Fry. For some reason, Jerry took it very personally that I had walked out on my physical exam and, along with it, on the prospect of being insured by GenMed. Somebody from Dr. Kolodny's office must have called to tell him. It certainly wasn't me. I was too busy calling women.

"You left? You just left? Just like that?" Jerry was beside himself.

I was in my office. He was in his office. His office was located less than three blocks away from my office, but our local telephone line, as tended to happen more and more since the breakup of AT&T, was breaking up itself. It was full of static and whine and all those nostalgic sound effects of long-distance calls of yesteryear. This sense of distance, although I knew for a fact he was only a couple of blocks away, prevailed and added a sense of urgency to every word he uttered.

"How could you do that, Saul? How could you leave just like that, when it was all arranged? It was all set. Why? Why did you do it?"

Hoping to placate Jerry, I told him that I had left "because I simply wasn't interested in being insured at this time."

This had the effect of squirting lighter fluid on an already overheated charcoal grill.

"You what? What did you say? Not interested, is that what you said? You're simply not interested in being insured at this time! Is that what you said?"

He was incensed, seething, screaming, and the combination of his voice and the crackling static on our line made it seem that he was calling me from a burning hotel in some tropical island paradise on the other side of the world.

"That's your explanation! That's it? You weren't interested! Can I quote you on that, Saul? Do you realize that a transcript of this conversation could land you in Bellevue or some other less reputable mental institution? What the hell is that supposed to mean? You're not interested. Nobody is asking you if you're interested or not. This is insurance, Saul. Health insurance. This isn't somebody asking you if you want your carpets cleaned, to which you could then reply that, no, you're not interested in having them cleaned at this time. This is insurance! Health insurance! You don't ask yourself if you're interested or not interested in having health insurance. You just do it. You just get it. Are you listening to me?"

I was. I really was. But I couldn't understand why he was so upset that I was left uninsured as a result of a choice I made when, if my memory served me right, he wasn't nearly as upset when Fidelity dropped me from its rolls and I was left just as uninsured as I was now, but without any choice in the matter.

Victims deprived of the blessings of health insurance he could understand. Blessings of any kind lost their significance if everybody was blessed. But to decide, to actually choose, for whatever reason, not to be blessed was a sign of a mad or subversive personality.

He called me once a day, sometimes twice a day, with fresh arguments and assaults on the position I had taken. And since the period in question coincided with my desperate attempts to get a date, I not only had to put up with the insults and sarcastic remarks of the women I called, I also had to put up with the insults and sarcastic remarks of Jerry, who kept calling me.

"You think you're a rich guy, don't you? Don't you, Saul? You think you don't have to bother with health insurance because you're so damn rich. Right? Let me tell you something, Saul, rich guys are my bread and butter. I know rich guys. All I do is handle rich guys and you want to know something? You're not so rich, Saul. Not rich enough to make do without insurance, that's for sure. That's for damn sure. There's diseases out there, diseases you and I don't even know about, which could, any one of which could, slurp up your liquid assets in a blink of an eye."

He was so worked up, he actually made a slurping sound of some disease sucking up my liquid assets.

He went on to talk about diseases at length (polio was making a comeback) and made it seem that diseases had a way of knowing when somebody was stupid enough to be uninsured and went after him first. Jerry seemed to hint that diseases actually worked for insurance companies, like Mafia goons, and were sent out in pairs to wreak havoc on the lives and liquid assets of men like myself who "weren't interested in being insured at this time."

Nor should I hope to seek comfort, he warned me, in the prospect of a quick death when it came to these diseases. No, no. No, sir. Months, years, probably decades of agony and suffering lay in store for me.

There were blood clots of various kinds, leading to countless combinations of physical and mental incapacity. There were rare tropical and subtropical viruses brought over by the influx of immigrants from those parts of the world, which caused blindness, disfigurement, loss of facial, genital, and body parts, and, in some cases, total shedding of the skin. All these diseases would require prolonged hospitalization and private nursing care.

"And who's going to pay for all of that? You, that's who. You, Mr. Rich Guy. While these diseases are chewing up your life, the bills will be chewing up your assets. Chewing them up, Saul. Are you listening to me?"

I was. I really was. It was just that as his assault on my position changed, so did the motive for my position. Our conversations never became totally pleasant, but I started enjoying them. They acquired an element of a theoretical discussion, a hypothetical case of someone rejecting health insurance, and as we argued, I saw motives I had not seen before. Being open to life, instead of protected and "covered" by insurance of any kind. Being "covered," I told Jerry, was not the way to live.

"You want open!" Jerry shrieked, "I'll give you open. Open heart surgery. Open brain surgery. Open-ended agony and pain. Open bank accounts and stock portfolios. Open hospital windows with assets flying out, while you lie in bed paralyzed and drooling. You want more open? I'll give you more."

And he did.

"I know what your problem is," he called one day and ripped into me without even a hello. "You think you're better than I am. You do, don't you?"

I didn't, but I didn't get a chance to say that I didn't. His voice was choked with rage.

"You think you're better. More sensitive. That's what you think. You think you're too sensitive, too artistic to put up with such mundane things like health insurance. You're an artist who can't be bothered with crap like premiums and policies. You ever hear of hubris? This is hubris, Saul. This is fucking hubris up the ass. This is you thumbing your nose at Zeus!"

I laughed, and it's true, I might have laughed the wrong way and said something to the effect that I had no idea that accountants worried about hubris. Whatever it was, my laughter or my words, Jerry took it wrong. He took it as a snide comment on his education and his MBA degree. His education and his MBA degree were the furthest things from my mind, but that didn't matter to Jerry.

"Listen to me, Mr. PhD in comparative literature, you're not the only guy around here with a quality education. Just because I've got an MBA degree doesn't mean I'm not familiar with the classics, Greek and otherwise. I went to Yale. So when I say hubris, I know what I'm talking about, and when I say Zeus, I know who Zeus is."

And, as if I were doubting him, he went on to tell me exactly who Zeus was. Zeus was (I discovered, thanks to Jerry) the son of Cronus and Rhea, the husband of Hera and father of Athene and Hermes, etc., etc. Jerry not only went through Zeus's whole family, he rattled off almost all the gods of ancient Greece and the names of their Roman counterparts as well. And somehow he made it sound as if all these deities were arrayed against me because I was a hubris-infested chump who needed to be taught a lesson.

The next day, he attacked me on purely sociopolitical grounds. Fine, it was fine for me, an affluent asshole, if I didn't want to be insured. But what about all those people working at part-time jobs in the service industry with no medical benefits? What about them? What about all those millions of destitute poor who couldn't afford health insurance? Men of goodwill (his phrase) were busting their chops trying to get a national health insurance bill passed in Congress, and here I was, making a mockery of the whole thing. What kind of a message did that send to all those underprivileged millions in our nation? Or did I give a shit?

I told him, or I tried to tell him, that I was a private citizen and not a political candidate and that therefore I wasn't sending any messages to anybody.

"What?" Jerry jumped all over me, as if he had been hoping I'd use that line of defense. "What? What was that? A private citizen! Is that what you said? Is that what you are now, a private citizen? There is no such thing! We're either a society and a nation or we're not, and the last time I checked, we were. The United States of America. Ever hear of it, Saul? Private citizen! Private citizen is an oxymoron, you asshole. You can't be both. You can't be both 'private' and a 'citizen' at the same time. Citizen of what? Do you have some private country, some private world, of which you're a citizen, where the things you do don't affect others? The only private citizens I know live in private padded cells and wear wraparound sleeves that tie in the back. Private citizen! Do you know what that is, thinking you can be a private citizen, having the goddamn nerve to think of yourself as a private citizen? It's hubris, that's what it is. It's hubris!"

And so, once again, but this time by another route, I was back among the vengeful gods of ancient Greece.

In the end, Jerry gave up on me. I received a fruit basket from him, whether as a peace offering or a symbol, I wasn't quite sure. It was delivered by a messenger to my office, and shortly after its arrival came the last phone call from Jerry on this subject. It was his view, he informed me, that I was a self-destructive maniac and it was his job, as my accountant, to make sure to invest and care for my money in such a way that when I did destroy myself, I would at least have something to fall back on. This he would do. But I should keep one thing in mind. It wasn't just the accountants of this world who were held accountable for their actions. He hoped I liked my fruit.

## 3

The end result of my telephone calls to all the women I had ever known was that no woman who had ever known me wanted to know me anymore. My only hope of getting a date for my dinner with Cromwell was with a woman who had never heard of me.

I was left with three choices.

Cancel the dinner altogether, maybe even leave town on some pretext and not come back until Cromwell was gone.

Get a date through an escort service.

Or resort to the unthinkable and ask my own wife.

I rejected the first option as being cowardly.

All the elite escort services I called only dealt with corporate accounts. This made me afraid of the kind of date I might get from an escort service that was willing to have me for a client.

In the end, the only option I had left was to do the unthinkable. But the more I thought about it, the better it seemed. Seeing as how, despite all my efforts, I was still married to Dianah, I should at least get something out of my marriage before it ended. Dianah, although not young anymore, was considered beautiful by one and all. There was a certain panache, I decided, about showing up with one's estranged wife that might even make up for her age.

I lit a cigarette and called her.

"Hello," she answered breathlessly, as she sometimes did, for no reason at all. This used to drive me crazy when I lived with her. We'd be sitting there in the living room, bored out of our minds, rereading old *New Yorker* magazines, but when the phone rang she answered it in that breathless way of hers, as if she hadn't had a moment of rest all day.

To make sure I didn't blow this, my very last hope for a date, and to get on her good side right from the start, I steered the conversation toward the topic of our divorce.

Yes, she agreed, we really had to get going on this divorce business. We had let it slide.

So we talked divorce.

Talking divorce always had a strange way of making us feel closer to each other than we had ever been in our marriage, except for that brief period when Billy came into our lives. Talking divorce brought out the best in us. We tried to outdo each other in caring, generosity, and consideration. We shared our visions about the kind of divorce both of us wanted. Amicable, yes, but more than amicable. Much more. Tender, deeply felt, full of love, that's the kind of divorce we had in mind. Fifteen minutes and three cigarettes later, we were still talking about it. The more we talked about divorce, the more married we seemed. Not just married, but happily married.

When I lit my fourth cigarette, I decided it was time to get around to the purpose of my call.

She found the abrupt change of topic offensive and inconsiderate and told me so. Not only that, she told me that she was going to a spa with Jessica Dohrn and wouldn't be in town the whole of next week anyway.

This was Saturday. She was leaving tomorrow, Sunday. My dinner with Cromwell was on Thursday.

"Can't you put it off for a week?" I pleaded.

"For you? No. Poor Jessica has been looking forward to this for weeks and I'm not going to disappoint her."

"What about disappointing me?"

She laughed.

"Oh, darling, if I could be assured of disappointing you, I would stay in town and do it, but I don't think you're capable of being disappointed, or even of knowing what the word means. When was the last time you talked to Billy?"

"Billy. What do you mean? I talk to him almost every other day," I lied.

"Oh, Saul," she sighed, "why do you lie?"

"I don't know."

"I talked to Billy yesterday and he told me he hasn't heard from you since the McNabs' party."

"How is he?" I asked.

She found my question egregious and told me so. If I really wanted to know how he was, I wouldn't have to ask her. What kind of man was I? What kind of father was I? What kind of creature was I? Her questions built up rhythmically and stylistically, like a piece of music culminating in:

"Oh, Saul," she moaned, she made a moan out of my very name, "what *is* the matter with you?"

"What isn't?" I replied, and then tried once again to get her to change her plans and come with me to Cafe Luxembourg on Thursday, to have dinner with Cromwell.

"You're pathetic, sweetheart. You really are. Didn't you tell me a couple of years ago that you don't like Cromwell and that you would never, ever, work for him again?"

"Who said anything about working for him again? Are you kidding? And I didn't say I didn't like him. I told you I hated him and I do. I hate the bastard."

"If you hate him so much, why are you having dinner with him?"

"He called me. He's coming to town."

"What's that supposed to mean? He's coming to town. What does that mean, Saul? If Hitler were alive and called you and was coming to town, would you have dinner with him?"

"I just want an opportunity to tell him to his face what I really think of him."

"I'm sure you do, darling. And I'm sure you're bound to be magnificent, as always. How unfortunate that I won't be there to share in your triumph. You must remember to tell me all about it when I come back. Bye."

# CHAPTER EIGHT

## I

Cafe Luxembourg was filled to capacity and in full swing all around us. The table where Laurie and I sat, waiting for Cromwell and his entourage to show up, was really three tables joined together to form one and covered with a single white tablecloth. It was set for ten people. In the jam-packed, elbow-to-elbow environment, our table for ten, occupied for the moment by just the two of us, was like some last piece of vacant real estate.

Our short, anemic-looking waitress, her makeup and hairdo in keeping with the Art Deco decor, stopped at our table to inquire if we wanted another round of drinks.

Laurie's Coke glass was still half full and she covered it with her hand.

"I'm fine," she said.

I ordered another gin and tonic, my third. Laurie frowned at me, then smiled, both admonishing me for drinking so much so fast and taking pleasure in revealing how long she had known me and how well.

I lit a cigarette and reveled in this strange, recently renewed relationship of ours.

## 2

Laurie was seventeen, a senior at Hunter High School, but despite her age I had known her longer than almost anyone else in my life other than Billy and Dianah. Longer, even, than I knew Guido. I've seen only two children grow up before my eyes: my son Billy and Laurie Dohrn.

Long before she was born, long before her parents were even married, they were Dianah's friends, and when I met Dianah, they became my friends as well. A little over nine months after we adopted Billy, Laurie was born. Two years later, her parents divorced. Her mother, Jessica, not only never remarried, she never had anything to do with men after her divorce. In her concern, however, for Laurie's welfare and her desire not to deprive her daughter of something she called "the masculine side of life," Jessica singled me out, with Dianah's blessing, as the father figure in little Laurie's life.

I was asked to do the kinds of things that dads did. Crawl on the floor on all fours with Laurie on my back. Throw her in the air. Play catch, with a soft cloth ball. At the top of the list of the "masculine side of life" was having Laurie watch me shave.

"She was only two when her father left, and he was neurotic about having to be in the bathroom alone, so she's never seen a man shave," Jessica explained. "So if you don't mind, Saul, I think it's something that would be very healthy for her to see from time to time."

I didn't mind. I loved shaving. I had never thought of it as a spectator event, but I didn't mind trying. It didn't take long before I became fond of the whole thing. Either born to be or genetically predisposed to be a much better father figure than an actual father, I came to love the role-playing I was asked to do and found that the artificiality that had bothered me in theory was quite enjoyable in practice.

Almost every Saturday or Sunday, between ten and eleven in the morning, until they grew bored with the ritual, I took Billy and Laurie to the bathroom to witness "the shaving of the dad."

Billy had no desire to watch me shave when Laurie wasn't there, but with her next to him, the two of them, sharing a seat on top of the toilet seat cover, watched me with the rapt attention of true theater lovers. Seeing their faces in the mirror while I shaved was something I came to look forward to and then missed when I had to go back to shaving alone.

Despite an almost full year difference in their ages, which with three- and four-year-olds can sometimes qualify as a generation gap, the two of them got on great. Even when Billy grew older and, emulating other little boys, professed to have no use for little girls, Laurie was excluded from that condemnation. The older they got, the closer they became.

It was Laurie who introduced Billy and me to chess. It quickly became apparent that she had a true gift for the game. Billy and I got better at it over time, but we never became anything more than competent. We plunked along, one move at a time, as if playing individual notes on the piano while Laurie played chords. Using two boards, she played both of us simultaneously, and so fond of her was Billy that he took enormous pride in the speed with which she dispatched both of us. It was from Laurie that I learned, although I never admitted it to anyone, that the word "endgame" was part of chess terminology and not, as I had thought, an invention of Samuel Beckett. I used this information to correct others whenever possible.

She and Billy didn't so much fall in love as become worn out trying to resist it. They became lovers at the beginning of his senior year at Dalton, her junior year at Hunter, but it ended abruptly, for some reason.

When I left Dianah, all contacts between Laurie and myself ended as well. I missed her for a while. I thought about calling her from time to time. But then other matters and other maladies took over and I forgot about her completely.

I might have never thought of her again had not Dianah brought up her mother's name. Hearing "Jessica Dohrn" reminded me of Laurie.

Burdened by my motive for calling her, I resisted calling for as long as I could.

It wasn't until Wednesday evening, the night before my dinner with Cromwell, that I finally picked up the phone.

I pretended I was calling just to see how she was. Just to chat. To catch up.

I pretended to be surprised when she informed me that her mother had gone off to some spa with Dianah.

When I asked her, as if the idea had just occurred to me, if she wanted to have dinner with me and some people from LA the following evening, she said, "I'd love to."

3

Instead of taking a cab to pick up Laurie, I rented a limo. I wanted to be free to smoke and I also saw the advantage of having a limo waiting for us outside Cafe Luxembourg, so that after I delivered my harangue to Cromwell's face, there'd be a limo waiting to whisk us away. It seemed neat and clean that way.

I told Laurie I would pick her up at seven thirty, but I was fifteen minutes early. As it turned out, she was looking forward to seeing me so much that, early as I was, she was all set to go.

She had let her hair grow. It fell over her shoulders like black velvet curtains. Her voice was deeper. Her neck seemed longer. She had always been pretty, but now she was an achingly beautiful young woman. When she smiled, her smile seemed to have the wingspan of a bird in flight.

The way she smiled when she saw me. The way she hesitated for a split second, as if considering the appropriate form of greeting between us. The way she then chucked appropriateness aside and threw her arms around my neck, her lips on my cheek. Her words, the way she said those simple, wonderful words: "It's so nice to see you again, Saul."

"It's so nice to see you too, Laurie," I replied.

Laurie lived on Thirty-second and Third Avenue, where she had lived since she was born, and so we had a leisurely ride in the limo, north and west toward Cafe Luxembourg.

On the way there, we touched on briefly, in a chapter heading kind of way, what we were doing, what we were planning to do, and what we had done with our lives since the last time we saw each other. She was going to Stanford in the fall, to study computer science. She was now a nationally ranked junior chess player. Her heroines were the man-beating, checkmating Polgar sisters from Hungary. She was glad her mother was out of town. It was a relief to be alone, all alone, for a week. It bothered her that her mother was becoming a professional "poor friend" of rich women. Laurie worried what would happen to Jessica when Laurie left to Stanford.

I smoked my cigarettes and brought up events and memories from a long time ago. Of course she remembered coming to watch me shave, what did I think? The ballets I took her to with Billy. The movies. The symphonies. The opera, that one time.

While we talked, the limo driver driving slowly, listening at times to what we were saying and reacting with a smile of his own, I felt something happening to me. My father-figure feelings were reviving, coalescing around her. I not only felt wonderful, but I suddenly realized why.

Of all the people I had ever known in my life, Laurie was the only one left to whom I had never lied, whom I had never hurt needlessly, never betrayed in thought or in deed. She was the last living witness on this planet who could testify on my behalf without having to perjure herself. I had been loving and decent toward her for all those years, and by some miracle I had not ruined it all the way I had done with every other man, woman, and child I had ever known. My record with her was still perfect and clean and reminded me that, diseased as I was, I still had a scrap of unsullied goodness inside me.

It was something I didn't know I had.

The joy, the overwhelming joy, of that discovery.

The promise it offered.

The possibility of renewal. Of rebirth. Of living out the rest of my life in some other way.

4

The waitress brought my drink. I took a couple of sips, feeling Laurie watching me intently.

"It takes a lot more booze these days, doesn't it?" she asked.

"What do you mean?

"To get you into orbit. That's your third and you still seem completely sober."

"I didn't know you were counting."

"Old habit," she smiled. "Billy and I used to keep track."

"The three of us went out a lot."

"Yes," she nodded, "yes, we did. Public events, Billy called them. And after every event, we'd have dinner, and he and I would watch you drink and nudge each other as soon as one of us spotted the first telltale sign that you were sailing away toward blotto land."

I shrugged and lit a cigarette.

"If I remember correctly, two quick ones was all it took to fire up your rocket engines. On the third, you were in countdown. On the fourth, you were in orbit."

I decided to confess. It seemed fitting that Laurie should be the first person to hear about my drunk disease.

"I don't exactly know what the problem is, but something's gone wrong with me. I can't get drunk anymore, no matter how much I drink."

"You needn't sound so sad about it."

"Did I sound sad?"

"Yes, very. It's not exactly a tragedy, if it's true."

"It's true, all right. Watch." I held up my gin and tonic and drained it in a gulp. "You see? Nothing."

I raised my empty glass to our waitress as a sign that I wanted another.

"I am scared," I went on. "It's one thing to be on the wagon as a choice, it's something else to have no choice in the matter and be condemned to sobriety despite myself. I don't know. I've heard of bodies rejecting transplanted organs, but I've never heard of any body rejecting alcohol."

She half frowned, half smiled, uncertain whether to take my remarks as clever banter or as something genuine. I was ready to go either way.

"If that's the case," she said, "then maybe you should listen to your body."

"If you had a body like mine, would you listen to it?"

She cracked up.

I loved the way she laughed.

I loved feeling capable of provoking so much joy on her face.

As her laughter began to subside, I hit her with a follow-up to my previous punch line:

"The truth of the matter is that my body and I haven't been on speaking terms for years."

She laughed again, this time in an obliging sort of way, out of respect for me. But even as she laughed, she was letting me know that she hoped this evening would not degenerate into an entertainment. There was a polite request in her laughing eyes for us to move on to other matters, if I didn't mind.

We fell silent. I lit a cigarette. My drink arrived. Around us, the din continued and above the din I could hear the dying black swan voice of Billie Holliday overdosing on the blues. Laurie, head bowed, deep in thought, was moving the salt and pepper shakers as if they were chess pieces. Then she looked up at me.

"I was so in love with Billy," she said.

How to describe her face as she said those words? The way in which every single feature of her face, every square inch of it was in perfect alignment with the words she had spoken.

A phrase, not my own, came to mind to describe the expression she wore. "The sweet seriousness of life," somebody had called it.

"Yes," I nodded, "I know. And he was in love with you, too."

"It bothers me how it ended. How it just ended. This may be stretching our friendship, Saul. He's your son after all and I wouldn't want you to betray his confidence, but if you do know, and if you're at liberty to tell me why it all ended like that, I wish you would. He opened his heart to me and invited me inside and then he suddenly . . ." She shrugged.

"There'll be other boys," I said.

She winced and shook her head.

"I wasn't fishing around for reassurance. Of course there'll be other boys. There already are. That's not the point. The point is this particular boy. Why did he do that to me, Saul? Can you tell me?"

I retrieved a line from Billy's letter and flashed it on the monitor of my mind: "Lovely girls come and go, friends come and go, love comes and goes and I never ask it to stay because I'm waiting for you."

Laurie sat there, waiting for me to reply.

The steady look in her eyes, the expression of her face left no room for me to maneuver.

I was confronting a question posed by a seventeen-year-old girl, but the quality of her question and the features of her face made me realize that I had, despite my age and the ages of those with whom I associated, been out of touch with the world of adults until now. I had been cavorting with middle-aged kids, thirty-year-old kids or forty-year-old kids, and to answer her question properly I would need to grow up.

She, on the other hand, wearing both the sweetness and the seriousness of life with ease, neither embarrassed nor proud of her maturity, waited for me to reply.

I don't know what I would have told her had Cromwell and his entourage not arrived at that moment.

He came at the head of his cortege, which fanned out on both sides of him, so that the whole procession was shaped like a letter V. Although aware of the scrutiny he was receiving, Cromwell looked neither left nor right, disdainful, indifferent to it, the prow of his forehead cutting through all that attention like a clipper ship through floating debris. Everyone in his entourage carried a little bell in their hands, which they shook merrily as the whole group moved toward us.

# CHAPTER NINE

## I

How to describe the rest of that evening, the way in which, and the speed with which, everything changed with Cromwell's arrival?

One moment I was who I was, sitting there with Laurie, and the next I was somebody else, standing up to embrace and be embraced by him.

The way we embraced. The way I sucked in my gut when I felt the pressure of his abdomen against mine. My realization, or his, which I perceived, that our relative heights had changed by the inch and a half I had lost.

The post-embrace position. The way he pushed me away from him to look at me at arm's length. The way he looked at me. The way he looked me over, as if to say, and then saying: "Let me look at you, Saul. It's been a long time. Too long, right?"

"Right," I said.

The way I said it.

His forehead. The size of his forehead. The sheer size of it.

The young Asian girl at his side, his date, his concubine. The mirthless glow of her doll-like eyes.

I introduced Laurie as "my old, young friend."

Cromwell shook her hand with his right and with his left he squeezed my shoulder as if my flesh were a surrogate for Laurie's, and his gesture, that repeated kneading of my shoulder, was a masculine sign of commendation for my choice of Laurie as my companion.

He winked at me and with his left hand he drew me close to him again to whisper in my ear. "Nice, very nice, Saul. Robbing the cradle, but nice."

The sound of his voice, the warmth of his breath, as he breathed those words down my ear. The physical sensation that he was not merely saying the words but making sure that each one of them entered the orifice of my ear without spilling.

There were three other men there. Maybe they were older men who looked good for their age, or maybe they were prematurely old Brads. They had wonderful white teeth. Maybe the teeth were theirs, maybe not. All three had little bells in their hands, as did the young women at their sides. Cromwell rattled off the introductions, but the names I heard failed to stick. I heard them all, but then, as if some memory magnet were suddenly demagnetized, the names slid off the board of my mind and fell into a common heap.

## 2

Drinks arrived. We drank, delighted with ourselves, congratulating each other on who we were and how wonderful it was to be spending an evening like this. We had to shout to be heard, but it was so much fun being who we were that we enjoyed shouting.

The three men, and to a much lesser degree the three young women with them, were familiar with my work and they all expressed a high regard for it.

A pro, Cromwell called me.

"A toast," he said. "To one of the true pros in the entertainment industry." He raised his glass to me and I, like a true pro, raised mine to him.

Drinking up, he glanced at Laurie over the rim of his glass and winked at me again ("Nice, very nice") and smiled.

The way he smiled. How to describe the innuendo of that smile, lips parted, teeth showing, eyes elaborating on what the lips and teeth were doing.

The way his attendants responded to his smile with little smiles of their own. The voting that took place while we bantered at the top of our lungs in the din of that restaurant.

It was secret balloting by little smiles, but it was a secret only to Laurie. Sensing that something to do with her was happening but not knowing what it was, she kept her eyes downcast. In her confusion, she even moved her chair a fraction of an inch closer to mine, as if I were still her father figure, her guardian from harm.

All the girls at our table were young. The Asian girl, Cromwell's girl, was younger than the other three, but Laurie was even younger than the Asian girl.

I had the youngest one there.

Laurie's youth was transformed into consumer goods, which I possessed.

It was I who had her youth, not she.

My popularity at the table was soaring.

The ease with which, and the speed with which, my relationship to Laurie, so recently renewed, so recently treasured as a potential source of my salvation, the ease with which, and the speed with which, its nature was reinterpreted by the drinks before dinner plebiscite.

The vote was unanimous: I was fucking the youngest one there.

I was declared the unanimous winner of this night.

And it was all done by smiles and glances, the whole plebiscite took less time than it takes to take a few sips of wine.

Why couldn't I, when I saw clearly what was happening, reject the results of the voting?

Cromwell's conviction, and by his extension the unanimous conviction of his attendants and their dates, of who I was and who Laurie was and what our relationship was, the unanimity of all those convictions was much stranger than anything I possessed and I could not counter it.

I had no way of holding on to my own convictions because I had no way of holding on to anything of my own for too long.

I went along with the new drift of things. Let them think what they want to think, I thought. I'll recapture my mood of salvation later.

The way Laurie looked, unable to understand the specifics of what was going on but sensing a smarmy plebiscite descending over her.

The way she kept looking up at me for guidance.

The way Cromwell looked at her. His zest, as it's been called, "not just for his own life, but for the lives of others." The size of his forehead. The Kissinger shape and size of his forehead and the frightening power of the damned-up thoughts behind it.

3

Drunk is what I wanted to be, dead drunk, or dead even, but since none of those choices was available to me, I slipped into the role of a drunk, a role familiar to both Laurie and Cromwell from the days when I didn't have to pretend. I played it for all I was worth.

Either my reputation as a legendary alcoholic rewriter had preceded me or Cromwell had made a point of acquainting his male attendants with it, because the more I drank and the drunker I pretended to be, the more I seemed to confirm their expectation.

The way I thought I was deceiving and manipulating Cromwell with my parody of myself. After all, I knew the truth, that I was cold sober, and he didn't. The way I thought that the possession of truth gave me an advantage.

The Asian girl sitting across the table from me, next to Cromwell, was the only one keeping up with me. For every drink I ordered, so did she. Whenever she noticed that her glass was empty, she raised her arm in the air and rang her little bell at our waitress. The drunker she became, the more she laughed. When she laughed, her eyes disappeared completely and she seemed to laugh for the pleasure it gave her to be temporarily blind. I had never before seen laughter used as a blindfold.

### 4

We ordered dinner, all except Laurie. She couldn't eat, she told me. Not even a little something? No, she shook her head. I ordered a country salad to start and lamb chops, medium rare, as my entree.

And then Cromwell explained about the bells.

He spoke to me, but he looked at Laurie while he spoke.

Prior to coming here, they had all been at the Cathedral of St. John the Divine, to attend the tribute to Vaclav Havel and the celebration of democracy in Czechoslovakia. (The Asian girl roared with laughter.) As part of the program, Cromwell went on, hundreds of little bells were distributed to those in attendance, so that when Havel made his entrance into the cathedral he could be greeted by the sound of all those little bells ringing in his honor. This part of the program was called the Ringing of the Bells for Freedom.

The food arrived as ordered.

Throughout dinner, somebody at the table rang one of those little bells.

When Laurie excused herself to go to the ladies' room, somebody rang a bell. When she came back, somebody rang a bell. When a waitress, not ours, dropped some dishes on the floor and they broke, almost everyone at our table rang their bells. It became a compulsion, and the compulsion finally resulted in a kind of crescendo.

The Asian girl became inspired. She gathered up all the bells at our table. They had little key chain clips on them, and she clipped them together into two clusters of four bells to a cluster. She looped the clusters over her earrings. One cluster of bells on the left earring, one on the right. And then she shook her head, making the bells ring. All of us except Laurie exploded with laughter and applause.

Laurie excused herself to go to the ladies' room. I don't know how many times she went. I lost track.

In her absence, we played a parlor game with her and my relationship to her.

Where *did* I find her, Cromwell wanted to know. She was delicious, he thought. She really was.

I made a big show, in Laurie's absence, of denying all the innuendoes and insinuations. Laurie, I told them, was like a daughter to me.

The way I said what I said. The way I smiled when I said it. The incestuous connotations of my defense of our relationship. The remarks with which it was greeted. The way the Asian girl shook her head, ringing all those little bells dangling from her ears, the way she shook and shook her head, laughing with an eyeless face.

"Really, really," I insisted. "She used to come and watch me shave when she was a little girl."

"And I bet she still does," somebody said.

The way we all applauded the remark and laughed. The way I laughed. The way Cromwell laughed. The way he flung back his head and laughed, so that all his teeth showed.

Laurie's return.

The way she looked, walking back toward us, her long neck seeming not so long anymore. The way in which, and the speed with which, our laughter subsided when she sat down again next to me. The way she looked when she absorbed, as she couldn't help absorbing, the smarmy leftovers of the conversation that had prevailed during her absence.

Her eyes. The way she didn't know what to do with them. Where to look.

5

After dinner, over after-dinner drinks, another parlor game began.

Could anyone guess, Cromwell wanted to know, his Asian girlfriend's country of origin.

We all took turns playing the game, all except Laurie.

Cromwell gave a hint. It was Southeast Asia.

Thailand?

No.

Laos?

No.

Vietnam?

No.

Cambodia, somebody finally guessed. Yes, she was from Cambodia. We all burst into applause.

The way in which, and the ease with which, the banter turned from her country of origin to movies. Somebody wanted to know, maybe it was me, if she had seen *The Killing Fields*.

### 6

Later, and only when asked, Cromwell regaled us with details of the various movies he was planning to make and the various stages of development of each of the projects.

The ravenous, empty hunger he created in me for an assignment, a rewrite job on one of them. A hunger for something for which I had no need, or use, or desire, but a genuine hunger nonetheless.

As an entertaining finale to our dinner, Cromwell told the story of our last collaboration and the last time we saw each other. His reenactment of the young writer's attack on us in the lobby of the theater in Pittsburgh. The way the writer wept and cursed and called us names. Cromwell's interpretation of that event as comedy. The way everyone laughed and applauded his performance. The way I laughed and applauded with the rest.

### 7

The parting outside Cafe Luxembourg. The waiting limos. The way I staggered as if drunk. The way Cromwell took me aside and asked me to meet him for lunch at two at his hotel tomorrow. The way he told Laurie how much he had enjoyed her. The Cambodian girl with the bells still dangling from her earrings. The way she laughed and laughed when she caught herself staggering toward the wrong limo.

The almost balmy February night.

### 8

The seemingly endless limousine ride with Laurie, back to her apartment on the East Side.

The way she either refused or could not bring herself to look at me. The silence between us.

My memory of our limo ride to Cafe Luxembourg. Our limo conversation. My memory of Laurie as my guardian angel. The last person on earth who could speak on my behalf. The way it all seemed so long ago. The same night, but so long ago.

The memory of that sweet seriousness of life I had seen in her face.

My growing desperation, the closer we came to her apartment, to part with her on terms that would enable me to call her again.

When the limo finally stopped outside her building, she recoiled in horror when I tried to give her a good-night kiss on her cheek.

The way she fled from me, out of the limo, as if running for her life.

The way the limo driver took notice of everything but, being a professional, made it seem he was oblivious to the whole thing.

The way I tried to chat him up.

The taste in my mouth. The way my saliva tasted like somebody else's.

Moods, I thought, moods was all I had. Waxing moods. Waning moods.

I could not hold on to anything.

I was not, I realized, a human being anymore, and had probably not been one for some time. I was, instead, some new isotope of humanity that had not yet been isolated and identified. I was a loose electron, whose spin and charge and direction could be reversed at any moment by random forces outside myself. I was one of those stray bullets of our time.

# CHAPTER TEN

## 1

My lunch appointment with Cromwell is at two, but I am earlier than usual, early even for me. It's one thirty by the large antique clock in the hotel lobby. I have half an hour before I pick up the house phone and call him to tell him I have arrived.

There is a lot of wood and wing-backed chairs in the lobby. Next to the chairs, there are large stand-up ashtrays. I sit down in one of the leather wing-backed chairs studded with shiny brass upholsterer's tacks and light a cigarette. For once I'm not the only one smoking. The well-to-do of Europe love this hotel, and the well-to-do of Europe still smoke. The lobby is fairly teeming with them. I hear Italian, German, and Spanish being spoken. The English I do hear has a heavy British accent. I smoke and let my free hand glide over those shiny brass tacks in my chair, whose heads are as large as the hobs on hobnail boots. I control the urge to count them.

The elevator is directly in front of me and the elevator doors open and close, bringing down new people, taking up the ones I have already seen. The perfumes of departed women linger for a while, and then are replaced by the perfumes of others.

## 2

I'm not just early, I'm way ahead of Cromwell in every respect.

He will come, I know, with a manila envelope in his hands. In the envelope will be either a script in need of rewriting or a videocassette of a film in need of recutting. The manila envelope will lie there while we talk of other matters.

I need nothing from him. I have no need of money or of an assignment. I have no ambitions. I cannot be flattered because I know the narrow limits of my so-called talent and, if anything, I resent others, as I resented Guido, who try to convince me that I'm better than I think I am. I'm not. I'm as good as I can be, as good as I'll ever be. I know all that.

If anyone is leading anyone on, it is I who am leading on Cromwell by being here when I haven't the slightest intention of working with him ever again.

My mascot, the moral man within me, is busy putting the finishing touches to his harangue, the moral monologue he plans to disgorge into Cromwell's face.

"Listen to me, Cromwell, and listen well . . ."

### 3

At exactly two o'clock I pick up the house phone and call him. He apologizes profusely and informs me that he is running a little late and suggests, not knowing that I have already waited for him for half an hour, that I go and wait in the restaurant adjoining the lobby. The reservation is in his name. He won't be long.

"Have a drink, relax, I'll be down as soon as I can. And sorry about the delay. I really am."

And he sounds as if he really means it.

### 4

The hotel restaurant is old-world elegance itself. It's barely a third full and the ratio of waiters to customers is heavily stacked in favor of the customers. Cromwell doesn't smoke, but he's reserved a table for us in the smoking section out of consideration for my habit. He can be very thoughtful that way.

The old-world atmosphere of elegance and dignity makes me feel, as I light my cigarette, that I am here not in some personal capacity but as a representative of some country or some cause and will shortly be signing an important treaty at The Hague, which is just across the street.

My waiter comes and, like one world-class diplomat to another, inquires if I would like a drink. It's an important question and he gives me time to think. I thoughtfully answer that yes, I would. A Bloody Mary. In his dignified way, he seems pleased by my decision and betakes himself toward the bartender to give him the happy news.

The walls of the restaurant are decorated with lithographs of old sailing ships. Schooners. Frigates. Men-of-war. Some of them seem to be the work of primitive, self-taught artists with bizarre notions of perspective. The hull of one clipper ship is shown in its entirety above the water, as if the weight of the ship could not make so much as a dent in the sea.

My waiter brings my Bloody Mary, bows, and departs. I light a cigarette.

## 5

Cromwell appears. His back is turned as he waves to somebody in the lobby. Then, turning around, he scans the restaurant. He sees me. He smiles. In his left hand he's carrying a yellow manila envelope.

I stand up. We shake hands. Pat backs. Chit our chat.

"I am really sorry . . ." He apologizes yet again for being late. What can he do? He's in town for only a few days and there are so many loose ends to tie up before he departs for Europe. Oh, didn't he tell me? Monday, he flies to Europe. He wants to see what's happening over there for himself. Romania, Hungary, Bulgaria, Poland, Czechoslovakia. The whole thing. Then on to Moscow. The world is changing and he wants to see the changes for himself. It's an exciting time to be alive, don't I agree?

I do.

He keeps the yellow manila envelope in front of him for a while and then moves it casually aside, where it stays. Whatever is in that envelope is meant for me, but we will not discuss it right now. Whatever is in that envelope will cause somebody great harm, because whatever Cromwell does causes somebody great harm. Being an old pro with manila envelopes, I can tell by its outward shape that the object inside is not a script but a videocassette.

Once again, I'm way ahead of him. Thanks to Guido's trip to LA and the gossip he brought back, I feel pretty sure, positive almost, that the cassette inside the envelope is a video transfer of the film that Cromwell had taken away from its director, Arthur Houseman. The Old Man. The national treasure of American cinema.

Meanwhile, we banter about the night before, the dinner at Cafe Luxembourg. How nice it was. How nice to see each other again after all that time. How great it is for Cromwell to be in New York again. Cafe Luxembourg is his favorite restaurant. They just don't have restaurants like that in LA, he laments. He wishes he could live in New

York himself, but his job makes it impossible. I sympathize. He compliments me for living here and staying away from the LA rat race unlike so many other screenwriters. He thinks it's very wise of me.

It's like a sit-down waltz, our banter. The rhythm is familiar. The dance steps are second nature. We chit our chat in three-quarter time and I feel as if I'm the one who's leading.

We chat on. Our remarks become interchangeable. He tells me, or I tell him, how good he looks. How I've never, or he's never seen me look so good. And I reply, or he replies that he feels good. The whole secret to looking good is how you feel.

I have a great affinity for this kind of mindless babble. Only my mouth is involved, leaving my mind free to think its thoughts.

I ponder the nature of evil while we waltz. The nature of Cromwell's monolithic evil. What makes it so attractive?

No, it's not merely that in comparison to him I come out feeling semidecent, virtuous almost, although that is one of the fringe benefits of associating with evil.

There is something else at work here.

I focus on the problem at hand (babbling along meanwhile) like Einstein performing one of his thought experiments. I seek a larger theoretical framework for Cromwell's irresistibility.

The answer I arrive at is this: Monolithic evil is irresistible because it raises the possibility of the existence of monolithic goodness as a compensatory force. I become aware of this only when I'm in Cromwell's company. It's his evil that makes goodness come to mind.

The same principle is involved in my chronic lying. I lie not because I'm afraid of truth but, rather, as a desperate attempt to preserve my faith in its existence. When I lie, I feel that I'm actually hiding from truth. My dread is that were I ever to stop hiding from it, I might discover that truth does not exist.

The same principle yet again is involved in my penchant for mindless babble. By saying nothing over and over again, in a variety of ways, I seem to be nurturing a hope that I have something essential to express at the right occasion. The one brings the other into focus.

And so while I waltz with Cromwell and match his banalities with banalities of my own, I feel positive that the next time I see my son, I will have something deeply felt and genuine to tell him. This man, Cromwell, whom I'm dying to hate, brings to mind the son I'm dying to love.

6

We order a light lunch. The soup du jour is clam chowder, Manhattan style. Soup du jour it is for both of us. Soup and salad.

Cromwell sticks to mineral water.

I order another Bloody Mary.

"You writers." Cromwell, impressed by my drinking, sighs and shakes his head. "I don't know how you do it, Saul. I really don't. After what you had to drink last night, I'd still be in bed. I would. And here you are, picking up where you left off last night, while I'm still trying to get over my hangover. You artists," he sighs, throwing up his arms in admiration. "You're made differently from the rest of us, you really are."

I go along with being called an artist so he'll think he's leading me on. Nothing he does or says can catch me off guard. I'm way ahead of him.

The talk turns, or rather, he makes it turn, to art. Literature.

He thanks me for recommending *The Asiatics* to him. It is a novel I had recommended to him over two years ago and he has finally found the time to read it.

"Brilliant," he says, "absolutely brilliant. I've never read anything like it."

Do I think *The Asiatics* could be a movie? The way he asks the question makes it seem that everything hinges on my answer. If I say yes, a movie it will be. If no, it won't.

We discuss the pros and cons of Prokosch's novel, the ultimate road novel, and the problems associated with trying to turn it into the ultimate road movie.

Cromwell is a well-read man, a man who has read as much as if not more than I have, despite my many years of graduate school and my PhD in comparative literature. He has read the great Greek and Roman writers of antiquity. He has read the Russians, and not just the Russian Trinity of Tolstoy, Chekhov, and Dostoyevsky, but Andre Biely as well, and Sologub and Kuprin and the poetry of Blok and Akhmatova.

He knows classical music. His ear can discern the difference between a good recording of one of Beethoven's piano concertos and a definitive recording. He can talk for hours about Wagner's influence on Thomas Mann. He loves the poetry of Elizabeth Bishop and has been known to quote long passages from her work. I know, because I know him so well, that when he visits those Eastern European countries he will spend a good portion of his time going to museums, theater, concerts, ballet.

He is an enlightened man. Cultured, well-bred. Well-read. Civilized. But evil. He is evil neither for lack of enlightenment nor because of it. He is evil in addition to it.

## 7

"This," he says, alluding to the yellow manila envelope to my left and his right, "is a real tragedy. It doesn't happen often, but every now and then a project comes along that's close to my heart and when it doesn't work out, it hurts in a way that a heartbreak hurts."

He's lying to me, of course. But he's doing it in his own way. He wants me to know that he's lying. He wants me to know that every single word he's telling me is a blatant lie. I sit across from him, feeling hopelessly old-fashioned, out of touch with current trends. When I lie, I still try to deceive others that I'm telling the truth. When Cromwell lies, he asserts that there is no truth.

The waiter has cleared away our lunch debris and brought the coffee we ordered. I drink mine and light another cigarette as Cromwell goes on.

"I not only produced this film," he alludes again to the yellow manila envelope, "I financed it with my own money. I almost never do that, but this was a special case and a special film. This was, after all, not just any film by any director, but a film by Arthur Houseman."

He pauses, as if out of reverence for the name he has just uttered. Looking right at me. Reading me. Gauging my response. I congratulate myself for having guessed right the content of the envelope and raise an eyebrow in mock surprise at Cromwell's revelation.

"*The* Arthur Houseman," I say.

"The one and only." Cromwell sighs. "The Old Man himself. The last living giant in our line of work. If I can't invest my own money in one of his films, then what's the point of calling myself a producer? The man's not only a genius, he is a seminal genius. I'm not a religious man, Saul. I don't believe in God, but I believed in Arthur Houseman."

(Maybe it's the light in the restaurant, or the absence of any other bright color to compete with it, because the yellow of that yellow manila envelope seems yellower than any manila envelope I have ever seen. It's as yellow as a highway warning sign illuminated by headlights in the dead of night.)

"But," Cromwell goes on, "I had to protect myself. The Old Man's age. His health. He was a little shaky even before the shoot began. The deal we made was meant to be a mere formality. Something to satisfy the insurance boys. As you well know, every film has to be insured against unforeseen contingencies. So we signed a document stating that should the unforeseen occur and should he be either physically or mentally incapable of delivering a satisfactory first cut of the film, the ownership of the film would revert to me and then I, as a producer, would do with it whatever, in my opinion, was best for the film."

He pauses. He shakes his head.

"Did I ever dream that such a thing could happen? No. Do I now enjoy being in this painful position of having to take away a film from a man I revere? You know the answer to that, Doc. It's tearing me apart. It's literally tearing me apart."

He sips his coffee. I sip mine.

"But what can I do?" He goes on. "This thing—" he gestures with his hand toward the manila envelope "—this chaotic thing he calls his final cut, not his first cut, mind you, but his very final cut, is not even a respectable assemblage. It's like confetti, Doc. I swear to you, that's what it's like. Celluloid confetti strung together at random. I tried talking to him, but there's no talking to the Old Man anymore. The combination of old age and disease, I don't know. The only thing I do know is that he's lost it, I'm afraid, but please, not a word about this to anyone."

I nod, signaling my pledge of silence. And then, as if in eulogy for the Old Man who's lost it, a respectful and full moment of silence follows. And then Cromwell goes on again.

"Like I told you, I've put up my own money to make this film, but you know me, Doc. You know me probably as well as anyone and you must know that I don't give a damn about money. I've lost money before and I'll lose it again. It's not a question of money. This man"—he points with his index finger at the yellow manila envelope—"was one of my idols. He's the reason I'm in this business in the first place. I grew up, as so many of us did, on his films, and now I feel like the guardian of his name and his reputation and his place in history. This will be his last film. He doesn't have much longer to live. Six months to a year tops. I just can't let him go out like this. He deserves better. It's a case where we have to save him from himself.

"I don't want to kid you, Doc. This is not just another easy fix. For all I know, and God knows I'm not an artist like you, but for all I know, the film may be unfixable. But if there's anyone who can salvage this great man's last work and let him enter the Pantheon in peace, it's you.

You have an uncanny facility with celluloid and a genius for the spine, the story line. Yes, you do. You know you do, so spare me your modesty. If there is a story in all this confetti, only you can find it and bring it to life. It's not much of a plot . . ."

He tells me a little about the plot of the film, but I'm only pretending to listen. I'm so far ahead of him that I know that there are always two plots in any project with which Cromwell is associated. There is the plot of the movie itself and then there is the plot of Cromwell's motives and maneuvers as a producer of that movie. If I accept the assignment, I will work on one plot. The other plot will work on me.

I am way ahead of him, but being way ahead of him is a problem in itself. I am mesmerized by my own foresight. Everything that is happening conforms with my predictions and my seerlike ability to foresee it all.

"I've transferred the film to a videocassette," he says, and moves the yellow manila envelope to table center. "In addition to what's on the cassette, there are thousands of feet of raw footage that the Old Man shot but never even bothered to edit. He wanted it destroyed when he found out what I was doing, but fortunately we managed to rescue it just in time. If and when you want to see any of it, just give Brad a call and he'll take it from there. Meanwhile, take the cassette home and have a look. Maybe it is hopeless. Maybe even you won't be able to fix this one. Think it over. There's no rush. I'll be in Europe for four to five weeks. We can talk when I come back or, if you want to reach me, just give Brad a buzz. He'll know where to find me."

He signals to the waiter for a check.

He winks at me while signing.

"That was some little girl you were with last night, you old goat," he compliments me.

I shrug.

He smiles.

I smile.

He checks his watch and gestures that we still have a few minutes. No need to rush my coffee.

I light another cigarette. I sit there and wait for something to happen. For some act of man or God to keep me from forming another alliance with Cromwell. For something or someone to intercede.

If knowledge is power, then all the power is on my side. I know Cromwell so well that a fraction of the information I know about him should suffice to make me recoil from the offer on the table.

And yet nothing happens.

There is something about being fully informed that's so satisfying that it becomes an end in itself. Instead of begetting a response, being informed precludes having a response.

We walk out together. I am carrying the yellow manila envelope in my hand.

We part in the lobby.

It's a little after four o'clock when I walk out of the hotel. Park Avenue is jammed with cabs going in both directions. The yellow of the manila envelope in my hand is yellower than any cab I see.

# CHAPTER ELEVEN

## I

From the moment I returned to my apartment Friday afternoon until I finally saw Arthur Houseman's film Sunday evening, the videocassette, removed from the envelope and lying on top of it, remained on my dining room table.

They remained there the whole time, one on top of the other. A videocassette. A yellow manila envelope. Two ordinary, mass-produced objects. As ordinary and as familiar as paper cups or disposable razors. There had to be hundreds of thousands if not millions of manila envelopes and videocassettes in circulation which were absolutely identical to the ones on my dining room table.

But after I had lived with them for two days, looking at them, picking them up and putting them down, their very mass-produced ordinariness began to invest them with a quality of foreboding. Not any specific foreboding but a kind of general mass-produced foreboding.

My own personal unease with videocassettes was something else entirely. Their submissive acceptance of all images and impressions to which they were exposed was a trait I also had. They came in various grades of quality, but as far as I knew there was no videocassette with a conscience that refused, on principle, to record some abomination or other. From the totally trivial to the truly sublime, it made no difference to any of them. Their reusability was particularly troubling. The way you could erase them by simply recording something else over them. What was there was suddenly there no more. Replaced by what was there now. I was uneasy because I had so much in common with these inanimate objects.

2

Sunday evening.

I unplugged the telephone so I wouldn't be interrupted while watching the film. I took a clean ashtray and a pack of cigarettes and placed them on the end table next to the couch. Then I inserted the videocassette into my VCR.

There were no credits. No music. Nothing even to tell me what the film was called. The film simply began.

A man in his mid-thirties is at the wheel of a car. He's driving slowly, both hands on the steering wheel. It's a narrow, residential street lined with houses, lawns, and trees. Judging by the trees, it feels like a small town in the Midwest. Judging by the light, it's early morning.

He stops for a stop sign and stays there a little too long. We're tight on his face and he seems to be thinking thoughts he knows he should not be thinking.

The tempo of the film as it proceeds is controlled and deliberate, but as hypnotic and unassuming as a river flowing. It is the story of a love affair between a man and a woman, both of them married to somebody else.

About fifteen minutes into the film, the scene shifts for the first time, to a local restaurant.

Our would-be lovers, who are not lovers yet, go there for a cup of coffee.

They seem very eager to demonstrate to others, as well as to themselves, that by going to a public place together they have nothing to hide.

They sit down in a booth.

A waitress, played by an actress I have never seen before, watches from a distance. There is nothing particularly attractive or even particular about her, unless it is the unusual whiteness of her face. The face itself is as ordinary as the decor of that restaurant.

She watches them. She likes both of them. She walks up to their booth to take their order.

"Hi," she says. "And how's every little itsy-bitsy thing with the both of yous?" And without waiting for a reply, she inquires in a mock-sophisticated tone: "Do you want to hear our specials for today?"

She knew the couple. They knew her. It was the kind of town where almost everyone knew everyone else and there was nobody who didn't know that there were no specials in this restaurant.

Having said her line, as if amused by it herself, the waitress laughed.

Everything stopped. The videocassette continued to roll, the scene in the restaurant continued to play, but I was deaf and blind to it all, undone and disoriented by the laughter I had heard.

I knew that woman. I had never seen her before, but I knew her. I didn't know her name and she didn't know mine, but I knew her.

## 3

Dianah and I met and married when we were quite young. I was at Columbia at the time. She was going to school across the street at Barnard College. We met at a party and fell in love at first sight, as we later described it to others. I was in graduate school. She was an undergrad. I was in comparative lit. She was in political science. She was blond and petite. I was on the dark and burly side. She was immaculate in her appearance. I was dressed in those days, not without affectation, like a tattered book jacket. Her parents lived in Santa Barbara, California, mine in Chicago, Illinois. Together, like a demographically correct presidential ticket, Dianah and I seemed to be in a position to have everything.

She graduated from Barnard at the same time that I got my PhD from Columbia. Shortly after that, we got married. Her parents were very rich. They were thrilled that their daughter was marrying a certified member of what they called "the intelligentsia." They bought us a huge apartment on Central Park West and endowed us with enough money that neither of us had to work for a living. They were both quite old, and when they died, the wealth Dianah inherited was substantial.

And so there we were. We were young, she was beautiful, I was an intellectual, we were wealthy, we had everything except a baby.

Dianah wanted to have a baby right away. She didn't want to be just a mother. She wanted to be a young mother. Her own parents had been quite old when she was born and she felt cheated that she had never known them as anything other than old her whole life. She didn't want her child to have to repeat that kind of an experience.

She was going to be a young mother. She loved that image of herself. "We'll take our baby everywhere with us," she kept telling me.

Freed by Dianah's wealth from the necessity of pursuing an academic career, I was trying to write something of my own at the time. I soon discovered that although I was considered a witty and amusing conversationalist, a talent much admired in the social circles in which we moved, I really had nothing to say. Even my talent as a conversationalist was that of someone capable of responding to other people's ideas rather than initiating any ideas of his own. It seemed that I lacked both the talent and the creative urge ever to become a writer.

To become a father, to create a baby, seemed at the time an artistic endeavor of which I was capable. I embraced the idea wholeheartedly. Dianah would be a young mother. I would be a youngish father. We would take our baby everywhere with us. We became passionate on this subject.

Passion produced pregnancy after pregnancy but no baby. One miscarriage followed another and was in turn followed first by a deep depression and than by a renewed and almost fanatical desire for a child.

After her fifth miscarriage, Dianah began to panic. We consulted several specialists, who all reassured her that there was nothing biologically wrong with her, that she was putting too much pressure on herself to have a baby and that if she just relaxed, waited a year or two before trying to have a child again, everything would probably turn out all right.

But Dianah couldn't wait. She felt time slipping away. She saw herself repeating the pattern of her own parents and becoming a mother when she was long past her youth.

She wanted to be a young mother.

We decided to adopt a baby.

We quickly discovered, however, that if we wanted to adopt a baby through normal channels, it would take a long time. A few years perhaps. Every adoption agency we applied to had a long waiting list and Dianah just couldn't wait.

There were, we learned, other ways of getting a baby and getting it quickly. There were lawyers who specialized in this field, and because they were certified by the New York State Bar and because they had diplomas from reputable Ivy League law schools hanging on the walls of their offices, it made it a lot easier to overlook the quasi-legal nature of their work.

We hired one of these lawyers. His fee was exorbitant but presented no problem to our resources.

In less than a month, he called to tell us the happy news.

I answered the phone in the living room, and once Dianah discovered the nature of the call, she ran to the phone in our bedroom and picked it up.

Our baby. Already it was ours. The lawyer kept referring to it as "your baby." Our baby was not yet born. It was still in the womb of its mother. The girl who was expected to deliver in a few days was only fourteen years old. She was from Charleston, South Carolina. Her boyfriend, the father of the child, was only seventeen. He had been killed in a car accident two months ago. Drunk driving. The girl's parents were very poor but very religious and wouldn't hear of an abortion.

Our lawyer kept on talking.

Confidentiality, he told us, was crucial in these matters. We would never know the name of the biological mother and she would never know ours. There were nasty legal ramifications and heartbreaking emotional costs when names were revealed. Therefore he, our lawyer, would be our representative. He would make the trip to Charleston. He would wait there until the baby was born. He would pick it up and he would bring it to us along with all the necessary paperwork.

We would have to pay the young girl's hospital expenses, our lawyer's travel expenses to and from Charleston, and any and all expenses he incurred while waiting there for the baby to be born, plus, upon delivery of the baby, the remainder of the mutually agreed-upon fee he charged for his services.

"Congratulations," he told us.

I heard Dianah scream with joy on the extension phone. I ran from the living room toward her and she ran from the bedroom toward me. We met in the corridor and flew into each other's arms.

She went on a mad shopping spree the next day. Every few hours it seemed, the door would open and she'd be standing there engulfed in packages of baby things. Toys. Blankets. Diapers. Baby bottles. Stuffed animals too big to wrap. And then out she went to shop some more. Delivery men brought a beautiful baby crib. Dianah hung mobiles above it. She was as happy as I had ever seen her.

Three days later our lawyer called again. Dianah was out shopping for more baby things.

Our lawyer told me that he was calling me from the hospital room where the young girl was now recuperating. His voice was very low. He was whispering almost. No, no, he said, there was nothing wrong. No problems at all. Everything was fine. The girl had delivered not long ago. The baby was fine. It had been quickly removed so that the girl didn't even have a chance to hold it or see it, which lessened the risk of her becoming attached to it. She didn't even know if she had given birth to a boy or a girl.

"It's a boy," he whispered.

There was just one thing, he said, and I could refuse if it made me uncomfortable. The young girl had pleaded with him to be allowed to hear the voices of the couple who were adopting her baby. Just to hear them. To hear what they sounded like.

Had Dianah been there, I would have passed the phone to her and let her, as one mother to another, talk to the girl. But since she wasn't, I agreed to do it myself.

"You don't have to do this if you don't want to," our lawyer advised me.

"I know."

"Remember," he whispered, "no names."

"Yes. I know."

There was a long pause and then a very sleepy, very young voice came on to say, in a soft Southern drawl, "Hi."

"Hello," I replied.

Another long pause ensued and then, not knowing what else to say, I asked her how she was feeling.

"Tired," she said. "I thought it would hurt more to have a baby. But it didn't hurt. Not nearly like I thought it would. It just made me tired. I could sleep and sleep. It's a real nice room they have me in."

"My wife's not at home," I felt obliged to tell her, so she wouldn't be wondering why she wasn't talking to the future mother of her child. "She's out buying baby things. She's been shopping ever since we heard."

"Tell me, mister, if it's all right for me to know this, are you folks rich?"

"Yes, we are."

"Really?"

"Yes."

"Real rich?"

"Real stinking rich," I told her.

Maybe it was the way I said it. Laughter just bubbled out of her in response. There was this raucous catch-in-the-throat quality to her laughter that not only seemed unusual for somebody her age and startling under the circumstances, but also caused her laughter to break up, seemingly to die, and then reerupt again an octave higher. It just trailed off at the end, becoming softer and softer, but raspy soft, like the sound of a soft-shoe dancer.

We talked some more. She kept calling me mister. I didn't know what to call her. She asked me to promise that I would love her baby, that it would have everything. I promised. I thanked her for giving us her child.

"You are welcome, mister," she told me.

And then, tired and sleepy, she said, "Bye."

When Dianah returned, I told her all about the telephone call. I left out the description of the mother's laughter.

## 4

I despise and have always despised the term "little masterpiece." It's a favorite category of film critics for certain foreign films. The term "little masterpiece" seems to suggest the existence of a whole spectrum of masterpieces ranging in sizes, like products on supermarket shelves, from small to medium to large, to jumbo-sized masterpieces. And yet, despite my aversion and detestation of that term, I could think of nothing more fitting to describe the Old Man's film. It is humbling, if not humiliating, to realize that there are occasions when we're all just as fatuous as any film critic.

The film was a masterpiece because it was perfect. It was "little" because its subject matter was love.

A man and a woman. They were both, in their own words, happily married. Then, by chance, they met each other. A vision of another kind of life and another kind of love was born between them. It was as if at some point in their lives their souls had been torn in half. Just when they had adapted and found a way to be happy living with half a soul, they met the very person who had the other half in his, in her possession. The serrated, torn edges, like the two halves of a treasure map, fit perfectly.

Once they had met, they could not unmeet. Once they had experienced the feeling of being whole, they could not pretend that it hadn't happened.

So they went on meeting and the affair began.

The mere act of being together, in a car, in a coffee shop, in a motel room, increased the wattage in their lives, made both of them burn with a different kind of light. Her whole face changed, became more beautiful, when he was with her. Likewise, he changed when she was with him. A third entity came into existence when they were together. A ghost. The holy ghost of love itself.

But to keep this kind of love alive required an inordinate amount of energy, both spiritual and emotional, because it was an inordinate kind of love they felt for each other. Each time they got together was almost a mutual act of self-immolation. They were both ordinary people, an ordinary man and an ordinary woman, caught in an extraordinary love affair that required terrifying amounts of inner resources to feed the fire of the love they felt.

It was not the infidelity that troubled them, or what the people in the town were saying about the two of them. It was the sheer amount of energy they needed if they wanted to keep on loving each other.

They discovered, in the course of the film, that the demands of this kind of love were too much for them. They tried to make do on less. They tried to ration themselves. They could both tell that as a result of this rationing, something divine was dimming and dying between them. But they could not shake off the entropy. In the end, it was just the two of them, sitting in that same restaurant where we saw them early in the film. Just the two of them. The ghost, the holy ghost of love, was not there with them anymore.

Unable to comprehend what had happened, to accept responsibility for what they had allowed to happen, both of them used their marriages as an excuse for ending their love affair. They both said that the guilt they felt, she toward her husband, he toward his wife, was the cause of their separation. They said this to avoid confronting the much greater guilt and the much graver infidelity toward their own souls, torn in half again.

We see them a few years later, at a Fourth of July celebration in the park in the center of the town. Her husband is there. His wife is there. Their children are there. In a scene full of heartbreaking ordinariness, we watch the fireworks.

They have both returned to the fold of their families and former lives, but it is clear that they will be haunted forever by the vision of the love they have allowed to die. And because the memory of that vision, and the part they played in its demise, is still with them, they both seem, in that final scene in the park, despite the fireworks and the festivities and their friends and families around them, as alone as any inmate on death row.

The film was a love story, but it would be more fitting to think of it instead as a story about love, a story that explored the expiration of love in us all. The tragedy of the limited resources of man.

The waitress in the restaurant, that woman I knew to be Billy's mother, appeared several more times in the film, but only as part of the background in a scene belonging to somebody else. She never had another line to say.

The movie ended the way it began. No end credits. No music. No THE END at the end. Nothing. It just ended.

5

Four days later. It's a little after three A.M. I sit on the couch in the living room, smoking, with an ashtray on my lap. I have one of those remote-control gizmos in my hand. On top of the TV set, where I have placed it, sits a framed photograph of Billy. His high school graduation picture. On the screen I watch, yet again, the scene in the restaurant. The waitress appears. She goes to the booth. She says her lines. She laughs.

The laughter just bubbles out of her. The same raucous catch-in-the-throat laughter of that fourteen-year-old girl on the telephone some twenty years ago.

And then I rewind and replay that same scene all over again.

I have been doing this for hours.

I think my thoughts or they think themselves, it's hard to tell the difference. I think the kind of thoughts that only God should think, but the remote-control gizmo in my hand makes me feel godlike.

The three of us, Billy, his mother below him on the monitor, and I sitting on the couch opposite them, the three of us are like three parallel rivers, three parallel lines, which in the old Euclidean geometry could never meet and intersect, but which in the modern time-bend and space-bend universe can. With a phone call or two (another remote-control gizmo) I can alter the landscape of all three of our lives. I can change the course of the rivers. I can cause a confluence to occur. I can, like God, bring mother and son together. There is something terrifying about doing this, meddling in their lives in this way, but I know that I can do it.

What would happen, I wonder, if I arranged to bring mother and son together without either of them knowing that they were mother and son?

Would something in them respond to each other?

Would they know in some way that they were flesh of the same flesh?

My thoughts move on as I replay the scene again on the TV screen.

Despite my many failures as a father, I now have (do I not?) something enormous and essential in my possession that I can give Billy and that will (will it not?) make up in one fell swoop for all the derelictions of my past. If I give him back his mother, that will (will it not?) more than make up for all the rest.

What greater gift could I give him?

And by doing so, would not a bond form between us, some new bond, loving in its own way? Would he not thereafter think of me as a true father, because who else but a true father gives back a mother to a child?

And she, would she not see in me a deliverer who gives her back something she foolishly gave away as a child?

It is possible (is it not?) that thereafter I will be an indispensable and cherished part of their lives. It is Saul, they will say (will they not?) who brought us together. We owe it all to him and we will always love him for it. And as a result I will (will I not?) finally have a home of my own in their hearts.

I think my thoughts, or they think me, it's hard to tell which, and because I'm in a mood to do so, I warn myself against setting such thoughts in motion.

There is something terribly wrong, I tell myself, about my godlike contemplation of intervening in their lives.

A man like me, incapable of playing the role of a man properly, should not try playing God with the lives of others.

My mood is one of judicious restraint and concern for the welfare of Billy and his mother.

But I know myself. I know that my mind revolves. I know that my moods are like phases of the moon. I know everything except how to stop being the way I am.

# CHAPTER TWELVE

## I

Her face grew on me. Either because I knew who she was or because there really were features in common, I came to see many similarities between the moving image of her face and the framed photograph of Billy on top of the TV set.

Billy was sixteen in the photograph.

When she was sixteen, Billy was two.

I didn't know her name. I didn't know where she lived. I didn't know if she was now married or not, with or without children of her own. I didn't even know if she was still alive. People die. And sometimes they die senseless, random deaths. The pages of the *New York Times* were full of stories of random bullets and random victims and there was no guarantee that this epidemic of randomness had not claimed her as well.

It was all I could do to keep myself from calling Cromwell's Brad in LA and getting all the information I needed about her, or at least enough to allow me to find the rest for myself.

As the crisis of what I should do intensified, my response to it was to let my beard grow. If this was not exactly dealing with the crisis, the sight of my hairy face in the mirror every morning was a useful visual reminder, lest I forget, that I had a crisis on my hands.

When Dianah called me, my scraggly beard was approaching its first full week of existence.

She had just returned from her spa. It was wonderful. Truly wonderful. They had both had such a wonderful time, especially "poor Jessica" who seldom got a chance to go to places like this.

We decided to meet for dinner that Saturday. Although I did not feel like seeing her, it seemed like a good idea to discuss with her in person the details of my dilemma. The least I could do, before I did anything about Billy's mother, was to inform Dianah about her existence. My personal feelings about Dianah aside, she had been a good mother to Billy and deserved to be consulted.

### 2

The French restaurant where Dianah and I go to discuss our divorce is located not far from my office, on Fifty-eighth Street.

The restaurant, when I get there, is packed. The din is pleasantly deafening. We agreed to meet there at eight, but I am early as usual. Dianah, I know, will be late, as always.

The maitre d' is a man named Claude who greets me warmly since I am an old customer, then apologizes that my table is not ready yet. He inquires, as he always does, about Dianah, and I tell him, as I always do, that she is fine and will be along shortly. Claude is aware of my scraggly beard, but in the best maitre d' fashion he manages to convey the impression, without saying a word, that a scraggly beard is just what I needed.

He leaves to greet other customers. I go to the bar and order a drink to pass the time while I wait for Dianah to show up. I have three bourbons in a row. I chug the first two. I sip the third. But the drinks have absolutely no effect on me. It's like pouring lighter fluid on myself, only to discover as I strike one match after another that I'm completely fireproof.

### 3

Dianah finally arrives. She is wearing a striking blue dress dotted with lifelike images of little endangered elephants. Whether African or Asian I'm not qualified to say, but there are dozens of them, all over her blue dress, beautifully replicated, tusks and all.

Although we've spoken on the phone, we haven't seen each other in person since the McNabs' day-after-Christmas party at the Dakota. She looks at me, and then she looks at me again and bursts out laughing.

"A beard!" she cries out and claps her hands. "My poor darling," she says, "it looks like a swarm of flies landed on your face."

We kiss. She pulls back. She strikes a pose. She is convinced, as she has told me on the phone, that her stay in that spa has done her a world of good and that as a result she now looks entirely different, younger, more beautiful, radiant. She looks exactly the same to me, but the sheer horsepower of her conviction that she has been rejuvenated overwhelms my perceptions. Who am I to say she doesn't look radiant?

"You look wonderful," I tell her. "I've never seen you look so good."

"I feel good," she says.

Claude appears. He leads us to our table. Dianah follows him. I follow her. If there's one thing at which she excels, it's the way she walks through a crowded room. I genuinely admire the way she does it. A kind of runway walk.

On the back of her blue dress too there are little doomed pachyderms. Her gleaming platinum-blond hair shines above them like the merciless sun over the defoliated, drought-stricken plains of the Serengeti.

We sit down at our table and check out the people at the tables around us. They return our gaze. We order drinks. Dianah, confident of her radiance, radiates. I light a cigarette.

The drinks arrive. We toast each other. I chug mine and light another cigarette. She sips hers and tells me about the wildlife conference she attended at the spa.

The natural habitat of countless species, she tells me, is being systematically destroyed.

"At least there's a system to it," I tell her.

She frowns.

"This wildlife expert from Seattle pointed out to us that once the natural habitat of a given species is destroyed . . ."

I drink my drink and smoke my cigarette and wonder, as she goes on, if I myself have ever had such a thing, a natural habitat.

The Eskimos have the Arctic. The Pygmies have their jungle. The rain-forest Indians have or have had their rain forest.

My co-op on Riverside Drive is very nice, very spacious, the maintenance is reasonable and the view is quite pleasant, but no, I wouldn't call it a home and I certainly wouldn't call it my natural habitat.

Maybe white people no longer have natural habitats.

"There are over eight hundred and fifty endangered and threatened species," Dianah tells me, "not including plants. If the list included plants, there would be over one thousand and seventy. In the past twenty years alone, over three hundred species were declared extinct while awaiting government approval to be on the endangered list. At this rate . . ."

Our waiter comes to take our order. Dianah falls silent and listens to the specials of the day. Some items on the menu are, it would seem, endangered as well. There is only one sea bass left. A couple of other selections are unfortunately extinct tonight. No more Dover sole. Ditto for brook trout.

We place our orders. It's absolutely pointless for me to keep drinking, but I order another bourbon and a bottle of wine.

The waiter takes our menus and departs.

Dianah, deeply concerned, admonishes me for drinking too much. She reaches across the table and places her beringed hand on top of mine.

"You must take better care of yourself, darling. You really must."

"Why's that?"

"Oh, Saul," she sighs.

My bourbon arrives.

I don't need this drink. What I need is to get drunk, but since I can no longer get drunk, it would be very easy for me to give up drinking altogether. Although I no longer love Dianah, I haven't got the heart to hurt her. And it would hurt her if I stopped drinking. She has invested so much time and energy popularizing the myth that it was my alcoholism that was responsible for our wrecked marriage, that to give up drinking now would almost seem vindictive. For me to show any personal improvement after our failed marriage would border on being spiteful. Although I am riddled with diseases and reprehensible traits, spite is not one of them. So I know that the best thing I can do for her is to uphold the myth that I am a hopeless drunk. I feel I owe her that much.

So I drink my drink. She is both concerned and reassured.

Our wine arrives.

I start in on the wine.

Our salads arrive.

4

Over salad, while I wonder when to bring up the subject of Billy's mother, Dianah launches into her lament. Her lament spills over from the salad to the main course, which is lamb chops for me, sea bass for her, with a side order of creamed spinach.

She interrupts her lament to inquire how I like my lamb chops. I in turn inquire about her sea bass. We're both delighted with our selections and then her lament continues.

Actually, "lament" is not the right word for it. It's some new genre. A divorce dirge? An oratorio for a long-lost marriage? I don't know what to call it.

She marvels at herself for having survived our marriage intact. Other women, she is sure, would have been completely destroyed by being married to a man like me.

"When I think of what I've been through," she says, shakes her head, and goes on.

I drink my wine and eat my lamb chops and listen to her version of that marriage of ours. She's in brilliant voice, absolutely brilliant. The story of our marriage is broadcast to diners beyond the immediate vicinity of our table. They become as enthralled by her telling of it as I am. Although I was married to her for all those years, I remember no such marriage as the one she is describing at the top of her lungs.

"Oh, don't get me wrong," she says, "there were moments of bliss. Conjugal bliss. We had more than our share of bliss, I suppose, but for the most part, correct me if I'm wrong, for the most part, our marriage was one long bloodbath in which we tore at each other. We tore each other to shreds time after time, and only then . . ."

I remember neither the bliss nor the bloodbath and although I am invited to correct her, I don't. It would be needlessly cruel of me to insist now, over lamb chops and sea bass, on the truth that our marriage was neither blissful nor bloody, but merely tedious.

There is an innate sense of fair play in me. Having lied to her for all those years, the least I can do now is not contradict her and let her lie to me. There is something else, too. Her need to lie moves me.

"I suppose," she goes on, "we were always closer to being a couple of wild animals than a man and wife. Our claws sharpened, our teeth bared . . ."

When a woman lies to me, as Dianah is doing, it's as close as I get to feeling loved. Whenever one of the women in one of my many short-lived love affairs faked an orgasm, I was always deeply moved by such a selfless act of generosity, genuinely moved to think that she actually cared enough about my feelings to go to the trouble of faking. Their occasional real orgasms were not nearly as moving.

Dianah's description of our marriage is not just a fake orgasm but a fake orgasm in public and as such even more appreciated. Hearing myself described as a wild animal with sharp claws and bared teeth, and knowing that those at the tables around me can hear the description, helps me to feel again like a burly six-footer with a manly beard and not someone whose spine is contracting and bulk is expanding as he sits there gnawing on his lamb chop.

A cake with candles goes past us, carried by a waiter, and a moment later we hear the "Happy Birthday" song.

## 5

Our waiter brings us the dessert menus. While I ponder what to have for my dessert and while Dianah ponders what to have for hers, while we read and reread the selections listed on the menu in both French and English, I listen in to the conversation of the four people, two couples, at the table next to ours.

They are talking about a recent event that to me seems like something that occurred years ago. The dismantling of the Berlin Wall. A woman at the table is telling her three tablemates that she was there at the Wall to witness the event for herself. People hugging each other. Crying with joy. History in the making. A multinational audience listening to Leonard Bernstein conducting a multi-orchestral performance of Beethoven's Ninth. A man sitting across from her remarks how strange it makes him feel, although he wasn't there, that a whole city once called East Berlin is not east anymore. In his opinion, there is hardly any east left in the world. A bit of south to be sure, and a bit of north, but in the main "there is only the West now. The West and the rest," he says.

Over coffee and dessert, which is a peach tart for Dianah, a heroic slice of gâteau au chocolat for me, I intend to bring up the subject of Billy's mother, but at the last second I change my mind and bring up the subject of my father's camel-hair overcoat instead.

I tell Dianah how I saw an old homeless man on Broadway wearing my father's overcoat, several Saturdays ago.

"I told you," she tells me, "I warned you repeatedly that if you didn't come to get your father's things, I would give them away. I'm not a warehouse, darling, for the living or the dead. I have my own life to live."

I don't know why I'm telling her this story, unless it's to avoid telling her another, more pressing one. I continue. I tell her how I followed the old man uptown. The turtle pace at which he walked. His overall turtlelike appearance. I tell her how I spent an hour or so sitting on a bench next to him, with my dry-cleaning bag draped over my lap.

"You are sick, darling," Dianah tells me. "You're a very sick man. A complete neurotic."

"I may be sick, but I don't think I'm neurotic in the least."

"Of course *you* don't think you are. That's because you're neurotic. Neurotic people never think they're neurotic. That's one of the side effects. Don't you understand that a man who goes around the city following his father's clothes is somebody who is totally out of control?"

"I wasn't out of control in the least. I knew exactly what I was doing."

"You *always* think you know what you're doing. You have this image of yourself as someone who's *always* in charge. But you're not. You're just a marionette, sweetheart, that's all you are, responding to the tugs and pulls of the strings from your subconscious mind. How many times have I urged you, pleaded with you to go see . . ."

She's off again. The people at the Berlin Wall table are all ears, and being unusually candid about being so. My kind of audience.

"The subconscious mind . . ." Dianah goes on.

She believes in the subconscious the way hard-line Catholics believe in the Trinity and the doctrine of transubstantiation. To her, the subconscious explains everything and it allows her, therefore, to issue recriminations and dispensations on subconscious grounds. You can be both doomed and redeemed by the same source, depending on the mood of the issuer.

"All your problems, darling, every single one of them . . ."

According to her, all my problems, every single one of them, are caused by the turmoil in my subconscious mind. My drinking. My faithlessness in marriage. My sorry record as a father. My constant lying to myself and others. My pathetic, scraggly beard. My disregard for the feelings of others. My lack of respect for the way I look.

"Look at yourself," she exclaims, and I feel the eyes of the foursome at the Berlin Wall table turning to look at me. "You're getting fat, darling. You are, you know. You really are. You're not just overweight anymore. You're fat, sweetheart. I can't even see the chair you're sitting on. For all I know, there is no chair. For all I know, you're just crouching there with your elbows on the table. And that miserable-looking beard you're growing isn't fooling anyone. All men who're ashamed of their appearance grow beards. Especially fat men. At this rate, God forbid, you'll soon start wearing black turtleneck sweaters as well. And why? Do you know why? Do you want to know?"

She knows. And she tells me. Lodged deep in my subconscious mind is a desperate need for self-expression that is constantly frustrated and aggravated by working as a rewriter on other people's scripts. This constant frustration leads to anger and hate. According to her, I am full of both.

"You are, darling. You really are overflowing with anger and hate. You're a potential madman with an assault rifle, who bursts into an all-night convenience store and guns down a dozen people in a fit of rage. What you need is professional help to help you to come to terms with yourself. Because if you don't . . ."

Her analysis of my problems is so sweet, so innocent of the true and terrible nature of my many diseases that I can only wish that she were right. I could cure myself completely in a matter of days, if all it took were coming to terms with myself.

If I am a madman, as I very well might be, then I am some new improved madman, with a new and improved madness that allows me continually to come to terms with myself. The millstones of my mind constantly grind and reduce to powder whatever disturbing matter enters its territory.

The matter of Laurie Dohrn is a good example. In a few days after that dinner with Cromwell I came to terms with what I had done and allowed to be done to her.

It was all for the best. It was a good thing I had done. Her attachment to me, had it continued, might have arrested her emotionally and caused her to feel an overdependence on me for the rest of her life. This attachment, although very flattering to me, was not in her best interest. As her father figure, I had performed a final act of selfless love by setting her free from my influence. Some day, when she was old enough, she would realize that . . . etc., etc., etc.

The last thing I needed was professional help in helping me to come to terms with myself. If anything, I have a nostalgic craving for that time in my life when terms existed that I could never come to terms with.

### 6

"Listen," I finally begin, as the whole dinner is coming to an end, "there is something I need to tell you. I need your opinion on this matter. It's something . . ."

And so I begin.

"It's about Billy's mother." I make the mistake of blowing the punch line of the story right at the top and then wave my hands stupidly as if trying to erase it. I begin again.

"I was asked, this man I know asked me to take a look at the first cut of a film he produced, to see if there's anything I can do to . . ."

Once again, I make a mistake and start getting sidetracked by telling her about the film itself. How wonderful it is. I'm not only talking about something that's not germane to the subject at hand, I'm doing a bad job of describing the film in question. I'm making it sound like any other film. So I light another cigarette and begin yet again.

I tell her about the video.

About the waitress.

About her laughter.

"As soon as she laughed, I knew, I mean, I really knew that she was the same . . ."

I stop in midsentence because I suddenly realize that although I told Dianah about my telephone conversation with that fourteen-year-old girl all those years ago, I didn't mention anything about her laughing on the phone. So I backtrack hurriedly and insert that piece of information into the narrative. I also try, because it's crucial to the story I'm telling, to describe the quality of her laughter that made it unforgettable. But try as I might, my description of her laughter is not successful. I'm doing a bad job of it. I feel like a nightclub performer who's losing his audience. Out of desperation, I bring up examples of actresses whose laughter has the approximate quality of the girl's.

By the time I get back to the subject of Billy's mother, I discover that I have nothing more to say on the subject. That I have said everything but somehow managed to leave out everything.

I worried all evening about the impact my story of Billy's mother would have on Dianah, and now that the story is over, I realize that it seems to have no impact on either of us. Neither on me who told it nor on her who heard it. The significance of the story is no more or less significant than anything else we said to each other over dinner.

I sit there puzzled, unable to tell if the story's lack of impact is the result of my having told it badly, or if its lack of impact and significance accurately reflects my current state of mind. Perhaps I waited too long to tell it. Perhaps by viewing that scene in the restaurant over and over again, I used up whatever significance it had to offer. I feel exactly as I felt when I pitched my Ulysses in Space movie to a studio executive and, in the process of pitching it, managed to lose not just his interest in my story but my own as well.

I light another cigarette. Dianah sits across from me, watching me smoke. She is scrutinizing me in silence, as if waiting for some further elaboration. I have none to give.

"You are worse than I thought," she finally says. "You really are. You remembered her laughter? You? After twenty years you remembered the sound of her laughter? Is that what you said?"

I nod my head, but not with conviction.

"You can't even remember to call your own son once in a while and you expect me to believe . . ." She leaves the sentence unfinished and sighs.

"Oh, Saul," she says and shakes her head. "You're a sick man. Much sicker than I gave you credit for being. It doesn't really matter if you actually believe in this fantasy you told me, or if you made it up just to hurt me. What it shows, all it shows, is the extent of your decline into some mental illness I'm not equipped to handle. It torments me to see you like this. It really does."

She sighs. Her lovely hand, with her lovely long fingers, flutters in the air and comes to rest gently on her chest.

"You know the way I am. You, of all people, must know that if I am anything, it's nurturing. Overly nurturing, in fact. It torments me to see suffering of any kind, but especially suffering which even I can't alleviate. You remember what it did to me, how devastated I was, when that seagull crashed into the windshield of our car on the way to Sag Harbor that summer. We stopped at that fish restaurant afterwards and you, you were fine . . ."

The people at the Berlin Wall table, having drifted away during my story, are back with us again. They're listening to every word Dianah says. They seem to know the restaurant in Sag Harbor. Perhaps they've eaten there themselves.

"You were perfectly fine. The poor dead seagull meant nothing to you. There you were, eating those crab cakes and your clam chowder and I, if you remember, I was so shattered, so devastated by its death, that I couldn't eat a bite. Not a single bite. And then, later on that evening, when we went to the McNabs' party, it was their twenty-fifth wedding anniversary, and we drove over to Southampton? Remember how both George and Pat thought that I was ill? They both commented on how pale I looked. How distraught I seemed to be. And that was over a seagull. I don't even like seagulls, and yet I was devastated by the incident, completely devastated. Don't smoke anymore. Put it away. Do it for me. Please. So, what I'm saying is this, a time comes when even I must admit defeat. It's not that I'm giving up on you, Saul, it's just that I have no choice. I wish I could nurture you back to health. I've tried. God knows, I've tried. I've spent the last couple of years of our marriage, while we were still living together, doing nothing but trying . . ."

I am enchanted by the fiction she is spinning, moved by whatever is moving her to tell me the lies she's telling me. In a way, I feel unworthy. Do I really merit lies this good?

"And I probably would have gone on trying, if you hadn't left. It was you who left me, Saul. It was you who moved out, and now look at yourself. You're worse than ever. Instead of taking some positive step forward and trying to come to terms with yourself, you're running around with that unattractive beard on your face, following your father's overcoat around New York, and now this. Either making up some fantasy about a girl who laughed on the phone or believing in the fantasy yourself. I don't know which is worse. All I know is that if I, with all my nurturing nature, can't nurture you back to health, then nurturing is not the answer. This is a job for professionals. You should commit yourself. There are many fine, reputable psychiatric institutions in the city and you belong in one of them. And don't think that I wouldn't visit you there. I would. Every day. But I just can't bear to go on seeing you like this, watching helplessly from the sidelines as you fall further and further apart. Don't you understand what it does to me to see you like this? I can't . . . I just can't. . . . Excuse me."

Tears well up in her eyes, she rises and departs with great dignity in the direction of the ladies' room.

I turn in my chair to watch her and admire, yet again, the dancelike way she has of crossing a crowded room. The stately swing of her shoulders in counterpoint to the sway of her hips.

## 7

The cigarette I had meant to light earlier, but which she had pleaded with me not to light, I now light.

My conviction that the actress in the scene in the restaurant was Billy's mother is no longer with me. Perhaps, I think, Dianah is right. Some kind of fantasy on my part. The chances of my remembering that fourteen-year-old girl's laughter seem very slim. We play tricks on others, memory plays tricks on us. It now seems highly unlikely that the waitress in the movie was anything but some poor actress in a bit part. There are so many of them in that age bracket. Mid-thirties to early forties. The conventional wisdom says that if they haven't made it by their mid-thirties, they never will. You're either a leading lady by then or, for the rest of your life or career, whichever ends first, you'll be acting in bit parts, in scenes that belong to others.

It's true, I've invested a lot of hope and time in thinking about her, and through her, as Billy's mother, in the prospect of my own redemption. Now that the whole central premise is in doubt, I have no idea what to think. I am temporarily in between thoughts until some new mood comes along to trigger a thought into being.

I turn my attention to my colleagues at the Berlin Wall table. They have been kind enough, with a few understandable lapses, to listen in on the melodrama at my table, and my sense of social responsibility bids me to return the favor.

They are discussing hate crimes at the moment.

A woman at the table says that hate crimes are on the rise. She offers statistics. Racial crimes are up sixty percent. Religious, overall, are up forty percent, but hate crimes against Jews are up a whopping ninety-two percent. Crimes against children are even worse. Crimes against children are up over two hundred percent. She is ready to continue, but the man opposite her interrupts. He does not think that crimes against children can be classified as hate crimes. And why not, she wants to know. Because, the man replies, crimes against children are a separate category. This doesn't mean that he doesn't deplore such crimes, it simply means that as a category . . . This time the woman interrupts him. What else but hate, she wants to know, can explain crimes against children? Is he also aware of the fact that children have become the victims of choice of most Americans? Yes, he is aware of that fact, he is also aware of the fact that children have become the victims of choice of other children as well, but that still doesn't mean such crimes should be included in the category of hate crimes. Hate crimes, in his opinion, and not just his alone, are crimes that . . .

My waiter comes. He brings my bill, bows, and leaves.

I have an account here and all I have to do is sign my name. I leave huge tips for anyone on the staff who so much as comes near me.

Dianah returns, fully composed, tears gone, hair brushed. She is Ms. Sisyphus incarnate. Ready to resume her unending toil of trying to roll me up the steep incline to the summit of health and happiness. She knows that it's a hopeless and thankless task she has set for herself, but she can no sooner turn her back on me than she can on those doomed elephants that adorn her beautiful blue dress. It's just the way she is. A nurturer at heart.

We leave together. I stagger a little, to keep up appearances. I lean on her for support, doing one of my better imitations of a hopeless drunk.

There are no hard feelings between us. None at all.

It's neither warm nor cold outside. It's March, but it feels like May. It's been May since January.

As in some huge illuminated aquarium, Sixth Avenue is full of cabs moving past us like schools of goldfish.

I hail one of them.

I open the door and hold it open for her. She slides across the seat, making room for me to come inside.

"I feel like walking," I tell her.

I light a cigarette and head uptown. My beard feels like a dog that I'm taking for a walk. It precedes me, as if it knows the way back to my apartment.

8

Lincoln Center is letting out as I go by. Hundreds of people with Play-bills in their hands. They run, hurtling themselves off the sidewalk, arms desperately waving at the taxicabs. It's like a scene from one of those disaster-at-sea movies. Only so many lifeboats to go around. The able-bodied men run on ahead to secure a taxicab, while the women and children and the infirm remain behind, huddled together in little groups. They can only hope and pray now.

A new mood is beginning to rise slowly inside my head.

Dianah's contention that the woman I thought was Billy's mother was just a fantasy or fabrication no longer disappoints me. The doubt I now feel about the woman's identity seems liberating. Whereas I had serious moral qualms in contemplating my pursuit of her when I was certain that she was Billy's mother, I now have none. I'm now free to set things in motion, should I choose to do so. To make my phone calls. To find out her name. Her address. To befriend her. To insinuate myself into her life. To find out who she is.

An ever-so-fine drizzle, so fine that it almost seems a mist, starts to fall.

9

Seventy-second and Broadway. Tomorrow's Sunday *Times* are stacked up outside the news vendor's on the corner. A steady stream of people are buying them, leaving with the papers in their arms.

The sidewalks are crowded with people. Heading home. Away from home. Homeless. All kinds.

The old man in my father's overcoat is nowhere to be seen. I pass the corner where I first caught sight of him, and the bench where we sat. I have not exactly been looking for him, but I have expected to see him again, as if we had made an arrangement to do so. I now recognize this idea for what it is. It's the Hollywood hack in me at work. A rewriter who sets up minor characters early on so that they can then reappear for the payoff. Nobody in the scripts I've rewritten appears just once. The only reason they exist in the first place is so that they can reappear for the payoff. Their whole reason for being is to be somebody's payoff.

I know, of course, that there is a big difference between real life and the scripts I rewrite. The lives of most people are neither character-driven nor plot-driven, but driven by random currents, trends, and moods. Lives that are moody rather than plotty. I'm well aware of this, but the rewriter in me wishes that life too could be rewritten at times.

It starts to rain for real.

Despite the rain, there's a line on the corner of Eighty-sixth Street to buy the Sunday *Times*. Those leaving with their papers clutch them to their bosoms to protect them from the rain. The image is almost maternal, or paternal, depending on their sex. It brings to mind, at least it does to my mind, an image from an old movie. The townspeople in *The Invasion of the Body Snatchers* leaving the distribution center where they picked up their pea pods and hurrying away, each holding the pea pod of his replication tightly in his arms.

I pay for my *Times* and, clutching it to my bosom like the others, I trot on due west toward Riverside Drive.

## 10

It's a little after midnight when I get to my apartment.

I stick the videocassette into my VCR and fast-forward to the scene in the restaurant. I light a cigarette and watch the scene yet again. My eyes go from her face to Billy's photograph on top of the TV. Whatever resemblance I saw between the two before, I now either don't see anymore or do see, but it no longer matters in quite the same way. I hear her laughter. It's either the exact same laughter as the laughter of that fourteen-year-old girl on the telephone, or it's not. The crisis I had about what to do with this woman on my TV screen is gone. I'm no longer aware of having any crisis.

I strip off my clothes and head for the shower, making a sudden executive decision as I get into the shower stall to shave off my beard.

The hot water feels wonderfully soothing in both the tactile and acoustical senses as it falls on my shoulders. Steam rises inside the shower stall. The steam covers the glass door. What had been transparent becomes opaque.

I have an office on West Fifty-seventh Street, but in many ways this is my office. It's in the shower that I resolve conflicts, gain insights, come to terms with whatever terms are left to come to terms with. It was in this very shower that I conceived of my Ulysses in Space movie, and it's in this shower that I return to the subject from time to time to embellish the conception.

I do so now.

I see the solar schooner with a mile-high solar sail sailing through space and time. I see the scene with the sirens as something from MTV. Ulysses, tied to the mast, gets to see videos of what he has missed by being away from home for all those years. He sees the scenes he could have had with his son Telemachus but can never have now. Or can he? The tantalizing images spun into being by the sirens' songs torment him with what could have been. He tears at the ropes that bind him to the mast.

I shave.

Having shaved, I move on and shampoo my hair. The shampoo I use is made especially for frequent users like myself.

I feel so relaxed that even the iron grip of my prostate loosens and I pee freely for the first time in a long time. I think of Dianah.

She was wrong to call me a potential killer who is full of anger and hate. I am angry at no one. I hate no one, not even Cromwell, whom I want to hate. I have never caused premeditated harm to anyone.

On the other hand, I do lack the willpower to stop myself from hurting others in passing, in the day-to-day living of my life, in the mere process of being who I am.

My ability to cause harm has been limited up to now only by my limited opportunities to do so. I know, because I know myself, that I'm capable of causing much greater harm than I have, perhaps even killing somebody, should such an opportunity arise. It's not that I want anyone's blood on my hands, it's just that I would be unable to keep myself from spilling it.

This character trait of mine is cause for concern, and I concern myself with it. It kicks around inside my head like a chunk of carrot inside a Cuisinart. But even as it kicks around, it gets smaller and smaller, until finally it loses all significance. It joins the list of other concerns, thoughts, and insights in the psychic soup of my mind.

My former crises and concerns are now indistinguishable from one another. There is a great sense of freedom and peace in knowing that I can do neither right nor wrong, because in the undifferentiated broth of my mind there is no difference between right and wrong.

The hot water continues to fall from the showerhead. The steam rises and thickens. In the egalitarian democracy of my mind, there is tranquillity and total equality. All is soup.

# PART TWO

# Los Angeles

# CHAPTER ONE

I

Her name was Leila Millar. Millar with an *a* but pronounced, as the ever-helpful Brad in Cromwell's office had hastened to inform me, "Miller."

I was flying to LA to meet her.

When I called Brad, my intention was only to get her name and phone number. The rest, I thought, would follow in the days to come. But the rest followed right away.

Brad told me that there were quite a few scenes "with the young lady in question" that had been cut from the print I saw. If I wanted to see any of those scenes, or any of the other scenes Mr. Houseman had cut, all I had to do was say when.

"She lives in Venice," Brad said and then laughed in that bleating way of his. "The one in California."

He gave me her address. I wrote it down.

I was about to thank him and hang up, when he asked, "Would you like me to take care of your travel arrangements?"

Why not, I thought. If I'm going to do what I'm going to do sooner or later anyway.

"Why not?" I told Brad.

Brad took care of everything, the flight, the limo to Kennedy and from LA, the hotel, the rent-a-car waiting for me in the hotel parking lot.

In the aria of accommodations, his mellifluous, self-effacing voice almost put me in a hypnotic trance. Hearing him talk was like getting a haircut, a manicure, and having my shoes shined at the same time. The details of my trip, as rendered by his voice, were made to seem matters of vital importance. It made me want to have a Brad of my own.

## 2

I was half-napping when our pilot announced over the PA system that we were flying over Chicago.

He sounded like an honest man and I took his word for it, because when I opened my eyes and looked down, all I saw were clouds.

Chicago served as a marker on my trips to LA, indicating that we were a third of the way there.

A pang for my mother, like the sound of one of those submarine sonar devices, bounced off my heart.

I was very familiar, too familiar, with the house down below in which she now lived alone. Perhaps she was at this very moment walking aimlessly through it, east to west, and, perhaps, as the plane flew over it, the two of us were in synch for a split second, heading aimlessly in the same direction.

I hadn't seen her since my father's funeral.

There were no unresolved issues between us. We had both resolved them a long time ago. We had come to terms with each other in what's popularly known as a very healthy way. There was no hostility between us. No scores to settle. No need to get even. My relationship with my mother was in many respects exactly the same as my relationship with Dianah. We were separated, but not completely divorced as yet. No hard feelings on either side.

The only real thing left between my mother and me was a memory of a single moment. For all I knew, she had forgotten all about it.

On my way to LA, I had stopped over to see my dad and her. He was still healthy and sane at the time and was working in court that afternoon. I sat in the kitchen, smoking and drinking tea, watching my mother wipe the dust off the wooden windowsill above the sink.

Our teas together were always like this. She would ask me if I wanted a cup of tea. If I said yes, she made a cup for me, but not for herself. If I said no, it was the other way around. One of us was always watching the other drink tea.

She had watched me drink mine and then, driven by some addiction for doing useless chores in my presence, she began wiping the dust off the windowsill with a damp cloth.

The kitchen window faced west, and by the light of the afternoon sun, as if she were illuminated by a spotlight, I saw how old she had become. The thought that this old woman had given birth to me made my own life seem as ancient as something written on clay tablets in cuneiform.

Suddenly, as she moved her hand across the wooden sill, she cried out in pain and pulled back her hand.

I stood up and said, "Mom, are you all right?"

She shuffled toward me, holding out her right index finger.

There, in that old index finger she brought for my inspection, I saw a thin splinter of wood and a small droplet of blood.

What I saw didn't look like a living human finger at all but a dead piece of wood which the splinter, wood itself, had entered. The thought that this old piece of wood could feel pain and bleed horrified me.

I pulled back from her. From that fingertip and that trembling droplet of blood. I couldn't bring myself to touch it.

My mother, realizing the mistake she had made in bringing her little hurt to me, came to her senses and almost apologized for the blunder. Contrite and embarrassed, she turned around and shuffled back to the kitchen sink, where she let some water from the tap run on her fingertip.

The next day I left, as planned, for LA.

The tiny splinter, I knew, had long departed from her flesh. The broken epidermal cells, even at her age, had long since replicated themselves and covered the break in the skin, so that no visible mark remained of the incident.

Like some miser, however, I clung to the memory of that afternoon, as if it were a precious stone.

It required a conscious effort on my part to keep my mind from dissolving the memory of that moment in the kitchen with my mother. It took work to keep the splinter in my mind. What I got in return was that each time I flew over Chicago, I had the satisfaction of feeling a little discomfort for the way I had behaved that day. This discomfort was neither intense nor prolonged, but it sufficed to persuade me that I was still an active member of the human race.

3

It was almost eight P.M. when we arrived in LA. A tall limo driver met me at the baggage area, holding up a sign with my name on it.

The baggage carousel began to turn. For the first time in my life at any airport, domestic or foreign, my suitcase was the first one to appear. I took it as a good omen of something.

The limo that Brad had arranged to pick me up was a stretch limo, but try as I might, I couldn't stretch myself out far enough to take full advantage of all the comfort and space it offered.

It was dark outside, and made to seem even darker by the limousine's tinted windows. I cracked open a window and lit a cigarette.

Venice was close to the airport, and as we drove past several exits that could have taken us there, I couldn't help thinking about Leila. But since I didn't really know her, I didn't really know what to think about her. Lacking any specifics, or freed from the burden of specifics, I let myself think anything I wanted to think about her, meaning, I suppose, that what I was doing was thinking about myself.

## 4

My lobster-pink sixth-floor suite was enormous, but I had expected nothing less. I have been flown out to LA enough times to be able to predict the sumptuousness of my accommodations by the size of the limo that picks me up at the airport. No limo means a single room. A town car means a junior suite. A stretch limo, a stretch suite.

Awaiting me were two bottles of champagne and two baskets of fruit. The smaller basket of fruit and the smaller, less expensive bottle of champagne were from the hotel management, a token of their appreciation for my being a loyal customer. The other, larger basket and the other, much larger and much more expensive bottle of champagne were from Cromwell. A faxed note came with them, written in longhand and sent from Leningrad.

"Saul, you bloody genius, welcome on board. If you need anything, just call Brad.

"Looking forward to seeing you in person next Saturday. Regards, Jay."

It was late. I was tired but not sleepy and there was nowhere to go, so I unpacked slowly, methodically, trying to stretch out the activity for as long as possible.

It pleased me to learn that Cromwell had been informed about my trip to LA.

After taking care of my accommodations, Brad had returned to the topic of the cut footage from the film. When was I interested in seeing it? I wasn't interested in seeing it at all but I had to justify my stay in LA somehow, so I agreed to see it on Monday. Brad told me that he would reserve a screening room for me.

Cromwell, I was sure, knew all about it and was probably interpreting my arrival and my arrangements to see the cut footage as a sign that I was seriously considering accepting the assignment. It wasn't often that I was in this wonderful fail-safe position of being able to arouse and then to dash Cromwell's expectations in such a pleasant way. It pleased me to think of him being somewhere in Leningrad and counting on me.

This was Friday. According to his note, he would be back in LA next Saturday. I would be back in New York by then. It pleased me to imagine him calling my hotel only to be informed that I had checked out the night before.

If there was one thing I was certain of, it was that I could do nothing to damage the brilliant film I had seen. Its integrity was safe from me, not because of any personal integrity I possessed but because the film itself was so perfect. Even had I been eager to alter it, I could have found nothing there to alter.

I had, it's true, been involved in the ruin of other films in the past, but they were all of a different kind. All of them, in one way or another, had been compromised in their very conception, before I ever got to them. The very best of these films, that young man's film in Pittsburgh, for example, had as their goal a certain level of commercial competence, and although my involvement lowered that level a notch or two, it did not deprive the world of any great work of art.

Arthur Houseman's film was something else. It was a masterpiece. It called upon the best in me just to be able to appreciate it properly, and even in that regard I felt a little inadequate. I was a hack, but I was not a vandal. I could as easily go to the Art Institute in Chicago and attack my favorite Van Gogh there with a butcher knife as be responsible for even the slightest change in the film I had seen. For once, I was protected from my own moody and unreliable nature by the artistic integrity of the work itself.

All Cromwell was doing was paying for my little getaway from New York. Although I knew that he could afford it, that the costs I would incur were negligible to somebody of his resources, it still pleased me that for once I was getting something from him in return for nothing.

## 5

Having unpacked, I uncorked his bottle of champagne.

A faint hope lurked in my mind that perhaps my inability to get drunk was a regional disease, confined to the East Coast. Perhaps here in LA, where I hadn't been since the onset of my drunk disease, things would be different.

I drank until both bottles of champagne were empty, only to reconfirm yet again that my mind was a fortress impervious to alcohol.

On the positive side, however, my drinking did use up time. It was now almost two hours later than when I began. Almost midnight. Time, even by LA time, to call it a night.

I lay in a bed that was large enough to be a small island. I lay waiting for sleep. Friday was over, but the remainder of the LA weekend loomed in front of me like some sea I would have to traverse.

The motive that had brought me to LA appeared to me in all its absurdity.

What in the world was I doing here?

Loneliness, like leaking gas, began to seep into the darkness of my suite.

# CHAPTER TWO

I

I woke up the next morning feeling better, cured of something or infected with something else, it was hard to tell which, but definitely in a better mood.

I took a long shower. I shaved. I called room service and ordered breakfast. I thanked the Asian boy who brought it and overtipped him. I thanked and overtipped the Latino boy who took the dirty dishes away. I lit a fresh cigarette and picked up the phone.

Dialing Leila's number on the touch-tone phone felt like typing. I had no intention of talking to her. All I wanted to do was to hear her voice and then hang up.

Her line was busy.

It was still busy five minutes later.

It was still busy when I called her again from the poolside. But the mere repetition of dialing her number three different times made her seem a lot more familiar. Like somebody I now felt I had a right to call.

The sun was shining. The sky was blue. The sound of water falling from the fountain into the pool was very soothing. There was a drought in California and the sign next to the fountain informed me that the water it used was recycled.

I sat at my table under a huge umbrella, smoking, thinking my thoughts which, like the water in the fountain, were recycled.

The air began to heat up, the high-noon sun to bear down. A young girl in white shorts and white blouse bearing a name tag and a bright smile approached me to inquire if I wanted to order something to eat or drink. I thanked her for asking, I thanked her as sincerely as if she had rescued my whole family from a burning building, but no, I did not wish to order anything. One of the side effects of staying in a luxurious hotel is that you wind up saying thank you so many times to so many people for so many trifles that after a while this mantra of thank-yous makes you feel grateful just for being there. It makes you feel generous in a lazy LA kind of way.

Leila's telephone number was written on the same piece of paper as her address, 1631 Crescent Place, Venice. I considered calling her again but then decided to do something else instead.

## 2

A young Asian boy brought my rented car from the valet parking lot and held the door open for me. I thanked him and slipped a five-dollar bill into his hand.

It had been a long time since I drove a car and it felt wonderful to drive one again. To press the cigarette lighter. To steer with one hand and smoke with the other. To have a rearview mirror and sideview mirrors, and the wind blowing through my hair. The faster I went, the more hair I felt I had for the wind to blow through. It made me feel young to drive a car again, or at least younger, as if youth were some recreational activity that could be rented in LA.

I started speeding as soon as I got on the San Diego Freeway. I flew past cars that were speeding themselves. I was not only breaking the speed limit, I was demolishing it. At times I was going so fast I forgot where I was and where I was headed. The speeding created a momentum of its own and the momentum created its own justification for whatever destination I had in mind.

I still had no health insurance, but so long as I stayed in my rented car, I was fully covered. I had liability and I had comprehensive. The irony of this just added to my reckless delight. I was insured. If I happened to plow into one of my fellow motorists, the ensuing carnage would be fully covered.

It almost came to that. A multicar collision was avoided only by the keen reflexes of the drivers around me when I swerved sharply from my far left lane to the far right lane in preparation for my exit on Venice Boulevard.

## 3

Around and around Venice I drove for almost an hour, as if caught in some whirlpool that kept spitting me out time after time back on Lincoln Avenue.

There was a very good map of LA and its vicinity in the car, and I consulted it every time I wound up back on Lincoln Avenue.

I had no problem at all finding her street on the map, or figuring out how to get to her street on the map. But getting there in my car was proving to be a multi-cigarette-consuming ordeal.

I kept driving around in circles, running into streets that were one-way the wrong way, or that dead-ended without warning at tall chain-link fences, on the other side of which were warehouses or lumberyards or junkyards guarded by big, barking junkyard dogs.

Finally, more by accident than thanks to any navigational skill on my part, I stumbled upon a small semicircle with several streets radiating from it like spokes from a broken wheel.

One of the street signs bore the name Crescent Place.

## 4

A single, very tall palm tree stood in the middle of the semicircle.

Not far from the palm tree was a large tree house, but a tree house in name only. It was freestanding and perched atop sturdy wooden beams. A wooden ladder, attached to the beams, led to the top.

I could hear the laughter of children from inside the tree house as I walked past it. Judging from the different voices I detected, the place was jammed full of kids.

Like the tree house, Crescent Place was a street in name only. Had there been no street sign there, I would have mistaken it for a sidewalk, and a narrow sidewalk at that. It was lined with old, one-story houses. Little lawns enclosed with fences. Little flower gardens in the lawns. The arm's-length proximity of one house to another reminded me of the houseboats at the Seventy-ninth Street marina.

The lawns, the houses, the little narrow street itself, were completely deserted. Or seemed to be. The only sound I heard was of someone hammering. And then that ceased abruptly.

It was getting to be very hot, and a hot wind, as if channeled by the narrow street, was blowing at my back.

I had been to Venice Beach before, several times, but I had never ventured inside Venice itself.

A story in the magazine section of the *LA Times* came to mind as I shuffled along with the wind at my back. It was about this man who at the turn of the century had a vision of building a Venice in the West, along the lines of the Venice in the Mediterranean Sea. It was to have everything the European city had. Canals instead of streets. Gondolas for transportation. Graceful bridges spanning the canals. His vision, however, was revised by others, until nothing remained of the original idea other than some bridges that now spanned nothing. And, of course, the name itself. Venice.

I followed the house numbers until I came to the address I had flown from New York to find: 1631 Crescent Place.

It looked no different from any of the other old houses I had seen. A chain-link fence. A little lawn. A little flower garden. A cluttered porch.

The windows were wide open and a draft from within the house caused the white, gauzelike curtains to fill with the wind and expand and then, losing the wind, to contract. I stood there, watching Leila's house inhale and exhale, watching it breathe as if it were a living thing peacefully asleep and dreaming and completely oblivious of my presence and purpose there.

Having come here, I had no idea what to do next. My usual supply of banal opening remarks seemed inadequate for the occasion. Nor did I have a handle on what the occasion really was. Who she really was.

Her telephone suddenly rang. I could hear it ringing through the open windows. In the hush of the street, I heard her answering machine come on.

"I'm not at home right now, but if you leave a message I'll get back to you as soon as I can. I promise."

"Leila, it's me again. This whole thing is getting ridiculous, isn't it? I don't know what's going on with us anymore. So please, at least call me and tell me so I know. That's not too much to ask, is it? Bye."

Although I was standing outside her house and although the message I had heard was not very intimate, I still felt like a burglar who had rummaged through her private things. The message I had overheard put me in the category of those who open other people's mail, and I shrank in shame from the petty indecency of it.

But it brought to mind the much larger indecency of my motive for being there. The man who had called her, if nothing else, sounded as if he had a right to do so. I no longer felt that I did.

Let her be, I told myself. Leave her alone. No human being has benefited by knowing you, so why add to the list? Fill your time in LA in some other way. Let her be.

It felt so good and right to follow my own advice that as I left her house I thought of myself and my actions in the third person.

He, being aware of his own unpredictable and unreliable nature and knowing full well that she would be better off never coming in contact with him, decided, out of nothing more than simple human decency, to leave her alone.

## 5

The air was filled with screaming, laughing, and bloodcurdling cries. What I saw when I emerged from her street was a battle scene. Little boys and girls, armed with rubber swords and squirt guns, were scrambling up the wooden ladder, brandishing their weapons like pirates and storming the tree house. The defenders inside, thrilled to be attacked, were screaming and laughing and trying to repulse the attackers with rubber swords and squirt guns of their own.

The energy of the kids was in stark contrast to my own. Maybe it was the heat, or the normal dip in energy I experienced at this time of day, or the bottom falling out of my plans for coming to LA, but whatever it was, it was all I could do to get back to my car.

My automatic impulse, as I sat down behind the wheel, was to reach inside the right-hand pocket of my trousers, pull out my car keys, start the engine, and drive away. But I couldn't get myself to do that. I just sat there, and the longer I sat there the hotter I got, and the hotter I got the harder it became to do anything.

If I had had some space-age remote control that could have fast-forwarded me to my hotel, I would have pressed the right button and transported myself there. But the thought of fishing the car keys out of my pocket, starting the car, finding my way back to Lincoln Avenue, driving back on the San Diego Freeway, in a mood different from the one that had brought me here, and then having the rest of the evening to fill up with activities of some kind, the thought of all that time I would have to fill or kill proved too daunting for me in my present state of mind.

I checked my cigarette supply. I lit one and watched the battle of the tree house.

It was hard to tell what the rules were of the game of war the kids were playing. The attackers climbed the ladder and, despite heavy resistance, stormed the tree house and vanished inside. Although the shouting and screaming and laughing never stopped, some arrangement must have been reached, sides were switched, and kids I had not seen until now, former defenders of the tree house, I assumed, spilled out of there like a bag of marbles and bounced down the ladder in disarray. Once on the ground, without pausing for so much as a breather, whooping and howling like wolves before a hunt, they charged up the ladder to storm the tree house they had defended only moments before. The former invaders, the defenders of the tree house now, tried to hold them off with rubber swords and squirt guns shot at point-blank range, but to no avail. The former defenders, invaders now, stormed the tree house and vanished inside. The old defenders, chased out by the new defenders, spilled down the ladder in disarray only to regroup and become barbarians, invaders once again, when they reached the ground.

The war continued. Although I watched with interest, I eventually lost track of who had been the original defenders of the tree house and who had been the original invaders. I suspected that the combatants themselves no longer knew.

And then a yellow taxi appeared in the right-hand corner of my windshield. It entered the semicircle on the other side of the palm tree, drove around it, and stopped at the curb, its nose pointed to the entrance of Crescent Place.

It wasn't so much that I had expected her to suddenly show up as that I wasn't at all surprised when she did. As soon as I saw her, it was like a continuation of something that had already begun.

She stepped out of the cab and stopped. When the car door started moving toward her, she gave it a swift bump with her hip and sent it flying back again. She then bent at the waist and reached inside the backseat of the cab with open arms.

The gesture, on its own, was not necessarily maternal, but it appeared very maternal to me. A baby, I thought. A baby in a bassinet. She's reaching inside to pick up her child.

Instead, she backed out with two large grocery bags in her arms. They were full and, judging by the way she held them, a little too heavy for her. One of the bags had a blue hat on top of it.

I watched her from my car in what in movie terms would be called a long shot. The easy but total concentration with which I observed her made me think that if I had been able to summon such powers of concentration in my work, I might have turned out to be more than a rewriter.

She stepped over the curb and headed for her door. She paused once, despite the weight of the grocery bags in her arms, to watch the continuing warfare in the tree house.

She looked at the kids spilling down the ladder while I looked at her. She thought her thoughts and I, looking at her, tried to imagine what those thoughts might be.

## 6

The kids continued their game of siege and resiege, but shortly after Leila's departure I could tell that things were beginning to wind down. Battle fatigue was spreading through the ranks. The bloodcurdling cries of the invaders and the defiant screams of the defenders were losing some of their earlier conviction. And then it was over. They all knew it. They wandered away in little groups, in various directions, much like a disbanded army of adults might have done after a war: a little weary, a little bored, but not at all eager for the rigors of peace that they knew awaited them at home.

## 7

The shadows of the palm tree and the tree house lengthened until they intersected. The wind died down. The sun, as a presence, dipped and disappeared from my point of view, but it would not be accurate to claim that I saw it set. Shadows gave way to dusk which absorbed them, the dusk to night. The moon rose slightly to the left of that solitary palm tree in the center of the semicircle.

I was down to five cigarettes and I lit one.

Being where I was, sitting behind the wheel of a parked car, was starting to feel much homier than being back in my suite at the Beverly Wilshire.

A taxicab swung off the street and into the semicircle, its headlights taking a quick swipe at my windshield. It stopped not far from where the other taxi had stopped. The engine kept running, the headlights stayed on. A minute or so later, Leila appeared. She was running as if she was late for something. She shielded her eyes with her hand from the glare of the headlights and got in the cab. The cab took off.

## 8

I had felt so good about myself when, earlier in the day, I decided to leave Leila alone. The memory of that high moral ground was with me now while I followed her cab, except now the memory was being re-worked to accommodate a complete repudiation of itself.

It was, I rationalized, a very rare thing for me to feel good and moral about myself, and yet the woman who had inspired such virtuous behavior in me and in whose name I had committed both goodness and morality earlier in the day was a woman I had never met. If without even knowing her I could be inspired to such high-minded behavior, then perhaps a whole new vista of moral behavior would open up to me if I befriended her. To leave her alone, therefore, would be tantamount to turning my back on that possibility.

I had no idea where the cab was taking her, and so none at all where I was headed in pursuing her through the streets of Venice, but pursue her I did, like a line of narrative I was in the process of writing while I drove.

# CHAPTER THREE

## 1

The place is called the Cove. It's a club of some kind where you can eat and drink and dance, and everyone I see is doing at least one of the above. Those not dancing are sitting at their tables and moving at least one part of their bodies, head, foot, hand, shoulder, to the downbeat.

I am easily the oldest, fattest person there.

I am sitting in a corner at the far end of the bar, from where I can see the whole place and follow Leila with my eyes without having to twist and turn on my barstool. I can stare at her without drawing attention to myself. I am staring at her now. She is moving through the crowd, leading with her shoulder, wedging her way through dancers returning to their tables. In quick succession, I see her in profile, then head on, then from the back as she makes a U-turn and disappears in the throng.

## 2

My pursuit of her cab through the night streets of Venice was neither hectic nor high speed. The cab in which she rode kept to the speed limit, seldom exceeding thirty-five miles an hour.

I was sure when the taxi stopped in front of the Cove that she was going there to meet someone, some man, perhaps the very man whose voice I had overheard leaving a message on her machine.

Instead, what I discovered when I entered the place and took my seat at the bar was that she worked there as a waitress. It took something away, hard to tell what, hard to tell from whom, from her or myself, but something was taken away when I saw her waiting on tables with a pad and pencil in her hand. It wasn't that she was lessened in my eyes for being a waitress. It was just that some comfortable supposition of who she was was taken away.

### 3

I order another drink and light another cigarette. I now have a whole pack in my pocket and an opened pack on the bar. Since nobody here knows me, I feel no need to play drunk. I just keep drinking as a way of paying for my seat at the bar. The bartender, ignorant of my drunk disease, is becoming a little annoyed by the amount of bourbon I am consuming without showing the slightest signs of intoxication. My sobriety bothers him. To him, I am an old cliché, the fattest, oldest cliché in the place, and he would like me to finish off the image by becoming a fat, old, drunken cliché. He brings me another bourbon, I thank him, he smiles, but he is tired of me. If I can't cooperate and get drunk, then I should leave. There's a nasty look to him, which brings on a nasty feeling inside me. My revenge will be to leave him a tip so large it will make his handsome head spin. A monster tip to remember me by, long after the memory of him and his teeth and his cheekbones and his hair is gone from my mind. I will erect a monument to myself with money inside his head.

The dancers dance, the diners dine, the waitresses make their rounds, there's Leila again, and the drumbeat beats on. The musical selections change, the couples dancing and the dances they dance seem to change, but the same drumbeat beats on. It becomes, after a while, an acoustical version of a strobe light pulsing, so that sight and sound, light waves and sound waves and brain waves become either interchangeable or indistinguishable one from another.

The thoughts I'm thinking are not necessarily mine. They could be anybody's thoughts. I could be anybody. A uniperson.

### 4

It's all over now. The plug has been pulled. The music has stopped. The dance floor is deserted.

It's not yet midnight, but it's already dwindling time at the Cove, dwindling time in Venice, dwindling time in LA and its environs.

The bar is closed. I have paid my bill. All that remains for me is to leave my monster tip on the counter and follow Leila out of the Cove.

The Cove is closed. You can only get out. You can't get in anymore. And when you get out, as some stragglers are doing now, the manager escorts you to the door, unlocks the lock, pushes the door open for you, and then locks it again with a flick of his wrist.

A few diehard diners still remain, but the waitresses now outnumber the customers. I can see Leila chatting with another waitress at the far end of the room. I can't hear a word they're saying, but they're leaning against the wall and chatting in that end-of-the-workday way of working people.

My problem is this. I know that as soon as Leila heads for the door, I will follow her out into the street but, having been beaten senseless by that drumbeat, I have only one opening line in my head, "Excuse me, please, but haven't I seen you in some movie recently?"

There is a big problem with that line, aside from its dreary overfamiliarity. The movie in which I have seen her will not be released for quite some time, if ever, and using the line would put me in a position of having to explain how I managed to see the film already. I would prefer not to have to explain anything, not my profession, nor my connection to the film. But I'm tethered to that line and I can't come up with another.

The only alternative would be to tell the truth. Excuse me, please, but are you the same person as the fourteen-year-old girl with whom I talked on the telephone from her hospital room in Charleston, South Carolina? Are you the one who gave her baby to me? Are you the mother of my Billy?

The manager of the restaurant is releasing everybody except for a skeleton crew. One by one, the waitresses are leaving. Parting gestures. Parting remarks. On her way out, Leila stops at the other end of the bar and uses the telephone the bartender hands her. She makes a quick call to somebody and hangs up. She waves, smiles at the bartender, and heads for the door. The manager is waiting to let her out.

I rise slowly, leave my monster tip on the bar, and follow her out.

5

She is standing at the curb when I come out, as if she is waiting for somebody. Her back is to me. Her head is turned toward the oncoming traffic. There is a stiffness to her posture, as if she knows there is somebody behind her and is aggressively ignoring him.

"Excuse me, please."

My words make her spine stiffen even more. I wait, but she shows not the slightest intention of acknowledging me. I walk toward her.

"I hate to bother you, I really do," I say.

"Good," she replies, still looking away from me. "We have something in common then. I'd hate to have you bother me. So why don't you just trot along."

"I'm afraid my trotting days are all behind me."

Partially, but only partially, disarmed by my reply, she turns her head and suddenly there is her face, in a close-up, in front of mine.

Her complexion is white. Not pale but white. There is a softness to her skin that makes itself felt without having to be touched. A face as soft and white as those seagull feathers one finds in the sand on a beach and picks up and carries and strokes with one's finger for a while before discarding them in the sand again.

"You sat at the bar the whole night, drinking and looking at me, didn't you? And then when I left, you followed me out, didn't you?"

I nod to both accusations.

"Are you trying to pick me up, mister?" She asks this question with all the sternness available to her, but somehow it is the sternness of a child playacting at being an adult rather than being one.

"No," I lie, "I'm not trying to pick you up."

"Then what do you want from me?"

"I feel I know you."

"Oh, dear." She sighs and shakes her head. "You are trying to pick me up. Don't do this. My cab will be here any minute, and when I get in the cab and it drives away, you'll feel like an idiot."

"I feel like an idiot most of the time," I tell her, but she's not interested in my sense of humor. "Just tell me one thing," I go on. "That's all. Just tell me this one thing and I'll go away."

"What one thing?"

"Haven't I seen you in some movie?"

She seems suddenly to grow very weary. Her shoulders slump, her face sags, she seems to age ten years. Only her eyes remain young and like the eyes of a child who's been tricked by an adult. She glares at me with open disgust. Then her disgust turns to anger.

I can read on her face what she is thinking. I might as well be looking at a face with subtitles.

You creep, she's thinking.

"If you have no fucking respect for yourself," she says, furious, "then at least have a little for someone who's worked all night."

Words don't suffice for her rage. Only in women who have known me have I seen such rage before, and so, in an odd way, her disgust and fury are familiar, as if we were involved in a relationship already.

Her taxi arrives. She rushes toward it. I follow, trying to get in a last word.

"I'm sorry, I really am, if my motives seemed suspect to you. I honestly did think that I saw you in this film by Arthur Houseman, a director I happen to revere."

She has opened the cab door and is about to step inside when she hears the end of my remark, and then, as if snagged on a hook at the end of a line, she stops. She looks back at me.

"You played a waitress," I tell her. "Your hair was different in the movie and you wore a lot more makeup, but it was you, wasn't it?"

"You saw me?" she asks, as if her whole life is wrapped up in that question. "You actually saw me?"

"Yes."

Having considered me to be some miserable lowlife, she now reverses herself completely and bestows upon me a look of such naked benediction (there are tears in her eyes) that I am made to feel, without exactly knowing why, not just a bearer of good news but an agent of her deliverance.

"Oh, dear," she moans. She pushes herself away from the cab and moves toward me. Then she stops and turns back to the cab, sticks her head inside, and tells the driver to start the meter but wait, and then she rushes toward me again. She does not embrace me, but I feel both embraced and kissed by the way she looks at me. She starts to apologize in a rapid but incoherent manner. I understand nothing at this point, except that something means too much to her. The depth of her emotion is of a kind in which a person can drown. There are tears in her eyes and they're the kind of eyes and the kind of tears that suggest there are many more tears to come.

"We have to talk," she tells me. "You don't know what this means to me. I want to know more. I want to know everything."

I feel trapped in her rapture, engulfed by her gratitude, knighted by her into some benefactor who with a single silly utterance has brought meaning into her life again. I seem to be doing her a lot of good, but the good I'm doing, its nature and substance, is beyond my comprehension.

She's thinking and talking, but there seems to be no difference between the internal and the external monologue she's making. She looks at her watch and considers the hour. Maybe it's too late. Maybe we should meet tomorrow.

"Fine," I say.

"But, no, no." No, she can't possibly wait until tomorrow to hear the rest. What rest, I don't know, but she's certain that there's a lot more to hear and she couldn't possibly wait until tomorrow to hear it. She couldn't sleep. She couldn't possibly sleep tonight. Was I in the movie business?

"Yes, that's how I saw your movie."

No, no, no, she doesn't want to hear another word about it, not a single word, not until we are seated somewhere so she can sit and listen, just sit and listen while I talk. Am I tired? Am I sleepy? Do I have somewhere to go? No? Wonderful! Then I must come to her place. I simply must. Fine, I agree. I'll come.

She considers the logistics.

Do I have a car?

Yes. I point across the street to where my car is parked.

I offer to drive her home but, no, no, no, she couldn't possibly come with me. The bartender Larry has told her that I consumed more alcohol than any man he has ever seen. She's afraid of drunk drivers and afraid for them. I really shouldn't drive myself. I'm too drunk to drive. I should come with her in a cab. I insist that I'm not drunk, but she has another argument against coming with me. She's called a cab already and the cab came and the poor driver is just sitting there, waiting for her, and although she told him to keep the meter running, she still feels she must go home in a cab. They don't make much, these poor drivers, and they work so hard.

"I know what," she announces a solution.

I should get in my car and follow her. That's what we'll do. She'll take the cab and I'll follow.

## 6

And so, once again, after making a sweeping U-turn, I'm sitting behind the wheel of my rented car and following her cab through Venice, only this time I'm doing it at her insistence.

I feel like a stalker who's been subverted, incorporated, into the life of the object of his pursuit.

# CHAPTER FOUR

## I

I followed the cab back to the semicircle it had taken me so long to find the first time. It was almost routine now, as if I lived there. The cab stopped and I, without thinking, as if I lived there, parked once again in my old parking space.

There was something charming and gracious, although a bit theatrical, about the way she inserted her arm under mine in that *Gone with the Wind* kind of way and then led me through the moonlight down that narrow sidewalk of a street toward her home. We did not and would not talk of "her movie" until we were comfortably settled inside. We chatted instead about how hot it had been earlier in the day and how much cooler it was now. There were always cool breezes in Venice at night, she told me. I realized, as she lifted the latch on the gate of her chain-link fence and swung the gate open, that we had not introduced ourselves and that she didn't know my name, but I decided not to spoil the ease and intimacy between us by bringing it up.

## 2

She seemed to have second thoughts about something, about everything, as soon as we were inside. About my being there. About "her movie." About the improbability of good news coming her way. I could see her worries and anxieties and her efforts to dispel them as clearly as if her face were a series of slides with captions of the emotions she was feeling. I had to keep looking away from her, breaking eye contact, and this just contributed to her unease.

But I had to keep looking away. The completely open window of her face made me feel like a voyeur of her disrobed inner life. Nobody should be that open, I thought. Nobody.

She ran around turning on every single light in the living room, little lamps with little shades of various colors, pale yellow, pale blue, pumpkin orange, as if all that illumination could dispel her anxiety. She talked the whole time, telling me things about Venice I already knew, and the whole time she talked, I could tell, anybody could tell, that what she really wanted to talk about was "her movie" but that having been burned once before kept her from bringing up the subject for fear that she would be burned again.

"I'll tell you what," she announced when there were no more lamps to turn on and she had nothing left to tell me about Venice, "I've got to get out of this dress. I only wear it to work and I feel like I'm still working when I wear it, so I'll go put something else on and then I'll be right back. And then—" she paused and summoned whatever courage she possessed "—you'll tell me all about my movie, all right?"

"All right."

I could hear her traipsing through various rooms, half-humming some song, staying in touch with me through the noise she was making. I heard the faucets run. I heard the toilet flush. I heard her opening doors and drawers. I heard the rattle of ice cubes falling into the kitchen sink and the clink of a bottle neck against a glass and knew, both by the state that she was in and by the sound, that she was having a drink in the kitchen to compose herself. Which was fine for her. But what could I have to drink, burdened as I was by my disease, to compose myself?

Breezes blew through the living room from various directions and at different elevations. Some of them carried my cigarette smoke away and expelled it through the open windows, others rubbed against my ankles, blowing the other away.

The living room was decorated with clutter. A clutter of couches cluttered with little pillows. A clutter of cocktail tables, three of them, cluttered with magazines. Fashion. Fitness. Interior decorating. The floor around the couch on which I sat was cluttered with books. Romance novels. With romantic titles. Written by authors with romantic pseudonyms.

There, among the clutter on top of the end table to my right, I caught sight of a box of English Ovals, a brand I used to smoke.

I leaned forward and reached for the box. I opened it. There were still two cigarettes inside. I took one out, tapped the end on the hard surface of the box, just as I used to do, and lit it.

What the taste of madeleines was to Marcel Proust, the scent and the taste of various brands of cigarettes were to me.

The campus of Columbia rolled into view with my very first puff. The way I dressed, the way I walked, the way I talked and thought, for I walked and talked and thought and dressed differently in those days.

Dianah came back as she was when we met, because I was smoking English Ovals when we met and fell in love. When we got married and when I had a cigarette after our lovemaking, it was still English Ovals that I smoked. I smoked them when I first tried writing. I smoked them when I gave up writing. I smoked them when we decided to adopt a child.

Leila reappeared. She wore a strapless black gown and high-heeled black shoes, bearing liquor bottles in her arms. She announced herself by tossing her head back and saying, "Ta-da!" In addition to the bottles pressed against her breast, she carried two tall glasses in her hands. She was a little less tense and a little more composed, as people who are a little drunk tend to appear at first. Even so, she couldn't quite pull off saying "Ta-da!" Dianah could do it perfectly. Dianah could "Ta-da!" with the best of them. But not Leila.

"This was going to be my gown for the premiere of the movie I was in, but the premiere went off without me, so I thought, why not premiere it tonight? What do you think?"

"I think it's a wonderful idea and a beautiful dress."

"Really?"

"Yes."

She placed the bottles and the glasses on top of the magazines on the cocktail table in front of me.

"I have vodka and I have gin and I have Scotch."

I meant to smile but wound up laughing. It was the way she pronounced "Scotch." She chirped it like a little bird. The sound of her voice tickled.

"What's so funny?"

"What isn't funny?" I replied.

She poured a Scotch for herself. Having no preference, and knowing that it was a complete waste of time to drink, I decided to go in alphabetical order and therefore started with gin.

## 3

It was she who did the talking.

She told me all about the movie she was in, which she hadn't seen and I had. And since I could not get drunk, she got drunker and drunker as the night wore on.

It was the longest single night of my life.

The lies I told her, or rather the lies she wanted me to confirm, were the easiest and the most catastrophic lies I've ever told.

Along the way, prodded only a little by myself, she told me the story of her life. It was, to borrow a phrase, the saddest story I have ever heard. It all began like this.

"Do you know what one of my favorite scenes in the movie is?" she asked. The fact that her question put "scenes" in the plural made me despair.

"No, I don't."

"Well, I shouldn't say it's my favorite scene. They were all so wonderful. But, on the other hand, why not say it? I mean, it is my favorite scene, so what's the big deal about saying it, right?"

"Right."

"Cheers." She drained her glass, poured herself another, and went on. "It's the scene, you know, when I drive home late at night after work, still wearing my waitress's outfit, and I go inside the house where my little girl is sound asleep, still clutching that silly stuffed dog I bought her, and I just sit by her bedside and tell her all about my day. What I did. What happened. Who came into the coffee shop. How they looked. Who said what to whom. I just loved doing that scene. Did you like it?"

"Yes," I lied.

"Did you really?"

"It was wonderful."

There was, of course, no such scene in the film I had seen, but there was no way I could tell her that. We were, after all, celebrating and she looked so happy, so involved, describing it to me, that I just couldn't tell her it was gone, that it had been cut, as so many scenes in films are cut.

"It really was wonderful, wasn't it?" she asked.

One confirmation was never enough for Leila, so in the course of the night I had to confirm everything, and lie about everything, in duplicate, sometimes in triplicate.

"Yes, it was. I don't blame you for liking that scene so much."

"It's my favorite," she said, clutching her drink with both hands and pressing the glass to her chest, "my absolute favorite." Her white, naked face beamed with pride as she thought about that scene. She looked so fragile, defenseless. I could almost see the dotted lines of demarcation in her features, like tiny cracks in a beautiful ancient vase. A wrong word, a single tap with some harsh truth, and the whole thing would shatter.

She drank up and had another and told me about a couple of other scenes. Both were gone, of course, but I loved them both, just as she wanted me to love them. She talked about Mr. Houseman, what a gentleman he was, the nicest director she ever worked with, "a gentleman of the old school," she called him, and how patient he was with her, and encouraging, and fatherlike, and what a shame it was that he was so ill as she had heard he was.

"There was that one scene, remember, where I just stood there in the coffee shop, cleaning off the tabletop with a wet rag and looking out the window at the two lovers walking away toward his car. Remember that scene?" I nodded. "We shot that scene I don't know how many times, because Mr. Houseman wanted a certain kind of close-up where he could read all the thoughts in my face, how I felt, you know, about the love story of those two and what memories it kindled in me. And it was such a long, long close-up that I just couldn't do it right because I lacked confidence that I had enough life in me to sustain the silent moment. So we kept on doing it over and over again, take after take. Finally, I don't know why, maybe because I was so exhausted and tired of worrying about my inner life, but finally I just did it. I forgot they were even shooting. I forgot everything. I just looked out the window while I wiped the tabletop with the wet rag and thought my own thoughts. The people I've known, the friends I've had, my childhood, my mom and dad, my little . . . well, everything. I thought about everything. And the close-up seemed to last forever this time, it was like waking from a dream, or like in a hospital, you know, when you wake up after anesthesia and don't quite know where you are or why everyone is smiling at you in that funny way. That's what it was like. The whole crew burst into applause. They did. They really did. They all burst into applause. And Mr. Houseman, that sweet, sweet man, he was not in the best of health even then, you know, but despite all that and despite his age, he got all excited. He looked like a young man again as he jumped out of his chair, shouting, "Print!" and ran toward me to give me one of the biggest hugs I've ever had. Did, did you like that scene?"

"Oh, yes."

"Did you really?"

"It was unforgettable."

My description pleased her, but the look on her face entreated me to elaborate.

"It was heartbreaking," I obliged her. "It was as if you were trying to look after the two lovers like some guardian angel, urging them to hold on to their love, as if you instinctively knew that . . ."

I blabbed on. Her face responded to every word I said. Ripples of joy appeared and, ripplelike, spread out in concentric circles until her whole face was consumed by delight.

"I loved the ending of the film, didn't you? I just loved it. It was so melancholy, I know, but I just loved it. Standing there in the park while the fireworks went off above us in the night, looking around and catching glimpses of my friends and neighbors by the light of the fireworks and feeling the life of the town flowing through me, flooding me somehow. I almost cried while we shot that scene. Part of it, of course, was that it was the end of the film, and that come tomorrow, we would all go our separate ways, but a part of it was the scene itself. The two lovers weren't lovers anymore. Something had triumphed which wasn't love, but life still went on and for all the fuss and the bother and the pain and the mess, there was still something glorious about life. Even when it's tragic, it's still a glorious tragedy. We had our wrap party that night. Everyone danced. You should have seen Mr. Houseman . . ."

She told me all about it. How he danced like a young man. How she danced with him. He took off the hat he was wearing, he always wore a hat, and put it on her head, and told her that he had never seen a woman who looked so good in hats the way she did.

I could not tell her that she had been cut out of the ending of the film that she loved so much. What did remain of her in the film, her one spoken line in the coffee shop, her laughter, and glimpses of her in the background of two other scenes that belonged to somebody else, these were so inconsequential to her that she never mentioned them. And yet they were all that was left of her. The rest was gone.

She poured herself another drink, most of it going into the glass but quite a bit of it spilling on the floor on which she was now sitting.

"Cheers!" She raised her glass.

"Cheers." I raised mine.

"You really don't know what this means to me. You see, I've been in so many films." She tried counting them on her fingers, but gave up and swept them away with a flick of her wrist. "Many, many. That's how many. Many, many films. And for some reason, they always cut me out of them. Out of all of them. Or they did up to now. Cheers!"

We clinked glasses again.

"All those films I was in, and they cut me out of every single one. Gone. From all of them. Simply gone as if I had never been in any of them. So many films. So many parts. Little parts, yes. Most were little parts, but still, I was there. I said things. I felt things. I wore costumes. My characters had names. Gone. Poof. And you see, they never even bother to tell you that you're gone. Not if you're somebody unknown like me. They never even bothered to tell me. So I'd go and buy a ticket to see the movie I was in and I'd sit there in the theater waiting for myself to appear only to have the film roll on without me. All those films. They just rolled on without me.

"And it's not just movies. I mean, it would be bad enough, right? Bad enough even if it was just movies, but it wasn't just movies. There is, or rather there was, knock on wood"—she rapped with her knuckles on the floor—"there was something about me, I don't know what other explanation there could be other than that there was something about me which followed me since I was a little girl. I swear to God, mister, these things have been happening since I was, what? Fourteen. Parts of my life are just cut out. Taken away. Just taken away somewhere. Whole sections. Whole big chunks. And what're you supposed to do then? Reconnect what's left. Just reconnect what's left and carry on as if nothing had happened. I've tried, mind you. But when you're constantly removing parts of your life and reconnecting what's left, you start feeling bizarre after a while. Like you're getting older and older and yet the life you've lived seems shorter and shorter. Know what I mean?"

"Yes," I said.

She frowned.

"I'm terribly sorry, mister, but I can't remember your name."

"Saul. Saul Karoo."

"And mine's Leila Millar."

"I know."

"You're in movies, right? You told me that, didn't you?"

"Yes."

"I thought so. What is it that you do?"

I explained what I did, that I was a rewriter, a movie doctor, and how, in this case, I had been asked by the producer to assist him in doing some work on the film that Mr. Houseman, because of his failing health, was no longer able to do himself. She listened with that smiling drunken benevolence of someone who doesn't hear a word you say because they're listening intently to their own voice in their own mind.

And then, out of nowhere, but perfectly consistent with the line of her own drunken thoughts, she exclaimed:

"Take my father, for example. He's dead now. He died, I don't know when anymore, but he died. And do you know what he told me just before he died? He told me how sorry he was that he didn't love me. He asked me to forgive him on his deathbed for not loving me. See what I mean?" She flung out her arms in both directions in one of those drunken gestures meant to encompass the whole of life.

"The thing is, I didn't have a clue. I had no idea until then that he didn't love me. I grew up thinking he did. I was sure he did. God knows I loved him and it never occurred to me that he didn't love me. Why the fuck couldn't he die quietly and keep his mouth shut about that? Why did he have to tell me? So he can die in peace? But what about me?

"I flew back to Charleston as soon as my mom called to tell me he was dying. It was late at night and I had to take a red-eye to Chicago and then hang around O'Hare waiting for my connection, worrying myself silly the whole time that I might arrive too late. But I didn't. I got there in the nick of time, running down that hospital corridor like a fool, in the nick of time so he could tell me, before he died, that he didn't love me.

"All those years, mister, what was I supposed to do with all those years I lived believing I was loved?

"And when I walked out of that hospital that day, exhausted by travel and lack of sleep and stunned by what my father had told me, I felt like some patient who had an amputation. I was a grown woman, but it was like all my growth was taken from me and I was a girl of fourteen again. It was just like that. I felt just like I did when I was fourteen, leaving the hospital, going home."

It didn't take much prodding, a few casual questions was all it took to have her tell me what happened to her at fourteen. I probably didn't even need to have asked. Leila, unprodded, would have told me everything by herself.

4

"I had a baby when I was fourteen. It was a love child, if there ever was one. The stories you hear about girls that age, you know, how they don't really know at fourteen what love is, how they don't really like sex but do it for other reasons, how they can't even have proper orgasms at that age, wrong, wrong, wrong. I loved that boy. I loved the sex. I loved getting pregnant and having that secret growing inside of me."

She told me a little about her boyfriend, her first love, Billy's father. His name was Jaimie Ballou. He was seventeen. Very tall, with a mop of hair that bounced up and down when he ran. A basketball star. Every college in the country was after him.

"Nobody knew that I was pregnant for the first couple of months. Nobody. Not Jaimie. Not my parents. Nobody but me. It was my secret, and it was the happiest two months of my life. It was springtime and there was life growing outside of me and inside of me. All was life and it was all growing.

"My parents were very religious people. When they found out, they were horrified. They had a harlot for a daughter, a sinner. But they tried to love the sinner in their midst as proof of their religion. They saw it as a test. My dad tried so hard to love me that I thought it was the real thing. I did. I thought he was crazy about me.

"Even if I'd been willing—which I wasn't—they wouldn't hear of an abortion. Or consider letting me keep the baby. They took turns talking at me, the way detectives do in crime movies. They brought in the parish priest, who talked at me too. It would be a bad thing, they all kept telling me. My whole life was still ahead of me. If I kept the baby, my whole life would be over. In the end, I came to see it their way. The thought that my whole life was over frightened me. I felt so full of life, and the thought that somehow, it would all be over . . .

"So it was arranged that as soon as my baby was born, this lawyer would take it. He was representing some couple who wanted to adopt. They would pay for everything, you know, medical bills and things like that.

"Although I agreed to give it up for adoption, my body didn't want to give it up. My time for delivery came and went and my body held on to the child as long as it could. They finally had to cut it out of me. A C-section. My baby was taken out like an appendix. I never even saw it. I don't even know if it was a boy or a girl, but I have this hunch it was a girl. It's just a hunch, but I trust my instincts."

"Do you know who adopted it?" I asked her.

"No. Some rich people. They didn't know my name and I didn't know theirs."

"How do you know they were rich?"

"I pleaded with the lawyer to let me talk to them so I could at least hear what they sounded like."

"What did they sound like?"

"The woman wasn't at home. She was out shopping for baby things. I only got to talk to the man."

"What was he like?"

"I don't know. Can't remember anymore. All I remember is that he said that they were stinking rich. I was still a little dazed. It was all like a dream. Before I even went to the hospital, Jaimie got drunk. He never drank in his life, but this time he got drunk and got killed in a car crash. He was gone. The baby was gone. It was all gone, but somehow my whole life was supposed to be still ahead of me.

"Nobody really warned me what it would be like afterwards. What it was like to go on living after you've lost so much. The boy I loved. The baby I loved. Nobody prepared me for that. The rest of my life, whatever that meant, was mine again, but I no longer felt that I could just live it. I had to do something special. Make something special of myself. Become somebody special. So that someday I'd be able to look back and say, 'There, it was all worth it.' I saw only two choices. I could become a saint or a movie star.

"Cheers," she chirped, raising her glass, and then suddenly she started crying.

"No, no, no," she waved me back. "I'm OK. I'm fine. Really, I am. It's not what you think. I'm just crying because all that stuff's finally behind me. All my life, things have been taken away from me. Until tonight. And then tonight, you show up and tell me that you saw my movie and that I was in it. For once I survived. So I'm not here falling apart. I'm celebrating, don't you see. That's what I'm doing."

She wiped away her tears with the back of her hand.

"You see?" She pointed at her new face. "See how good I feel? I'm going to sleep so nice tonight."

She did not mean this as a cue for me to leave, but I chose to take it that way. I got up.

"I better get to bed myself."

She saw me to the door.

"Are we going to see each other again?" she asked, holding the screen door open with her hand. "I'm not petitioning, you understand. Just asking."

"I think we should," I told her.

"What a coincidence." She clapped her hands. "I'm just breaking up with this man, so I happen to be emotionally available at the moment, you lucky dog."

She laughed, as if making fun of herself.

"Thank you. Thank you ever so much for everything."

"No need for that." I shrugged.

"Yes, there is."

"Good night, Leila."

"Good night."

She stayed in the doorway, watching me open and close the gate.

"I'm in the phone book," she shouted after me. "My last name is Millar but it's spelled with an *a*. Drive carefully."

# CHAPTER FIVE

## I

He was everything you ever wanted in a Brad: affable, congenial, polite, deferential. He wore a wide grin and one of those white-man Afros. He was obsequious in a committed way, so that it looked like a calling. He created the impression that he could look me right in the eye and kiss my ass at the same time without undue hardship or inconvenience to himself.

He was Brad. Young Brad. Cromwell's Brad.

"It's an honor. A real honor to meet you in person at last," he told me as he shook my hand.

We were in Cromwell's office at Burbank Studios, but since Cromwell was in Europe, Brad played the part of the sorcerer's apprentice.

I'd been in Cromwell's office before, when he had another young Brad working for him, and it bothered me then, just as it bothered me now, that the office was so modest by Hollywood standards. You wanted Cromwell, I wanted Cromwell, to have one of those huge, ostentatious offices, so that I could despise him just for the kind of office he had. It was always the same problem with Cromwell. If you wanted to hate him, you couldn't hate him for the trappings of power he exhibited, because in that regard, by Hollywood standards, he was almost a Buddhist monk. If you really wanted to hate Cromwell, you had to find and define something at the center of his personality. The risk there was that whatever it was you found to hate at the center of Cromwell might be identical to what lay at the center of your own being. Cromwell was somewhere in Europe, but his presence in absentia was more substantial than Brad and I put together.

Brad, a perfect combination of hustler and hostess, took it upon himself to talk enough for both of us. He told me things about myself, he told me things about himself. Being an underling, he conveyed the impression while he talked that I was under no obligation to listen. Every once in a while, he laughed out loud at something. The gurgle in his voice while he laughed, like someone drowning in his own blood, had a cheerful, energetic quality.

"Shall we?" Brad finally asked and jumped off the corner of Cromwell's desk, where he had been sitting.

"Let's," I replied.

I had been here many times before, in the service of Cromwell and others, and I knew where the screening room reserved for me was located, but Brad insisted on taking me there himself.

We had to leave the building and walk across the vast Burbank lot. It was close to three P.M. Close to the heat of the day. Through the heat ribbons, the sand-colored buildings on the studio lot shimmered like the mirages that were manufactured inside them. Brad kept talking.

We walked past astonishingly beautiful girls, young starlets or starlets in the making, as beautiful as apparitions. They were or seemed to be all in between auditions or interviews with casting agents on the lot. In between jobs. In between all kinds of things. They all seemed to have been created by biogeneticists for certain body parts currently in demand.

Young. So young. All of them.

Even now, in my condition, they eyed me and not the young, rather attractive Brad at my side. I fit the type of man they thought had the influence and the power. All Brad had was youth and good looks. He was no better off than they were, and they knew it. But I was fat, sweaty, middle-aged. I was the very image of some wealthy industrialist turned studio head and therefore, in their young, street-wise eyes, the man to know.

The screening room was cool, very plush, intimate, the seats wide and comfortable. The configuration of the seats and the type of seats were reminiscent of the first-class section on a Boeing 747.

Brad, having urged me to enjoy, left. I took out my cigarettes. I came prepared. Two packs.

I lit one while the projectionist dimmed the lights slowly to black. I felt goose bumps all over my body, as I always did at these times. Although I wasn't there to fix anything really, merely going through the formality of seeing the excised footage, habit was habit, and from years of habit the fixer in me surfaced and fixed his eyes on the screen. Sitting in a dark screening room and waiting for the reels of film to roll was like being in a darkness like no other. Anything could happen when the projector began turning. It was like sitting in darkness and waiting to be born, or waiting to die, or waiting for something less definite but more terrifying and exhilarating than either.

## 2

The wheels of the projector kept turning. The reels of film rolled on.

I sat alone in the screening room, watching scene after scene and take after take of scenes that had been deleted from the film.

Normally in these situations there was an editor or an editor's assistant in the projection booth who made sure that the cut footage I was seeing had been arranged in its proper chronological order. This time, there was nobody in the projection booth except the union projectionist. The editor of the film and his assistants, I later discovered, had all resigned, out of respect for Mr. Houseman. As a result, the projectionist, having no idea which scene followed which, kept slapping on reels of film in no particular order. We began somewhere in the middle and skipped around from there, backward and forward.

Fortunately I had seen the completed film so many times in my apartment in New York that I had it almost memorized, shot by shot and line by line, so that I could make intelligent guesses where in the film the various scenes were supposed to have been before Mr. Houseman deleted them from the completed work.

Leila's scenes were not the only ones that had been cut. Everybody in the film lost something in the editing room, but nobody lost as much as she did.

In the original scheme of things, as the vanished scenes clearly revealed, hers was one of the pivotal parts of the movie. In that conception, she was to have been the town observer and commentator on the unfolding dream of the two lovers and their story. Originally, the whole film was to have been a flashback of Leila's character, allowing her to comment intermittently upon the action we were seeing.

It was as if, in that original conception, Mr. Houseman, who was the sole screenwriter as well as the director, had lacked confidence in the central love story or had failed to predict, until he began putting the film together, the power that the little love story would assume. The device of the waitress storyteller, a kind of lovable busybody narrator, was there to allow him at crucial points in the film to leave its seriousness and pain by cutting back to her and giving the audience a little respite and a laugh or two before returning to the tragedy of the love story.

But as he worked on the film in the editing room and observed, as he could not fail to have observed, the power that the little love story began to assume, he mercilessly deleted everything that stood in its way. He no longer wanted relief, comic or otherwise, to detract from the love story itself. He no longer needed, nor would tolerate, an observer or a commentator. Therefore he had no more use for the waitress or for the actress who played her.

Her one tiny moment in the film, the scene in the restaurant, was left in place because Mr. Houseman had shot the scene of the two lovers in such a way that he could not cut her out of the scene and thereby out of the film altogether. Had he shot an alternate take from another angle, there would have been no Leila at all in the film. And, needless to say, no Leila at all in my life.

Leila's acting (as the wheels of the projector kept turning and the reels of deleted scenes rolled on) was not what I had thought it would be. She was not a potentially great and as yet undiscovered actress. In truth, she was in the wrong field, because she was essentially not an actress at all.

But it was all too easy for me to understand how any director, how all her previous directors, could be smitten by Leila in real life. Her inner life in real life was so rich and textured and so overwhelmingly true to the moment at hand, that any director would assume that such naked truth would play beautifully on the screen.

It didn't.

What was so right and powerful and at times heartbreaking in the three-dimensional realm of real life was all wrong and over the top on the screen. Leila's tragedy as an actress was that she was only real and right in real life.

Acting is not, despite persistence of talk to the contrary, being true to yourself. Acting is the art of assuming the burden of truth and the limitations of being somebody else, and Leila had no capacity for being true to anyone but herself.

Every scene in which she appeared meant too much to her. It should not have meant that much to the character she played to go home and pick up her little daughter in her arms and tell her about the things she had seen and heard during the day. But Leila was not playing that character. She was not playing any character. She was not acting. Having that little girl in her arms meant too much to her, far too much, and on the screen it showed as something embarrassingly exaggerated. In real life, the same scene would have been very touching and moving. On screen, it wasn't. The same was true for every other scene in which she appeared. Observing the gradually deteriorating love story of our two lovers in the movie seemed to pain her more than it did them. Her heart seemed to be breaking for people whose hearts were not breaking at all.

It must have been a shock to Mr. Houseman to see how much she lost in translation to the screen.

Some of her moments were comic, but not comic on purpose, not funny in a good way. If she had a future in films, it was in roles in which she would be properly misused. In films that were entertaining and de-meaning distortions of the human experience (the kinds of films I rewrote), her depth of feeling, if exploited properly, could be turned into belly laughs. Few things are funnier, if the context is right, than somebody on the screen to whom everything in life means so much.

The reels of film rolled on. I saw several scenes with several very good actors that had been totally cut out. A policeman. A priest. A won-derful scene with a wonderful actor playing the part of a Little League coach. Gone. All three. I saw many variations of scenes that had been cut and many variations of those that had been kept.

The Old Man's reputation was that he shot a lot of film, filmed many takes, and this deleted footage bore out the truth of his reputation. As much as I loved the film the first time I saw it in my living room in New York, I found myself loving it even more when I realized (as the wheels of the projector kept turning) what he had gone through in order to create his masterpiece. Considering his age and his illness, I could only marvel at his capacity for completely reconceiving his film in the edit-ing room and finding a way to create a great work of art despite the fact that he had written and shot a relatively pedestrian movie. Such relent-less pursuit of perfection was incomprehensible to me.

The lights finally came on. There was no more film to see.

It was dark outside, almost as dark as it had been inside the screening room. The studio lot was deserted. In the distance, I saw my rented car.

# CHAPTER SIX

## I

There were two restaurants in Beverly Hills that I considered for my dinner with Leila. Both were appropriately pretentious and suitably overpriced, but I had eaten at Spago's too many times before, so I chose Nestor's. The chances of running into movie people were not as high at Nestor's, another reason for my selection. I made a reservation for two at eight o'clock.

Since she neither drove nor had a car, I offered to come and pick her up, but Nestor's was located in the heart of Beverly Hills and she thought it would be silly for me to drive all the way to Venice to pick her up and then all the way back to Beverly Hills.

"The more you drive," she told me, "the more likely you are to have an accident and the last thing I want on my conscience is to have somebody killed or maimed in a car wreck while coming to pick me up for dinner. I'll take a cab."

You had to wear a jacket and tie to Nestor's and so I did. On my way there that evening, I tried to delete from my memory all those deleted scenes of hers I had seen in the screening room the day before, but it sometimes happens that the very effort to forget something enhances its presence in your mind.

I arrived at Nestor's, as was my way, ten minutes too early but, approaching the canopied entrance of the restaurant, I was stunned to see Leila standing outside. She was chatting with a tall young man in charge of valet parking.

Never, not once in my entire life, had a woman with whom I had a date arrived before me.

I stopped the car just to savor the sight of her standing there.

She was dressed for an evening out in a fancy restaurant, but the way she stood there, chatting with that tall young man, the way she held her purse by the straps so that it hung down to her ankles, the way she kicked the purse playfully while she chatted, now with her foot, now with her knees, made her seem like a schoolgirl kicking her school bag.

## 2

Our table in the smoking section, like all the other tables at Nestor's, had a candle burning in the center, and although it was there more as decoration than as a source of light, in the mood I was in, it was by candlelight that I saw Leila that evening.

We started drinking. Since it no longer made any difference to me what I drank, I joined her by drinking Scotch. After several stumpy glasses of Scotch, we decided to move on to taller, more graceful glasses of champagne. Her posture, her whole appearance, changed and lengthened with a champagne glass in her hand. We had two bottles before dinner. She got higher and higher and I did my best to appear likewise.

She wore her hair up in a style I associated with classical ballerinas. It made her long white neck seem longer and very fragile, as if it could be broken with terrifying ease. Two shiny black earrings dangled from her earlobes. She kept worrying them with her fingers, as if checking to make sure they were still there.

Her fancy black dress was cut low, revealing two-thirds of her breasts. As she inhaled and exhaled, her breasts rose and fell like white-plumed, sleeping seabirds nestled down for the night inside her bodice.

But it was her long white arms that tempted me more than anything else. Her black dress had long sleeves gathered at the wrist, but the sleeves were made of transparent gauze which created the illusion (by candlelight) that each arm was a body of a young, ravishing girl encased in a negligee. Whenever she moved one of her arms, my center of gravity shifted to the pit of my stomach and blood disgorged into my groin.

The drunker she got, the more her eyes narrowed, until they became almost Asian in appearance. She kept them focused on me the whole night, peering into my soul or letting me peer into hers.

When I talked, her lips moved ever so slightly, as if she were taking the words from my mouth into hers to see what they tasted like.

It thrilled me that she was, or appeared to be by candlelight, so beautiful.

And it thrilled me, of course, that this beautiful woman with those ravishing arms (like two young daughters, one on either side of her) could be attracted to me. Her attraction for me, which I could not but notice and which grew as the night went on, was not based on any physical allure I possessed. What she was attracted to, I concluded, was something else. Something spiritual within me. The real me. Since I had no idea who that person was, feeling, as I had always felt, that I could be anybody, the possibility that somewhere deep within me the genuine article existed, the real me, and that perhaps Leila saw it, made me hope that in time I too would get to know it.

In time, I told myself. In time, I will not only tell her everything but share with her things I have not shared with anyone else.

Rebirth. Renewal. It seemed not only possible but imminent, by candlelight.

### 3

Over dinner, I told her about my apartment in Manhattan. How big it was. How it was too big for just one person. I described the view I had of Riverside Drive and Riverside Park and the Hudson River.

I was a fount of information. Since the essentials between us could not be discussed (her child, her movie), I described the inessentials in great detail.

I told her that I had six large windows facing the Hudson and that if I opened one of them and looked right, I could see the George Washington Bridge to the north, and, if I looked left, the Seventy-ninth Street marina to the south, and further south, the piers where the big liners docked. Circle Line boats, I told her, went past my windows, loaded with sightseers. Barges. Oil tankers. Tugboats. Foreign vessels with foreign flags. I told her how I had seen Long Island ducks flying south for the winter and how, when I opened my windows, I heard the sound of their ghostly cries. I described the intense but short-lived cold spell that hit New York right after Christmas and how, when it was over, I saw huge flotillas of ice moving down the Hudson from upstate New York, as if the Adirondacks were some arctic continent breaking up and drifting in pieces into the Atlantic.

"I've never been to New York."

"You'd like it there," I told her.

"Really?"

"Yes, I'm sure of it."

In this way, in my own way, I was inviting her, and in her own way she was considering the invitation.

I told her about my marriage and about my separation from Dianah. How long had I been married, she wanted to know.

"Over twenty years."

"Only once?"

"Yes, only once."

"Any children?"

"He's not a child anymore, but yes. A son."

(It occurred to me that between the three of us we only had one child.)

I told her all about Billy, or all that I could tell her. How handsome he was. How tall. How self-conscious of his height. How bashful he could be and how eloquent. How much I loved him.

Smiling softly, her quarter-moon eyes glistening by candlelight, she listened to me. It was my impression that she could have listened to me talking about Billy and my love for him for hours and hours.

A man who loves his son.

I could see the impression I was making.

The more details I divulged of my love for him, the more she seemed to be handing herself over to me, falling in love with me, with the father within me who loved his child.

My bill arrived.

When we stood up to go, Leila had to grip the back of her chair in order to steady herself. And then, although drunk, she let go of the chair and, performing a half-curtsy, leaned her rigid torso forward at some precise angle known only to her and blew out the candle on our table. She did it with such dignity and grace, complying, as it were, with laws of some higher etiquette known only to the drunken few, that even the haughty waiters were impressed by what she had just done. It seemed right. As soon as she had done it, it simply seemed right that the candle should be blown out before we left.

4

She gave the tall young valet in livery two smacking kisses, one on each cheek, when he brought my car.

"Take good care of yourself," she told him.

Inside the car, while I drove, she told me about him.

"I got here early. I was going to go inside and wait for you, but I started talking to him. He's so sweet. He really is. From Iowa. Wants to be an actor. What else? He kept calling me ma'am. Yes, ma'am. No, ma'am. Boys like that—" she sighed "—I don't know. You just want to . . . I don't know. But you just want to . . . something, when you see boys like that. Like a sweet ear of corn, that's how sweet he was. And I kept giving him advice about the movie business." She laughed. "Me!"

"Careful!" she screamed suddenly and gripped my shoulder.

I slammed on the brakes just as I was about to pass a slow-moving car. She apparently didn't realize that I had two lanes to myself and that the oncoming traffic was not a threat.

We continued, but whenever I approached the legal speed limit, she got nervous.

"Not so fast."

"We're not going fast."

"Feels fast to me. This is why I take cabs everywhere. Nobody ever gets killed in a cab."

Her anxiety bothered me.

"Don't worry, I'm an excellent driver," I tried to reassure her.

"How could you be, you're drunk."

"I'm not drunk."

"But you drank as much as I did."

"I can take it," I told her.

I got on the freeway and headed toward Venice.

"Do you think I'm going to be a movie star?" she asked.

"Maybe."

"A big star?"

"Maybe."

"Then it'll all be worth it."

She slid down in her seat, her knees pressed against the dashboard.

I was taking her home, but I didn't feel like taking her home. I felt like driving and driving. I felt like getting lost, getting both of us lost, and having a common starting point for ourselves, a brand-new beginning for both.

It took me a while to realize that she was crying.

"Are you all right?" I asked.

"This is not what I had in mind," she sobbed.

"What's not?"

"This life I'm having. When I was a young girl, I had a whole other life in mind."

Moments later, smiling through tears, she said, "Your face looks like a ratty old sweater. But a nice ratty old sweater."

And then she started crying again.

I slowed down and came to a gentle stop on the shoulder of the freeway.

"What're you doing?" she wanted to know.

"I can't bear the thought of you being home and crying alone. I thought we'd stop here for a while so you can cry your eyes out."

With an exuberance that belied both her age and her drunkenness, she sprang to life and flung her arms around my neck. Sobbing and laughing, she began kissing me all over my face. I had never been kissed like that before. Rapid little kisses, too fast to count. Kisses all over my face and eyes, as if there were no end to them.

"You know how to sweep a woman off her feet, don't you," she said, and kept on kissing me. "Most men go stiff and cold when I start crying. They feel all put upon. But not you. You're a strange man, mister. Yes, you are. Maybe we're meant for each other."

How was it, I wondered, that I had lived as long as I had lived and never been kissed like that?

She just kept crying and kissing me.

When we kissed on the lips moments later, an odd thought accompanied the kiss.

I'm putting my lying tongue in her mouth, I thought.

"We're too old to be doing this on the shoulder of the freeway," I said.

She didn't want to go home. I invited her to spend the night at my hotel.

I drove back as slowly and carefully as I could bear to drive. We rode in silence, as if everything had been said that could be said until after we slept together.

Headlights from oncoming cars came and went, and although they looked nothing like projector lights they brought back memories of the cut scenes I had seen in the screening room yesterday.

She stumbled and almost fell as we walked across the nearly deserted lobby of the Beverly Wilshire Hotel. I caught her just in time.

"How drunk am I?" she wanted to know.

"Very drunk," I told her. "But don't worry. I'll take good care of you."

"You will?"

"Yes."

"Will you take me under your wing?" she asked as we got on the elevator.

"I will."

"I was just a little girl when I heard that expression and ever since then I've yearned for it to come true. To find someone who would take me under his wing. Oh, God, dear God, how lovely it still sounds." She started crying again, as only drunks can cry.

## 5

Being undressed, I had come to think, was the same thing as being naked, but Leila reminded me that night that it was not the same thing at all.

I was coming out of the bathroom, where I had taken a hurried shower in order to be fresh and clean before I got into bed with her. The lights were on in the bedroom when I came out, and I saw her lying there on my huge bed.

The sight of her stopped me dead in my tracks.

The closest I had ever come to seeing human nakedness before was in a movie. A documentary. It showed hundreds and hundreds of naked Jews, men, women, and children, being escorted by armed Nazi guards and barking German shepherds to their deaths. All the Jews were naked. Not undressed. Naked. And it seemed to me then, while I watched that documentary, that it wasn't just the Jews that the Nazis wanted annihilated but the very concept of nakedness as well. What was troublesome to me was that I found myself approving of the annihilation of that concept. I am no historian, but as far as I can tell, I was not alone in feeling that way. As far as I can tell, those images of those naked people stumbling to their deaths were the last recorded images of human nakedness in the twentieth century.

I had of course come to terms with all that a long time ago. With history. And with the history of history that followed. And with my own feelings about it all.

So it was not pleasant to be confronted with something I had assumed no longer existed.

Leila lying naked on my bed.

Her nakedness covered not just the huge bed but filled my whole suite. It wasn't just that her eyes, looking directly at me, were naked. Nor that her long white arms and her breasts were naked. Nor that her legs were naked and parted. It was as if she had brought her whole deleted past with her, and her past lay there alongside her, naked as well. The fourteen-year-old girl to whom I had only talked on the telephone lay there alongside her and she too was naked. The young mother. The young mother deprived of her child. The woman. The actress. The parts she had played in life and in films were all there on the same bed, waiting for me to take them under my wing, and all were as naked as those Jews trekking across that barren landscape to their deaths.

I hurriedly turned off the lights in order to clothe myself in darkness and avoid the suffocating multiplicity of meanings of that one naked body on my bed.

And then, a few fumbling moments later, either because I lacked the capacity or the courage or the wingspan to take all those Leilas under my wing, I had to decide which Leila I would embrace in the darkness and to which Leila I would make love.

I chose, for the record, the fourteen-year-old girl. When I say chose, I mean I consciously imagined myself making love to that young girl, and while I made love to her, the rewriter in me was rewriting the screenplay of her life. The two of us were reconceiving Billy. I was rewriting the events that would follow, so that in the end there would be a happy ending for everyone. I was fixing it all.

# CHAPTER SEVEN

## I

It was Friday again, just as it had been Friday when I arrived in LA. Cromwell was coming back from Europe tomorrow and I was supposed to be in New York when he arrived.

But that would not happen. I no longer had any hopes of leaving. I was stranded by circumstances.

Most of the time, I come to terms with things after the fact, after I have done the wrongs I've done. This time was different. This time, I had to come to terms with things ahead of time in order to free myself to commit the wrongs I planned to do.

I chose the poolside of the Beverly Wilshire Hotel as my designated spot for coming to terms with my future crimes.

It was not yet noon, but it was hot. It would turn out to be the hottest day of the year, but it was plenty hot already. Not a hint of breeze. Heat fell down from the hazy blue sky like a torrential downpour. A deluge of heat.

Following the young pool attendant (in white shorts) to my poolside chair, I was sure that I would be unable to take the heat for long. A few minutes at best and then I would return to my air-conditioned suite and come to terms with things there. But once I lay down in my chaise longue, it was all over. A Niagara Falls of heat fell upon me, pinning me in place. I was trapped. I might as well have been strapped to a poolside electric chair.

There were others there, lying in chaises longues of their own all around me. Men. Women. Young girls. A little boy with red hair. All of them, I assumed, were trapped just as I was. They too had probably thought that they would only stay a few minutes and then leave. Scattered around the pool, we lay in our reclining chairs like so many victims of nerve gas.

The sound of falling water from the recycled water fountain had a hallucinatory quality to it in all that heat. Like the sound of something sizzling.

## 2

I had Leila on the brain. Her life. The many losses of her life.

Her baby was her first loss, and that loss paved the way for all the others. That loss led to a choice of a career, and that career in turn turned out to be nothing but one loss after another.

In my own defense, I could not be blamed for anything. I did not take her child away either by force or cunning. It would have been taken away from her by somebody else if not by me. I was merely a random man who paid, with his wife's money, for the implementation of its removal, and was therefore, at worst, only the recipient of her loss, not the cause of it.

As far as that original loss went, I was now more than willing, eager in fact, to do the right thing and reunite her with her child. To serve as the agent of their reunion.

But to do that was not enough anymore.

She had incurred too many other losses along the way. If she got Billy back, but at the same time discovered that she had yet again been cut from a film and not just any film but a film in which she finally got to play a major part, that might turn her reunion with her son into yet another loss. The reunion, I was determined, had to be a triumph. A total triumph. Nothing must be allowed to detract from the joy of that occasion, or undermine the happy ending I had in mind for the two of them.

Had I known at the start what I knew about her now, I never would have come to LA.

But it was too late now. We can't unknow what we know.

I agonized over my dilemma (as I lay there by the poolside) not out of any genuine irresolution about what I planned to do but merely to be on record with myself that I had agonized over it. It was part of the procedure of coming to terms with things ahead of time. It was important to leave a trail of torment behind, so that if unexpected consequences occurred as a result of my actions, I could exonerate myself on the grounds of the torment I had felt prior to causing them.

I agonized over the unthinkable act I was prepared to commit in order to have a happy ending for Leila and Billy.

The more I agonized over it, the more familiar the unthinkable became, until it was not unthinkable anymore.

But it was not easy, even for someone as gifted as myself with coming to terms with things, to contemplate desecrating a work of art.

Being an out-and-out hack who had never even come close to conceiving a true work of art, I worshiped Art in a way that a practicing artist could not possibly understand. To a practicing artist, it was something one did. To me, Art was a miracle, the only man-made miracle on earth.

How then was it possible, I agonized by the poolside, that I could lie there and plot its undoing?

The more I castigated myself and the more I agonized over something I knew I would do, the more I came to terms with it. My savage self-criticism licensed me to proceed.

Most of the horrors committed in my time (I waxed philosophical) were not the work of evil men bent on committing evil deeds. Rather they were the acts of men like myself. Men with moral and aesthetic standards of high order when the mood was upon them. Men who knew right from wrong and who did right when the mood was upon them. But men with no moorings to hold those convictions and standards in place. Men subject to changing winds and moods, who were doomed to reverse themselves completely when another, contradictory mood was upon them. They would always, these mood men, find a way to justify their actions and come to terms with the consequences. The terminology they used in coming to terms with their crimes constituted, in large part, what we referred to as history.

Listening to myself, while I lay there by the poolside, was an education. The philosopher within me philosophized, the psychologist within me psychologized, the moral man moralized, but all to no avail. Their voices had a fatalistic keening quality, as if they had all gathered within me to eulogize the victim of my upcoming crime rather than to keep me from committing the crime itself.

Throughout the long hot afternoon, while I lay there sweating in my poolside chair, a woman's voice came over the poolside PA system to say that one of us lying there had a telephone call.

"Telephone call for Mr. Stump."

"Telephone call for Ms. Florio."

"Telephone call for Mr. Messer."

Those called, as if paged back to life, awoke from their deathlike stupor and arose to answer the call. Not one of them came back from his telephone call to lie there among us. They were saved. The rest of us, the damned, the uncalled, remained to broil in that terrible heat.

Perhaps, I thought, Judgment Day would be something like this. There would be no trumpet blasts to raise the dead. Telephone calls instead. You'd either get called or you wouldn't.

The earth revolved around the sun (while I lay there), spinning on its axis and creating the illusion that the sun above me was sailing across the sky, east to west.

Shadows lengthened, creeping across the pavement like sprung leaks. The heat of the day began to subside.

I lit a cigarette. Some process had been concluded. Something within me had been metabolized, digested, eliminated.

So much life (the third-person narrator within me narrated) had been sacrificed over the years for the sake of Art, that it was high time for Art to be sacrificed for the sake of someone's life.

I arose and left the pool, having successfully concluded the business I had come to accomplish.

And so Friday came and went.

# CHAPTER EIGHT

## I

Saturday morning begins the way Friday afternoon ended, by the poolside. Only now it's by the poolside of Cromwell's house in Coldwater Canyon, where I've arrived a little too early for our working breakfast and am, as I sit there, a little too eager to get going.

I sit at a wrought-iron table with a glass top, in a wrought-iron chair with a thick, soft seat cushion. Cromwell's housekeeper, another Maria, is bringing out the breakfast. English muffins. Canadian bacon. A big pitcher of freshly squeezed orange juice. A basket of pastries and coffee in a large ceramic pot. I sit and smoke and wait. Through the glass tabletop I can see the light-blue Spanish tiles on which the wrought-iron table rests.

A handyman is repainting the tall wrought-iron fence that surrounds Cromwell's property. I can see that the paint he is using is black, but it smells yellow to me, and when I look away from the fence and the handyman, it's a manila-envelope-yellow fence I see in my mind.

There is a hint of a breeze, just enough to carry the scent of paint fumes from the fence toward the poolside table where I sit.

Cromwell appears. He is clean-shaven and fully dressed for work, so that when he is finished with me, he can get into his car and drive to his next appointment without having to go back inside the house.

Everything about him says that he has a busy day ahead and that there is a definite limit on the time he has for me. Knowing that I know the score, he is free to create the impression that he has nothing but time for me.

He greets me graciously, unhurriedly, as if we had made no appointment to meet here at this time, as if I were an old friend who dropped in uninvited and unexpected but a friend he is thrilled to see.

"How nice of you to come," he tells me.

"Look at you," he tells me, "you're all tanned. You look wonderful, Doc. You really do. I've never seen you look so good."

"I feel good," I tell him.

He sits down. Having stood up to greet him, I sit down again myself.

We drink coffee and orange juice and eat English muffins. We talk about Europe. He gives me credit for knowing everything he tells me, but he tells it to me anyway, as if seeking corroboration for his impressions from a post–cold war expert of Eastern Europe like myself.

He tells me about the Russians, the Czechs, the Slovaks, the Poles, the Hungarians, the Bulgarians, the post-Ceausescu Romanians. (He pronounces it perfectly: chow-SHESS-koo.)

He tells me about the cities of Eastern Europe, about Budapest and Prague and Moscow and Leningrad and Sofia and Bucharest and Warsaw. The museums in the cities. And how, despite all the economic and social turmoil in those countries, there are still some wonderful hotels where one can stay.

"It's mind-boggling," he tells me, "the changes that are happening throughout Eastern Europe. Monumental. Absolutely monumental. I was just on the phone with a playwright I'd met in Prague and I was telling him . . .

"It's heartbreaking," he tells me, "the way they have to live in this period of transition from the old to the new without so much as a pause to catch their breaths. The poverty. The anxiety. The suffering, both physical and mental . . .

"And yet," he tells me, "it was exhilarating. The humanity, the unadorned and undisguised humanity of the people I saw was worth the trip. It makes you think, to see people like that. It makes you wonder that perhaps for all their suffering . . ."

It's always a shock to see Cromwell again, even after a relatively short separation. Although I know him well, and although his physical appearance is tattooed on my brain, the confrontation with his forehead, that damlike structure holding back millions of gallons of thoughts, is not something for which I can ever prepare myself ahead of time.

Nor can I prepare myself ahead of time for the way he looks at me as he is looking at me now. He is pleased to see me. Pleased for reasons I can imagine, but pleased also for reasons beyond my comprehension. He doesn't just look at me. He sees me. I feel seen when he looks at me.

I might have doubts as to my identity, but he has none. He knows who I am. He alone knows.

There was in Greek mythology a being called a daimon, an attendant spirit that stood behind us, our true self that we could never see. Only others could see it. This attendant spirit seems to materialize whenever I'm with Cromwell. He alone sees it.

He does this to others, not just to me. You are seduced into being what he sees in you. I can easily imagine Jay Cromwell, for the few days he was in each of those countries of Eastern Europe, leaving a lasting impression among its peoples that he alone knew what it was to be a Hungarian, a Pole, a Russian, a Romanian. When he circumscribes a man, a country, or a continent, he does it with such certainty that there is no room for doubt. There is not a trace of doubt in Cromwell's whole being. He is made, or seems to be made, of some new man-made material called certainty. One hundred percent certainty.

A young woman comes out of the house in a black Lycra bathing suit. Her thick blond hair is combed back into a single, thick braid reaching down to the small of her back. I see a face (with melting blue eyes) that is so beautiful, I know instantly that this is the most beautiful human being, male or female, the most beautiful living thing, I have ever seen and am likely ever to see.

She is heading toward the pool on a diagonal line designed to pass the table where we sit. Cromwell calls her.

"Vera." He gestures for her to approach.

She does.

Her beauty is so outrageous that I don't know where to look, so I reach for a cigarette and light it to avoid looking at her. Extremes of this kind, be it beauty or ugliness, make me feel ashamed of something. But when she stops in front of us, I have to look up at her.

She is so young. Totally different from the Cambodian girl whom she has replaced as Cromwell's concubine.

"Vera, this is Saul. Saul, Vera," Cromwell introduces us.

I half stand, she half bows.

"How do you do," she says in that slightly startled way of Slavic immigrants, finding four words to stress in a three-word sentence.

"Vera is from Leningrad," Cromwell tells me.

"Vera, I am told," he tells me, "means 'faith' in Russian."

I look at him while he speaks, and when Vera leaves, to continue her interrupted journey to the swimming pool, I continue looking at him watch her walking away.

"How I managed to get her out of the country on such short notice is a story in itself," he tells me.

"Her parents," he tells me, "are intellectuals.

"You should have seen the scene at the airport," he tells me. "Intellectuals or not, Russian parents are first and foremost true parents, if you know what I mean. Real Old World parents. Close. All those families over there that I met were real close." He makes a fist to demonstrate just how close. "Her mother was crying, her father was crying, Vera was crying. But it wasn't until she had to say goodbye to her baby brother Sasha that she really started crying. It was very moving. It really was. The show of emotion. The humanity. It was worth the trip itself.

"She's still a child herself," he tells me.

"Her parents understood," he tells me, "that a girl as beautiful as Vera would be wasted over there. No opportunities.

"I met her at the Hermitage," he tells me.

He waves to Vera and gestures with his chin that I too should look. I turn around and look. Vera waves from the diving board and then performs an unspectacular but efficient swan dive into the pool. She is not a very good swimmer. She keeps her head too high out of the water and she's all arms and no kick.

## 2

Cromwell and I eat Canadian bacon and socialize while Vera swims some mandatory number of laps she has set for herself. Back and forth she goes while we talk. We talk about the weather. How hot it was yesterday.

"Hottest day of the year so far," one of us says.

"Not so bad today," the other says.

We talk about the drought, global warming, crime, homelessness, the growing anarchy of everyday life everywhere.

It grates on me again that a man as corrupt and evil as Cromwell does not indulge at least in that ostentatious bad taste of other corrupt Hollywood producers I have known. Not in his office and not here at his home. I want his swimming pool (where Vera swims her laps) to be shaped like a huge letter C or be heart-shaped or amoeba-shaped. Instead, his pool is simple and rectangular, the proportions soothing and pleasing to the eye. His outdoor telephone is neither cellular nor pink, as I would want it to be. It's black, with a cord. He has no tennis court. He doesn't even play tennis. He doesn't even have one of those tans. I am the one who has one of those tans.

A few minutes later, Cromwell segues from socializing to the business at hand, but he does it so casually, in such an offhand manner, that the business of the film I have come there to discuss is made to seem no more than a by-product of my visit to an old friend's house.

Seeing as how you're here, he seems to be telling me, and seeing as how I value your opinion so much, Doc, there's a little something I'd like to discuss with you, but only if you have the time.

And so we begin.

Something disquieting is revealed as we talk about the Old Man's movie. I realize that in Cromwell's opinion, the film really is a mess, in desperate need of massive recutting and reshaping. He is not aware that the film is a masterpiece. He is not, therefore, sitting there by the poolside advocating the undoing of a work of art. I am the one who is doing that, because I am the one, not Cromwell, who is aware of the beauty and the brilliance of this work.

And so I can't help but wonder (as we continue our discussion) that if Cromwell is evil, as I know that he is, if he is the most evil man I know, as I know him to be, what, then, does that make me?

His memory of the film, despite his trip and his recent return, and his memory of all the deleted scenes, is as fresh and precise as if he had seen it early this morning, prior to my arrival. He remembers every single shot. He just doesn't know what to make of it all.

"I don't get it," he tells me. "Maybe the fault is mine. Maybe I'm the one who's obtuse and the film is wonderful. I really don't know. What do you think, Doc?"

He leans back in his wrought-iron chair and, with a gesture of his hand, indicates that the stage is mine.

I light a cigarette before I begin. My agenda is simple. It is to gut the work I love and to put back into the film as many, if not all, of Leila's deleted scenes. To find a coherent new structure that accommodates this desecration.

I need a lot of enthusiasm and energy if I want to be able to sell Cromwell on the merits of my case. It's not enough to be a slut. I need to be a Salome. And so I begin my song and dance.

"I see the movie," I tell him, "as a warm-hearted comedy. A romp.

"I see the movie," I tell him, "as a story of a lovable waitress. A coffee-shop cupid of sorts, who wears her heart on her sleeve and believes in Mom, God, America, and apple pie, but who most of all believes in love.

"It's a throwback," I tell him, "to the movies of old. It's an old-fashioned movie for the new times.

"The heart and soul of the movie," I tell him, "are all those scenes of the waitress that the Old Man cut out. Why he did that I don't know, but I do know that without them there is no movie. Those scenes should not only be reinstated but reinforced. Without the waitress, the film not only lacks focus, but what's even more damaging, it lacks humanity, if you know what I mean."

Cromwell, fresh from his trip to Eastern Europe, nods as if he knows exactly what I mean by the word "humanity." The two of us are experts on the subject.

"The movie as is," I tell him, "is too relentless. Too much of a piece. Too mercilessly wedded to some dissection of life instead of its celebration . . .

"The movie," I tell him, "should be a celebration.

"It should ramble a little," I tell him.

"It should be Capra-esque," I tell him.

My enthusiasm, or whoever's enthusiasm it is I'm doing, is becoming infectious. Cromwell nods and smiles. He is as amused as a king watching his favorite court jester.

"The music," I tell him, "the whole score for the movie should be classical music. Beethoven's *Leonore Overture No. 3* would be perfect for the opening credits."

I hum a little of the overture, just to create the atmosphere.

"The 'Blue Danube' waltz," I tell him, "would be wonderfully over the top for that scene where all those working-class men are getting into their cars in the parking lot at the end of the day and driving home.

"The 'Waltz of the Working Man,'" I call it.

"The 'Waltz of Husbands returning to their Wives and Kids,'" I tell him.

I hum a little of the waltz and sway in my chair. Cromwell does not sway in his but he seems to like the way I sway in mine.

He nods. He smiles. He raises his eyebrows. He throws back his head and laughs, revealing all his teeth.

Stravinsky's *Firebird Suite.* A theme from Copeland's *Appalachian Spring.* Wagner. Mozart. Bach. I blab on, humming snatches of musical themes and describing the scenes to be underscored by them.

I provide a theoretical framework for my decision to go with an all-classical music score.

Using familiar and recognizable pieces of classical music to underline the everyday, mundane moments in our movie would (I tell him) send a clear message to the audience that we were gently poking fun at our characters, while at the same time saluting them. It's a send-up, I tell him, a spoof of sorts, but a lovable spoof.

"The use of classical music," I tell him, "would help sway the film critics and give them an excuse to like the movie, and a little movie like this, in my opinion, can only benefit by quality reviews. The thing we must do is to take the art out of the movie and yet have it be reviewed as an art film, but an art film accessible to everyone.

"And the thing is," I tell him, "our choice of classical music fits because our movie is really a movie about a waitress in a small town with a yearning for a classical love story. Her romantic yearnings are over the top, just like the music we're using.

"The love story that's there now," I tell him, "would have to be trimmed back a lot and recut, so as to appear as something she invents for the couple involved. She thrills over their love affair. She is really a female version of Walter Mitty, but far more generous at heart, because she is generous enough to imagine these wonderful romantic moments for others. Not for herself, not just for herself, but for others as well.

"The grim love story that's there now," I tell him, "once it's trimmed back, way back, once it's underscored with music that sends up the whole love affair, and once we understand that we're seeing it all through the eyes of our waitress, will play like pure comedy. But it will always be tastefully funny, that's the thing. It's Americana. Pure Americana. It will make love look like the great American pastime."

Cromwell shoots his index finger at me.

"That would be a wonderful copy line for the movie. Love, the great American pastime. Or maybe the other way around. The great American pastime, love. What do you think, Doc?"

"I think," I tell him, "the first one's better."

"So do I," he tells me.

We're the souls of generosity. We argue over who deserves the credit for the copy line for our movie. He insists on giving me the credit for it. They were my words. I beg to differ. They might have been my words, I tell him, but the credit belongs to him for spotting their appropriateness instantly.

And so I move on to the ending of the movie. I chastise Mr. Houseman, but with reverence for his past accomplishments, for cutting Leila's character from the last scene.

"We have a chance here, not just for a good old-fashioned upbeat ending, but for a truly satisfying ending on a variety of levels. It's a Fourth of July. All the characters from the movie are there in the park awaiting the fireworks. We see it through our waitress's eyes, just as we have seen the whole movie through her eyes. And we see through her eyes that all are back with their families, where they belong. The family unit, the basic building block of humanity"—I actually say this—"has been tested and strained, but it holds. The collective unit, the town, the community, holds as well. And they've all come together to celebrate the continuation of an even larger unit, the country, America, and the idea behind it. And then we have the fireworks. They light up the sky over our little town. In my opinion, the Old Man didn't have enough fireworks at the end. What I think we should do, because I think we've earned the right to do it, is get as much stock footage of the greatest fireworks displays available and insert them into the ending, as our waitress's final POV. There must be great stuff available that we can get. The Bicentennial stuff on TV was great. We use only the best of the best. Our little town goes cosmic at the end. The screen literally explodes with fireworks. Maybe we underscore it with Sousa, maybe not, but I do know that we want to go out big, with a bang, with a thousand bangs."

I am done. I have finished the movie, but I don't feel finished myself. New gimmicks occur to me for various portions of the movie and I have a compulsion to share them with Cromwell. Gimmicks, like maggots, are swarming through my mind.

Fortunately, Cromwell glances at his watch. He is heartbroken. So much time has passed so quickly. He has a meeting at the studio he must go to, and the way he says it is designed to tell me that he would give anything if he could get out of it and stay with me. But he can't. Somebody has to do the boring business part.

He walks me to my car, parked in his drive.

Vera has vanished. She's not in the pool anymore.

Cromwell tells me how thrilled he is by everything I have told him. We make a midweek appointment to meet at his office to consider, in greater detail, the implementation of my ideas. He mentions hiring a team of editors and putting them at my disposal and under my supervision. That way, working overtime, if need be, we could maybe finish the film in time for its original release schedule.

I know that I'm pressing, and I know that I'm being obvious while I do it, but I pitch Leila to the very end. I tell Cromwell that one of the hidden assets of our film is its potential for making the actress who plays the waitress into a big star. I remind him how invaluable it is for a movie, from a selling point of view, to have a fresh face, a brand-new star in the making in the lead role.

We part.

I cruise down Coldwater Canyon, tapping lightly on my brakes.

The maggots, the unused gimmicks, continue to swarm through my mind, begetting new ones.

# PART THREE

# Sotogrande

# CHAPTER ONE

I

Billy and Leila are playing tennis down below and not far away. I sit at my table, drinking yet another cup of espresso, stirring in the little cubes of sugar with my little espresso spoon. The outdoor restaurant of our resort hotel is deserted. I am the only customer. It is still early morning. A little after nine. The sky above me is cloudless and blue, but because I'm in Spain I do my best to think of it as being Iberian blue.

The coffee I'm drinking couldn't be better or stronger. There are four choices: single espresso, single espresso but double in strength, double espresso, and a double-double espresso, that is, double in size and strength. I've had a couple of each already and am now drinking my third double-double of the day.

I light a Spanish cigarette. I brought along many cartons of my own cigarettes on the trip, but I smoked all of them a long time ago. I am now smoking a Spanish brand called Fortuna. I use locally made wooden matches to light them.

A handyman is hosing down the tiles of the terrace restaurant where I sit. The hotel is called Sotogrande, but Billy, in a moment of inspiration, has dubbed it Notsogrande. Which is what Leila has called the place ever since.

The handyman drags his hose past me, turning the nozzle away from my table. We nod to each other and then he moves on to spray the stairway leading down to the next level. Sotogrande is all levels. The dining room has three levels. The outdoor restaurant where I'm sitting overlooks the swimming pool. The swimming pool overlooks the tennis courts where Leila and Billy are playing tennis now.

They always play in the early morning or late afternoon. Leila is allergic to the sun. Even moderate exposure to direct sunlight can cause her to break out with the cold sores she dreads. So concerned was she about getting cold sores in a foreign country (the technical name for this affliction is herpes labialis) that before we left on our trip to Spain she persuaded her Venice dermatologist to overprescribe the quantity of Zovirex she would take along with her. Just in case. It is the only treatment for these fever blisters of hers. She has half a dozen little tubes of the ointment in her makeup bag in our room. Enough Zovirex for a whole ward of cold-sore patients.

She never played tennis before I introduced her to Billy, but thanks to him she has developed a passion for the game. This passion began almost as soon as they met in LA. When we left for Spain, they took their tennis racquets, stowing them in the overhead bins. Since I was a smoker and they were not, I sat behind them on the plane and observed, to my delight, how wonderfully they got along. Although Leila was still young, she seemed a lot younger in Billy's presence.

We flew to Madrid out of Boston.

2

From Madrid we drove east to Guadalajara and then south to Toledo. And then farther south, on to Granada. Wherever we stayed along the way, I made sure ahead of time that there would be a tennis court where the two of them could play.

Sotogrande has three tennis courts. It is a sprawling resort hotel situated, as its brochures proclaim, "on the magnificent Costa del Sol" of southern Spain. The Rock of Gibraltar is not far away. Across the Straits of Gibraltar is Morocco. There is a ferry service to Tangiers.

Despite the tennis courts, both Leila and Billy grew bored with Sotogrande and the area around it. Bored with the narrow and not-so-clean beaches of Estepona. Bored with the boutiques of Marbella. Bored with the hotel dining room and bored with dining in the nearby restaurants specializing in fish dishes. But bored primarily, I think, by the break in the rhythm of travel, of moving on every few days to another place.

The fault was mine. It wasn't so much that I loved Sotogrande and felt like staying there as that I felt even less like packing up and moving on.

While I waited to regain my enthusiasm for travel, I rented Billy and Leila a car of their own. This way, with Billy driving, the two of them could take day trips or overnight trips to wherever it was they wanted to go without feeling guilty that they were leaving me stranded and carless in Notsogrande.

Today, after tennis, the two of them went to Ronda. I always took it upon myself to make the reservations for these little overnight trips of theirs. The manager at Sotogrande knew the best hotels everywhere. In Ronda, he assured me, Queen Victoria was *the* place to stay. I booked them two rooms there for the night.

3

I finish my espresso and order another double-double. My waiter brings it, along with a clean ashtray.

I stir in the little cubes of sugar with my little espresso spoon and watch the lemon rind twirl like some ancient vessel in a black whirlpool.

I light another Fortuna.

I take a sip of espresso.

I look up at the sky. It's one of those things you can't help doing if you're a tourist. Looking up at the sky as if something momentous is riding on the kind of day it will be. As if I were nothing less than Agamemnon.

The sky is still blue, but a regatta of clouds is sailing northward across it. The clouds are scattered but in a loose confederation, suggesting a common goal. Because I'm in Spain, they bring to mind the doomed ships of the Spanish Armada, sailing toward England once again.

I take another sip of coffee, but the old caffeine kick just won't kick in anymore.

Obviously it's not the coffee. It's me. Something new is wrong with me. Not terribly wrong. Nothing to be alarmed about. But something is definitely wrong.

It's as if my old drunk disease has spawned its own, completely opposite counterdisease. Alcohol can no longer get me drunk. And now caffeine can no longer wake me up. Not fully, at least.

I first became aware of the symptoms of my caffeine disease in Madrid. We stayed there five days, and for the first couple of days I thought it was simply a case of jet lag. The symptoms were very similar to those I'd had before during my first couple of days in Paris or London. My assumption was that on the third day I would feel like myself again.

But it didn't work out that way. The jet lag itself went away, but a residue of some other lag remained.

I wasn't dysfunctional. I could and did function normally, despite this new disease. When we left Madrid, I did more than my share of driving. I carried on lively and meaningful conversations with Billy and Leila. I joked. I made sweeping generalizations about Spain and its people. I ate well. I slept well. I made love to Leila and was very animated in my lovemaking.

So it wasn't that I either felt or looked dazed or drugged or narcoleptic. It was just that I wasn't open for business. Any business.

I was so good at keeping my symptoms to myself that neither Leila nor Billy seemed to notice that I had anything the matter with me. I saw no point in telling them. The two of them were having such a wonderful time.

Besides, what exactly could I tell them?

That caffeine no longer had the kick it once had?

That when I woke up in the morning, I wasn't really awake?

That I wasn't open for business?

What made it even harder to bring up my new malady was that they both had noticed a change in me. But far from perceiving it as a problem that I was having, they happily concluded that I was finally beginning to unwind, to let go.

"I have never seen you look so happy, Dad," Billy told me.

It wasn't simply a matter of not wanting to disappoint him and hurt his feelings that made me go along with such remarks. It was also the possibility that, for all I knew, Billy was right. A very real possibility existed that what I considered to be symptoms of some new disease were in fact due not to a disease but simply to a case of happiness.

Maybe I was not sick. Maybe I was happy.

Even a partial list of my blessings would warrant happiness.

My former theoretical daydreams about the kind of relationship I wanted to have with Billy were now an actual, almost daily, occurrence. We had nice, long, easy chats. Just the two of us. We talked about life and literature and Leila. I gave him a hug almost every night when he went off to bed in his room, which was right across from ours.

"Good night, son."

"Good night, Dad."

Very often, I kissed him on the cheek at these times. And sometimes, because we were in Spain, I kissed him on the cheek three times, the way the locals did. More than once, he kissed me back. And for a boy his age to do that to his father was no small thing.

He knew that I loved him.

I could tell that he loved me.

Both of us loved Leila, each in his own way, and she loved both of us.

For the first time in my life I felt like a member of a loving family and sometimes even the head of it.

There was every reason to assume that this little family unit of ours would prosper and last a lifetime and that the bonds of love between us would only deepen with the passing years.

I light another Fortuna. I take another sip of espresso. I check out the sky again.

I consider giving happiness a whirl.

But the problem, given this exotic new disease I've contracted, is that to do anything I first have to decide to do it, go through the business of deciding, and then, having decided, go through the business of holding on to the decision I've made. And even when the end result of all that deciding (and all that holding on) is happiness itself, the work required to achieve it has become a little too much for me.

Too something.

How to explain?

Being happy, deciding to be happy, is one thing. Staying happy is something else entirely.

Everything, it seems to me, is suddenly a conscious choice, requiring conscious decisions. To be happy. Not to be happy. To be miserable. Not to be miserable. To feel guilty because I haven't yet told Leila and Billy that they are mother and son. Not to feel guilty about it, because the right time to tell them has not yet come and a thing like that should only be done at the right time.

Once we return to America, I think to myself, this whole thing will pass. This inability ever to fully awake during the day. This sense that nothing is involuntary. This strange sense that even when I am asleep at night, I am conscious of what I am doing.

## 4

A tall chain-link fence surrounds the tennis court. Outside the fence is a little wooden bench where I sit and smoke my Fortunas and watch them play.

It's almost ten thirty now, but because the tennis courts are situated on the lowest of the many levels of Sotogrande, the shadows cast by those other levels help to keep the courts in shade until well after eleven o'clock. There's some sun now, on Billy's side of the net, but that's all.

They don't mind my sitting here and watching them play.

If they did, I wouldn't do it.

But they don't.

Leila's white outfit seems whiter than Billy's because of the whiteness of her skin and because Billy's oversized tennis shirt (it's enormous) is soaked with sweat. The dampness darkens its appearance.

Leila is bone-dry. It's a problem she has. She gets hotter and hotter and, depending upon the level of exertion, redder and redder, but she can't sweat.

Her face is covered with red blotches, as if somebody has slapped her around. The same red marks appear on her face after prolonged love-making. I think of that now while I watch her play. She makes the same little noises, little grunts and yelps, while chasing a ball as she does when she's nearing her orgasm. I think of that too while I watch her play. The similarities.

"A-a-a!" Leila screams and chases a lob from Billy.

She kills me, the way she plays. She's all heart and no skill. Her game hasn't improved a bit, but her passion for the game has intensified.

She's running after the ball now, which has sailed high over her head, and it's over her head that she carries her tennis racquet now, while pursuing the ball, like some screaming lepidopterist chasing a butterfly.

## 5

The tennis game, such as it is, goes on.

Nobody, as far as I can tell, is keeping score. They're just playing, pretending to abide by the rules when it suits them, and abandoning them when it doesn't.

This absence of structure makes me a little uneasy in my role as the observer, but that's my problem, not theirs. I'm a stickler for law and order in sports. For standards. For tradition. For structure. The game they're playing is anarchy. There, just now, Leila's return is out by two or three feet, but Billy doesn't call it. Played this way, tennis looks no better than life itself.

It's not a big deal. It just makes me a little uneasy to see the game played this way.

## 6

Leila, her face still a little blotchy, is undressing in our room. Slipping out of her tennis things.

She is completely naked now. Hers is one of those pre-aerobic bodies. No definition, nor discernible muscle tone anywhere. Everything is soft and round, just as her breasts are soft and round. Her stomach is not hard and flat but softly rounded like the rest of her. What makes her body so erotic is the sense that it is completely connected to the rest of her, so that when she smiles, her whole body smiles.

The proximity of her nakedness is provocative in theory, but I'm not open for the business to follow.

Grabbing a dry towel, she heads for the shower. Her bare feet slap on the red-tiled floor. She vanishes. The shower comes on. The acoustics of our room in Sotogrande amplify the sound, turning it into the sound of a large fountain.

The thought of telling her about Billy always comes up when there's something else that's coming up. Their trip to Ronda.

The trip to Spain was my idea, because I was going to tell her about Billy right before we left. My whole motive for the trip was to have something waiting in the wings that would absorb the telling of the truth and allow us, after the truth was told, to move on from there.

I have a terrible problem with truth. I can't imagine what will follow the telling of it. I see everything stopping and the spoken truth, like some avalanche, blocking all roads forward and back.

I should have told them right away. I should have done it when I introduced them to one another, although the word "introduced" is really not the right word under the circumstances.

I meant to do it, but the logistics of the telling got in the way.

I couldn't decide how to do it. Should I first tell one and then the other? And if so, should I first tell Leila and then Billy, or the other way around? Or bite the bullet and tell both of them at the same time?

It had to be done right. There had to be the perfect moment and the perfect way in which to do it.

Leila starts singing in the shower, not so much singing as vocalizing some Andalusian melody we heard on the radio the other day.

## 7

Billy's room is right across the corridor from ours and is shaped, to all intents and purposes, like ours. Same components, different configuration.

He has already showered and is beginning to pack when I enter his room without knocking.

His hair is still wet. Long and black and shiny. His chest is bare, he hasn't put on a shirt yet. Long baggy shorts are all he's wearing.

His torso is at once flat as a surfboard and full of little valleys and hollows, all those little unfilled-in places where youth resides. I could easily imagine birds drinking water from the two hollows under his collarbones.

His shoulders are a joke. I have never seen shoulders so skinny and yet so wide. His arms as long as the sleeves of a straitjacket. He packs his duffel bag without moving his feet at all. He simply reaches out for things around the room with those long arms of his and zap, the thing is in his hand and then in the duffel bag in one motion.

As tall as he is, he seems even taller now, because he is standing above me. I'm sprawled out on the couch in the sunken living room level and he's up there in the bedroom level by himself.

Leila is with us in spirit. There are three of us here, as there always are when I'm with either one of them. The other is always present in spirit. This physical absence but spiritual presence of the other allows me to relax and enjoy the illusion that it's just the two of us, whichever one of the two I'm with at the time.

"You're not going to fall asleep down there, are you?" Billy calls to me.

I yawn, playing along with the part that he thinks suits me.

"I just might," I reply. "If I can't wake up, I might as well go to sleep."

"Go right ahead then." He smiles and continues packing.

Silence falls between us, but it is an easy silence. Like roommates in college. He's off on a date. I'm staying home.

"I've never seen you like this, Dad."

"Like what?"

"Like that. You look like Buddha under that tree, whatever that tree is called, where he lay down and went to sleep."

"I envy Buddhists," I tell him. "It must be so nice to have a religion founded by an overweight man for once. The thing about Buddha . . ."

I banter on. Billy pretends to listen, laughing an occasional busy little laugh just to inform me that he's paying attention.

My banter about Buddha runs out of steam. I light a cigarette.

He puts on a loose polo shirt and instantly takes it off and puts on another one. I've seen him do this at least half a dozen times with the same shirt. He bought it in Madrid and feels obligated to wear it, but as soon as he puts it on, he rips it right off again.

"What's in Ronda?" I ask him.

"It's not so much what's in Ronda as what's not in Ronda. And what's not in Ronda is this place. This Notsogrande."

He pauses. He looks down at me. There is a change in his voice when he speaks again and inquires, "Do you want to come with us, Dad?"

### 8

Back in my room again. Leila is cool and showered and almost ready to go. The red blotches are faded from her cheeks. She is wearing a long white sun dress, with bare shoulders and arms.

Still barefoot, slipping into her sandals, as I look at her.

The straps on the sandals are thin (she bought the sandals in Marbella) and the holes in the straps are small. She is having a bit of difficulty notching the notches.

She crosses her legs and moves her foot this way and that, as if enjoying the way her feet look inside those dainty sandals.

Seeing her completely dressed is even more provocative and erotic than the sight of her naked flesh was earlier. She looks gift-wrapped.

### 9

Out in the parking lot of Sotogrande, the three of us do what we always do when they go off on a little trip of their own. I escort them to their rented car and dispense unwanted advice like Polonius. Although Billy has three credit cards accepted worldwide, whose billing address is that of my new accountant, Jerry, I make a point of stuffing a wad of pesetas into the pocket of his baggy shorts.

"Oh, Dad," he complains.

"Just in case. You never know."

Leila is wearing her big blue hat, the same hat she wore when I first saw her getting out of that taxi in Venice.

There is no protocol as such on these occasions, but when I position myself to take my leave of them, I always kiss Leila goodbye first. I do so this time. It feels so cool in the shade of her big blue hat. I find her lips and kiss them. Like drinking water from a stream.

"Saul," she asks, "are you sure you don't want to come with us?"

I shake my head.

"C'mon, Dad," Billy does his bit. "Go grab a suitcase. We'll wait."

I decline.

They insist.

I decline again.

Finally I win.

We always do this and, although I know I'm not coming, I enjoy being coaxed.

It's Billy's turn now to be kissed. He bends his legs to lower his cheek to my lips. His arms are so long, I feel willowy in his embrace. I kiss his cheek and he kisses mine. Memories of his childhood flood my mind.

Their bags are in the trunk. Leila is sitting in the car already. And now Billy, like a tall tripod collapsing, shrinks himself into the driver's seat where, as if by magic, his long limbs telescope out again.

His window is rolled down and I put my hand on top of the door frame. I bend over and stick my head inside the car as I speak.

"Do you have a road map?" I ask.

He does.

"Call me when you get to Ronda so I know you made it safely?"

He says he will.

"Promise?"

He promises.

"Drive carefully," I tell him. "No speeding."

"Oh, Dad," he moans. "Are you kidding? With Leila next to me? If I go over forty, she opens the car door and starts dragging her foot on the road."

He puts on his sunglasses. He starts the car. They can't leave until I take my hand away from the door. I keep it there a beat too long and then let them go.

I wave.

They wave.

I see Leila punching Billy on the shoulder in playful retaliation for something. They're having fun already.

Everyone I love, everything of any meaning to me at the moment, is inside that rented car that is pulling out of the parking lot. And yet, the only true response I feel as I watch them depart is one of relief.

A relief of some kind.

It's as if having people who mean so much to me were a burden. Like a pressure, like a tumor on the brain, which I now feel receding as the distance between us grows.

How to explain?

When they're around me, either one of them, or both, I'm so conscious of them, so conscious of the need to appreciate, and rightly so, the newfound meaning in my life. But appreciating, counting one's blessings, is hard work. A constant squinting of the psyche to keep it all in focus. A point is reached when you want a sabbatical from meaning.

# CHAPTER TWO

## I

It took a while, after that "working breakfast" with Cromwell, actually to start working on the film. Editing rooms and equipment had to be rented. A team of editors and assistants had to be hired. There was some difficulty in hiring the staff because most of the reputable editors refused to have anything to do with the recutting of Mr. Houseman's last film. A couple of them showed up for the interview just for the pleasure of telling me what a reprehensible sonovabitch I was to be cooperating with Cromwell in the ruination of a film by a great man. I didn't need them to tell me this. I knew it better than they did.

It took almost a month, but a staff of young editors eager to work on a feature was found. Three young men and two young women. Nice kids, all of them. Hard workers. Their first big chance.

And so we began.

My recutting of the film was one thing in theory, but something else when the first day came to put the plan into effect.

A dread accompanied me and everything I did that day. A horror, not an intellectual horror but a physical horror, made me shake like an old drunk when the time came to cut into the first scene and undo the perfection of its form.

I was sure I wouldn't be able to continue. I was positive that something within me would recoil and refuse to go on with it. But I was wrong.

Working was working. Working on the desecration of something required as much dedication, was just as time-consuming, as if one were working on a masterpiece.

I got lost in the details.

Undoing was doing too.

The drive to and from the Burbank studio where our editing facilities were located was exhausting at first, but soon became soothing and reaffirming. Driving in the rush hour in both directions gave me the sensation of being a part of the great tidal movement that swept millions of people away from their homes in the morning and then deposited them back home again in the evening. It was like being a part of some great daily cycle. Of being a working man.

And having Leila to come home to at the end of the day gave me the feeling of having a home. A family, in fact. I was a working-class family man. I was doing it all for my family.

We alternated. She spent nights at my hotel suite. I spent nights at her house in Venice. All that was missing was Billy.

2

And so one day I picked up the phone in my editing room and called him.

It was four o'clock in Burbank, seven o'clock at Cambridge when I picked up the phone. The members of my young crew were walking about with strips of film hanging around their necks. They were splicing scenes together. Tearing other scenes apart. They were all around me.

I hadn't spoken to Billy since the night of the McNabs' party and, as I dialed his number, I had no idea what I would say to him.

He answered the phone on the third ring.

"Billy," I said, "please don't hang up. It's me."

It was a good opening on my part. By putting myself at his mercy, I rendered him speechless. Before he could recover, I continued talking.

The members of my editing team, not wishing to appear to be overhearing a very painful, private conversation, continued working around me, but I knew that they were listening to every word I said.

"Listen to me, son, I can imagine what you must be thinking to get this phone call after all this time, but I beg you to . . ."

I went on.

On the Steembach editing machine to my right (we had two of them) I saw a close-up of Leila's face from one of her cut scenes that we were putting back into the film.

"I know, believe me, I know, what a miserable father I've been. Father, indeed. As far as I'm concerned, I don't even have the right to use that word anymore, considering the nature of my derelictions, but . . ."

I went on.

I told him how he had every right to hate me for the rest of his life. That what I was doing now was too late. That I neither deserved nor expected another chance.

Every word I uttered was utterly sincere, but at the same time the confession I was making was a travesty. What I was doing to the film in the editing room, with the help of five assistants, I was now doing to my relationship with my son. I was snipping away at its complexity and integrity and reducing it to something as banal as a bowl of soup. But every word I uttered was sincere.

I told him that although I neither deserved nor expected another chance, I wished with all my heart that he would give me one, just one more. I told him that hardly a day went by that I didn't think about him. I told him how hard it was for a man like me to show love for others when, in the deepest recesses of my being, I had no love for myself. I retraced briefly, but without assigning a bit of blame to her, my relationship with Dianah, and how the limbo of that relationship, being neither a marriage nor a divorce, nor even a real separation, had created a limbo in my soul.

And then I told him about the woman I had met. And how, because of this wonderful woman, I had dared to think that perhaps there was something worthwhile about me after all. Something worthwhile I could do with what was left of my life. And the one thing that was uppermost in my mind right now was to be allowed to love him again.

"That's all I ask," I told him. "I'm not asking you to love me, son. I have not earned the right to ask you that. All I'm asking of you now is to allow me to love you again. Maybe I have forfeited the rights to that privilege. Maybe . . ."

I got so moved by my own words, or whoever's words they were, that I started crying. I could hardly go on.

"Maybe I won't get a second chance. It's up to you. Whatever you decide to do, I'll understand. Good night, son."

"Good night, Dad," he stammered.

When I put down the phone, the members of my editing team reached to embrace me in that support-group kind of way. Then we all went out for pizza.

## 3

From that day on, Billy and I talked on the telephone almost every other day. I called him from my editing room, with my young crew now listening freely.

I called him from my hotel suite, with Leila listening from the other room.

With Leila listening from the other room, I told him how much I loved him, how much I loved her, how much they both meant to me, and how I hoped when they met they would like each other.

There were at least two separate occasions when, after talking to Billy on the phone and putting down the receiver, I saw Leila, returning from the bedroom where she had been listening, with tears in her eyes.

"Oh, Saul." She walked toward me, her face contorted with grief and joy. "Oh, Saul," she sobbed my name.

And there were times when, drunk out of her mind, she wept that her father had not been a man like me.

Over and over again she told me—without knowing, of course, that she was speaking about her own child—how lucky Billy was to have a father like me.

All that remained was to bring the two of them together. To introduce them to each other.

## 4

Billy still had over a month of school left, but he had no classes on Fridays and so he jumped at the chance to have a long weekend in LA.

Days before his arrival, Leila was in a complete tizzy. It was the only time that she ever reminded me of Dianah. The same nervousness. The same excitement. The identical rush of anticipation. It was like that time many years ago, when Dianah and I were waiting for the little and as yet unnamed baby to arrive in our apartment.

Leila was terrified that she wouldn't make a good impression. That she didn't look right. That her hairdo was all wrong. That she didn't have the right dress to wear, as if there were a right dress for such an occasion. Not the least of her terrors was the prospect of meeting a boy from Harvard, because Leila was positive that kids who went to Harvard "knew everything, absolutely everything, there is to know."

In the end, I also got caught up in the excitement and the terror.

There were two of us again, waiting for a child to enter our lives, only now the child was a young man. The same moment, but with a different woman.

We stayed at my suite at the Beverly Wilshire, where a guest bed awaited Billy in the living room.

The whole time that he was there, on his first visit, Leila religiously refrained from turning on the TV, because she was positive that kids from Harvard didn't watch TV. I didn't have the heart to tell her that some of the best and the brightest Harvard graduates were in LA writing episodes and pilots for TV series.

When Billy came back for another long weekend two weeks later, he and Leila simply picked up where they had left off and went on from there.

They started playing tennis.

The trip to Spain was my idea.

# CHAPTER THREE

## I

I took a long, aimless stroll around Sotogrande and then returned to my room.

Leila had left a mess behind. Her things were all over the floor. Never exactly neat to begin with, she was getting messier and messier the longer we stayed in Spain. The ratio of things that got scattered around the room to the things that she packed in her suitcase was about five to one.

I didn't mind picking up after her. It was exactly the kind of mindless activity I enjoyed doing.

I put her tennis dress into the dirty laundry hamper.

There were several skirts and blouses she had considered taking to Ronda but at the last minute had decided to leave behind. I hung the skirts on skirt hangers in her closet and folded and put away the blouses in the dresser where she kept them.

I picked up the crumpled wet towels from the floor, which she had used after her shower, and hung them on the towel racks to dry. There were blood red stains on the white towels.

Sotogrande was a very expensive hotel, luxurious in many respects, but the red tiles in our room were not glazed properly and bled into anything wet that was left on the floor.

I thought about the two of them, on their road to Ronda. The words had a nice alliterative sound. The two of them on their road to Ronda.

When I finally told them, how would I explain having waited so long to tell them?

The logistics of telling the truth were getting ever more complex and the right time to tell it harder and harder to define.

The room looked better now. Everything in need of folding or putting away was folded and put away. I even found Leila's sunglasses, which she couldn't find and had to leave without. I put them on top of her dresser, next to a small wooden bowl full of Spanish coins.

They always called me when they got to where they were going. I checked my watch. I knew where and how far away Ronda was. They should be getting there soon. I lay down on the bed and began waiting for my phone call from Ronda.

## 2

I'm not a man who believes in premonitions or forebodings. So when I lay on the bed and after a while began to worry that Leila and Billy might have had a car accident, it was not the presentiment of a disaster of any kind, it was simply the worry of a worry-prone mind. All those who stay behind while the ones they love leave on a journey know what it's like to wait for a confirmation of safe arrival, and the worries that are loosened when that confirmation becomes overdue.

In my case, the potential for some disaster on the road was enhanced by years spent rewriting other people's screenplays. In those rewrites, I had more or less perfected the use of certain hackneyed devices, the primary one being the setup and the payoff. By focusing on a seemingly innocuous object or event, I imbued it with consequence as a way of picking up the tension in a sagging story line.

I now found myself falling prey to that same device.

Leila's sunglasses.

She hated driving in a car without them. The glare of the sun in sunny Spain exhausted her and made her irritable if she didn't wear her sunglasses.

And today she had left without them. Billy was wearing his when they drove off.

I could easily imagine Leila reaching over and trying to snatch away Billy's sunglasses from his face. Playfully, of course. And Billy, just as playfully, resisting. And the car, while their playful tussle continued, going its own way.

It was of no help at all to remind myself, while I waited for that phone call from Ronda, that my disaster scenario was too contrived and far too improbable to ever occur in real life.

It was this very improbability that was worrying me. Because anything was possible.

# PART FOUR
# Pittsburgh

# CHAPTER ONE

## I

Who knows how long I might have remained in Sotogrande had it not been for Billy. August was winding down. His school year was to begin in a few weeks and he wanted to get back to New York so he could spend some time with Dianah before he left for Harvard.

From Sotogrande we drove to Malaga. From Malaga we flew to Madrid and caught a connecting flight to New York.

Billy and Leila sat in the nonsmoking section of the first-class cabin. I sat four rows behind them, smoking the last of my Spanish Fortunas.

There were still a few hours of daylight left. The sky was blue. The Atlantic below looked even bluer than the sky.

The farther I got away from Spain, the better I felt. There was something unreal about vacations in general, as if nothing that happened on vacations really mattered.

There was nobody sitting next to me, so I let my body sprawl over both seats. When the stewardess offered me a drink, I asked for a coffee.

It was your run-of-the-mill airplane coffee and lukewarm at that, but it did me more good than all those countless demitasses of espresso I had drunk at Sotogrande. I felt the caffeine elbowing its way through my sluggish system and a long-dormant, almost forgotten, sense of alertness returning.

I ordered another cup and lit another cigarette, and sip by sip and puff by puff I enjoyed the sensation of becoming wide awake for the first time in a couple of months. Open for business again.

But nothing, apparently, was all benefits and no drawbacks. The more coffee I drank (I ordered yet another cup) and the more I enjoyed feeling like a fully functioning human being, the more it seemed to me that I had neglected taking care of some business during my semi-comatose stay in Spain.

I found myself in the strange position of feeling anxious and worrying about something without knowing what it was.

A couple of hours later, we had our in-flight meal. Leila stood up at her seat with a champagne glass in her hand and toasted me.

"Cheers," she chirped, smiling.

The heads of the passengers between us turned to look at me.

"Cheers," I toasted her back.

After the meal, the stewardess announced that our in-flight movie would begin shortly. For some reason she asked us to pull down our window shades although it was now dark outside, and for some reason we all obeyed and pulled them down. The cabin lights were turned off.

It was during that brief interval of sitting there in darkness and waiting for the movie to begin that I realized the cause of my anxiety. It was so obvious, I was dumbfounded that I could have blocked it out for so long.

And then the movie began.

2

It had taken me over three months, working long hours with five young and energetic assistants, to recut the Old Man's film to my satisfaction. I discovered in the end that it had taken me longer to destroy his film than it had taken him to create it.

When the three of us left for Spain, there was still a lot of work to be done. The classical music choices I had picked out for various scenes had to be arranged and scored. Opticals had to be added. The film had to be mixed. A title sequence, if any, had to be designed and shot by an expert in this field. But my job was over. What work there remained was in the hands of technical experts of one kind or another.

Before I left, Cromwell wanted to see what the new version looked like, with allowances, of course, for all the missing technical elements.

We saw the film in the same screening room where I had seen Leila's cut footage for the first time.

Just the two of us.

I was very nervous.

The film had no musical score yet, but I had asked my editing team to underscore several scenes with a put-together temp track.

When Cromwell started roaring with laughter during the "Waltz of the Working Man" sequence, I relaxed.

Cromwell kept laughing out loud throughout the film and I, relieved that he liked it, laughed right along with him.

All those scenes that had meant so much to Leila, that she had found so moving or heartbreaking, were now hilarious. A couple of times, I heard the projectionist laughing.

What can I say about my version of the Old Man's film?

That it was a travesty? A desecration? A lobotomy of a work of art?

Those denunciations, although accurate, did not go far enough.

It wasn't merely that I had taken a masterpiece and, for motives of my own, turned it into a banality. I had taken something and turned it into nothing.

The only just description of what I had done was that I had created nothingness, but a nothingness of such accessible and broad appeal that it could pass for anything.

Cromwell was ecstatic. I had exceeded all his expectations. I was a genius. A bloody genius.

"You've really done it this time, Doc," he told me.

Even as I basked in his praise, I felt I had more in common with Doctor Mengele, the Black Angel of Auschwitz, than with any Hollywood hack I had ever known.

But I came to terms with it. My work on the Old Man's movie was a rare example of having to come to terms with something both before and after the fact.

My anxiety, as we flew on toward New York, had nothing to do with what I had done.

My anxiety was of another kind.

What if, while the three of us were in Spain, Cromwell had second thoughts about my version of the film?

What if, during my absence, he had shown the film to somebody else, some other hack, who had entirely different ideas of what the film should be?

What if, and this was the most terrifying possibility, what if, as an act of courtesy, he had shown the film to the Old Man himself, and what if the Old Man, with the authority and the eloquence of a dying genius, had persuaded Cromwell to return it to its original state?

What if, without my knowing it, Leila had been completely cut out of the film once again, except for that little moment in the restaurant?

I no longer had any misgivings about the role I had played in the annihilation of what I considered to be a masterpiece. My only dread was that the annihilation had been reversed in my absence.

It was possible. I was a random man living in a random world where anything was possible.

## 3

Leila couldn't believe her eyes when we landed at Kennedy and cleared customs.

She laughed. She cried. She did both at the same time. Billy applauded, shaking his head and smiling at me.

The cause of all this commotion was a large piece of white cardboard on which, written in large black letters with a Magic Marker, was her name: LEILA MILLAR.

She had told me in Spain how wonderful it must be to be one of those famous people with limo drivers holding up your name at airports for everyone to see.

It was an easy enough wonder to accomplish.

I called my limo service from Sotogrande before we checked out and requested that the driver who met us outside customs carry a sign with her name on it instead of mine. I requested a very large sign, printed in very large letters.

The shock on her face when she saw it was Christmas morning itself.

Having forgotten all about the arrangements I had made, I surprised myself.

She hugged me. She hugged Billy. Then she hugged the limo driver. She had to have the sign. Simply had to. She took it in both hands and looked at it at arm's length. She swaggered around as we made our way through the airport, holding up her name for everyone to see, striking sexy poses like some starlet at Cannes and then cracking up at her own antics.

She wouldn't dream of letting the limo driver put the sign in the trunk with the rest of our baggage. It sat there on her lap during our drive to Manhattan. She kept looking at it as if it were some priceless work of art.

We dropped Billy off at Dianah's.

Leila remained in the limo. I got out.

I suddenly felt dizzy, as if some gyroscope in my head were beginning to wobble.

Here we all are, I thought.

Here was I. Here was Billy and his two mothers, one in the limo and the other waiting upstairs for him. And here he was, without knowing it, leaving one for the other again.

It was here, in this very building, in the apartment upstairs, that I had heard Leila's voice for the first time on the telephone. Her laughter.

Before we parted, I gave Billy a hug, but I was really holding on to him to keep from falling.

"It's just us old fogeys now," Leila said when I got back in the limo.

She used the pucker of her lips in saying "fogeys" to give me a sweet little kiss on my cheek. Then she put her head down on my shoulder and kept it there until we came to a stop in front of my apartment building on Riverside Drive.

## 4

It had been, in our absence, one of the hottest summers in years, and the heat wave continued without showing any sign of a letup. It was almost biblical in its relentlessness. A strange kind of heat too, because it seemed to have little to do with the sun.

The sun itself, like some scrambled egg, was almost never in clear sight. It was somewhere up there, amorphous and diffused, in the haze of the constantly hazy sky, so that it wasn't the heat of the sun you felt, or at least you didn't associate the heat with the sun. You didn't know what to associate it with. It was just heat. Heat from somewhere.

When the sun set and night came, the heat of the day gave way to the heat of the night and the sounds of boom boxes and police sirens and ambulance sirens and the sirens of fire trucks that usually traveled in pairs.

There were numerous heat-related stories in the newspapers. Heat-related deaths. Heat-related crimes. Things going wrong. Little things. Big things. Murders were described as heat-related acts committed by men without any motive except the heat, as if men were no more than molecules of gas living out their lives at the mercy of the laws of thermodynamics.

My office, unoccupied in all that time, was like a pizza oven. I let the air conditioner run for well over an hour before picking up the phone.

It was so hot I couldn't even smoke, a first for me.

I had no reason to be in my office other than to make this phone call. I could have called from my apartment, but my anxiety was such that I couldn't bring myself to do it. Not with Leila there.

"Mr. Karoo," Brad answered the telephone, "how very nice to . . ." He went on, his minimum greeting to me now being a short paragraph.

Then Cromwell came on.

The fiber optics of telecommunication were at it again, destroying any sense not just of long distance but even separation between Cromwell and myself.

He asked about Spain. About the various museums and various paintings in those museums, and although I hadn't seen any of them, I lied and said that I had and that I had loved them all. He seemed to know Spain better than I knew New York. His description of the Spanish countryside made me feel that I had never been in Spain.

We talked about everything except the reason for my call.

I was unable to bring up the subject of the movie for fear that some catastrophic revelation awaited me if I did.

"Vera," Cromwell told me, "has been having a hard time of it adjusting to the U.S."

I couldn't remember at first who Vera was and when I did, I didn't really care how hard a time she was having. I only cared about what I cared about.

My stomach was slowly contracting into a rock-hard little ball.

Had Cromwell not brought up the subject of the movie, I don't know if I ever would have.

"By the way, Doc," he told me, "in case you don't already know, your reputation has taken a quantum leap forward. I showed your cut to some of my close friends and their reaction was to die for."

"Really?"

"To die for," he repeated. "You're the talk of the town."

"Any changes from the last time I saw it?"

"What's to change? You're a fucking genius. It hurts me to say this, but it's going to cost me a lot more money if I want you to work for me again. Your price, when this movie comes out, is going to skyrocket, you sonovabitch."

He laughed.

I felt a burden falling away from me and the resulting euphoria of relief caused me to laugh along with him. I laughed as if I had no intention of stopping.

He told me that he had decided to call the film *Prairie Schooner*.

Prairie Schooner was the name of the restaurant where Leila's character worked.

"It's wonderful," I applauded his choice.

The title, he told me, had market-tested very well. He planned to release the film just before Christmas, but only in a few select theaters.

Then, when the big Christmas movies began to die like flies, as he thought they would this year, it would go to more and more theaters around the country. This was a release pattern predicated upon the assumption that we would get wonderful word of mouth and rave reviews from the critics.

Cromwell thought we would get both.

He had a hunch.

We had a sleeper on our hands.

As always, he planned to have a few sneak previews in several cities prior to the release, just to see how the movie played in front of a real audience. Our first preview ("Call it a world premiere," he said) would be in Pittsburgh. In that very same theater where we had had our last preview together.

"Call me superstitious," he said, "but we did great starting there the last time we worked together, and I see no reason to change."

The exact date of the preview was still being worked on, but it would be sometime in mid-November. He would let me know.

"If I don't see you sooner," he told me, "I'll see you in Pittsburgh."

Even before I hung up, inspired, perhaps, by the euphoric relief I felt, I began to feel something else as well.

Something coalescing.

A swirl of themes from my whole life moving through me as if toward some long-delayed and much-desired resolution.

It was Pittsburgh.

That was where I would tell Billy and Leila that they were mother and son.

In a single, blinding moment of total clarity, I saw the perfection of Pittsburgh, both as a time and a place, for the telling of the truth.

I saw it all.

I saw the three of us at the world premiere of Leila's movie. Billy and me dressed in tuxedos. Leila wearing a brand-new evening gown for the occasion.

I saw Leila watching herself for the first time on the screen.

The loud, maybe thunderous applause at the end of the film.

Leila crying, covering her face with her hands, standing up to receive even more applause from the public. Billy and me sitting down, looking up at her.

And then afterwards, back at our hotel, when in her giddy delight she was positive that nothing could possibly top this wonderful, magical night, I would top it.

I would tell them the truth.

At first, they would wonder if I was joking or not, but as I continued to speak and elaborate, the expressions on their faces would slowly change.

Leila, I decided, would be the first to break down. Her long-lost child was here again. And then Billy, weeping himself, would envelop his mother in those long, gangly arms of his. At that moment, Leila would have everything. Everything that had happened to her would now be worth it, for it had made this moment possible.

And I?

I saw myself, the agent of their reunion, withdrawing a few paces from them. Standing there. Saying nothing. Asking for nothing. I would not intrude until they, on their own, turned to me in love and gratitude for all that I had done for them.

Maybe then I would cry a little myself.

"Oh, Dad," my Billy would say.

"Oh, Saul." Leila, squinting, would open her arms.

The three of us would embrace (I could see it) and become, in that moment of embrace, a real family, thereafter indivisible.

In the years to come, Leila and I, happily married now, would make yearly pilgrimages to Pittsburgh, in celebration of that unforgettable night.

Maybe, just maybe, I would even write my Ulysses movie.

Nor was I unaware, while I sat there in my office, happily smoking my head off, of the symbolic aptness of Pittsburgh as our rendezvous. The three of us converging upon that city of the three rivers. The Allegheny, the Monongahela, and the Ohio. Leila, Billy, and I.

# CHAPTER TWO

I

My apartment building, like all the prewar buildings along Riverside
Drive, has it charms, but it has no central air-conditioning. I have four
large air conditioners in four different rooms and they're all on. They
run night and day. The noise is not deafening, but there's no getting
away from it either. I don't mind the noise, but Leila does. It's getting
on her nerves. It's like being in a jet plane, she claims, with all the engines running but without going anywhere.

I'm sitting in the living room (Leila's in the bedroom) waiting for
Billy to walk through the door.

The doorman has just called to tell me that Billy is on his way up.

I have left the door unlocked, as I always do when he comes, so that
he can just walk in without knocking or ringing the doorbell. In this
small way, I'm trying to make it as comfortable as possible for him
when he comes to visit us. As if, so to speak, my home is his home.

Poor kid.

It hasn't been easy for Billy coming back to New York.

Knowing Dianah the way I do, I know she is furious (and who can
blame her?) that Billy has spent almost his entire summer vacation with
Leila and me. The little time he has left in New York she wants all to
herself.

I am positive that every time he comes to visit us, he has to lie to
Dianah regarding his destination. It's either that or run the risk of having a big fight with her. The lie shows on his face. It's the first thing I
notice when he comes through the door, the lie and the confused look
of guilt in his eyes, as if he's betraying someone by being here.

I understand what he is going through better than he does, because he is a little overwhelmed by it all.

It is all very simple, but at the same time very painful. He loves us both. And both of us love him. In a way, not in a good way, but in a way life was probably a lot easier for him when he had only one parent who returned his love. Now he has two. And since Dianah and I are a mess, he is an unfortunate victim caught in the middle of it. He is either betraying Dianah by coming to visit me or (in his mind) betraying me by staying away. I have felt like explaining all this to him on several occasions, but since his days in New York are numbered, and since after Pittsburgh everything is bound to change anyway, I have refrained. But I feel for him. It bothers me to see him tormenting himself needlessly when the fault isn't his.

The door opens and, for a moment, Billy's tall figure and broad shoulders fill the doorway.

He's all sweaty. His loose-fitting polo shirt clings to his body.

"It's hot as hell out there," he says, avoiding eye contact with me by wiping the sweat off his face with his hand.

Leila comes out of the bedroom wearing culottes, a long T-shirt, and her Spanish sandals.

"Better not hug me," Billy says. "I'm soaked."

But she hugs him anyway and then pulls back, making a big show of being scandalized by the imprint of dampness he has left on her T-shirt.

I can tell by his body language that he doesn't plan to stay for long. But then he never does.

Who knows what lie he told to get here? It's there on his face, whatever it is.

We sit there, the three of us. I sit on one end of the couch. Leila on the other end. Billy sits in the swivel easy chair in front of the air conditioner. He can't sit still. He swivels a few degrees north and then a few degrees south.

We talk about the heat and the latest heat-related stories we read in the papers.

Old people dying from heat.

The depletion of the ozone layer.

The greenhouse effect.

The upsurge in crime, in murders especially.

In the haze outside my window, the Hudson River looks like a river of haze and the sailboats upon it seem to be sailing in midair.

Leila suddenly does a wickedly accurate impersonation of an unusually obnoxious Englishwoman named Doris who was at Sotogrande
while we were there.

We all laugh.

Leila milks the moment with an encore.

We laugh again.

One of us says, "Notsogrande," and the three of us laugh yet again.

Spain as a topic of conversation gives every promise of being suffi-
cient to see us through a substantial portion of Billy's short visit but, for
various reasons, it doesn't take hold.

Maybe it's the heat.

Or maybe we've talked about Spain too many times already. Spained
out.

A silence falls.

I light another cigarette. When our glances intersect, we smile.

The silence continues. Gains in strength. It threatens to become
prolonged, if not permanent, if I don't come to the rescue.

So I start talking about world events as a way of getting them to forget about whatever little personal problems they have (soon to be resolved in Pittsburgh) by focusing on the big picture.

"One reason for the fall of the Soviet Union," I begin, "is that the
government, by becoming the country's economic system as well, managed to ruin both, the government and the economy. I don't want to
jump to any hasty conclusions, but I think we face the opposite danger
here. The economic system in America is threatening to become the
government and in the process . . ."

Suddenly, in mid-discourse, I feel this strange . . . what? Something.

It's as if the acoustics in my living room had suddenly changed. As if
there were no live bodies there to absorb the sound of my voice. As if I
were talking to myself and hearing the sound of my voice bouncing off
bare walls.

Billy and Leila are there in front of me. They are not only looking at
me but making a point of doing so, as if determined to convince me
that they are paying attention to every word I say.

They are right there in front of me, but somehow they're not there at
all. The who of who they are seems to be somewhere else, and this sense
of duplicity in the faces of the people I love brings on a mild disturbance.

The disturbance (panic, almost) lasts for a second or two. But a second or two is all it takes for me to understand what is really going on.

It's not them. It's me. I am the duplicitous one. It's not Billy or Leila who is keeping something from me, but the other way around. I am projecting my own symptoms upon them. There is that secret I can't share with them until Pittsburgh, and so until then I am bound to see in their eyes the projection of my own uneasy conscience.

Satisfied by the brilliance of my diagnosis, stunned by the speed with which I can comprehend such a complex psychological problem, I continue my analysis of capitalism and democracy and the gradual abdication of power of the latter to the former.

## 2

The day before he left for Harvard, Billy came to say goodbye. He came in the early afternoon. He couldn't see us that night because he and Dianah were going out to a musical and having dinner afterwards. And he couldn't see us tomorrow because he was leaving early in the morning and Dianah was escorting him to the airport. So this was the only possible time.

He hoped that I understood.

I was, of course, understanding itself.

When somebody comes to say goodbye, the purpose of the visit dominates the scene and no matter what else is being said, it's the unspoken goodbye that's the topic.

So it was with Billy's visit.

The whole thing turned out to be one endless goodbye.

Leila and I rode the elevator down with him (in silence) and walked him out to the street.

I was sure that he was going to get a cab, but Billy thought it silly to get a cab. It was only a fifteen-minute walk (the way he walked) to Sixty-ninth and Central Park West and he said he felt like walking. Stretching his legs a bit.

I should have let it go at that, but I couldn't. I had a certain kind of a farewell in mind, a neat and clean goodbye, with a taxicab taking him away while Leila and I stood and waved. Deprived of the anticipated image of our parting, I conjured up a longer version of the same scene.

"We'll walk with you a bit," I told him.

It was hot. As hot as it had been yesterday. As hot as it would be tomorrow.

We talked about the heat. At least I did. For all I know, I was the only one doing any talking.

I wondered how people lived before the advent of affordable air-conditioning. I advanced a thesis (not my own) that the architectural landscape of modern cities was shaped by Freon.

Who could argue with that?

Nobody did.

We turned down Broadway. Past the panhandlers, the derelicts, the trashmen selling their recycled trash. Past the wild-eyed and wild-haired Jeremiahs. Past the phone freaks carrying on bogus conversations with phantoms at the other end.

I hadn't intended to walk this far, but it now seemed almost impossible to stop and say I'd walked far enough. The downtown current of Broadway was pulling us ever more southward. Past Harry's Shoes. Past the Shakespeare bookstore. Past Zabar's.

I had no idea that I would be taking this walk when I left my apartment and so I hadn't come prepared. I had no loose change to hand out. I had no money on me at all. It almost felt chilling (in all that heat) to find myself penniless in public.

We were drifting.

Past the Apthorp building. And the Apthorp Pharmacy. Past the little traffic island where I had sat in silence with that old man wearing my father's overcoat. Where, in silence, we sat "like two chess pieces of an abandoned game."

I was following Billy. If something or somebody didn't stop me soon, I knew that I was quite capable of following Billy back to Dianah's apartment, as if all of us, Leila too, could spend the night there.

Fortunately for me, Billy came to his senses. He stopped.

"I think you better take Leila home, Dad," he said with authority. "Look at her."

Billy and I were bathed in sweat. Leila, true to form, was bone-dry, but her face was swollen and covered, as if with bruises, with red blotches.

"I'm fine," she protested.

"I'm not," Billy said in a no-nonsense voice. "I'm going to take a cab the rest of the way. It's too hot."

He hailed a cab.

For such an extended farewell, it suddenly became very abrupt.

He and Leila embraced and kissed and muttered some words of farewell. Eager not to make my embrace any longer or better than Leila's, I made it short and manly. No kiss at all.

Billy got in the cab.

"We'll see you in Pittsburgh," I shouted and waved.

And then he was gone.

It all felt messy and wrong, parting like that, and wishing to alter the mood and hoping to elicit a smile from Leila, I turned to her and said in my most engaging manner, "Phew, I thought he'd never leave."

"Oh, please," she snapped at me. "Don't! Just don't be clever for once. It's too fucking hot for clever. All right?"

I offered to get us a cab, but then I remembered that I didn't have any money on me. Neither did she. Nor had she brought her blue hat and the sunglasses to protect her from the heat and the glare.

We walked on uptown, past all those places and people we had walked past before.

It was so hot. The term "nuclear winter" seemed apt but misplaced. A nuclear summer is what it felt like. The bubble of our mood, our own private little biosphere that moved with us as we moved, just added to the heat.

Her face, gorged with blood, got redder and redder.

# CHAPTER THREE

I

The next morning, Leila woke up with a fever blister. I was still in bed when I heard her cry out in anguish from the bathroom. It sounded horrific, as if some long-evaded destiny had finally caught up with her.

I rushed inside to find her face-to-face with her reflection in the mirror, examining something on the left side of her lower lip, touching it gently with her fingertips.

"Oh, fuck! I don't fucking believe this," she screamed.

I still didn't know what the problem was and asked for an explanation.

"Look!" she screamed, full of rage.

I looked.

She stuck out her chin and turned her head so that I could have an unobstructed view of the little red inflammation in the corner of her mouth.

"It doesn't look so bad," I told her.

"What's that got to do with it?" she snapped at me. "So what if it doesn't look bad now? Who cares how it looks now? It's throbbing! And I know what that means."

She seemed ready to cry. Or to smash something. Or somebody.

By noon, the fever blister had grown considerably larger, puffier.

Just before bedtime that night, she spotted the beginning of another one next to it.

By next morning, the two blisters had merged, forming a sprawling multifaceted sore that essentially took over the left side of her lower lip.

She had to keep her mouth open at all times to avoid touching the lower lip with the upper. The slightest contact resulted in wincing pain. She was also terrified that the infection, as it had done in the past, might spread to her upper lip as well. Mouth open, wearing a grimace that at times looked like a sinister grin, she spoke like a ventriloquist.

She applied Zovirax hourly, but the prescription ointment made an already terrible-looking thing look even worse. The heat from the fever blister melted the ointment, coating the sores with a milky-white ooze and imparting to the whole thing an appearance of some strange imported fruit that had latched on to her lower lip and would not go away until it had ripened and burst.

Driven by some need to find the silver lining in everything, I saw even in this attack of herpes labialis a cause for consolation, if not outright celebration.

Better, I thought, that it should happen now than at the premiere of her movie in Pittsburgh.

When I shared this thought with Leila, she started screaming. It was much easier for her, much less taxing, to scream than to talk.

Then, on the third day, or maybe it was the fourth, she woke up feeling sick all over. She was shivering. I turned off the air conditioner in the bedroom. But then she got too hot. So I turned it back on. I didn't have a thermometer, so I ran out to the drugstore and bought one.

She had a temperature of 104. Aspirin knocked it down a few degrees, but then it came right back up again.

No, she wouldn't hear of going to see a doctor, or of having a doctor come to the apartment to see her. She knew what this was, "and there is nothing doctors can do because I've been through this before and there was nothing the doctors could do then either. So please," she half pleaded, half threatened, "just stop with the doctors or I'll go check into some hotel so I can have a little peace."

2

Her confinement to the apartment while she recovered from whatever it was she had (a flu of some kind) led to my confinement as well. Instead of going to my office, I stayed home. I came to enjoy it while it lasted. I only went out for groceries, cigarettes, or to buy the papers.

She lived on apple sauce, bananas, and ice cream. Things you didn't have to chew.

To help her pass the time, I read her stories from the newspapers, magazines, and periodicals I was now beginning to read. (The problems of the world fascinated me and my reading list of daily and weekly publications expanded to keep up with them.) I also read her poetry. When she confessed that she had never read a single play of Shakespeare's, I took it upon myself to read some Shakespeare to her. She couldn't bear to hear any one whole play, but she loved having me skip around and read my favorite passages. Which is what I did.

Of all the lines I uttered from the volume of Shakespeare's collected works, only one made her cry and it was, as far as I was concerned, an odd choice, because my reading of it was not very good.

"Nymph," I read Hamlet's line to Ophelia, "in your orisons be all my sins remembered."

"Oh, dear," she started blubbering, "but that's so sad. It's too sad."

I went in and out of her room over a dozen times a day, and there were times when I returned to find her asleep.

Even in sleep, she kept her mouth open to avoid aggravating that fever blister. Her now permanently parted lips gave her face (whether asleep or awake) a strange, disturbing intensity, an expression of some arrested intent, as if any second, despite the pain it might cause her, she would put her lips together and deliver herself of some devastating utterance.

### 3

Leila recovered. Her fever blister vanished. Everything was now fine, except for Leila herself.

She picked on and found fault with everything I did. The nicer I tried to be to her, the more unbearable she found me.

"Just don't!" she kept saying.

*Just don't* became her refrain.

"Please," she hissed, seething, "I beg you. Just don't be so goddamn charming all the time."

"I didn't know I was."

I made a little theatrical bow as I retreated. She blew up.

"That's it. That's just it. That's what I mean. That fucking little bow you just made. What's that supposed to be?"

I, of course, knew exactly what she was going through and why. She was dying to get away from New York and go back to Venice for a while. But she couldn't just go. She had to torture herself (and me in the process) and agonize over it, as if she were in some way betraying me by leaving.

Feeling guilty for wanting to leave, she was trying to pick some horrible fight with me so that she could justify her departure. By not obliging her, by being considerate and tolerant and kind, I was making her feel even more wretched, even more guilty.

In the end (Saul to the rescue again!) I had to step in and clarify the crisis in which she found herself.

"Leila," I addressed her one evening, "listen to me, please."

"What now?" she snapped.

"Please." I gestured to a chair. "Sit down."

"My, my," she said, rolling her eyes, "aren't we polite. Is that what we're going to do now. We're going to be polite till bedtime. We're going to sit here and listen to the air conditioner roaring and be polite to each other."

She sat down in the swivel chair and began swiveling.

"All right," she said, "I'm sitting. Now what?"

"Why don't you go to Venice for a while?" I told her. "I think you need to get away from here."

Not having said a single word herself about wanting to leave, she seemed shocked by my ability to penetrate into her private thoughts. She stared at me in that squinty-eyed way, as if wondering how much I knew.

I lit a cigarette.

"You're telling me I should leave, is that it?" she finally said.

"No, I'm telling you that you don't need an excuse for wanting to. You want to go. I can tell. It's not something you should feel guilty about."

My use of the word "guilty" caused guilt to appear instantly on her face. She could hide nothing. She tried, but she just couldn't do it.

I then proceeded, in an admittedly professorial manner, to analyze the situation in which she found herself at the moment.

"This is a whole new crisis for you," I told her, puffing away on my cigarette. "Up to now, your whole life, from what you've told me about it, has been a series of losses and disappointments. Something was always cut, taken away from you. From your life. From all the movies you were in. And this has happened over and over again. If something happens enough times, no matter how painful it is, it becomes normal. It ceases to be a crisis and becomes, through repetition, a way of life.

"But now," I went on, "all that is about to change. For once, all the scenes you shot are not only still in the movie, but you're the star of the movie. You were thrilled when I first told you about the preview in Pittsburgh. But you've had time to think about it. You see, you've become comfortable as a victim and are now terrified at the prospect of having to abandon that role and assume a new one. The role of a woman who is loved. Whom life rewards instead of robs. It's this crisis of fulfillment that's making you anxious . . ."

I lit another cigarette and continued.

"I'm not blind. I know what you've been going through. I know you well enough to know that you haven't been bitchy toward me just for the sport of it. That we haven't made love in all this time just because of the heat or whatever. You are too honest to fake your emotions. To fake love and goodwill when you're churning inside. You need to be off by yourself. To take stock of things. To mess around Venice for a while. See your old friends. Do some of the old things you used to do while you prepare yourself for the next phase of your life. You'll see, Leila. Something glorious, but something you richly deserve, is awaiting you in Pittsburgh."

She couldn't take any more. She couldn't bear to hear another word. Sobbing, she flapped her hands at me, gesturing for me to stop.

She threw her arms around my neck, those white, soft, seemingly fragile arms of hers that on occasion (this being one of them) could be as strong as steel cables. It almost hurt to be embraced with such force.

She buried her face in my neck and shoulder and, although she was sobbing louder than she spoke, I heard every word she said.

"I do love you," she told me. "You do know that, Saul, don't you? I really do."

She left the next day. But not for Venice. She changed her mind. Said she felt like visiting Charleston and seeing her mom and some of her old high school friends again before she became famous. She would go to Venice after that.

She would not let me arrange her itinerary through my travel agent or pay for the tickets.

And no limo either.

We had a lovely, unhurried farewell outside my building. I stood under the canopy and waved as the cab whisked her away.

During her absence, I resumed my former life. Going to my office. Having lunches with Guido at the Tea Room. Picking up my clothes at the cleaners and strolling down Broadway, handing out money to the panhandlers along the way.

But whatever I did was tinged with a sense that all this was time in the interim and that real time would begin only in mid-November in Pittsburgh. In a way, I was there already, waiting for Billy and Leila and Leila's movie to join me.

# CHAPTER FOUR

## I

It was meant to be my very last divorce dinner with Dianah. I was determined to stick to the business at hand and insist that either she get a lawyer, or I get a lawyer, or we both get lawyers. Whatever divorce settlement she wanted, she could have. I, for one, would contest nothing except further procrastination on the matter.

To underscore my businesslike mood, I wore a businesslike suit for the occasion. Dark blue suit. Rust red tie. Light blue shirt. The expression on my face was one of firm resolve offset by a touch of fairness.

Our dinner at our French restaurant was at eight. I was early as usual.

"Ah, Monsieur," Claude the maitre d' greeted me with the fullness of emotion one normally associates with Muslim pilgrims beholding Mecca. "Monsieur Karoo, so wonderful to see you. So very, very, wonderful. It has been so long since . . ." He went on, wanting to know how I'd been. Was Madame joining me tonight?

He clasped my right hand with both of his and didn't so much shake it as cherish it for a while.

Instead of going to the bar, where I normally waited for Dianah to show up, I told Claude I would prefer to wait at our table.

"But of course," Claude said.

He led. I followed.

In my many years of dining here, I had never seen the place so deserted. It was less than half full. Either it was an off night, or our French restaurant was in decline. Those things happened. Empires, restaurants had diseases of their own and once the decline set in, it was next to impossible to reverse.

It seemed fitting that my last divorce dinner with Dianah would take place in an atmosphere such as this.

I had my choice of tables, but force of habit made me choose one next to a table that was occupied. Two couples in their late thirties or early forties.

The last thing I wanted for this last divorce dinner with Dianah was privacy. An audience, even a small one, was an indispensable component of my being alone with her and her being alone with me. Our kind of privacy demanded a public.

My waiter came and he, like Claude, expressed jubilation at seeing me again. Despite my long absence, he hinted at an ongoing intimacy between us by offering to bring me my usual drink.

"A gin and tonic for the monsieur?" he asked with a knowing grin.

I hated to disappoint him, I really did, but I was determined to have my last divorce dinner with Dianah without the charade of playing drunk and without the device of a drink in my hand. I was turning over a new leaf and I wanted Dianah to know it.

"No, thank you, Bernard," I told him. "Not tonight."

Instead, I ordered a large bottle of domestic mineral water.

Bernard bowed, but in a funereal way, and left. I lit a cigarette and gave myself over to the conversation at the table next to mine.

The foursome there were having a roundtable discussion (around a square table) about the swastika. The history of the swastika. The varieties of swastikas to be found. They talked as if they had all read the same book on the subject.

"It's a very ancient sign, much older than the Christian cross. It predates Christianity by . . . I'm not really sure . . . by a lot. It's eastern in origin."

"Mayan, wasn't it?"

"I'm not really sure if it was Mayan, although . . ."

"Tibet, I thought."

"The word itself is Sanskrit. It means well-being in Sanskrit . . . "

"But the sign itself came to be seen as a sign of creativity, creation in general."

"What I thought was so ironic was that in England they gave away these little swastika pins during World War I to those who exceeded some goal for selling war bonds. Isn't that just . . ."

Bernard arrived with my mineral water. He was the picture of despair. Not only was it an off night at the restaurant, but one of his most reliable customer-drunks had switched from gin to Poland Spring.

I sipped my mineral water and lit another cigarette.

I had to keep reminding myself, as I waited for Dianah to show up, that it was mineral water I was drinking, not alcohol, and that no symptoms of intoxication were expected of me. Force of habit was such that just by holding a glass of something with ice in my hand, I was ready to playact the part of the doomed drunk. It was not something I had foreseen. There were apparently withdrawal symptoms even when one was no longer addicted to anything other than oneself.

## 2

At eight thirty (I checked my watch when I saw her), half an hour late, Dianah showed up.

She looked stunning. So stunning, and so aware of it, that as she walked toward me in that inimitable way of hers, she made it seem that the restaurant was packed and that the empty tables were all occupied by discerning men and women gazing at her, admiring her beautiful green off-the-shoulder dress, her stunning hairdo, her regal carriage, her deep, dark tan.

Her platinum blond hair was like Halley's Comet coming toward me. It was shinier than ever. It had been regilded or re-platinumed or something, and its fiery glow, especially in contrast to her deep, dark tan, was dazzling, intimidating. It was like the glow of the Burning Bush.

"Thou shalt not," her hair, her eyes, her whole being radiated a single message my way. "No, no, no, darling, whatever it is that thou thinks thou will, thou shall not. Not today. Not tomorrow. Not ever, sweetheart."

We exchanged kisses the way sworn enemies exchange prisoners of war.

She took a moment (as if out of her hectic schedule) to take in the suit I was wearing and the mineral water I was drinking. Pursing her lips, she measured me with her eyes.

"I haven't seen you wear that blue suit since the last time you tried to put your life back together again. Looks good on you, darling. A bit snug, but nice."

"If that's a compliment, thank you."

"If that's a thank-you, you're welcome."

Comfortably seated, she unburdened herself of a long significant sigh, whose lush sound underscored the brief silence that followed between us.

Smiling a sumptuous smile, she looked at me. I looked at her.

The foursome next to us were now talking about Singapore.

"I'll tell you one thing," one of the two men said, "there's no malaise in Malaysia, that's for sure."

His quip was greeted with a peppering of appreciative laughter. Dianah and I responded with appreciative smiles of our own in his direction.

She sat across from me in silence as if she were sitting for a portrait. There was a look of pity in her eyes. Pity for me. For the kind of man I was. Had always been. And, as far as she was concerned, always would be.

Always.

She wasn't indicting me. She was merely reintroducing me to myself, just in case I had forgotten who I was.

All I was when I was with Dianah was my past. To sit at a table with her was to be swept back in time to the mausoleum of our marriage where, as in the Bible, alterations were not tolerated. She was so certain that my destiny was something that had already occurred, so positive that my character was incapable of change of any kind, that I found myself succumbing to the narcoleptic nostalgia of it all, as if to the strains of an old love song.

Her eyes, her smile, her whole knowing air invited me to play the part she considered to be my true identity. The doomed alcoholic. The worthless husband. The man manqué.

There was a promise in her eyes of loving devotion to that man.

I felt myself slipping to accommodate her.

This was, after all, our very last divorce dinner.

What harm could there be in making this woman happy, whom I'd made miserable for so many years, by now accepting her assessment of me? If she still had the capacity to pity me after all these years, the very least I could do was to have the generosity of spirit to be worthy of it and be pitiful. This one last time. For old time's sake.

The arrival of our waiter, Bernard, broke the silence and the spell, and with the ordering of the wine and, later, dinner, our bloodletting began.

## 3

The waiter wants to pour some wine into my glass to let me taste it, but I cover my glass with my hand. None for me, thank you. He pours a glass for Dianah.

Dianah sips her wine. I sip my mineral water.

"You're not drinking?"

"No, I quit."

"Really?"

"Yes."

Little migrainelike wrinkles of anxiety appear in the corners of her eyes. If what I'm saying is true, then her whole theory of my doomed character is in question.

"I'm so proud of you," she says.

"Thank you."

"When did you quit?"

"Just this minute," I tell her. "This will be the first drink that I didn't have all day."

She breathes a little easier now and smiles.

I light another cigarette.

"So," she sighs. "Here we are. I'm sure you have so much to tell me. You seem to be bursting with news and I'm dying to hear it. I hope you don't mind me drinking while we talk."

"No, not in the least. Please, sip away. How is the wine?" I ask, as if desperate for a glass.

"It's wonderful. It really is." She turns the bottle and reads the label.

"Nice tan you've got there," I tell her and stare at her bare brown shoulder. "It's one of the most splendid early October tans I've ever seen."

"Thank you, darling. Good of you to notice."

From her shoulder, my gaze rolls downhill and comes to a full stop in the crotch of her cleavage.

I know those breasts well and know the heart that beats under them. They remind me that when I'm with Dianah I'm like one of those spotted owls whose natural habitat no longer exists. The sight of Dianah sitting there across the table from me makes me feel profoundly homeless but, at the same time, through some emotional alchemy, this very homelessness becomes, in her presence, my natural habitat.

Bad marriages are a marvel. They can make even homelessness feel homey.

I realize (too late) that the only way for me to get a divorce from Dianah is not to be there when the divorce happens. To be with her is to be married not only to her but to the man I no longer want to be.

It was folly, I now realize, to think I could come here in my business suit and discuss divorce with her. Merely to talk with Dianah is to renew our marriage vows.

I could have come there with a team of lawyers and this divorce dinner would have been doomed because it was doomed from the very start.

I raise my arm and signal to Bernard. He comes. I order a gin and tonic. He couldn't be more pleased.

My capitulation to a reconfirmation of who she thinks I am has a very beneficial effect on Dianah.

She is now free to try to save me from myself.

She reaches across the table and places her hand on mine.

"Maybe you shouldn't have that drink," she says.

"Of course I shouldn't. But I will."


4

And I do.

I swill my drinks one after another. In between my drinks, I swill the wine. When the bottle is emptied, I order another and the waiter comes and brings it to our table and then the waiter goes.

We are, or Dianah is, discussing my life now. And the woman in my life. "This Lilly person," Dianah keeps calling her. I keep correcting her and telling her that it's not Lilly but Leila. Leila Millar.

A few other couples arrive while we talk and they occupy the empty tables around us.

"And how long have you known this girl?"

"She's not a girl, Dianah."

"Oh, I'm sorry. This woman. What's her name again?"

"Leila. Leila Millar with an *a*."

"Is that her real name or her stage name? You did say she's an actress, didn't you?"

"Yes, I did. Yes, she is."

"I bet she is. I bet she's a brilliant actress. But it does sound like one of those names that a starlet might assume. Leila Millar." Issuing out of Dianah's mouth, Leila's name acquires a fictitious quality, belonging to someone I don't know.

I drink my drink and light another cigarette.

"Her name is Leila Millar," I say.

"I don't really care what her name is," Dianah says, "or how many she has. I was just curious how well you knew her, that's all. I suppose it's not really any of my business how well you know her or don't know her. That's your affair. But I'm forced to make it my affair when you involve our son in these pathetic little affairs of yours. You've never done that before. You were always a perfectly miserable husband and a perfectly miserable father, but at least you exercised some sense of propriety in the manner in which you carried on with your sluts. You kept

Billy away from them. You had a talent for being decent while doing deplorable things. But now . . ."

I am dead drunk as far as Dianah is concerned, as far as our waiters are concerned, as far as the people sitting at the tables around us are concerned. But the more I pretend to be this besotted caricature of a worthless husband on the outside, the more certain I become and the clearer I see the Saul Karoo on the inside, that other Saul whom I fondly regard as the real me, the worthwhile and loving Saul whose salvation and synthesis awaits him at the confluence of the three rivers in Pittsburgh.

The more I present myself to Dianah in this false light, the closer I feel to the true Saul within, who's incapable of falsehooods and lies. Faking one brings the true one into focus.

The waiter comes and the waiter goes.

I've played drunk around Dianah before, but I feel inspired tonight to outdo myself and be not just a drunk but a bravura drunk. The way I see it, this will be my farewell performance to the role I've created for myself. There'll be no more impostors to play after Pittsburgh, so I might as well give it all I've got tonight.

I am only sorry that this last performance of our farewell tour is being played to a half-filled house. But we're troopers, both of us. Public professionals. Low attendance isn't going to deter us. If anything, it's a challenge to be overcome. Dianah's vocal delivery improves. Sharpens. Her selection of assumed poses gains in precision. The very wattage in her glowing platinum blond hair increases. It's not the Burning Bush anymore. It becomes a forest fire. She's a diva. A diva with a death dress on.

I try to hold up my half of this marriage we're performing. I pull out all stops. I premeditate and then execute knocking over a full glass of wine. No inebriated buffoon, no matter how drunk, could have pulled it off better. The wine spills on the tablecloth. The glass rolls off the table and breaks on the floor. Heads turn.

The waiter comes and performs gracious housekeeping. He mops up. He sweeps up. He brings me another glass. He pours me some more wine.

And then Dianah and I resume the performance of our marriage in concert.

"All your sluts," Dianah is saying.

We don't mind the waiter anymore. We go on in front of him while he serves us our dinner selections, medallions of venison in wine sauce for her, half a roasted chicken for me, with French fries.

"And another gin and tonic for the monsieur." I tap him on the shoulder as he's leaving. To my ear, at least, I'm slurring my words with pissed-to-the-gills authenticity.

As if for latecomers, Dianah sings out again:

"All those sluts, all those sluts of yours . . ."

She makes the *s*'s of the "sluts" sizzle. My God, she's in such good voice tonight. Clear as a bell. The voice of Schwarzkopf and the dramatic delivery of Maria Callas. I almost feel unworthy to be dismembered by so much talent. Drunk and disgusting as I'm pretending to be, I feel my stature growing in the eyes of the rapt onlookers.

Sensing, as any great artist can, that she has the audience in the palm of her hand, Dianah then proceeds with the litany of my many, many sluts.

She knows them all. Knows the names of all the women I ever slept with. I have forgotten them, but she hasn't. She is my memory. She goes in chronological order, beginning with the sluts I slept with in the early years of our marriage. Moving on then to the middle years, and so on.

"Mona, that slut Mona, that slut Sally, and then we have the Rachels, three of them, three sluts of three different sizes and shapes . . ."

She goes on like this, on and on, building up a rhythm and a cadence that, knowing her, will probably result in some grand summation after the last slut has been named.

". . . that squinty-eyed slut, Peggy, that you picked up at the McNabs' party."

She pauses at the end of the list, and it is a dramatic pause. The question hangs in the air: What does all this mean? All these sluts? And who is that man, that creature, that drunken slutmonger who is sitting across the table from her, eating French fries with his hands?

The foursome at the table next to ours are sitting on the edge of their seats. They want to know what kind of a miserable beast I am.

I myself am dying to know.

Having created and then controlled the length of the suspense by her silence, Dianah shifts gears and goes into her denouement.

"You seem to be looking for somebody, darling. Some holy grail of a girl or a woman or whatever. It is a sad and infantile practice among men in general to behave as you have behaved, so I can find it in my heart to justify your behavior on the grounds of pack-rat conformity and arrested emotional growth. But what piques my curiosity is not so much that you want to fuck all these sluts . . ."

One can feel a tremor run through the room and see spines stiffen at the sound of that word, "fuck."

I have to hand it to Dianah. She is magnificent. She pronounced that four-letter word unflinchingly, keeping her dignity intact, managing to convey its sewer connotation without being tainted by it in the least. The word has tainted the object of her scorn, me, not her. It is dazzling.

". . . but," she goes on, "that these unfortunate beings should want to fuck you. I have fucked you, darling, and frankly, I'm mystified that women exist, other than myself, who want to have you in bed with them. There are, at least, mitigating factors in my case. We are married. We have a son. I have overlooked your shortcomings as a lover in the hope that some day . . ."

I burst out laughing at this point and miss the rest of her indictment. I don't want to laugh. The last thing I want to do is interrupt Dianah in mid-diatribe, but I can't help myself.

Even while I'm laughing helplessly, I try to reassure Dianah (and our onlookers) that I'm not laughing at anything she has said, but, rather, at the sudden appearance at our table of a waiter bearing in his arms this siege cannon called the pepper mill.

"Some fresh ground pepper for you this evening?" he asks, and his request makes me hysterical. I laugh so hard, I can't catch my breath. I just wave him on to pepper away.

And he does.

I laugh and laugh like a drunken old fool in an amusement park.

5

"I'm glad you find all this so funny, darling," Dianah tells me. She is trembling a little as she speaks, trying to hold on to her self-control. "I really am. The humor of your life escapes me completely, but I'm gratified that you can still manage to find something amusing about it. I suspect you'll need that sense of humor and then some when you discover, as even you inevitably must, what awaits you in the end."

She seems to have something in particular in mind for my inevitable end. And the way she says it, with that knowing air of hers, makes it seem that she sees it. My end. That it's not far off.

"What is it that awaits me in the end?" I roar. "Is it death, is that what it is? I bet it's death. Death runs in my family, you know. My dad died. His dad died. And so on."

"You'll find out, sweetheart," she says. There is savage satisfaction in her eyes. Her knowing air and the fiery hair suddenly give her an oracular quality. She knows something I don't.

A dread goes through me, but lasts only a fraction of a second, and then the law of opposites comes to my rescue.

The real Saul inside me is immune to her calamitous prophecy.

"Dianah, Dianah." I say her name twice, and then I say it a third time. "Dianah," I say, gesturing with my arms all over the place like some inept Shakespearean actor demented with booze. "You see before you a man who is sorry that he was ever born. But having been born, and having it on good authority that I will someday die, all I have ever done was to try to find a little happiness. In between the bookends of my birth and demise. A little happiness. Just a little. Surely," I roar, determined to be heard by my fellow diners, "surely, even a man like me deserves a little happiness in his life."

She ponders my argument as if it were an application to a country club and then says:

"That's where you're wrong, darling."

She seems to be sorry to have to be the one to tell me this, but tell it to me she must, because that's the kind of woman she is. Honest to a fault.

"Wrong!" I roar. I'm in a bit of a vocal rut. Vocal variety eludes me. I can only roar. "Wrong? What do you mean, I'm wrong? How can I be wrong? Everyone—" I spread my arms wide open and turn my torso left and right, as if trying to embrace every single diner in my rebuttal "—and I mean everyone, everyone has a right to be happy."

My manifesto is designed to be greeted by general applause from the sparse but attentive crowd. But, alas, none comes. Not even a polite smattering. What comes instead is Dianah's reply.

"No," she says, "not everyone." And she says it as if she has not only the common law but the constitutional and the moral law also on her side.

"A man like you does not have a right to be happy. Not after all the harm you've done to others. For you now to sit there and have the nerve to claim a right to happiness is to abandon even the rudiments of being a responsible human being. In your former wretchedness, you were at least worthy of compassion. In your present insistence that you have a right to be happy, you can only inspire contempt from your many victims."

"Victims," I roar. "What victims?"

"Darling, darling," she sighs, "my poor, pathetic darling, don't you realize that everyone you ever get to know becomes your victim? This Lilly person will also become your victim if she's not already. Every woman, man, and child who was ever touched by your life has become your victim. Yes, even children. Not even children are safe from you. I hate to bring this up in public," she says, upping the volume of her voice with ease, so that everyone around us can hear just how much she hates bringing this up.

"But you leave me no choice," she says. "You and your right to happiness. What about the happiness of that sweet little girl? I don't know what you did to her and I don't want to know, but . . ."

"What sweet little girl?" I roar. "What're you talking about?"

"Laurie. Laurie Dohrn." She nails the *n* at the end of Dohrn as if with a hammer.

I fumble for another cigarette, while the visage of the girl in question flutters like a sail in front of my eyes.

The way she looked when I picked her up.

Our limo ride to Cafe Luxembourg.

The way I felt in the limo.

The way it all . . .

"I don't know what you did to her and I really don't want to know. All I know is what she told her mother, and what her mother told me. The poor child was hysterical. She kept saying over and over again how disgusting you were that night. Her word, not mine. How disgusting you were, how wrong it all was and how she never wanted to see you again. This wasn't one of your sluts, Saul. One of your women. This wasn't even a grown-up. A child, that's what she was. A mere child who looked up to you as to a father she adored, and you . . ."

She shakes her head. She sighs. She can't go on. Another dramatic silence ensues.

Dianah has her audience in the palm of her hand. They're waiting for the gory details. In the sudden sepulchral silence of the restaurant, there is a sudden, salivating hunger to hear more. There is a craving for the flesh of children.

Laurie, despite her youth, was not a child, but Dianah's use of that word and the response of those around us to it have created in an instant an atmosphere almost identical to the one that prevailed at that ill-fated dinner with Cromwell at Cafe Luxembourg.

Then and there, Laurie was debauched in person. Here and now, in another restaurant, she is being debauched and devoured by proxy. Everyone wanted a little piece of Laurie that night. Everyone wants a little piece of her this night. I pretended I was drunk then. I'm pretending that I'm drunk now.

"What in God's name did you do to her, Saul?" Dianah asks me.

They all wait for my reply.

"I can't remember," I say.

I remember it all, of course.

The way Laurie looked at me. The way Cromwell looked at her. I had the youngest one there. The Cambodian girl. The sight and sound of those little bells.

"I really can't remember."

My evasion is a disappointment to our onlookers. It makes them angry at me. I had a duty to give them the details.

"The thing is, Dianah, the thing is this. It's not a question of what I've done in the past and to whom, but rather who I am now. You see, I'm not the same man anymore. I've changed."

"Changed?" Dianah says and leans back in her seat.

"Yes, changed."

"You?"

"Me."

"I'm all ears, darling. I really am. I'm all eyes too, but since I can't discern any change in you with my eyes, other than the excess weight you're putting on, I'm fully prepared to be all ears." She pauses, smiles, tilts her head to the right and says, "I'm listening."

"On the inside," I tell her. "I've changed on the inside."

My words, by design, sound shallow and lacking all conviction. Dianah's raised eyebrows mock me. But I don't need her to mock me. I am mocking myself for reasons of my own. The more I make it seem that my change is a complete fabrication, the easier it is to see myself as completely changed. The one brings the other into focus.

"How long have I known you, sweetheart?"

"Feels like centuries," I tell her.

"And in all those years, how often have I heard you tell me about the treasures that lie buried 'deep, deep inside of you'? How often have you promised to change? How often have you gone through the charade of going on one of your treasure-hunting expeditions to look for the jewels that lie buried in the deep, deep—yes, you're so very deep, darling—in the deep portions of your soul? Has anyone ever benefited from all that promise that lies buried deep, deep inside of you? I'm not really picking on you, darling, if that's what you think. I'm really not."

She has another bite of venison and another sip of wine and then continues:

"But you really must face up to the consequences of your character.

There is nothing deep, deep inside of you. At least, nothing worthwhile. There really isn't. If your ship has sunk, sweetheart, as I think it has, then it has sunk empty. So please, have a little respect for my intelligence. Don't tell me how you've changed on the inside while at the same time pursuing what you call your right to happiness with yet another slut."

"She's not a slut. She's a wonderful woman."

"Fine. Let us assume for a moment that she is."

"There's no assuming. She is. She just is."

"All right. So be it. She's a wonderful woman. But can you, before you pass out, can you answer me just one question? What would a wonderful woman see in you, Saul? Surely you're not a complete fool, darling. So tell me. What is it that you have, or think that you have, to offer to any woman, wonderful or not?"

I pretend to be stumped by the question.

She is amused in a merry-eyed and malignant way. Her lips move, as if she's savoring something she could say but prefers not to.

It bothers me, this look of hers. Her knowing air. It's as if she's come armed this evening with something beyond her usual arsenal.

I light another cigarette and wonder, should I spill another glass of wine? Should I lean back in my chair and fall backwards to the floor? Or maybe run my fingers through my hair, as if forgetting about the lit cigarette I'm holding, singeing my hair, setting it on fire, as a diversion from the malignancy of her eyes?

"How well do you know Billy?" she finally asks.

"We're very close. Getting closer and closer all the time."

"Really?"

"Yes, really."

"Closer to what, darling?"

"What the hell is that supposed to mean? 'Closer to what?' What are you talking about, Dianah?"

"It stands to reason, if people are getting closer and closer, that they must be getting closer and closer to something, right?"

"To each other. To the truth of who we are."

By trivializing the word "truth" for her benefit, I experience the beauty and the full meaning of the real truth awaiting me and Billy and Leila in Pittsburgh.

"Mmmm," she says, nodding. She's in such wonderful voice tonight that she can even make her consonants sing. "The truth, is it?"

"Yes, the truth," I shout. I can't roar anymore.

"Just checking. And this truth is something wonderful, is it?"

"Ask Billy, if you don't believe me."

"I don't have to ask Billy anything. He confides in me, you know. He has all along. He had to confide to somebody, and since he had no father to speak of—or to speak to—he confided in me, his mother."

"You're not his real mother, Dianah." I can't help saying this. It's a cheap way to hurt her. I regret it as soon as I say it, but I probably would have regretted it had I not said it.

"Ah, Saul," she sighs, and shakes her head. "That's not like you, darling. To say something like that. Maybe you have changed after all. But let us not stray from the topic at hand, and the topic, I believe, is truth. Of all the people on this planet, you alone seem to have this childlike conception of truth as something wonderful. Probably because you've never experienced truth. It's as if you were separated from truth at birth and have been longing for it ever since, confident that when it finally comes back into your life, it will do so as a loving nurse with soft arms. That's not how truth works, sweetheart. Billy confides in me. He tells me everything."

"What's that supposed to mean? He tells you everything. Everything what? You seem to want to tell me something, but I don't know what you're talking about."

"You don't?"

"No, I don't."

She wipes the corners of her mouth with her napkin.

"I'll say no more," she says.

"Why not?"

"I don't want to spoil the surprise."

Her lips pinched, her hair aglow, her eyes gleaming with malevolence, she sits across the table from me like an image of Nemesis come to life.

And then her features soften. The image of Nemesis vanishes. There is pity in her eyes again. For me. Shortly, I know, she will make me an offer.

The offer comes.

"Do you know what I think? I think we should go home, darling."

She glories in her ability to make such an offer to a man like me after all I've done to her. Glories in the act of self-sacrifice she's making. She's a marriage martyr, offering to take me back where I belong. To bear me away. Like a cross it is her destiny to bear.

I know I'm not a mighty cross. Not really a burden to her. Not a blessing, certainly, but not a burden. A lesser cross of some kind. Something small, but always in fashion as a distinctive accessory to her lifestyle. Like a nice little cross, fashioned at Tiffany's, dangling from her neck on a simple golden chain. A doomed, worthless husband. I would go so well with almost anything.

The offer sits there, as it were, on the table among the leftovers of our meal.

It is, in its own way, a tempting offer.

The great So What of the soul speaks within me and urges me to accept it.

It's not Leila or my love for her that makes me resist. Nor is it something called personal integrity, a trait I've never had. It is, instead, a dread. The dread of the virtual reality of our marriage. The dread of the virtual life we would live were I to return to her. The dread that when death finally comes, it will be virtual death as well and I will discover that not even death has divorced me from Dianah.

She awaits my reply.

I gather myself and, in my very best drunken laughter, I laugh at her and her offer and then say, "I wish I were a Muslim. I love their divorce ceremonies. All they do is this"—I gesture toward her as if blessing her—"I divorce you. I divorce you. I divorce you."

I laugh as if my laughter were part of the divorce ceremony I am performing.

Her face stiffens. She stands up. I remain seated. Her hairdo glows above me like a full moon.

"I guess there's nothing left to say, then," she says.

"No," I reply. "Not a thing. But that's never stopped us before."

She stands, and remains standing, looking down at me.

"I hope you have a wonderful life with your whore," she finally says. "I really do."

"She is not my whore."

Her face goes Cubist at my response. Becomes broken-up facets of a single face. A smile detaches itself from the rest of her features and becomes independent, free-floating, ferocious.

"Whose whore is she, then?" she asks.

Then she departs. With dignity. With such dignity and grace that I turn in my chair to admire the way she exits the restaurant.

The show, our show, is over, and our audience, such as they are, are now forced to resume their own lives again, at their own tables.

My waiter comes with the bill. I look it over the way a drunk might look at the driver's manual for a rocket ship. I'm in a generous mood. I top the tips I left last time I dined here. If I could, I would leave tips for the diners who have remained.

Then, ever conscious of the need to be consistent in my portrayal of myself, I get up pretending to be so drunk that I have to hold on to the empty chairs I pass for support.

My slow departure has a unifying effect on the dozen or so diners scattered around the room. They consult each other with their eyes, as when a doomed but not very dangerous passenger stumbles through a subway car late at night.

# CHAPTER FIVE

## 1

Like an omen of good tidings, the weather changed a week before Leila's return. A new, cool wind began to blow, blowing the heat wave out to sea. Almost overnight, there was an autumnal feeling in the air. The large sailboats docked on the north side of the Seventy-ninth Street marina began sailing away one by one for their winter ports. Leaves on the trees in Riverside Park changed colors. And then one morning, I saw through my living room window a small contingent of geese flying south over the Hudson in a lopsided V formation. I opened the window and the wind blew their ghostly cries into my apartment.

## 2

I fussed for a couple of days getting the apartment and myself ready for Leila's arrival. A happy time full of happy anticipation. Leila was arriving on Wednesday and since Maria wouldn't come to clean until Friday, I cleaned the apartment myself. I vacuumed. I changed the sheets and pillowcases on the bed in our bedroom. I put out new towels and washed the old ones. I bought flowers for the dining room table. While cleaning the mirror in the bathroom, I was struck by my own reflection. I looked so happy that I had a hard time recognizing myself.

## 3

In addition to getting the apartment ready for her homecoming, I had a homecoming present waiting for her. I had that sign, held up by the limo driver with her name on it, framed at Lee's frame shop on West Fifty-seventh Street. I added a couple of words above her name with a black Magic Marker, trying to duplicate the style and size of the letters in her name. The words I added were the ones that would be used in her first screen credit: AND INTRODUCING.

I made a point of not being at home when she arrived. I stayed in my office until late in the evening and even called the doorman of my building to make sure Leila was there before rushing out of the office and getting a cab.

I just felt like doing it this way. Going home, having her there already, was my homecoming present to myself.

## 4

I unlocked the door to my apartment quietly and stepped inside. Almost instantly, I caught a scent of her perfume. Maybe it wasn't perfume at all but just the scent of my apartment being inhabited, not empty as I had left it this morning. A wonderful feeling that life was in progress and that I could partake of it.

Was this, I wondered, what home meant? That all I had to do was announce myself, and life, as if by magic, would begin?

"Is anybody home?" I called out.

She ran out of my bedroom like a run of good luck. That's what she looked like to me. Arms spread out. Lips parted. Smiling and screaming her head off as she ran toward me. She launched herself like a broad jumper from at least five feet away and literally flew into my arms.

How I managed to catch her, why I didn't topple over like a bowling pin when her body hit me, I'll never know. In a long sedentary life devoid of athletic accomplishments, this was my one Olympic moment. I caught her. I staggered backwards, but I caught her and held on.

## 5

She was thrilled with the framed sign, my homecoming gift to her. Thrilled with the words I had added above her name. She walked around the apartment saying, "And introducing, Leila Millar," in a variety of ways. A couple of times she introduced herself to me. "And introducing, Leila Millar," she said and extended her hand. I shook it, as if meeting her for the first time. "I've heard so much about you," I told her. "And who are you?" she asked. "Saul," I said, shaking her hand, "Saul Karoo."

## 6

She had changed her whole hairdo while in Venice. Its texture. Its color. The brown was now a bleached light brown, almost blond in places. Knowing her aversion to direct sunlight, I knew that it wasn't caused by the sun.

Her hair was shorter, rounder, bouncier. She had bangs halfway down her forehead.

She looked younger. Almost like a coed strolling across the campus. Almost like a complete stranger.

She was either nervous or overflowing with some newfound exuberance, it was hard to tell which, and easy to mistake one for the other.

When she brushed her teeth, she did it with vigor, humming along.

When she sat down, she sat so quickly that the bangs billowed off her forehead.

When she got up, she almost jumped to her feet.

And when the telephone rang, she had to restrain herself from running to get it, as if forgetting for a moment that she was in my apartment.

## 7

We didn't have sex for the first few days. It was as if she was too nervous or too exuberant, or, as happened one evening, too ticklish for sex. What we had, instead, was foreplay, which properly speaking wasn't foreplay but an end in itself. The way she looked, the sound of her laughter, the way her eyes narrowed when she smiled, it all made me want to kiss her. Not just kiss her but bother her with kisses the way one might be impelled to bother with kisses an irresistibly lovely child. I bothered her often in this way. We played at love. We made a game of it. I chased her around the apartment like some would-be monster. She ran, screaming for help, until I caught her. And then I kissed her and kissed her until she became ticklish and squirmed and wriggled out of my arms, laughing, screaming for help again. It reminded me of games I used to play with Billy when he was just a little boy.

## 8

On this particular night, thanks to many little signals sent by Leila and received by me, I know that we are finally going to make love again. I come out of the bathroom, having showered in preparation and anticipation.

Leila lies there naked on my bed. She is watching me coming toward her. We're both completely undressed, but she is naked. Her nakedness is so complete that in comparison to her I feel fully dressed, dressed in my past, in my plans for Pittsburgh, if nothing else.

She watches me.

I don't know where to look. She is so naked, so white, so wide open.

The lights are on. She likes to have them on when we make love. I don't. But since she likes to have them on, and since I love her, I leave them on. It's not the lights I mind so much. It's just that I don't know where to look when I see her like this.

Her openness, her nakedness, is too much for me, and, since it is, it ceases to be openness. It becomes something else. Her eyes, for example. They're so open (as she watches me) that they're not telling me anything. They're not like an open book but like a book open to every page at the same time. They're so open that they're telling me everything. Absolutely everything. But it's impossible for me to comprehend everything that she's telling me. It can't be done. So the effect of her openness on me is exactly the same as if she were hiding something.

It seems unnatural to think it, but openness of this kind seems like the ultimate camouflage.

It's not a thought I like to have while walking toward the naked body of the woman I love.

There is no time to analyze the thought and its implications. Things have been set in motion and I am committed to the lovemaking at hand.

When I kiss her, I shut my eyes. I now see nothing. I feel enormously relieved. I keep on kissing her.

### 9

We talked to Billy on the telephone every few days, with me on the phone in the kitchen and Leila on the extension in the bedroom. There wasn't any set rule about doing it like this, but it always worked out that way.

Our conversations were essentially banal gabfests and very enjoyable. There was no agenda or form. It was just talk. Life at Harvard. The classes he was taking. The ones he liked. The ones he didn't. An inevitable allusion or two to the premiere of Leila's movie in Pittsburgh. Billy asking Leila if she was getting nervous and Leila replying, "What do you think?"

There was something very enjoyable about these telephone calls. The three of us on the line at the same time. The electronic togetherness of it. The rotation of talking and listening.

But there was also, or came to be after a few of these conversations, a strange and totally unwarranted reaction on my part. Whenever I dropped out of the conversation for a while, to light a cigarette or simply out of courtesy, not wanting to monopolize the conversation, whenever I just sat there in the kitchen and listened to the two of them talking, I had this uncomfortable feeling that I was eavesdropping on them. I wasn't, of course. They knew that I was there on the line with them. It was just banter. Back-and-forth banter between the two of them. Telephone tennis. Talk about what kind of tuxedo Billy should rent for the premiere. Traditional or modern. Talk about Leila's dress for the premiere and her excuses for not having bought one yet. Things like that. It wasn't the content of their banter but the quality of their voices that made me feel uncomfortable, like some smarmy wiretapper overhearing a private conversation. To rid myself of this unpleasant feeling, I wound up butting into their conversation even when I had nothing to say. Just to remind myself that all three of us were on the line at the same time.

## 10

For the premiere, my old tuxedo—it had been hanging undisturbed for a year—was cleaned and pressed and encased in a plastic dry-cleaning bag in my closet. When I showed it to Leila, she seemed genuinely, almost childishly thrilled at the prospect of being escorted to the premiere of her movie in Pittsburgh by "two dashing men," as she called Billy and me, in formal attire.

She had never been anywhere where men wore tuxedos and women wore evening gowns.

The buying of Leila's dress for the premiere proved to be a mini-saga in itself.

"Yes, yes, yes," she agreed with me. She really had to buy something special for the occasion. "One of those once-in-a-lifetime dresses" was how she described it.

We spent hours discussing the kind of dress it should be. We talked about colors, fabrics, styles. We even consulted several fashion magazines for "ideas."

But she made no actual move to go shopping for it. Tomorrow. She would go tomorrow.

"I promise," she said.

But tomorrow came and went. And the day after tomorrow. She seemed weary of the subject when I brought it up again.

No matter, I decided. Even if she didn't buy and wear a special dress, it would be fine. The nature of the event that awaited her was guaranteed to enshrine the occasion as the single happiest night of her life.

And just when I gave up on the dress and the whole image of the three of us in formal attire, she fooled me again.

The dress she wanted was a bridal gown, but a modern, nontraditional bridal gown. There was in fact nothing particularly bridal about it except for the nature of the shop in which it was displayed. But perhaps that was what had caught Leila's eye in the first place.

It was mid-calf in length and slightly longer in the back than in the front. In another era it might have been called a cocktail dress. It was white. White satin, or some such fabric. Sleek. Shiny. Possessing one of those textures that seem impervious to stains. I could easily imagine a glass of red wine spilling on that dress and the wine beading up, rolling off the fabric without leaving so much as a trace behind.

"What do you think?" Leila wanted to know.

"It's wonderful," I said.

"You like it?"

"I love it."

She lit up with joy, as if I had validated her inspiration.

The dress had to be fitted. There were supposed to be two fitting sessions, but I think Leila contrived to make it four. She loved going to her fittings. At those times she was delighted with everything. With herself. With me. With life. My plans were that after Pittsburgh I would buy her designer dresses on a monthly basis so that she could go to fittings the year round.

## I I

When the dress was done, the manager called and offered to have it delivered. Leila didn't want it delivered. She wanted to pick it up herself. But then she made no move to do so. A day went by. Two. Three. Finally, the day before our departure for Pittsburgh, I managed to mobilize her into action. We would both go and pick it up. She consented, but put off going until late in the day. It was Thursday and fortunately the store was open late. We arrived at eight thirty, half an hour before closing time.

They offered us a choice of box or bag. Leila didn't care. She just shrugged.

"A bag," I said.

The manager nodded and bowed, as if complimenting me on my discerning choice of container.

We walked out (the manager escorting us to the door and holding the door open for us) with me carrying the plastic bag slung over my shoulder.

Fifth Avenue was fairly deserted. It was that in-between time in New York. Those dining were already in restaurants. Those going to concerts and shows were in theaters.

A steady breeze out of the northwest blew in our faces as we walked slowly uptown. An occasional gust, when it came, parted the bangs on Leila's forehead.

A jogger ran past us, but it could have been youth itself. One of those achingly beautiful creatures (male or female, I couldn't tell) running with such ease that he or she couldn't be bothered with making contact with the earth.

We turned west on Fifty-seventh Street.

No, she didn't want a cab. She felt like walking.

"Accompanied or alone?" I asked her, in that disgusting bon vivant tone I knew I shouldn't use around her but sometimes found impossible not to.

"Please don't," she said.

I lit a cigarette.

We stopped outside the Coliseum bookstore on Fifty-seventh and Broadway because Leila stopped. She stood there looking at the books in the window, as if she had no intention of ever moving again.

The books on display were the usual crop of bestsellers, so I couldn't understand the cause of Leila's apparent fascination with them.

"Must be nice," she finally said.

"What's that?"

"Oh, she sighed, "you know. The whole thing. Going to college. Having a roommate. Walking across the campus. Talking about this and that and feeling smart."

I had no idea what made her bring up this topic now. I could understand how someone like her who had dropped out of high school could think of college in such romantic terms, but it seemed completely incongruous to be talking about higher education while staring at those bestsellers in the window. But then maybe she wasn't really looking at those particular books. Maybe it was books in general, the sight of so many books, that reminded her of all the gaps in her life.

"I didn't think going to college was all that wonderful," I said.

"Sure. And millionaires don't think money's everything either," she said, without looking at me.

"Nothing's everything," I wound up saying, with only the vaguest notion of what it was I wanted those words to express.

"Have you read Flaubert?" she asked.

I almost laughed. It seemed like such an outlandish question for her to ask.

"Do you mean Gustave Flaubert?" a nasty little pedant in me couldn't resist inquiring.

She looked at me, her face wrinkling with worry. It was clear she thought that there were many Flauberts and that I knew them all.

"I don't know," she said. "The one who wrote what's supposed to be the best book there is."

"A novel, is that what you mean?"

"Yes, a novel. What did I say? Oh, yeah, I said a book. A novel. I meant to say a novel."

"What made you think of that now?"

"I don't know." She shrugged, wiping her bangs.

"It's a toss-up," I told Leila, "which is the best novel ever written, *Madame Bovary* by Flaubert or *Anna Karenina* by Tolstoy. There are those who think that *Madame Bovary*, because of its relative brevity and precision, and the merciless pursuit of its theme, is the better of the two. However . . ."

I could have gone on like this for quite a bit, and I did. In the end, Leila decided that she should read both of them. The store was still open and we went inside.

I knew the layout of the store well and where to go to find the books we wanted to buy.

There were clearly printed signs, like chapter headings, for the various sections in the store. HISTORY. BIOGRAPHY. RELIGION. SCIENCE. PSYCHOLOGY. FICTION. LITERATURE. TRAVEL.

Something came over me as I strolled through the store with Leila toward the subsection of the Literature section called Classics. Maybe it was just the memory of the many bookstores and libraries of my life. A semi-vertiginous sensation caused not so much the store to spin as my mind to whirl inside my head, forming a little whirlpool of books, in the center of which I saw, as if in a vision, a tiny speck of total clarity.

If God were now to reveal Himself, along with a handful of uncontestable truths, almost all these books would vanish.

The Philosophy section would be gone.

All the books on religion would be taken off the shelves.

Goodbye to physics and astrophysics. Goodbye to science and the Science section. A handful of truths from God would render all the books on science ever written totally superfluous.

The Travel section would remain.

The great books, the great works of art concerned with the great questions of life, would vanish, because the great questions would no longer exist.

There would be no role for humanity and civilization if truth were to reveal itself. It was as if mankind were a biologic response to the absence of truth.

If I were God, I thought, I wouldn't have the heart to appear now. Not after all these books and millions like them had been written. No, I wouldn't have the heart to appear at this late date and say: Here I am. I have come to tell you the truth and make superfluous the centuries you spent searching for it. No, if He were truly a loving God, He would stay away. It was too late now.

The tragedy of the poor lonely God who had waited too long to appear overwhelmed me. There He was, somewhere out there on the edge of the ever-expanding universe, getting farther and farther away from us, receding from us at the speed of light. There He was, with His handful of truths for company. And here we were, down below, guessing at the truth, trying to answer the great questions that confounded us because even the clues we had were wrong.

How to explain the love I felt for all mankind at that moment? The sense of tragic futility that bound me to every living being with ties closer than blood and brotherhood. And my heart went out as well to the lonely God above, who could not return to make things right without undoing man in the process.

# CHAPTER SIX

## I

Leila and I were on the plane bound for Pittsburgh.

The airplane was brand-new. In all my years of flying, I had never before flown on a brand-new plane.

I sat next to the window. I had offered Leila the window seat, but she preferred to sit on the aisle.

The sneak preview of Leila's movie was set for 8:00 P.M. tomorrow, Saturday. We were going a day early because I wanted to savor being there a day ahead of time and to make sure that all three of us were well rested before the big event.

Billy was flying in from Boston. We had reservations in the same hotel. His room was right next to our suite, and both his room and our suite (I had made sure to request) looked out on the confluence of the three rivers. The three of us were to have dinner tonight. I looked forward to seeing him again. I looked forward to everything.

It seemed so appropriate that the premiere of Leila's movie and the reunion with her son that awaited her after the screening were to be followed in less than a week by Thanksgiving.

My favorite holiday.

I glanced over at Leila. She was dozing.

The pillow she had requested from the stewardess was in her lap, her arms wrapped around it.

We would have Thanksgiving dinner in my apartment. The three of us. A real Thanksgiving dinner. And all of us would have so much to be thankful for.

## 2

The sounds of the jet engines come and go. I hear them and then I don't hear them, depending on the degree to which I'm absorbed in my thoughts.

Through a gap in the clouds I see the mountains of southeastern Pennsylvania bathed in twilight. Even from the air, I recognize the serpentine curves of the Pennsylvania Turnpike. The highways home. Pennsylvania. Ohio. Indiana. Illinois. Driving home from college for the holidays. (The tug of that sound still: Home for the holidays.) And no matter what eventual disappointment greeted me as I entered the house of my mother and father, next year in November I'd be speeding along the highways full of hope again, certain that this time it would all be different. Unlike Ishmael in *Moby Dick*, I looked forward to November in my soul.

## 3

Leila is awake. She is examining her hands, looking at them at arm's length.

She tried reading *Madame Bovary* and *Anna Karenina* in the same way. Lying on the couch, holding the books at arm's length, first one, then the other. I don't think she got past the introduction of either one of them.

"Do you think I have beautiful hands?" she asks.

"I certainly do," I tell her and only then do I look at them.

Her hands, I discover, really are beautiful.

I don't know how many times I must have seen her hands without noticing how beautiful they were.

Long white fingers. Narrow wrists.

She is captivated by them, as if they were holding a love letter she is reading in front of me.

Somebody must have told her she has beautiful hands. While I was thinking my thoughts, she was thinking hers. The memory of someone telling her that she has beautiful hands.

There is no room in my mind for any more details, if they're new, of parts of her body. I don't want to be forced to notice things about her that I haven't noticed before. I lack the storage capacity, for the time being, for any new information.

## 4

The voice of the stewardess comes over the PA system: "Ladies and gentlemen, in preparation for our landing . . ."

When the wheels of the plane touch the runway, I can't help thinking, exclaiming inwardly: Pittsburgh!

I reach over and take her hands in mine. My purpose is not necessarily to cover up her beautiful hands, but it does have that effect as well.

5

We stand and wait by the baggage carousel downstairs, along with the other people from our flight who checked their bags.

We're all waiting for the carousel to start moving.

This little hitch in an otherwise flawless getaway from New York is beginning to bother me, because it is totally unnecessary.

My tuxedo and whatever other items I needed for our weekend in Pittsburgh were packed in one of those large garment bags designed to be taken on board. Which was what I had intended to do. But Leila didn't want to take her suitcase on board. Despite my pleas, based on years of flying, she had to have her bag checked. "I don't want to lug it around with me through two airports," she told me. "If you want to lug yours, that's fine."

Since we were going to have to wait for her bag in Pittsburgh anyway, I saw no point in taking mine aboard with me. So I checked mine as well.

And so now, while I wait for the baggage carousel to start turning, I can't help fussing about having to stand there and wait. If we had done as I suggested, we could have been in a cab already heading toward our hotel.

It's not the waiting per se that bothers me. It's the interrupted rhythm of our trip. We had such a nice rhythm going. Everything was moving right along. We left on time. We arrived on time. And now this.

Standing and waiting. The rhythm of motion replaced by this totally unnecessary immobility.

The moribund crowd comes to life as the baggage carousel starts to turn.

As luck would have it, as luck tends to have it on these occasions, Leila's soft blue bag is one of the first to arrive. I snatch it off the carousel and wait for mine.

The carousel keeps going around and around. I wait.

A cramp is forming in my stomach.

Had she only listened to me . . .

I think I see my garment bag but no, it's somebody else's, not mine. It's snatched off the carousel by its owner. I see other people snatching theirs. I see one bald man snatching one suitcase after another off the carousel. Five. I count them. Five suitcases and he's still not done. He's waiting there for more. The random dispensation of justice and injustice is making me sick. Five suitcases. The bald sonovabitch has five and I can't even get my one and only. And I flew first class and I know he didn't.

I'm beginning to feel like a one-man riot in the making. If I see that motherfucker get one more suitcase before my garment bag arrives . . .

I look away from him to keep myself from . . . God knows what. From something.

"Relax, will you," Leila tells me.

She rubs my back with her hand.

I know that she's right. I know that I should relax. I know that if there's one thing I mustn't do it is to tarnish this weekend by my infantile overreaction to this insignificant little glitch with my garment bag. The last thing I need and the last thing I want to do is spoil the celebratory nature of our reasons for being here. Nothing, absolutely nothing must undermine the upcoming event.

The rational man within me knows this and I know that the rational man within me is right.

There is nothing in that garment bag that is of any value anyway. The single most important item is the tuxedo. But tomorrow is Saturday, and if worst comes to worst and my goddamn garment bag never comes, I'll be able to rent a tuxedo somewhere in Pittsburgh. Razor, shaving cream, toothbrush, toothpaste, I'll be able to buy those at the hotel.

I consider leaving. I consider smiling at Leila, putting an arm around her shoulder and saying: "To hell with it. Let's take a cab to the hotel."

But I linger and wait. I want this to be a perfect weekend, and to leave without my bag would taint things. I just want the status quo. Leila with her suitcase. Me with my garment bag.

Leila leaves to go look for a ladies' room. Her parting words to me are "You'll see. As soon as I leave, it will come."

I light a cigarette.

The carousel goes around and around.

The bald man with his caravan of suitcases has mercifully left without my seeing him go. Most of the passengers have gone. The group that remains waiting for their bags is composed (I count them) of seven people besides myself. I have no idea how I look, but the others either look frantic or fatalistic. One man just keeps shrugging.

A modern-day Dante, I think, would have a circle in hell that was the baggage carousel. And there, while it turned, the doomed and damned would be damned and doomed for eternity to wait for their bags which would never come.

Finally, I see my garment bag sliding onto the turning carousel.

I am relieved. I am thrilled. I couldn't be happier. But the time and passion spent waiting for it to appear have taken their toll.

I get my bag back, but the carefree rhythm of travel is gone. The sense of being in a state of grace where nothing can go wrong.

# CHAPTER SEVEN

## I

There were three telephone messages waiting for me at the hotel desk when we checked in. Two were from Cromwell. The first one asked me to call him as soon as I arrived. The second informed me that he had gone out to dinner and that we should talk in the morning. "How about breakfast?" he inquired.

I hadn't anticipated Cromwell's being in Pittsburgh a day early.

The third message was from Billy, only there was no message. Just the fact that he called. But called from where? There was nothing on the pink telephone message slip but his name and the time he called, a little over fifteen minutes before we arrived.

On the off chance that he had changed his travel plans and arrived at the hotel ahead of us, I asked the receptionist if he had already checked in. She informed me that he hadn't. So I left a message for him to call me as soon as he arrived.

It was almost 8:00 P.M. His plane, if he had kept to the original schedule, was not due until after nine. Perhaps he had called me from Boston. Perhaps there was some delay and he didn't want me to worry.

"That's probably what it is," Leila agreed with me.

I couldn't help thinking, of course, that if it hadn't been for the time spent waiting for my garment bag to arrive, I would have been there to receive his call. But not wishing indirectly to blame Leila for anything, I kept that thought to myself.

There would be no arguments over trifles. No arguments or bad feelings between us of any kind.

As master of the upcoming ceremonies, the first thing I had to do was to master my own self and my own moods.

Our happy rhythm of travel may have been lost, but that did not mean that I had to pout and fuss over it. I would replace it with another, even happier rhythm of my own making.

If I overdid it, it was because there was no other way to do this kind of thing.

I became aggressively amusing, entertaining, irrepressible.

I chatted up and chummied up to the young woman at the hotel desk.

I chatted up and chummied up to the bellboy who carried our bags. I harkened back (as we rode up in the elevator) to the glory days of the Pirates and the Steelers. Franco Harris. Mean Joe Greene. The Steel Curtain. And those Pirates! How about those Pirates! That wonderful motto of theirs: We are family!

"I tell you, son," I told him, "we'll not see their like again."

I actually said this to him.

## 2

The color orange, burnt orange to be exact, served as the unifying decorative theme of our huge, luxurious suite.

In addition to the huge bedroom (with a burnt-orange bedspread) there was a huge formal dining room with a dark cherry-wood table in the center of it. The tabletop gleamed like a frozen moonlit lake. Above the center of the table hung a crystal chandelier.

The huge living room (with burnt-orange curtains) ran the length of the entire suite. Shaped like a long and narrow rectangle, it could be entered at either end. If you were so inclined, you could circumnavigate the suite, entering at one end and exiting at the other and then reappearing once again from where you began.

There were lamps throughout of various shapes and sizes and styles, some with dimmer switches and some not. Subtle variations on the burnt-orange theme unified all the lampshades into an orange grove of lights.

There were two extra bathrooms in addition to the one off the master bedroom.

There were three TV sets and in the master bathroom a wall-mounted mini-TV.

Flower vases of various shapes and sizes and styles, with flowers of various kinds in them.

Strategically located mirrors everywhere.

Ashtrays throughout. You could smoke a pack of cigarettes without ever using the same ashtray twice. Almost as many telephones as there were ashtrays.

The walls of the suite were covered with abstract paintings of various shapes and sizes. The kind of abstract paintings found in the corporate headquarters of multinational companies. Abstract art, but without being an abstraction of anything in particular. Art once removed from everything. Nondenominational, nonsectarian, nonpolitical, nonideological, nonregional, nonnational art. Perhaps it was universal.

### 3

I couldn't stop talking.

Since there was nobody else there to chat up and chummy up to, I chatted up and chummied up to Leila.

It was as if I were trying to sell myself to her, or sell myself to myself, I couldn't tell which.

I couldn't tell if I was in total control of what I was doing, or totally out of control. There seemed to be enough evidence to warrant either conclusion.

It was not the case of somebody babbling away because he was in love with the sound of his own voice. Just the opposite. My voice, pitched a bit higher and much louder than normal, grated on my ears. It was irritating to hear myself chatter, but I chattered on. There seemed to be no way of stopping me, short of putting a bullet in my brain.

My reasons for behaving like this were either all too obvious or completely inexplicable, it was impossible to tell which.

The little we had to do, actually, physically do, was done very quickly. We had so little luggage, we managed to unpack in a matter of minutes. My chatter, while we unpacked, was at least connected to some real point of reference.

I harkened back, while Leila hung up the dress she had bought for the premiere, to how she had resisted going shopping for the dress.

I wondered out loud, as I took my tux out of my garment bag, if my tux would still fit me. Minutes later, I checked myself out in the wall of mirrors in the master bathroom and, patting my stomach, I laughed and made some ingratiatingly self-deprecating remarks about my swelling figure.

Once we unpacked and there was nothing to do anymore, my chatter, by necessity, became divorced and disassociated from anything except some ongoing need to narrate my existence.

I vamped.

I vamped the way I had once seen an actor vamp upon a stage when a member of the supporting cast failed to make his entrance on cue. I remember feeling very sorry for that actor then. I felt very sorry for myself now. It felt terribly lonely to be chatting with and chumming up to the woman I loved. It was like vamping in a void.

## 4

Leila, unlike me, was the picture of composure. It was as if our roles had suddenly been reversed in regard to the events that had brought us to Pittsburgh. Whatever anxieties she might have had in New York about the premiere of her movie were gone now, or seemed to be gone, and were instead being played out by me in her presence. And just as I had once been in a position to "understand" what she was going through, she now seemed to "understand" what it was that was causing me to chatter away the way I did.

The only response she made to my behavior was to regard me with silent compassion and, unless I was mistaken, a kind of loving understanding. There was a look in her eyes of a mother comforting an unhappy child.

"There, there, Saul," she seemed to be saying while words and sentences tumbled out of my mouth like Ping-Pong balls from a Lotto bin.

She made discreet and painfully diplomatic attempts to get away from me to another part of the suite and give me a chance to settle down. But I followed her from room to room, from the bedroom to the dining room, from the dining room to the living room, jabbering away about this and that.

About the view from our living room.

"It's too bad, it really is," I jabbered on, "that we didn't come just a couple of hours earlier, because then we could have seen the confluence at sunset. It's a stunning view. Truly stunning. You'll see. Tomorrow morning, we'll see the sunrise and I assure you it will be something you'll never forget. I know I haven't since the first time I saw it several years ago from this very hotel. I had no idea what was there because I had checked in late the previous night. But then I pulled open the curtains in the morning and there in front of my eyes was one of the most beautiful . . ."

She stood there listening to me with that look of compassion for what I was going through.

I had no idea what I was going through, or why, but she did. Or seemed to. And because she did and I didn't, because our roles were somehow reversed, it also seemed that it was she who had brought me to Pittsburgh for a presentation of some sort. That she was the master of ceremonies and not I.

This impression and my speculation on what the nature of those ceremonies might be made me chatter away all the more.

## 5

There is no hut, office, apartment, nook, or cranny on earth that does not become a waiting room where a man waits for something to happen.

I had waited so long for Pittsburgh and now here I was waiting in Pittsburgh.

Waiting for my compulsive chatter to cease.

Waiting for Billy to show up.

Wondering what was keeping him, worrying, and since I could neither worry nor wonder in silence (a temporary condition, I hoped), I worried and wondered out loud.

At first Billy was just a little late. I chattered away about Friday being the busiest travel day of the week and that as a consequence delays were to be expected.

"I know, from personal experience, from all the flying I've done, that given a choice I'd never fly on Friday. Saturday is the best day for travel by far. Unless we're dealing with holiday weekends, Thanksgivings, Christmases, things like that, in which case . . ."

I had followed Leila, while I talked, to every part of our suite. Eventually, realizing perhaps that wherever she went I would follow her, Leila gave up trying to elude me and sat down in the middle of the huge living room. She was sitting there now, as if she had no intention or strength to ever move again.

I sat opposite her, chattering away.

A rectangular glass cocktail table stood between us. We sat in identical easy chairs. Leila had her legs curled up under her and she had a small, burnt-orange throw pillow in her lap. Her hands, spread out like a book she was reading, lay on top of the pillow. She either looked up at me as I talked, or she gazed down at her hands in contemplation, the way she had done while we were on the plane.

The expression on her face when she looked up at me was always the same, or a new variation of the same thing. It wasn't really an expression at all. It was openness. Such total openness that all possibilities were contained within it. The terror or the joy, it was hard to tell which, of beholding such infinite richness in another human being made me chatter away all the more.

It was now well past ten o'clock. Billy was not just late, he was over an hour and a half late and there was still no word from him.

The three of us were supposed to be in the middle of our dinner by now.

I asked Leila if she wanted me to call room service. Have a little bite while we waited?

She shook her head.

A light snack or something?

No, she smiled, and shook her head.

"I wonder what could be keeping him," I said.

She shrugged.

And then somewhere along the way I made the transition from worrying about Billy to just babbling away about him. What a great kid he was. ("Kid nothing, he's a giant, right? Ha, ha, ha.") How proud I was of him. How much I loved him.

"It hasn't been that easy for him, it really hasn't. Having the kind of father, or lack of father, that he had for all those years. The thing is, I've always loved him. Always. It's just that . . . I don't know. Something kept me from giving him that love. But all that's behind us now, thank God. We've gotten to be real close this year. He tells me everything and I tell him everything. We couldn't be closer, he and I. We're like this." I crossed my fingers. "We really are."

I was near tears while I talked, either from my depth of feeling for him or from the frustration that I wasn't able to stop talking.

There, there, the motherly compassion in Leila's uplifted eyes washed over me. There, there, Saul.

Hearing myself talk and trying like some disinterested third party to discern some sense in what I was saying, I had the impression that the person in question (I) was pleading his case. That what he was really saying was this: Despite my faults, I am a good man who should not be hurt.

Please don't hurt me, I seemed to be imploring somebody in so many, many words.

The notion of my pleading and imploring intrigued me. There is something there, I thought. Something very revealing. And then I forgot all about it.

The next time I wondered (out loud) what time it was, it was an hour later.

The luxury suite where Leila and I were waiting suddenly felt like a wake.

A convulsion of symptoms gripped me and all of them sought expression. I would have needed half a dozen mouths to give voice to them all.

Panic. Despair. Grief. A fury of some kind. A pleading of some kind. A desire to make a deal of some kind.

Then I remembered an incident from the past and brought it up for discussion as a way to soothe my troubled mind.

I brought up Spain. Sotogrande. Leila and Billy's trip to Ronda.

"Ronda?" Leila asked, puzzled by what Ronda had to do with anything.

"It's just like Ronda," I was almost shouting, so thrilled was I by the similarity. "Don't you remember? The two of you went off to Ronda and didn't call me when you were supposed to. I stayed up half the night worrying and wondering what happened to you. Imagining terrible accidents in which both of you died. Anyway, it's just like this. I'm sitting here now and worrying and wondering about Billy when there's probably nothing to worry about at all. I'm sure there's a simple explanation for Billy's tardiness, just as there was a simple explanation why the two of you didn't call me when you were supposed to."

I clung to this comparison as if my salvation depended on it. And just to show Leila and myself that I was no longer worried about anything, I started talking about Spain in general, about that strange drowsiness, that tourist disease I had while we were there.

"I don't know what it was, I still don't, to tell you the truth, but I just couldn't wake up to save my life. I remember I kept drinking those double-double espressos until I thought I would . . ."

The telephone rang. Or rather, all the telephones in our suite rang. The two in the bedroom. The one in the master bathroom. The one in the dining room. The three in the huge living room where we were sitting.

It took me several seconds to mobilize myself into action. The ringing of the telephones had silenced me and I felt such relief not to be babbling that I almost didn't want to answer the phone and have to start talking again.

But of course I picked it up and, in a voice suddenly hoarse from all my talking, I said, "Hello?"

It was Billy.

"Billy," I said. "God damn it, Billy, I've been . . ."

I managed to shut up and let him talk. I felt the sound of his living voice commuting the sentence of catastrophe my worried mind had passed on him. I started crying.

Leila stood up and gestured that she was going to bed. She let her hand slide over my shoulder as she went. It was a loving thing to do, letting her hand slide over my shoulder like that, but it touched some nerve and caused an involuntary shudder.

6

The phone call was brief, rushed, and matter-of-fact. Billy was calling from downstairs. He had just arrived. He had driven down here from Boston. Driven? Yes, he had borrowed a friend's car. He felt like driving. He had a little car trouble on the way, something about a rotor cap, and he called to tell me he'd be late. He was sorry about having me worry. He said he was very sorry. He sounded more tired than sorry, which was understandable, just as it was understandable that he felt like going straight to bed. But I couldn't let him do that. I couldn't wait until morning to see him. I had to see him tonight. Now. And I told him as much. He said he would stop by for a minute. He said he was very tired.

"Of course you are," I told him.

Our meeting in my suite was almost as short and rushed as our telephone conversation.

When I opened the door and saw him, I was rendered speechless, and for somebody in my condition to become at a loss for words required a potent image.

Which is what Billy presented.

His lovely long black hair was gone. Completely gone. In its place was hair so closely cropped that I saw more scalp than hair.

A two-day growth of beard on his face.

Glazed, bloodshot eyes.

He wore a long military-style overcoat full of buttons. The coat was too narrow for his wide shoulders and its sleeves were too short for his long arms.

He looked more like somebody named Boris than Billy, an asylum-seeking defector from a Bulgarian basketball team.

I hugged him. Whoever it was he was portraying, whatever image he was projecting, he was still my boy, my Billy, and so I hugged him. Or as much of him as I could manage to hug through that barricade of an overcoat. He let himself be hugged in much the same way that a skin-head lets himself be frisked by the cops.

He didn't want to come inside. He was too tired. Just came to say hello.

I thought I detected a scent of alcohol on his breath when he spoke.

So we stood in the doorway and talked briefly in that unnatural way that people have when talking in doorways.

His eyes looked over my head as if examining my suite.

We went over the car business again.

He had borrowed his friend's car because he needed to take a long drive by himself.

"To clear my head."

"From what?"

"Things."

"What kind of things?"

"All kinds."

When I asked him about his haircut, he shrugged.

"I got carried away. I don't know."

Towering above me physically, he had something in his attitude as well that wanted to tower above me.

When I asked him if his room was all right, he snorted. He grunted when I inquired if he had had dinner, as if food and lodging were middle-class values he had jettisoned long ago.

There was this put-on punkish disdain for me and my questions and concerns. He seemed eager to offend, dying to displease, his whole fa-cade clamoring for attention, yet when the attention was given, it was greeted with the studied indifference of a surly lout possessing the taunting virility of youth. Any minute, I expected him to turn his head and spit a huge gob of spit on the carpet in the hallway.

His image was neither new nor original for a Harvard sophomore, but it was new for Billy. Unexpected. But because it was Billy (my boy), I found the affectation of it neither hostile nor troubling. There was something sweet about it, which I was eager to understand at my leisure. Only his exhaustion seemed genuine. He looked spent. Like a lone survivor of some legendary binge.

"I gotta get some sleep," he said by way of good night.

"Of course you do. Off with you, then. Go. Go sleep. I'll see you in the morning, OK? Good night, Billy."

For a brief fraction of a second, our eyes met as he turned to go and I saw Billy, my Billy, the old Billy I knew so well, peering out at me from that cumbersome suit of armor that was his new image.

7

I wasn't sleepy, tired, or hungry, even though the last thing I had eaten was a light snack on the plane. Adrenaline flowed through me.

No sooner did I shut the door to my suite following Billy's departure than a door opened in my mind, leading to an immediate and complete understanding of Billy's motives for looking and behaving the way he did.

It was all so obvious.

A clear-cut case.

An archetypal textbook case, in fact.

He had not been able to rebel against me, his father, when it was the proper time for such rebellion to occur, because I, his father, had not been there in any real sense for him to rebel against. The only rebellion open to him was hatred of me, an option he tried but found (thank God) unacceptable.

And so a bubble formed within his psyche, full of tantrums untried and rebellions unexplored, a bubble of adolescent behavior.

The immature boy became a mature young man on the outside, but the trapped bubble of immaturity remained on the inside.

Liberated, as he now was at last, by the certainty of my unconditional love for him and confident that I was there to stay in his life, Billy was finally free to burst that bubble within him.

Finally, finally, he was free to reject me, to rebel against me, to see me as somebody to be supplanted instead of needed and respected. He was free to do this because he knew that no matter what he did, I would love him and continue loving him.

It was, in my opinion, a very healthy and necessary thing that he was doing. Better that he should do it now than when he was my age.

How fitting it was, then, that Billy should revert to childish behavior the night before I reunited him with his mother, who, as a child, had given him away.

I was dazzled by my ability to understand everything so well and so completely and yet so effortlessly. Understanding flowed forth from me like music from Mozart.

I stretched out on the couch, wiggling my toes in delight. I contemplated getting up and going to bed, but the couch I was lying on felt perfect. Gradually, as if in conscious and discrete increments, I fell asleep.

# CHAPTER EIGHT

## I

The telephone rings.

I pick up, still half asleep.

"Hello," I say, in a voice alien even to myself.

It's Cromwell at the other end.

His voice, unlike mine, is showered and shaved and full of bristling vitality.

What, what's this, he wants to know, don't tell him (I haven't told him anything) that I'm still asleep. At this hour! Ha, ha, ha, he laughs, like reveille in a boot camp. Still in bed at this hour!

"No," I defend myself as best I can. "No, no, no, I'm not."

I clear my throat and feel around for cigarettes I can't seem to find.

"Breakfast. It's breakfast time. I'm downstairs waiting for you. You got my message, didn't you? So c'mon, put on some clothes and get your ass down here, you profligate bastard. Ha, ha, ha."

He hangs up laughing.

I check the time. It's nine forty-five.

It doesn't matter that I'm late for a breakfast appointment I neither made nor accepted.

I start rushing around. I had fallen asleep on the couch in my clothes, so I'm fully dressed, but I can't find my left shoe or any of my cigarettes. My rushing is tinged with futility. No matter how much I rush, it's too late to be on time. I can't make up for lost time.

First, I find my cigarettes and then my left shoe, and then, smoking, I rush to the master bathroom.

Leila is not there, but I have no time to wonder why not, or where she might be.

There is no time to shower or shave, but I have to brush my teeth.

Toothbrush in one hand, a lit cigarette in the other, I brush away, foaming toothpaste from the corners of my mouth.

There's a burning sensation in my penis, but there's no time to relax and play with the probability that I might have to pee. I'm at an age when physiological signals sent out by my body cannot be trusted anymore. My prostate gland is a source of ongoing disinformation. So I don't really know if I have to pee or not. I only know that I have no time to find out for sure.

I rush out of the suite and rush down the long corridor toward the elevators. En route, I have time to wonder where Leila is, but no time to come up with a likely explanation for her disappearance.

"She's probably just . . ."

I rush on.

## 2

The restaurant in the hotel lobby is large and almost filled to capacity. The tablecloths are white, the waiters dignified and well dressed, the atmosphere formal. The scent of food, bacon and maple syrup, leaves me in a quandary. Am I ravenous or stuffed? There is no way to arrive at an answer.

I look around for Cromwell and I don't have to look long or hard. There he is.

He is talking. His huge head is talking to somebody at the table with him. He is turned on. The power is on. He is smiling, laughing, reaching across the table with his hand to make a point.

Before I'm even halfway there, Cromwell senses my approach. His head, not the rest of him, just his head, much like a giant console TV with a swivel base, turns in my direction. He sees me. He takes me in. He incorporates me.

He waves and smiles.

I smile and wave back.

## 3

There were three of us at the table, Cromwell, myself, and Cromwell's new concubine.

His new concubine was a young black man.

A very young and very slim and very beautiful black man. He was light-skinned, more light brown than black, but Cromwell was determined that the blackness not be lost on me. Nor on the young man himself. Throughout breakfast, he used superfluous phrases to keep the issue of that young man's blackness alive.

"As my young black friend here will tell you . . ."

"Although he's young, my black friend has lived a lot more than . . ."

". . . my young black friend . . ."

The repetition became oppressive.

The young man's most striking feature was his eyes. They were as enormous as the eyes of Byzantine saints and so dark blue as to seem purple.

Despite his youth, he had thinning hair. His reserved semi-Afro was receding at the temples.

He wore a knowing expression on his face, like a sign that read that he was so well-informed and so wise to the ways of the world that nobody could put one over on him.

He was sure that he was way ahead of the game he was playing with Cromwell.

Whatever his name was, and it wasn't Brad, it went out of my head as soon as I heard it. As far as I was concerned, his name was Brad.

## 4

"Doc!" Cromwell stands up to greet me. "Goddammit, Doc, it's good to see you, even though you look like a human hangover, you old sinner."

We embrace.

"Sit down, sit down," he tells me, "you look like you're having a helluva time standing up." He laughs and slaps my back. "You really hung one on last night, didn't you?"

"What can I say?" I say and shrug, my shoulders demonstrating how lightly I bear the reputation that precedes me.

"What did I tell you?" Cromwell tells Brad. "Didn't I tell you he'd come down here with a hangover?"

He flatters both of us in one sentence. He flatters me that he had taken time out of his busy schedule to discuss me in my absence, and he flatters his young black friend by reminding him that he had discussed intimate details of my life with him.

It is a masterly demonstration of a master host. He flatters us both effortlessly and then rolls on.

"I just can't get over you," he tells me, and then he tells Brad, "He's indestructible. He's been this way ever since I've known him. The man's a legend . . ."

A waiter comes. Cromwell orders a fruit plate with plain yogurt and unbuttered toast, Brad a blue-cheese omelette.

I'm still in a quandary about what to have, but Cromwell comes to my rescue.

"I don't think our friend here is having anything to eat." He smiles at the waiter. "Unless I'm mistaken, he'll have a Bloody Mary to start," Cromwell says and turns to me for confirmation.

I nod once, as if the state of my hangover is such that to nod twice is out of the question.

## 5

It is relaxing, playing the image Cromwell has given me to play.

I had forgotten the mindless comfort of being an image instead of a human being.

It's not a lack of willpower that makes me go along with the charade of playing the image I've been given to play.

There are benefits.

I need a break from being.

Everyone, I think, needs an occasional break from being.

Even though I neither was drunk last night nor am hungover this morning, the image of a hack with a hangover is so comfortable that by assuming it I experience the peace that comes from finding a temporary respite from all the meaning crowding into my life.

From Leila and Billy, who mean so much to me.

From all the understanding I've had to do in the last few months.

I drink my Bloody Mary and smoke my cigarette and give myself over to Doc. He has fixed and streamlined so many screenplays and characters, transplanted so many spines into characters' lives and caused so many happy ending to occur that I want the same treatment for myself. Fix me up, Doc. And if you have to hack away, then hack away at me, but fix me up, Doc.

We talk on.

Our talk is talk-show talk.

There's a rhythm to the talking, an ancient rhythm, and there's a rhythm as well to the laughter. It's all very mellifluous and polyphonic, an acoustic massage for the mind. There is no content as such, but the tone is so pleasing that it becomes the content.

We're neither so loud that we offend the people at the tables around us nor so inconspicuous that we lack an audience.

We attract the proper amount and the proper kind of attention.

Our group image is enhanced by the fact that we're two white men and one black man (practically a boy) sharing the same table. It speaks well for us. It makes us feel and allows us to be perceived as goodwill ambassadors of some kind, of racial harmony if nothing else. And if the young black man at our table is Cromwell's concubine, that is not apparent in the image we project.

We're celebrating something at our table, life perhaps, or perhaps the fact that we're all in the entertainment business, the unifying religion of our time.

## 6

Here I am having breakfast with Cromwell and his young black friend because I was asked to be here and I came. I rushed to come, but there is neither rhyme nor reason for my presence except to be a witness of Cromwell's fucking of his young black friend.

In order to justify my presence, the topic of tonight's sneak preview comes up every now and then. Cromwell initiates the topic and he terminates it as he pleases.

He tells me that all the signs point to our having a big hit on our hands.

"Knock on wood." He smiles and raps the table with his knuckles.

The word of mouth on the movie is to die for. His friends and even his enemies in LA are calling him up and wondering when they can see it.

The ad campaign, built around the copy line "Love, the All-American Pastime," is going great. He had the copy line market-tested and it tested out even better than the title of the movie.

A sleeper, he's certain of it. An art movie with mass appeal.

As if as an afterthought, he turns to Brad and tells him that the credit for the copy line belongs to me.

I protest. It was just something I said, I say. I had no idea it was a copy line until Cromwell said it was.

Young black Brad watches us with his big blue Byzantine eyes which bring to mind the portraits of Christian saints.

Our banter, the way we so easily and generously give each other credit, the way Cromwell pats my shoulder, the way I respond, it all has the charming markings of a long and close friendship. A professional relationship, but a personal relationship as well. It is an appealing image we project, of two talented men fond of each other, and the black Brad, I can tell, feels good to be sitting there, being a part of this camaraderie. It is lost on him, of course, that I detest (loathe, hate, abominate)

Cromwell, but why shouldn't it be lost on him when, for all practical purposes, it is lost on me?

But the focus of Cromwell's enormous forehead and the dammed-up power behind it is not on me. I'm there as a diversion for the real business of this working breakfast, I'm nothing more than an observer who can be counted on to watch Cromwell fuck Brad in public. For a man like Cromwell to fuck somebody in private where only he and the victim are aware of the transaction would be a waste of time. Why even bother fucking somebody if there are no witnesses?

"Mmm." Cromwell savors the breakfast he's eating.

He forks little pieces of fresh fruit from his fresh fruit plate and dips them into his plain yogurt bowl and then pops them into his mouth.

"Mmm."

The zest with which he eats his food makes me doubt my hatred for this man. Makes me doubt my right to hate him. It seems un-American to hate somebody who loves what he's doing, who relishes who he is.

I have no idea what kind of hard-on Cromwell has for the Brad at our table, nor what part of Brad's life he wants to fuck. All I know, because I know Cromwell, because I have been repeatedly fucked by him, is that he wants to fuck that black boy, fuck something in him, or fuck something out of him, and he wants me to see him doing it over breakfast.

He has a zest for the life of that black boy.

The boy's a wunderkind of sorts.

Self-educated. He quit school as soon as he could. Went to work in one little theater after another. Started reading scripts for a large nonprofit theater where he became a dramaturg. Cromwell met him at the opening of a play in that theater and took, in Cromwell's words, an instant shine to him.

"I could tell right away . . ."

"As soon as we started talking, I knew that . . ."

"There was no doubt in my mind that he . . ."

And so on.

All this happened very recently, a little over a week ago. Cromwell asked him to lunch. They had lunch. Then Cromwell asked him to come to Pittsburgh with him to see a sneak preview of *Prairie Schooner*. So here Brad is in Pittsburgh, having breakfast with us.

Is it the artist in Brad that Cromwell wants to fuck? Or perhaps he wants to fuck the artist out of him. (Cromwell has a hard-on for arts and artists of all kinds). Or perhaps Brad's offense is that he has no need of Cromwell. Cromwell has a real hard-on for those who have no need of him.

"I need somebody like him in my office," Cromwell tells me, so that his young black friend can sit there and absorb the delight of being discussed. "I really do. I need the input of youth. Especially black youth. It's so easy to become insular and cut off, living the white life I live, and I feel a sense of responsibility to represent not just the mainstream white-bread culture but the black experience as well in the films I make. But you know this, Saul. I've told you this a hundred times . . ."

(This is the first I've heard of it, but I nod.)

"But I know nothing about movies," the black Brad-in-the making says. "I don't even like movies. I don't."

"Who can blame you for not liking the junk that's out there? If you liked it, we wouldn't be sitting here talking. And as for knowing nothing about movies, you know more than you think you do. You want to know who knows a lot about movies? All those film-school grads with their MFAs, that's who. They know all about them. I have one of them working for me now and it's a disaster. They haven't got the heart or the gut instinct I need. But you do. That play you produced . . ."

"I didn't really produce it. All I did was . . ."

"Oh, c'mon now. Let's not play games. You produced it and you know you did. It was your play."

"It was a play, not a movie. I really know nothing about movies," he says, but with not quite the same conviction as before. "I'm a theater animal, is what I am."

"If there's anything our culture needs, it's an infusion of that animal spirit, that raw vitality that you possess, not as an attribute but as an essence of who you are. That essence is the essence of art, be it film or theater or radio plays or rap or opera." The power and authority with which Cromwell speaks roll out of him as easily as the acceptance speech of a political leader elected by a landslide. He creates the impression that he knows the greatness in you that you are too timid to acknowledge.

Having been fucked by Cromwell in much the same manner, I now watch fascinated. It is as if I am being fucked again.

Fucked by having to observe this.

I should intercede, I think to myself.

And on it goes.

Cromwell no longer refers to me, looks at me, or acknowledges my presence at the table. He knows I'm there. He knows I'm observing it all. That's all he needs from me now. The little boost of energy that only an audience can give you.

Cromwell bites off little precise pieces of his unbuttered toast and shamelessly butters up Brad. He butters him up in such a blatant way that it can't escape Brad's attention.

And therefore Brad, knowing that he's being buttered up, wears a knowing expression on his face, as if that will make him immune to Cromwell's onslaught.

As if he could see through Cromwell with those beautiful purple Byzantine eyes.

Cromwell loves it when you see through him.

"What you have," Cromwell tells him, "is something so rare that . . .

"It's not just that you're talented," he tells him, "it's that you're also . . .

"You could be the first black man in the movie business to . . ."

He offers him image after image. And image after image, Brad refuses with a shrug or a smile or an amused knowing expression on his face.

But each refusal gives Cromwell an insight into the image that's needed to entomb his young black friend.

"Look," Cromwell tells him, and the tone of his voice suggests that he understands and accepts ahead of time Brad's refusal.

"Look," he says, "you've done just fine without me and I've done just fine without you, and I wager to say that we'll both continue to do just fine without each other. But that's not the point. I understand your reluctance. You, young man, were meant to be a young black warrior. I'm not telling you anything that you don't know a hundred times better than I do, nor am I about to lie and tell you that to be a young black warrior in the movie business will be easy. Because it won't. Our country, our society, the whole white corporate structure of the entertainment industry is on automatic pilot to crush the young black warrior whenever and wherever he appears. And so I have to admit that a part of me, the rational part of me, would urge you to stay away from it for your own good. But there's another, deeper part of me that knows that when young black warriors stop appearing in our society . . ."

I can see the change in Brad.

Detect some internal reappraising.

This image of himself as a young black warrior appeals to him. Those words have struck a chord.

The image, like some parasite, attaches itself to him as if to a host organism.

Cromwell, with a single glance of his upraised eyes, takes in his new black Brad who, he can see, is now there for the taking.

# CHAPTER NINE

## I

Cromwell and Brad are going to take a drive around Pittsburgh. Cromwell likes Pittsburgh. "It's a very interesting city," he says. "Far more interesting than people think."

He invites me to come along.

I can't, I beg off. My son's here.

We part in the lobby.

"See you at the movies tonight, Doc."

"I'll be there," I tell him, and extend a hand to Brad. "Nice to've met you."

He tells me that it was nice to've met me too.

They go one way and I go the other.

It's Billy I spot first. I become aware of him in the corner of my eye before I actually see him. His height. His newly cropped hair. Something has made me turn my head.

Had I not seen him, I would not have seen Leila, but now I see them both. There against the far wall. Both of them standing. Billy in profile, leaning against the wall, Leila full out, leaning against the wall too. Between them is a small table with a house phone, white, on top of it.

The lobby is enormous and very busy at this time of day. People checking in, checking out. Scattered throughout the lobby are little islands of furniture, little living rooms almost, with sofas, chairs, end tables, lamps, and rugs of their own.

I move through the crowd toward one of those little living room areas in the lobby. I sit down in an easy chair, it even swivels like the one in my living room in New York, and, lighting a cigarette, I begin to observe Leila and Billy at my leisure.

Billy is talking. Leila is listening. Billy's left hand is rubbing the top of his head as he talks.

Although there is something undeniably surreptitious about what I'm doing, my motives for doing it are innocent, pure family-man motives.

It's not often (strange as it may seem) that we get a chance to observe freely those we love.

It feels like ages since I've seen them.

Being with them is not the same as looking at them, as I'm doing now. You can't just look at people when you're with them. They say something. You say something. Your presence alters their behavior and your own as well. You see very little of the people you love when you're with them.

Or so it seems to me, sitting there, luxuriating in this opportunity to watch them, for once, to my heart's content.

I love them so.

I love the way they're talking to each other. I have no idea what they're saying, but there's a vitality and an urgency in their conversation that's apparent even at a distance.

Billy keeps rubbing the top of his head.

Leila is talking now.

He wants to interrupt, but doesn't.

Then she stops talking.

Both are silent for a while.

Then Billy says something. He seems to be asking her a question. She looks down at her shoes.

I either notice or imagine that I see a physical resemblance between them. The slightly swaybacked curve of their spines. With their heads bowed, as both their heads are now, they look like two graceful question marks.

Mother and son.

I sit there smoking, envisioning the happy ending to this day.

They stand in silence and then, without another word being spoken, Billy picks up the white phone. There is only one person he could be calling in the hotel. And that's me.

I'm sorry to give up my comfortable observation post, but it's time to go.

I head toward them.

Billy is leaning against the wall with the receiver to his ear and Leila is looking down at her shoes when I arrive.

"There you are," I say.

I've spoken too loudly and the sudden sound of my voice, and my sudden appearance, startles Leila. She is literally shaken. Billy spins around.

"Dad, I was just . . ."

All three of us start speaking at the same time and all three of us seem to be saying the same thing.

Then we laugh. Or I do. Or they do. There's laughter among us.

Explanations follow laughter. We all seem to have some explaining to do and we're all eager to state our case. Leila, still a little shaken, is explaining how she woke up starved and saw me asleep on the couch and didn't want to wake me but she just had to have something to eat. So she went down to have breakfast and who should she run into in the lobby but Billy, who . . .

Billy takes it from there and starts explaining how he too woke up starved, but as starved as he was, he just didn't like the look of the hotel restaurant. Instead, he decided to take a drive around town to look for a less pretentious place to eat, but just as he was heading out of the hotel, he saw Leila stumbling out of the elevator and . . .

"I was not stumbling," Leila protests.

We all laugh for some reason.

Then Billy and Leila take turns telling the rest of the story. How they drove around Pittsburgh looking for just the right place. How a lot of places were still closed. How cool and autumnal the air was. How they finally found this diner not far from the river. A real blue-collar kind of place, with a jukebox and a lot of trucks parked in the parking lot.

They shower me with details about the diner.

When my turn comes to explain, I tell them what I did with my time and with whom. I leave out the essentials of what occurred over my breakfast table. Instead, I repeat what Cromwell told me: how the word on the movie is that it is to die for. How we might have a big hit on our hands. How this day will mark the end of Leila's anonymity.

They both seem overly attentive while I talk. I'm not saying much, babbling away, but they're hanging on every word I say, nodding, responding.

We all seem overly excited about something.

It all seems slightly artificial, but it's hard to tell. Perhaps it's genuine. I either detect or think that I detect the scent of alcohol on Billy's breath. It's hard to know for sure, because I myself have been drinking.

We seem to be standing too close together as we talk. Billy's hands look enormous suddenly. They're the same hands he always had, of course, but now, for some reason, they seem to be massive. Maybe he's using them more. Big unruly hands, like the wings of a creature he can't quite control.

He's wearing a beat-up old fleece-lined athletic jacket and he keeps pulling up the zipper and then pulling it down and he doesn't seem aware that he's doing this.

I miss the distance I had while observing them without being with them.

I feel both crowded and, God knows why, lonely at the same time.

And I feel overwhelmed by the need to process, evaluate, and interpret the data I detect in their eyes, in the sound of their voices, the language of their bodies.

The way Leila keeps looking down at her shoes.

The way she looks up and then down again.

The way she seems ready to leave, to rush off somewhere, and the way she just manages to keep herself in place.

Billy looks as rebellious as he did last night (a skinhead, a Liverpool hooligan, an East European mafioso), but he no longer behaves according to his rebellious image. He seems confused, pathetic. As if he doesn't have a clue how to behave around me, what pose to strike.

I see a multiplicity of Billys in his eyes and I feel besieged.

I've done my part. I went through a rather exhausting process of understanding him and his rebellious image last night. The least he can do is stick to it for a while.

I feel incapable, not unwilling but incapable, of any new understanding at the moment, and I resent being called upon to provide it.

At the moment, I lack the resources to handle any deviations from what I consider to be their current characters.

I feel out of breath. Mentally out of breath.

As if caught in a vortex, or held together by gravity, we remain standing there, too close to one another for comfort.

In desperation almost, I suggest we do something.

"It looks like such a nice day," I shout, having not had a single glimpse myself of the kind of day it is. "Why don't we do something?"

Billy stammers and then speaks.

"I was just . . . I mean, just before you showed up . . . that's what I was calling you about. We were thinking of going for a drive to see

Frank Lloyd Wright's Fallingwater House. It's supposed to be not far from here and I've always . . ."

He starts explaining himself again, apologizing almost, telling me how he's become interested in architecture at college and how Frank Lloyd Wright is one of his . . .

I can't tell if I'm being invited to come along with them or not, but I assume that I am and I accept.

"That's a great idea," I tell him. "I've always wanted to see the Fallingwater House. Let me just shower, shave, and change my clothes and we'll be out of here. Won't take me more than fifteen minutes. Twenty, tops."

I thought they would wait for me in the lobby while I got ready, but instead all three of us get on the elevator and ride up together. Billy keeps zipping and unzipping the zipper on his jacket until I'm almost ready to slap his hand.

## 2

Standing in the shower, I bend my head as if in prayer.

I enjoy the sensation of hot water falling on my shoulders and the sight of steam rising, enveloping me.

There is no time to take a long shower because Billy and Leila are waiting for me in the living room. I picture them standing there.

It's puzzling. I'm taking a shower in private, but there's no private person within me. There's only the outer man taking a shower, playing some public persona.

I can't tell if it's just the mood I'm in or if it's a new malady.

I dry off, using many towels. I put on clean clothes.

## 3

I had left them standing and now found them sitting.

I never thought of either of them as massive before, but they seem massive to me now, as massive and as immobile and as burdened with some oppressive meaning as the two marble figures of Michelangelo atop the tomb of Giuliano de Medici.

No more meaning, please, I felt like screaming. Enough! I'm not a young man anymore.

They were sitting on the same long couch, Leila at one end and Billy at the other. Directly opposite the couch was an easy chair.

The chair faced them and seemed exactly equidistant from both Billy and Leila.

That chair was meant for me.

I was meant to sit in that chair (there was even a clean ashtray on the end table in front of it) and serve as a receptacle for whatever was oppressing them.

Everything pointed in this direction. The look in their eyes. The silence in the room. The triangular seating arrangement.

Our agenda to go sightseeing had been changed while I was in the shower.

I neither knew nor cared to know the details of the new agenda because I was not in a position to do anything about it. I was, for the time being, a completely one-dimensional creature trying to do his superficial best for both of them. There was no inner man within me. No one was on duty inside to handle this emergency.

Tomorrow, perhaps tomorrow, I would be able to deal with it. But not now.

To bog down now, to sit in that chair and listen to them disgorge themselves of whatever was oppressing them, was beyond my psychological resources. And I couldn't allow them to jeopardize the happy ending I had in store for them. I had to save them from themselves, to keep them from spoiling the glorious surprise that awaited them tonight.

The silence in the living room was about to be broken, and, I could tell, by Leila. She shifted her position on the couch ever so slightly, and ever so softly she sighed, exhaled, as a prelude to speaking.

I knew that if I let her start speaking, some genie would be out of the bottle, some jig would be up, some other story, not the story I had in mind, would begin.

And so I struck first.

What a wonderful day it was, I told them, and how wonderful I felt. I hadn't felt this wonderful in years. And how great it was to be going for a drive with the two of them again.

Not since Spain, I told them, had we been for a nice drive together. A drive in a car. One of my favorite things in life, especially with two of my favorite people.

I'd always wanted to see the Fallingwater House. It was one of my favorite works of Wright's.

I asked Billy if he knew how to get to the Fallingwater House, but before he could answer I suggested that we stop downstairs and talk to the concierge. Just to be on the safe side. They probably had road maps and things. And they probably knew of some quaint out-of-the-way country restaurant where we could have lunch.

I was frankly surprised at the ease with which I managed to browbeat them into compliance, and herd them out of the suite and into the corridor.

## 4

It was a most memorable sky, dotted with hundreds, perhaps thousands, of little white clouds. Identical in size and shape, they made the mauve sky seem like a field of chrysanthemums through which the sun shone down upon the earth.

I don't know if they looked or not, but as we walked across the hotel parking lot, I pointed up at the sky and, turning first to Leila and then to Billy, I said, "My God, would you look at that sky."

## 5

The car that Billy borrowed from a friend at Harvard was an old Checker cab. I didn't know much about cars, but I could tell that a lot of money had been spent on it. Repainted. Reupholstered. Reappointed.

The only yellow car in the parking lot. Not the yellow of yellow taxicabs but some other shade of yellow, with bits of reflecting granules mixed into the paint so that the exterior sparkled and glimmered with a combination of gold dust and mother-of-pearl.

Black leather interior.

A nice big steering wheel, the kind that made you want to keep your hands on the wheel just for the pleasure of it.

Maybe it was the alcohol I detected, or thought I did, on Billy's breath that morning, or maybe I didn't like the nervous way he twirled the car keys around his index finger as we walked across the parking lot, or maybe it was simply that I wanted to be the one in charge of the tempo of our drive, but whatever the reason, I asked Billy to let me drive. I said I had never driven a Checker and had always wondered what it was like to drive one.

I would drive out. He would drive back.

Instead of giving me the keys, he tossed them to me. It was one of those "guy" things that a boy his age might do. There was nothing hostile about it. It's just that I didn't expect it and therefore failed to catch them. The keys went right through my hands and fell on the pavement.

I bent down to pick them up and on my way up, with the keys in my hand, I could see Billy and Leila's commiseration directed toward me, as if I had been treated unfairly.

Although it was only Billy who tossed me the keys, they both seemed to want to apologize.

## 6

Despite my wealth of associations with the city of Pittsburgh, I had been there only once before. I now felt a little at sea sitting behind the steering wheel of our Checker cab and looking for a way out of Pittsburgh.

They didn't have any more free maps to give away at the hotel desk, but a certain Ms. Caan, consulting a road atlas, wrote out the directions for me on a sheet of hotel stationery. The directions had seemed perfectly clear while I was reading them in the hotel lobby and, in theory, they were still perfectly clear. It's just that the reality of the city took away some of the clarity.

The streets I was on meandered like rivers, and the names of the streets changed for no apparent reason, like the streets in Paris. One block they were called one thing, the next block something else. I drove up streets steeper than anything I had seen in San Francisco, only to drive down them again in search of an intersecting street that had failed to materialize.

Finally, either by accident or a process of elimination, I wound up heading west on (appropriately named) Western Avenue. I crossed the Ohio River over Wiend Bridge and there on the other side of the bridge was state highway 51 heading south.

According to my directions as written down by Ms. Caan, all I had to do was stay on 51 until I got to Uniontown.

I lit a cigarette and stepped on the gas.

We quickly left Pittsburgh behind.

Rolling along toward Uniontown, I even allowed myself to gaze at the scenery, because Ms. Caan had advised me that the route she picked for us was the scenic route.

I did all I could to appreciate the scenery. The rolling hills. The open fields. The groves of autumnal trees.

We crossed the Monongahela over Elizabeth Bridge (at the town of Elizabeth) and, with my foot gently pressing on the gas pedal to increase speed without alarming Leila, we sped on toward our next destination, Uniontown.

## 7

A Checker is a very roomy car. There's a lot of headroom, legroom, elbowroom.

Leila sat up front with me, but not next to me. This is not meant to sound like a criticism of any kind. She is simply taking advantage of the room the front seat offers to be comfortable. To stretch out.

Her cheek is nestled in the palm of her right hand, which is pressed against the rolled-up car window. Her body is stretched out toward me. Her legs are bent, and the hillocks of her knees under her dress are provocative. I keep thinking I'm going to reach out and touch them, alight on them, but I don't.

I don't know why I don't.

Perhaps it's because I can't tell for sure if my desire to touch them is a desire to touch them or a desire to demonstrate that I can if I want to.

But I can't tell if I want to.

I keep waiting for the situation to clarify itself. For some irresistible impulse to be born and to impel my hand toward her knees.

She seems too far away where she is. Her body so close and she so far away.

Billy is in the backseat, which is so far back that he seems like somebody following us rather than traveling in the same car.

I catch a glimpse of his face every now and then in the rearview mirror.

## 8

I speed up at times and then, when Leila starts to stiffen and show signs of alarm, I slow down again. I do this in order to control the atmosphere in the car and prevent a buildup of something.

A buildup of what?

I speed up until the focus becomes what I'm doing, and then I slow down again.

For a while, for a few scenic miles, the atmosphere returns to status quo.

And then the buildup starts again.

I respond by putting more pressure on the gas pedal.

There's a happy ending awaiting them at the end of this day and I will do whatever it takes to keep them from spoiling it.

## 9

I keep up a steady flow of superficial chatter.

It flows from me like cheap white wine from a bottle.

I have instant access to millions of bits of information stored in my memory. Everything from grade school to grad school and beyond. Almost everything I ever read in the *New York Times* is there. The genocides. The musicals. The movies. The sports in the Sports section. The science in the Science section. The diets. The drive-by shootings. The emergence of fashion models as famous personalities. The evolution of basketball and the emergence of the point guard and the power forward as the cornerstones of the game.

The episodes, the incidents, the encounters, the dialogues, the story conferences, the breakfasts, lunches, and dinners from the life I've lived.

They're all there.

It has no meaning for me but it's all there, and I draw upon it as I drive in order to entertain, divert, and engage.

There's no hierarchy of importance, no dictatorship of themes, no need to bridge diverse topics.

I regale them, as I smoke and drive, with an ongoing narrative of my life and times.

## 10

Approximately fifteen miles after Uniontown, we turned onto state highway 381 at the little town of Farmington.

From Farmington, according to Ms. Caan, it is another fifteen miles to the Fallingwater House of Frank Lloyd Wright.

Trees, forests of trees, on both sides of the road. Sudden flocks of birds rising up from the fields.

The road was a narrow two-lane blacktop, full of curves. Wonderful to drive on.

The three of us, by this time, were all a little punch-drunk. We burst out laughing at the slightest provocation. When no provocation occurred, we desperately reprised past provocations at which we had laughed and laughed at them once again.

I quoted Billy's many childhood malapropisms. Baa, baa, black sheep, have you any wolves. Robin Hood and his married men.

The traffic along 381 thickened. Weekend drivers enjoying the scenery. Young couples. Old couples. Cars full of kids.

I kept passing them and, in the faces of the people I passed, I saw ourselves through their eyes. We looked the very image of one of those happy families you sometimes encounter on the road.

When we drove through a little town called Ohiopyle, the name of the town was enough to make us hysterical with laughter. Leila's eyes disappeared completely from laughing so hard. Billy had tears in his.

We were laughing ourselves silly when we crossed the Youghiogheny River.

I passed some more cars as the road suddenly jogged eastward.

And then, just as I went around a blind curve in the road, I had to slam on my brakes and come to a screeching stop to avoid hitting the car in front of me.

In front of that car were other cars lined up bumper to bumper.

I couldn't tell how long the line was because the road vanished off to the right up ahead.

## II

It's just a slowdown of some kind, I think to myself. Some rubber-neckers taking in the scenery, or a car with a broken fan belt that has to be pushed off the road.

Soon, I'm sure, we'll start moving again.

I express this view to Leila and Billy and they concur.

We're all agreed. Any second now we'll start moving again.

I light a cigarette and think to myself that before I have finished smoking it we'll be moving on.

## 12

Our punch-drunk, rollicking mood is on hold for the time being. It's there, idling like the engine of the car, ready to be engaged again.

## 13

The smoke from my cigarette, while we were moving, was sucked out of the car through the windows, but now it accumulates inside the car. Leila fans it away from her face. I offer to put out the cigarette, but she says it's all right.

I put it out anyway.

## 14

The cars are bumper to bumper on my side of the road. However, there is a completely deserted lane on the other side. Not a single car going by.

Nothing is moving. Nothing except those chrysanthemum clouds.

I keep tapping lightly on the gas pedal to keep the engine from shuddering. This could easily develop into a nervous tic. I have to make sure not to allow that to happen.

## 15

Up ahead, a couple of drivers get out of their cars. Hitching up their pants. Tucking in their shirts. Ex-servicemen probably, they now look like perfect casting for washing-machine repairmen.

Trying to figure out what's holding up the traffic.

They join forces and walk together down to where the road bends to the right.

They stop. They survey the territory ahead. They shake their heads.

They amble back to their cars, gesturing to the rest of us with broad operatic gestures that they haven't a clue about what's holding up the traffic.

## 16

I keep tapping the gas pedal. The mood, the atmosphere in our car is changing. Some other atmosphere is slowly asserting itself in our car, and I don't know what to do about it.

My only hope is that we start moving again.

And soon.

## 17

The car in front of me is rapidly becoming a permanent fixture in my life.

It's a burgundy-colored Buick Riviera.

The couple inside the car have a dog that has taken a shine to me.

I try not to look at it, because I don't like the looks of this dog, but it's hard not to look at it when it keeps looking at me.

It appears, disappears, reappears.

There it is again.

And the damn thing is looking right at me.

It's a small, skinny dog, black and white. It must be standing on its hind legs on the backseat. All I see of it are its head and front paws through the rear window.

## 18

I'm desperate for a cigarette, but out of consideration for Leila I refrain.

I have the option, or course, of getting out of the car and smoking my cigarette outside, but I no longer feel comfortable about leaving the two of them alone in the car.

## 19

Once again I am beginning to detect the telltale signs of their agenda. They're getting ready to confront me with something.

I turn the radio on and off.

As if by accident, I hit the car horn.

I say something.

I say something else.

Anything to distract them.

## 20

I'm engaged in a valiant struggle against an unaccountable feeling of loneliness. It seems all wrong and unnatural. How can I be lonely when I'm sitting here with the only two people I love? If I have a family, this is it. If anyone loves me, it's the two of them.

All the evidence against loneliness is in my favor and yet I'm getting lonelier than ever.

There's that damn dog again.

## 21

Years ago, I rewrote an already rewritten screenplay (currently being rewritten yet again by a husband-and-wife team) that belonged to a then-new genre called a Mafia buddy movie.

One scene in particular now comes back in vivid detail.

Two Mafia guys are taking a third Mafia guy for a ride. They're all buddies, but the third guy has to die.

They're driving to a designated spot where the killing is supposed to occur.

They're telling jokes and talking about various parts of women's anatomies along the way, as they tend to do in these scenes, their doomed buddy not having a clue, of course, that he's taking his last ride.

They're driving along, having a wonderful time.

And then (this was my contribution) they have to stop suddenly at a railroad crossing.

And merely by the virtue of the fact that they have to make this un-planned stop, the mood inside the car changes. The jokes they were telling, the banter, the laughter that had been in keeping with the motion of the car suddenly seems forced and inappropriate.

Tony, that was the name of our fall guy, Tony Russo, starts to sense that something is wrong. His two buddies aren't saying much, but he can feel the current of silent sentence fragments going back and forth between them (or so I wrote in my stage directions). And as they all wait for the train to pass, he realizes what the real agenda is.

## 22

I remember Tony now because I am beset by the feelings I had ascribed to him in my stage directions for that scene.

The panic. The loneliness. His bewilderment at suddenly dreading the two guys he loved. His family.

I feel the same way.

Leila and Billy are going to hit me with something. I don't know what it is, but I suspect that it will hurt.

Despite the layers of flab that cover my body, it is tense and hard, in anticipation of a blow.

If I grip the steering wheel any tighter, my fingers will break like pretzels and fall into my lap.

## 23

I have never felt the slightest anxiety about the possibility of a nuclear war.

What terrifies me about atomic bombs is not their destructive potential but rather this aspect of them, that once a chain reaction begins inside a bomb, it cannot be stopped.

Anything irreversible is a source of terror.

I feel that some chain reaction has begun in our car.

I feel the currents of communication between Leila and Billy. Between the front seat where she sits (not quite beside me) and the backseat where Billy is sitting.

Without looking at each other, without speaking to each other, they are communicating.

The shuffling noise Billy makes as he rearranges his body.

The little cough he coughs.

The half-suppressed sigh Leila sighs.

Billy is opening and shutting the ashtray cover on the ashtray in the backseat.

Leila, having been slumped over in the front, now sits up.

She is now gathering her thoughts before starting to speak.

She is looking down at her hands, where the thumb of one hand is rubbing, worrying the fingers of the other.

Any moment now, she will raise up her eyes and look at me.

I brace myself.

She lifts up her head, turns it slightly, and looks at me.

The look I get from her is as soft as cashmere.

There are, or seem to be, tears welling in her eyes.

And then, in that catch-in-the-throat voice of hers that I associate with the sound of her laughter and memories of happier times, she says, "Oh, Saul."

The sound of my own name, as said by her, jolts me like a heart attack.

## 24

"Oh, Saul," was all she said.

I was stricken by the beauty and tragedy of it.

It is a rare thing, after all, to hear the true, unabridged sound of one's own name. It happens, if it happens at all, once or maybe twice in a lifetime.

In that "Oh, Saul" I heard a catalogue of all the names of all the men I had tried to be.

The pain was almost unbearable.

And yet l could tell that if I allowed her to continue, there would be more pain. She was just beginning.

## 25

I wish I could say that what followed was caused by something snapping inside of me and that therefore I did what I did as a result of being out of control.

Unfortunately, that was not the case.

Nothing snapped. There was nothing left to snap.

I began howling.

"Oh, Saul," I howled.

My cry, or shriek, or howl aborted Leila's speech. She winced and drew back from me. She flashed a frightened look of inquiry at Billy in the backseat and received from him, or not, some reply.

"Oh, Saul," I howled.

My only thought (I could think and howl at the same time) was of escape.

Escape from the point we had reached.

From the road we were on.

From the pain I was feeling.

My hope was that once we were in motion again, it would once again provide a distraction from the pain. Distraction from everything. And so I set us in motion.

Bookended by cars, trapped in an endless sentence of cars, I made the decision to break out of there.

I put the car in gear and, stepping on the gas, slammed into the car in front of me, just as that little dog appeared in the rear window. Then I put the car in reverse and slammed into the car behind me.

I had to repeat the procedure several times before the drivers of the cars in question, despite a manly show of outrage, provided me enough room for my getaway.

Since I couldn't go forward, I made a U-turn and, with the whole lane to myself, I set off in the direction from which I had come.

Back toward Pittsburgh.

As if the happy ending I had conceived for the three of us still awaited us there.

As if the consequences of things irreversible could be eluded by a deftly executed U-turn on a two-lane highway in southwestern Pennsylvania.

## 26

I was driving fast. My aim was to drive fast enough to cause a distraction from any story in the car requiring further development and exposition.

I could not stop howling my name and, once I started, I could not stop crying.

I was sobbing, keening, weeping, blubbering, out of frustration or grief at being unable to summon with the sound of my own voice the chordlike resonance my name had possessed when it was uttered by Leila.

"Oh, Saul!" I kept howling.

"Oh, Saul!" I kept crying.

But it was a hollow sound that I produced.

Like a single finger plinking away at a single piano key.

And no matter how I tried to discover some biographical intimacy with all those Sauls I had been or tried to be in my past, I couldn't.

The public, Leila and Billy in this case, had (I suspected) a much deeper and a much more personal appreciation of what I was going through than I did.

It wasn't that my connections to my past were severed or impaired in any way, but rather that those connections conveyed nothing.

My memory was still perfect. Even under the stressful circumstances in which I found myself (howling out my name, weeping, and driving at a pretty good clip), I could recall at will almost any episode from almost any period of my life.

It was a summer afternoon and I was maybe three or four at the time. A stout, tall woman came to visit my mother. She wore a long-sleeved polka-dot dress and because she was so tall and I was so tiny, she loomed above me like a magnificent tower of polka dots. She stopped in the kitchen when she saw me, smiled, and said, "There you are. You must be Mrs. Karoo's little boy, Saul."

The whole of that long summer, I walked around as if I had been knighted at a very early age. I was set for life. I was Mrs. Karoo's little boy, Saul.

"Oh, Saul," I howled, weeping like a fool, not because that memory from my childhood meant so much to me but because I couldn't get it to mean anything.

"Oh, Saul," I cried. "Oh, Mrs. Karoo's little boy, Saul."

Leila and Billy sat in silence, neither looking at me nor saying anything. By now they were like hostages who were either paralyzed into inaction from fear or had adopted inaction as the best way to keep from provoking me into even more extreme behavior.

## 27

The car held the road and I held on to the steering wheel of the car with both hands, howling.

The road seemed to have a current of its own that made us pick up speed without any action on my part.

Like some rolling river accelerating as it rolled along.

The only other car I ever drove that reminded me of this Checker cab was an old Packard Clipper I drove once with a friend in the summer of '59.

I was smoking Pall Malls at the time.

The thought that there was such a thing as the summer of '59 now struck me as one of the wonders of the world.

I was Billy's age.

"Oh, Saul!" I howled.

But the sound of my name, as uttered by me, caused no resonance. It was like dropping a pebble into a pond with ripple-proof water.

Leila and Billy sat in silence, not looking at me or out the window or at each other.

They seemed arrested in some midhowl of their own.

I could tell that they thought I had lost my mind.

I didn't blame them for thinking that, or take it personally.

I only wished that they were right.

Unfortunately, the human mind can't be lost as easily as most people think.

So there we were, the three of us speeding down a highway we had traveled in the opposite direction not that long ago.

There was clear sailing ahead of us as far as the eye could see.

High above our heads, those sunlit chrysanthemum clouds rolled across the sky of southwestern Pennsylvania.

PART V

# Here and There

# CHAPTER ONE

## I

He opened his eyes.

He had no idea where he was or who he was. He was lying flat on his back on a single bed in a room somewhere. It was, or seemed to be, night.

His room was dark, but there were shadows on the ceiling cast by the night lights below his field of vision.

A telephone ringing outside his room caused him to turn his eyes in the direction of the sound.

He saw that the door to his room was open. Light from the corridor spilled into his room, creating a carpet of light on the floor.

The carpet of light delighted him, as if the ability to see, simply to have eyes that could see, was cause for joy.

Knowing neither his identity nor location, he stared at the rolled-out carpet of light on the floor, as if any minute a messenger would arrive to answer all his questions. In the meantime, until the messenger arrived, he gave himself over to the joy of seeing.

## 2

It didn't take him long to determine that he was in a hospital.

He was strapped to the bed so that he could not move his body, or raise his arms. The image he had of himself was of someone lying at attention.

A tube, its diameter the size of a little finger, ran out of his body. It meandered upwards, riverlike, and with his eyes he followed its course to its source, a glass or a plastic container above his head, attached to a stainless-steel apparatus. The shape of the container, transparent and half-filled with liquid, reminded him of a hummingbird feeder.

Nurses in white uniforms and white shoes walked noiselessly past his doorway. Their images appeared and disappeared like full-length living portraits stepping in and out of a picture frame.

When he saw the same nurse twice, he experienced the thrill of recognizing somebody he neither knew nor would ever get to know, but the joy of seeing her again, the joy of seeing in general, was a joy in itself.

As far as he was concerned, he could just go on, happily seeing forever.

Every now and then, a telephone rang in the corridor and then stopped.

3

If he was, as he had determined that he was, in a hospital, then it followed that something was wrong with him. People were not dragged off to hospitals in this day and age, in any day and age for that matter, if there was nothing wrong with them.

He felt so good, he couldn't imagine the reason for his confinement. Strapped to the bed and all.

He wondered what the matter with him was.

A heart attack?

An aneurysm?

Maybe he was a victim of a random shooting.

He was not worried or anxious about it. Merely curious. Just as he was curious about the location of the hospital.

Chicago?

LA?

New York?

Paris?

His hospital room's nondescript decor provided no clues. For all he knew, he could be anywhere.

Another, but related question: When he was released from the hospital, as people always are, where would he go?

He didn't have a clue.

The only answer that came to him was "Home." But where was that? He had no idea.

He would know when the time came for him to check out of the hospital.

Out in the corridor, he heard the telephone ringing and he gave himself over to the joy of hearing the sound before it stopped. He could see. He could hear. He could think. All three at once, in fact.

What joy.

He wondered if perhaps he had been brought to this hospital not because of some physical affliction but because there had been no joy in his life.

4

From time to time he wondered who he was.

He knew, although he didn't have one yet, that he was supposed to have an identity. He even knew the general components that made up an identity.

A first and last name. A birthdate and birthplace. Current address. Occupation. Somebody to call in case of an emergency. Daytime phone number. Favorite author. Favorite quote. And so on.

It struck him as a curious thing, this concept of an identity. Curious in the sense that the components that made it up didn't seem all that personal.

If he were never to have an identity, would it be such a loss?

Of what significance was it that he didn't have one now?

Or did he?

Here he was, after all, seeing, hearing, thinking, full of joy. Was that not an identity?

Or was the joy he felt a substitute for an identity?

If so, then he wasn't all that keen on acquiring one.

5

Though he was bound fast to the bed on which he lay, his head was free to move in any direction. There was nothing external, no clamp or vise, to keep his head from turning this way or that.

And yet he kept his head perfectly still.

It was as if some precious and precarious balance existed inside his head that would not only be upset should he move it, but upset with dire consequences. Something would topple. Some peace within would collapse. Some flood of calamitous information would invade him and make him drown, should the balance be compromised. Therefore, when he looked to his left or to his right, only his eyes moved, turning within their sockets like floating compass balls.

Inside his head was his brain and within that brain was his mind and within his mind was his mind's eye looking back at him. It seemed like a friendly presence, both familiar and strange. Like a third parent we all have but seldom see. He saw love in his mind's eye. Love extended to him for no reason at all. Simply because he existed. Love without a motive or cutoff date.

A nurse came into his room, humming a Bob Dylan ballad. He still didn't know his own name but he knew it was a Dylan ballad she was humming.

She stopped humming the moment she saw that his eyes were open. She seemed startled, almost frightened by his steadfast gaze, and then she smiled and grew quite excited, as if some unexpected but significant phenomenon had occurred.

"You're awake," she said, implying by her tone that being awake was a major accomplishment. "I better get Dr. Clare." Even as she said this, she was backing out of his room as if unable to restrain herself from broadcasting the news of his awakening. In the next second, she was out the door and he heard her voice in the corridor.

"The guy in 312 is out of his coma. Where's Dr. Clare?"

## 6

He was not really surrounded, but he felt surrounded. Dr. Clare, a woman, was on his right. On his left, keeping her distance, was the nurse who had found him awake. Neither of them was pressing in on him, but he felt invaded by their curiosity. It was as if he were a story they knew better than he did.

Initially, he had tried to resist, to dismiss, to deny everything that Dr. Clare was telling him, but he found himself incapable of keeping up the effort. He found himself weakening. Succumbing to something in the weary monotone voice, in the weary, almost motherly eyes of Dr. Clare. The black circles under her eyes testified to sleepless nights spent looking after patients. Had she not seemed so overworked and been more businesslike, had she been a man and not a woman, he would have perhaps found a way to trigger his anger and outrage and tell her to get the fuck out of his room.

But as it was he felt helpless to be anything less than pleased with what she was doing because she seemed so certain that she was making him feel better. How could he tell her that he wanted no part of this identity that she was so kindly and yet mercilessly administering to him?

"Can you speak, Mr. Karoo?" she asked.

As soon as he heard Karoo, he remembered Saul and knew that he was Saul Karoo.

She waited patiently for him to reply, urging him to try with a weary smile and eyes kindly disposed toward him.

"Yes, I can speak," he said, and the sound of his own voice was like a signal that caused whatever resistance he had left to collapse.

From the far corners of the world, or so it seemed to him, came caravans and cargo planes bearing back into his mind the trivia and the tragedies of his past.

The speed of this reintroduction to himself was like a nuclear chain reaction. Nothing could stop it. A blur of details invading him at the speed of light. Names, places, people he knew, books he had read, the many poolsides of his life. His once spacious interior was being furnished with the seemingly endless clutter of his life. The more there was of it, the less there appeared to be of him. It was like being buried alive in the details of his past.

The joy of life is dying, he wanted to scream out, but couldn't bring himself to disappoint the weary-eyed Dr. Clare, who mistook the look of remembrance in his eyes for joy.

"It's all coming back to you now, isn't it?" she asked.

Yes, he nodded, saying nothing.

"Good," she said. "You've been in a coma for almost twelve days. A concussion. It's hard to tell with comas. We never know how long they'll last. We don't even know what makes one person come out of it and another stay in it forever. In case you're interested, you have no major injuries. No broken bones. The fingertips of your hands were scraped off completely and will require time to heal. I'm afraid," she smiled knowingly, "you won't be doing any typing for a while."

He wondered how it was that she knew his occupation. The trio of nurses standing in the doorway and the nurse to his left all smiled identical little smiles. They all knew too. They all seemed to know something about him and regarded him with eyes usually reserved for the famous.

"Considering the nature of the accident," Dr. Clare told him, "it's really a miracle that you're still in one piece."

There was something in the sound of the word "miracle" as pronounced by Dr. Clare that was too clipped and hurried and lacked the quality of expansiveness one usually associated with the meaning of that word.

This miracle sounded lonely on her lips.

A miracle for one.

Like a lonely Thanksgiving dinner for one.

The implication of it caused him to contract his conscious mind into a compressed dot of matter that nothing could penetrate. The fury of his denial met with momentary success, but its futility was a foregone conclusion. His teeth clenched with such force that several of them buckled and broke. The tip of his tongue, which had been pressing against them, now pushed forward. The broken tooth splinters tore at his tongue, drawing blood. Bits of broken teeth mixed with the broth of saliva and blood in his mouth and then the whole mess began to slide magmalike down his throat. He gagged. Then he began to vomit.

This was how he acknowledged to himself that both Billy and Leila were dead.

## 7

A police officer came to see him. They went to the third-floor hospital lounge to talk, Saul's hospital-issue slippers snapping at his heels as he walked down the linoleum-covered corridor.

They sat down on chairs upholstered in green Naugahyde that had been worn smooth and discolored by a countless procession of patients and relatives sitting and squirming on them over the years.

The police officer was young and handsome and possessed the athleticism of a former high school star.

His last name was Kovalev.

"Russian?" Saul asked.

The officer nodded.

"There's supposed to be a large Russian community in Pittsburgh," Saul said.

"Not as large as it was," the officer told him.

Saul had no idea at whose request this meeting was arranged and wondered if perhaps its purpose was to inform him that he was to be prosecuted for murder. He felt like a murderer and welcomed the prospect of being carried away by the assembly line of justice. On his own, he had no idea what he would do with the burden of years left in his life. Perhaps this handsome young policeman would tell him.

He was not only disappointed but felt betrayed when Officer Kovalev not only informed him but went to some trouble to assure him that the accident was not his fault.

Officer Kovalev produced a sketch, a Xeroxed copy of the original, and using it as some authoritative document on loan from the Library of Congress, he described to Saul how the accident that had taken four lives occurred.

Here was the road that Saul was on. Here was the blind curve. And here was the dirt road going off to the right.

Saul nodded, eager as always to please.

There was a stop sign right here, the officer indicated with a ballpoint pen. The driver of the other car, there were several witnesses who saw the whole thing, failed to observe the stop sign, intent on making a left turn, and entered the road down which Saul was driving. The Checker hit the Oldsmobile. There were skid marks indicating that Saul had tried to stop before the impact. The driver of the Oldsmobile, a male, was found in the autopsy to have been legally drunk, as was his companion, an out-of-state female. Both were killed instantly.

"I was speeding," Saul said through broken teeth. "I'm positive that I was."

Officer Kovalev looked up from the sketch in his lap and bestowed upon Saul a long, lingering look. Those eyes spoke of many things. Of his glory days as a high school hero. Of the disappointment that the glory days had been so short-lived and led nowhere. Of the gradual diminution of his athletic prowess. Of his attempt to make the best of things in his current occupation. But his gaze also informed Saul that this case was closed, that the blame, during Saul's comatose days, had been assigned and that Saul's opinion that he had been speeding was now neither here nor there.

Saul began to insist on his guilt, but reducing his guilt to a mere case of speeding seemed even more loathsome than being declared innocent of the crime.

His whole life had been a life of crime. To insist now that his responsibility was limited to exceeding the speed limit had the corrupt sound of plea bargaining. He would not stoop that low.

The question of speeding vanished in the silence between them.

The instant death of the couple in the other car caused a frightening question to be born in his mind during that silence.

"You said," he stammered, "that they were killed instantly."

"Yes. Both of them."

"The couple in the Oldsmobile?"

"That's correct."

"And what about . . ." He could not bring himself to pronounce their names. "In my car. The couple in the car I was driving?"

"Same thing."

"Instantly?"

"Yes."

"Both of them."

"Yes."

They sat there in the hospital lounge on the third floor, both dressed in uniforms, the police officer in his blues and Saul in his official hospital-issue green. Both wore name tags. The officer had his on his chest. Saul wore a plastic ID around his wrist.

He didn't know how to phrase the next question properly. It seemed obligatory that even questions should wear proper uniforms.

"Concerning the current status, I mean, as far as the remains of the deceased are . . ."

The officer understood and appreciated the form in which the question was put and took it from there.

Consulting a steno notebook (with a list of often misspelled words on the back cover), Officer Kovalev described the chain of events that had brought the mothers of the deceased to Pittsburgh and the manner in which the remains of the deceased had been taken to their final destinations.

All this was told to Saul in Officer Kovalev's polite and neutral police prose, a genre of communication that was beginning to grow on Saul the longer he sat in the hospital lounge.

They had found Billy's driver's license in his wallet, giving his home address. They got the telephone number for that address from the telephone company. Dianah answered the phone. There were no details about her response to the news. She flew out to Pittsburgh in order to identify the body at the morgue and to claim the remains as her own.

It took longer to notify Leila's mother. The only items of identification on Leila's person were a social security card and a card of a member in good standing of the Screen Actors' Guild.

Both of these, when traced, led to an address in Venice where the telephone recording of the deceased was the only reply in their repeated attempts at trying her number.

A gentleman from the film industry, Mr. Jay Cromwell, showing up at the police station after he heard of the accident, offered his assistance. Through his intercession and several calls to Los Angeles, he was able to determine that Leila's birthplace was Charleston, South Carolina, in which city Leila's mother still resided. When the prospect of travel to Pittsburgh on such short notice and for such a purpose proved both emotionally and financially too taxing for her, Mr. Cromwell interceded again and chartered not only a private plane to fly her out but a driver and a car to take her to the airport. He also made all the arrangements for the transport of Leila's remains back to Charleston. Billy's remains were flown back by Dianah.

The status of the personal belongings left in the hotel was this. Billy's were signed for and taken by Dianah. His own and Leila's things were still in storage at the Four Seasons Hotel, where they could be picked up at his convenience.

No, Officer Kovalev did not know anything about the nature of the funeral arrangements of either Billy or Leila.

Was there anything else he could tell him? Any other questions?

No, Saul shook his head. But he wished he could keep the young officer as a permanent companion who would render into neutral police prose the remainder of his life.

As soon as Officer Kovalev left, Saul's capacity to focus departed as well. A dull, incoherent, but widespread pain engulfed him. A pain without a center or precedence or a proper person to feel it.

He meant to get up, to leave this hospital lounge, and return to his room, but he didn't know as who.

So he sat there, in his Naugahyde-upholstered chair, with his hands in his lap, as if waiting for somebody. All eight of his fingers and both thumbs were capped with white bandages down to the knuckle. He remembered a movie of a criminal who had tried to burn off his fingerprints with acid and grow new ones so that he could elude the FBI and start a new life. Unfortunately the experiment didn't work. After much pain, the fingerprints regenerated themselves into the exact same pattern as before.

Saul now knew what that felt like. The old was intolerable and all hope for the new was gone.

## 8

His telephone had been disconnected while he had been in the coma. There were many messages for him taken by the hospital switchboard. He didn't want any of them. He took them but didn't read them. Nor did he want his telephone to be made operational. There was no one he wanted to call, nor was there anybody he wanted to call him.

## 9

On his last Sunday in the hospital a priest appeared in his room, just as he was waking up from another dreamless sleep. The priest, another man in uniform, was tall and thin with thinning hair. He was almost a one-man exemplar of thinning, he seemed to be thinning as he stood there, his voice thinning as he spoke and offered Saul the services of a nondenominational chapel on the fifth floor. The service would start in forty-five minutes and then again at eleven fifteen.

"Sometimes," the priest said, "it helps to turn to God in times of woe."

"God," as pronounced by the priest, sounded so thin and insubstantial that Saul agreed to come to the early service.

He took the elevator to the fifth floor and followed the signs to the chapel. It was a small chapel with benches on which sat people in pajamas and bathrobes, all facing the same way, as they would in a movie theater or a concert.

Something about this image struck him as wrong and self-deceiving.

The whole notion of turning to God struck him as absurd. If there was a God, then surely you were surrounded by Him and couldn't avoid turning to Him even if you tried. If there was no God, then turning in some agreed-upon direction in order to find him was a gesture of such futility that he was better off without it.

So he took the elevator back to the third floor.

## 10

Two days later, after undergoing some final tests in regard to the sequence and the pattern of his brainwaves, he was pronounced fit to resume his normal life and released from the hospital.

His room was by now half filled with flowers sent by secretaries of people he knew in the movie business.

Before checking out, he made the necessary arrangements for the hospital bills he had incurred. No, he told the woman in charge of these things, he had no insurance. He had no health insurance of any kind. But his accountant would take care of it. The nonexorbitance of the hospital bill disappointed him. He would have preferred something in the astronomic range of hundreds of thousands of dollars. His need to pay for what had transpired would not be easily satisfied.

He took a cab to the Four Seasons Hotel. He had spent Thanksgiving in a coma and now Christmas decorations festooned the business district and he heard the sound of Christmas carols. He gave the cab driver a tip so preposterous that there was something underhanded and ugly about the generosity of the donor which the driver perceived and which thus robbed him of whatever joy he might have had in getting such a tip.

"Merry Christmas to you, too," the driver parroted back Saul's greeting, but it was strictly pro forma and without even a hint of sincerity.

At the front desk of the hotel, Saul settled his account for the ill-fated luxury suite in which he and Leila had spent one night. The bill for Billy's room had apparently been paid by Dianah.

A bellboy brought him his garment bag and Leila's suitcase and he, also, was made uneasy by the tip he received from Saul.

Despite the bandages on his fingers, Saul insisted on carrying the bags out of the hotel himself. The pain he inflicted upon himself by doing so was all too slight for his appetite for pain.

Another cab to the airport.

He still had his and Leila's return tickets to New York, but the date of that return had come and gone. His ticket was still valid, but its validity was a joke compared to everything else that had perished and expired. Having no reservation, he bought a ticket on the next available flight to New York City.

It would be a considerable wait, he was told.

Carrying his bags like a traveling salesman defeated by the size of his territory, he went to the gate and sat down to wait.

Flights arrived. Those waiting greeted those disembarking. Other flights took off. New travelers arrived to wait where he was waiting and then they too got up and left and were replaced by others.

From time to time, he regarded Leila's suitcase like some crazed terrorist who knew there was a bomb inside of it.

He didn't know what to do with it. With that dress. That wedding gown. That once-in-a-lifetime dress meant for the premiere of her one and only film.

Once again and for the last time the film had rolled on without her. And Billy.

As on a tape loop, a single thought kept going around and around in his mind. A son separated from his mother at birth and then separated again from her, their remains flown to different destinations after their deaths.

He, Saul, had brought them together for a brief period of time. For what?

What had he done, what had he done, by trying to play God?

His pain was so huge, he couldn't get at it to feel it. All he could feel was a profound depression at his inability to rise to the occasion and be savaged by the pain. Be torn to shreds.

When his plane began to board, he took the name tags off his garment bag and Leila's suitcase and dropped them into a trash container. Then, after making sure that there was nothing in either piece of baggage to identify its owners, he left the bags where they were and boarded the plane with nothing in his hands except a boarding pass and the bandages on his fingers.

The plane took off on time, shortly before sunset, and in making a sweeping turn it dipped its wing to Saul's side. With his forehead pressed against the window, Saul beheld the confluence of the three rivers below. Nor was he spared the memory of the metaphorical meaning he had assigned to that confluence in happier times.

All gone.

For so long, it seemed, and with such high hopes, he had waited for the trip to Pittsburgh and the happy ending he had conceived.

And now?

Now he felt like some doomed, hubristic voyager who had endeavored to journey through time and space so that he could behold his own future. Defying the odds and the gods, he had set his course for nothing less than that. The price for his arrogance was high. His spacecraft collided with his future and in the resulting explosion his future was destroyed and everyone on board perished except for himself. He alone was rescued and was now being flown back to earth, where he would have to live out his days in the knowledge that he had no future.

# CHAPTER TWO

## I

Some families just keep on growing in wealth and power, as if each successive generation is genetically driven to outdo the previous ones. Other families begin well, gather momentum, seem destined for greatness, only suddenly and inexplicably to lose their vitality and sink back into mediocrity.

Individuals are subject to the same unpredictable laws of rise and fall.

In the beginning, the story lines of individuals are almost always epic in nature, beginning with the drama of birth. What could be more epic than that?

The epic of growing takes it from there. The sense of progress and overcoming challenges is a daily thing when the hero is a toddler. The hero walks. The hero talks. There is much applause and cheering from his parents to convince even the most modest toddler that he's bound for some glorious destiny.

The oral tradition of recapitulating every deed the young hero performs is not lost on him. A day spent saying a few barely coherent words and taking a dozen or so stumbling steps on his own takes on the aura of heroic accomplishment. He hears his name mentioned over and over again. His illnesses are catastrophic. His recoveries, festivals of rejoicing.

To the hero, to the toddler, to the child, he is not just a child. He is made to feel like a redeemer come to rescue the kingdom of the household from certain destruction. Just by being born, he has accomplished much and is made to feel like the child of whom it was said, "And unto us a child is born."

The epic continues. The epic of the young body growing. The mind expanding. The metamorphosis of both.

Somewhere along the way, he develops his own internal narrator, the I of the hero, the storyteller who speaks in his name. The narration of this personal story line almost always favors the epic genre as the only one suitable for the job.

The I of the hero proclaims, "I am," "I like," "I don't like."

Certain epic phrases are used to connect disparate episodes into a coherent story line. Phrases such as "And then I . . ." or "And after that I . . ."

The epic of puberty. The epic of first love. Of sexual initiation.

Somewhere along the way, the cheering that attended his every act tapers off.

But that's all right.

The epic of leaving home picks up the story line just in time and takes it to a new and higher level. Oh, the epic of leaving home. What could be more epic than going off to college in a car of one's own with the hero at the wheel, captain, navigator, and crew all in one. The car radio is playing, but the real music the hero hears is the music of the first-person narrator, the I inside his mind, the voice that says, "And then I . . ." or "After that I . . ."

There is a sense of progress again as the hero works his way up through the ranks from freshman to sophomore and so on. He is asked to join a Greek fraternity. Not the undisputed number one fraternity he wanted to join, but it's one that's right up there with the rest. He is disappointed, to be sure, but he thinks of his disappointment as a learning experience and his accommodation to reality as something that sharpens his skills of survival. In no time at all, his disappointment is transformed into the "best thing that could have happened to me."

"It taught me that I . . ."

"After that I never again . . ."

The epic of going home for the holidays.

How small the kingdom of the household now seems to him. Claustrophobic, almost. How much taller he is than his father. He takes to draping his arm around his father's narrow shoulders and assuming classical poses in doing so.

The growing distance between the hero and his parents only confirms to him that he is growing himself, branching out, heading forth, and that they're not.

But they are still, after all, his parents. He still loves them and is moved profoundly by his capacity to love them.

And then he's off again, back to the campus.

Car radio playing.

But the song that's being sung is a song of himself.

"And then I . . ."

He has no idea where his story line is going, but what epic hero ever did? Destiny awaits.

The girl he falls in love with on the campus, madly in love, from the number one Greek sorority, is unfortunately in love with someone else and nothing the hero does seems to convince her that she's in love with an out-and-out barbarian. An animal. A dumb jock. A human genital. The hero suffers much over this unrequited love, but not for long, because he has developed a mechanism for dealing with such episodes. In no time it becomes "the best thing that could have happened to me."

There are not only many fish in the sea but there are many seas as well, and so he's off again on yet another voyage.

Away from that provincial Midwest campus to the city of the rising sun. New York City. Grad school. The first apartment of his very own. What could be more epic than that?

New York City, he discovers, is full of epic heroes like himself. Their numbers suggest a swollen army of heroes gathering there for some epic campaign against the established order.

There is a sense of progress again, but not as exhilarating as before. From master's degree to PhD dissertation in three years. He becomes a doctor without a practice. In the meantime he has fallen in love with a girl who has also fallen in love with him. He is thrilled by both aspects of this love affair, but more so by the latter than the former.

For reasons that he can't quite explain, his story line starts to lose its epic quality. There is a sense that he has arrived somewhere without having reached any destination in particular. The comfort of arrival, however, feels pleasant. He thinks of it as temporary. Just a little pause before he sails away again in pursuit of his destiny.

The epic story line of his life remains in his mind. It's vivid for a while. Then it starts to fade. First from reality and then from memory.

The first-person narrator within him, the I within him, begins to sound like the I of other people he knows, as if his I were interchangeable with theirs.

He comes to terms with this. He discovers that he has a genuine talent for coming to terms with things. He takes to drink, and in an unconscious homage to his lost story line he becomes an epic drunk. His talent for coming to terms with things allows him to come to terms with being a drunk. Once again, he has a sense of progress as he succeeds in coming to terms with an ever vaster array of things in his life. Without much fanfare, his story line goes from the epic genre to the tragic and from the tragic to the tragicomic, until it finally settles down to farce.

Whatever journey he had been on is over. There is no sense of direction or motion in his life anymore. Only the years roll on, like waves washing away the I'm-still-young phase, the I'm-not-yet-old phase, bringing on middle age.

He comes to terms with it all.

And just when he has accepted and accommodated himself to both the brevity and the banality of his life, just then (let's suppose) something happens.

A story suddenly presents itself to him.

The story is perfection itself. It has a beginning and a middle and a glorious happy ending, which promises (as he sees it) to be an even more glorious beginning of the rest of his life.

When this happens to a man in midlife, it's like falling madly in love for the first time. The passions aroused, actually, are even more profound. No young Romeo ever loved a Juliet with more abandon than a middle-aged man loves the story line of his one last grasp at salvation.

But when, for whatever reason, such a story line suffers a sudden and catastrophic conclusion, more than a story line is lost. All is lost.

There is no falling back upon the comfortable despair where one has lived before. Not now. There is no fall-back position this late in life.

This, more or less, was the situation in which Saul found himself after Pittsburgh.

## 2

Saul has survived. Billy and Leila, on the other hand, are dead. But their story, unbeknownst to Saul, unbeknownst to anyone at the moment, is just beginning.

These things happen.

They have happened in centuries and countries other than ours: the premature and catastrophic end of a life coincides with the birth of the story line of the deceased. In the old times (real old times), deaths gave rise to legends. In our times, the legends are called newspaper stories.

For the moment, whatever moment this may be, the story of Billy and Leila is confined to a modest newspaper article in the Pittsburgh *Sun*. It is the story of an ill-fated traffic accident, the death of an actress by the name of Leila Millar, and the preview of her movie, *Prairie Schooner*, that very night in a theater in Pittsburgh. The producer of the movie, Jay Cromwell, is quoted as calling the accident a real tragedy. In his opinion, Ms. Millar was poised to become a star, perhaps even a superstar, as all those who see her performance in this movie will agree. He hates comparisons, since all human beings are unique, but in his opinion Leila Millar had the talent and that ineffable something to become another Judy Holliday.

Billy's name appears in the same article as someone who was also killed in the car.

It gives his full name and age and the fact that he was a sophomore at Harvard.

Saul is mentioned as the sole survivor who is currently in a coma and whose condition is described as serious. He is further mentioned as being Billy's father and a well-known script doctor in Hollywood.

Not much is said about the couple in the other car, other than their names, ages, and the fact that the driver of the car was legally drunk at the time of the accident and failed to heed a stop sign.

And that, essentially, is that.

A modest story.

But such a modest beginning is in no way indicative of the eventual sweep that an initially tiny story can attain. Once a story becomes public, anything can happen to it.

It's not just people living in Pittsburgh who read Pittsburgh newspapers. Some traveler from somewhere, pausing at the Pittsburgh International Airport to wait for a connecting flight, can easily pick up the local paper to while away the time. Who knows who he or she might be, or for whom he or she works or used to work? There, in the local paper, is the story of Leila and Billy and Saul. Maybe the name of one of them rings a bell. Or maybe all three names ring a bell. Maybe the reader doesn't know any of them personally but knows someone who does.

There are public telephones everywhere at the airport. With one phone call, the story of Leila and Billy and Saul can go directly from the Pittsburgh International Airport to the desk of some adoption lawyer in New York or some other individual who has information not included in the story as written.

Public stories are different from private stories. Public stories, by their very nature, are not really stories but stories of stories, once or twice removed from the individuals in the story. And just as second or third generations of computers are deemed superior to the original prototypes, second- or third-generation stories are likewise deemed superior in every way to the original story of some private person who has become public.

And so, although both Billy and Leila are dead, the story of their story has just begun.

# CHAPTER THREE

I

Saturday night, mid-December.

He's standing on the corner of Eighty-third and Broadway, right next to Harry's Shoes, shivering. It's a chilly night, but his shivering is caused more by the anxiety of what he's contemplating than by the cold air. A fear similar to stage fright is making his mouth dry.

He looks like somebody who's both paralyzed and out of control at the same time. A man capable of doing anything or nothing at all.

The once-clean white bandages on his fingers are now dirty and frayed and have the appearance of makeshift gloves favored by the lunatic fringe of the New York City homeless.

Northbound and southbound, the crowd moves past him along the crowded sidewalk. Christmas is less than a couple of weeks away and the spirit of pre-Christmas is in the air. Shiny, freshly minted shopping bags swing past him heading uptown and downtown. Not far away, to his right, half the width of the sidewalk is taken up by a little forest of Christmas trees for sale. The vendor of the trees has a little black boom box out of which issue instrumental arrangements of Christmas carols. The tape is either stretched or Saul's ears are playing him false, because the music sounds wobbly and elongated, as if there were no individual notes, just something called music.

People come and go and Saul stands there shivering, waiting for the moment of inspiration or desperation to propel him forward and make him do what he has come here to do.

He tried to do it the night before and failed, just as he failed the night before that.

Loss of nerve.

Even a man who has lost everything still has his inhibitions. They're the very last thing to go.

His appearance, the dirty, frayed bandages on his fingers, the broken teeth suggestive of some violent encounter, the constant working of his facial muscles as if he is engaged in some ferocious inner struggle with himself, all this causes the people on the sidewalk to give him a wide berth as they walk past.

In a revival of a Jacobean play in modern dress, Saul Karoo would now be perfect casting for an assassin with a dagger in his hand and murder in his heart, waiting in ambush for his victim to appear.

## 2

This transformation in his physical appearance took only a few weeks.

Upon his return from Pittsburgh, Saul tried to resume his former life, only to discover that there was no former life there to resume. Whatever story line or plot had driven his life perished on that road in Pennsylvania.

The word had gone out about the accident and while he was lying in a coma in that hospital in Pittsburgh people called and left messages on his answering machine.

Expressions of regret. Condolences. Offers of sympathy.

On his first night back in his apartment, he sat down next to the answering machine and listened to all the messages on the cassette.

Some were long. Some short. But he couldn't listen properly to any of them.

Somebody was required to be there listening to these messages and he seemed incapable of being the Saul to whom these messages were addressed. The Saul in question.

He sat there listening, but it was as if he were not there at all.

It was as if his responses to the messages he heard were prerecorded themselves, as if he were a machine listening while another machine spoke.

His insomnia began that night.

Even sleep, it seemed, required an identity to be relinquished as one fell asleep. But he could not conjure up an identity to relinquish. There seemed to be nobody to let go of.

So he stayed awake. He walked around the living room. He sat down in the swivel chair by the window and swiveled.

But being awake without being anyone in particular didn't seem like being awake.

He was neither asleep nor awake, neither this nor that. It was some new state that he was in, some new kind of nonexistence.

He tried, as a way of actualizing himself, to come to grips with his guilt. He tried, as a way of feeling something, to feel the pain of Billy's and Leila's deaths.

He could not.

The guilt was there. The pain was there. But he could not get at them. They seemed to be once removed from him, like the sound of a television one hears in a hotel room next door. It seemed to him that he had come out of one kind of coma in that hospital in Pittsburgh only to fall into another kind, the conscious coma of everyday life from which there was no recovery.

## 3

There were many phone calls in the days that followed from people he knew and from people he had known a long time ago and almost forgotten. Some who called, like Guido, had already left messages on his machine and were calling again to talk to him in person. Others were calling for the first time.

The McNabs, George and Pat, called.

His former accountant, Arnold, and his current accountant, Jerry, called.

Dr. Bickerstaff, his former doctor, called.

Various studio executives for whom he had worked on scripts at various studios called. Knowing there was nothing they would be asked to do, they asked if there was anything they could do for him. Anything.

Although he initially resented answering the telephone, he discovered that the loneliness of his nonexistence was lessened when he listened to someone talking or talked himself. This led him to look forward to people calling and he spent the intervals between calls waiting for the phone to ring and bring him back to a life of some kind.

It mattered very little to him who called. Since the art of extending telephone condolences tended to make everyone sound alike, it was like getting the same call over and over again. But that was fine with him.

Listening to the person at the other end created, if nothing else, the illusion that Saul too was a person. Since it required two people to carry on a conversation, it stood to reason that he was, if nothing else, one of the two.

The banalities that the callers by necessity used in expressing their sympathy did not seem banal to him. Far from it. He embraced them wholeheartedly and he became whoever it was the caller said he was.

"It's very hard for you right now, I know, but as hard as it is, you must . . . ," a caller would say, and to Saul's mind the caller seemed to know the exact quality of hardness that he, Saul, was experiencing.

And so, while the call lasted, Saul became a Man Who Had It Hard.

"I know you're suffering right now," another caller told him, "but you must be strong and see this thing through. It's times like these that test us and make us stronger so that when we come out at the other end we can . . ."

And while the caller talked and Saul listened, he became a Man Who Was Suffering, but a man who had to be Strong because he was being Tested. He had to See This Thing Through so that when he came Out at the Other End . . . and so on.

And there were calls that, as long as they lasted, made him behold the possibility that somewhere in the future another story line awaited him. It didn't matter to him what the story would be so long as he could hitch a ride.

4

And then Cromwell called.

And he called himself, with no Brad, white or black, to announce him.

"Saul," he said. "Jay."

"Jay," Saul cried out as if he were being rescued.

It had been a bad week. The calls had gradually dried up. Yesterday there had only been one. It was early evening now and Jay Cromwell was the first person to call that day and extract him from his nonexistence.

Cromwell made it seem that it had taken enormous self-discipline and consideration not to have called earlier. As he explained, "I knew what you were going through and I knew that you didn't want to talk to anyone for a while."

Saul thanked him for not having called. Although Saul would have gladly talked to anyone on the face of the earth who wanted to call him, he had no difficulty in molding himself now around the banality Cromwell offered and seeing himself as the man Cromwell thought him to be, a Man Who Had to Suffer in Silence because That's the Kind of Man He Was.

This version of himself was just as valid as its opposite or any other version in between. The beauty of banalities, as Saul was discovering, was that they allowed you to be somebody for a while. The horror of truth was that it didn't.

"What can I say," Cromwell said, "what in the world can I say? I'm still in a state of shock over the whole thing, so I can only imagine how you feel."

Tell me, Saul felt like asking, please tell me how you imagine I feel so I can feel it too.

"The only thing I can tell you," Cromwell told him, "is that I feel humbled by the awesome proportions of your tragedy. I truly feel humbled just to be talking to you. I hope you don't mind my saying that."

Saul assured him that he didn't.

"I hope I'm not intruding."

Saul assured him that he wasn't.

"If I am, just say so."

Even in his current condition of psychic disintegration, Saul still had the presence of mind to remember that he should be grateful to Cromwell. After all, it was Cromwell who had made the necessary arrangements to have Leila's mother flown to Pittsburgh and then back to Charleston with Leila's remains.

Saul tried to thank him, but Cromwell refused to be thanked.

"Please," Cromwell cut him off in mid-gratitude. "Surely you're not going to thank me for acting like a simple, decent human being. I did nothing that somebody else would not have done in my place, so, I beg you, Saul, out of respect for our friendship which I treasure, let this be the last time that the subject of gratitude of any kind comes up between us."

"All right, Jay, but still . . ." Saul stammered.

They talked some more about life and pain and the inexplicable manner in which catastrophes occurred in the lives of men.

And then, after inquiring several times in several ways into Saul's current spiritual state and after listening patiently to Saul's replies, Cromwell segued, but almost as an afterthought, into another but tangential topic.

There seemed to be a growing interest in Leila's story, he told Saul. In the story of this ill-fated actress who was struck down suddenly on the way to the screening of her first film.

"I know, I know," Cromwell said. "I realize that I must sound ghoulish to you to be talking about newspaper stories at a time like this, and to tell you the truth I feel a little ghoulish about it myself. I can't think straight. That's why I'm calling you. I need some help in this matter. Some guidance. You see, the way I feel is this. Leila was someone special and people should know about her and her movie. I guess what I'm saying is that, in my opinion, anything that we can do to make sure that as many people as possible see her in her one and only film is a duty we cannot ignore. We owe it to her . . ."

"I'm not talking about publicity," Cromwell went on. "That really would be ghoulish under the circumstances. No, all I'm talking about is having her story known, because I think her story deserves to be known. What I'm talking about here is something on the order of a testament to her and her tragically aborted career. However, if you think I'm off base here and if, in your opinion, the whole thing seems inappropriate, then just say so and I'll never mention it again."

The idea of a testament to Leila struck a responsive chord in Saul's heart. He had no idea what story it was that Cromwell considered to be Leila's story, but if it was a testament of some kind, then he was all for it.

And he said as much.

Cromwell accepted his approval as the authoritative statement on the subject and thanked Saul for helping him out of this moral dilemma.

"In that case," he told Saul, "if you're for it, we'll proceed."

The rest of the conversation was devoted once again to topics of life and pain and the inexplicable manner in which tragedies occurred in the lives of men.

"What a tragedy," Cromwell kept saying.

"It's a real American tragedy is what it is," he said, and he said it in a way that implied that there was something inherently more tragic about American tragedies than there was about tragedies of other nations.

The conversation ended with Cromwell's plea for Saul "to hang in there."

Saul promised to try.

Hanging in there seemed like a vivid and a purposeful activity until he hung up the phone and then, alone again, he had no idea what it meant "to hang in there" nor how such an activity was to be carried out by him.

Nor did he have any idea about what it was that had been concluded in his telephone transaction with Cromwell.

## 5

And then the telephone calls dried up completely.

Nobody called.

His insomnia made him nervous and edgy.

The noose of privacy tightened around him. Sometimes it seemed like an actual noose around his throat.

A phone call would save him, but the phone didn't ring.

He considered calling somebody himself but couldn't decide who it should be.

After much thought, he resolved to call his mother in Chicago. He picked up the receiver and extended his index finger to dial.

But then he just sat there with his index finger frozen in midair, because he didn't know who was calling her.

He had to be somebody in order to make the call, but he couldn't decide who to be.

Life of any kind, existence itself, seemed impossible.

Privacy suddenly revealed itself to him to be a dying planet that could no longer sustain life.

His only hope for survival was to flee. To go public. Which was what he did.

## 6

It's still the same Saturday night in mid-December and Saul is still standing shivering outside Harry's Shoes on the corner of Eighty-third and Broadway.

Snatches of monologues roll through his mind, and his lips move as if he is rehearsing them aloud.

Monologues addressed to all kinds of people, alive and dead, including several to himself.

Right across from Harry's Shoes, where he is standing, is a public pay phone.

His nerve failed him last night and the night before that but, as if in compensation for his failure, his need to give voice to his monologues has grown as well.

He goes to the pay phone and picks up the receiver, but he suddenly becomes confused. He forgets completely that he doesn't need to put any money into the box, or actually dial any number in order to have the conversation he plans to have. But for verisimilitude he drops a quarter into the slot and dials his own number.

The telephone rings five times and then it stops. The answering machine comes on.

"Hi, this is Saul Karoo. I can't answer the phone right now, but if you leave a message I'll get back to you as soon as possible."

The recording he hears was made when he first moved to his new apartment on Riverside Drive. His former voice, at the time the recording was made, now sounds to his ears like the voice of some happy, innocent fool living happily in a fool's paradise.

The innocence and optimism in that voice cause Saul on the pay phone to gasp in pain for the poor man who made the recording.

Although he doesn't feel that he knows him well, or ever did, his heart now goes out to him for the reverses and losses he has suffered.

"Oh, Saul," he says. He starts out softly, still lacking confidence as a phone freak, but his voice rises as he goes on.

"God, Saul, I just heard what happened! Is it true? Tell me it's not true. It is. Really! Not both of them. Oh, no. Oh, dear God, not both of them, Saul. Not Leila and Billy as well. Both dead. No. How? Why? . . ."

Initially hesitant to give expression to his pain in public, Saul feels all hesitation fall away as he goes on.

"But they were both so young, so very young, and their whole lives were . . ."

It's not that he's so carried away by his performance as to become blind to the people, the spectators, the audience moving past him in both directions on the crowded Saturday-night sidewalk. Just the opposite.

He sees the people who see him. He sees them looking at him and he feels transformed into a living entity.

He feels something very elusive and very personal, very private, on the corner of Eighty-third and Broadway, something that had refused to materialize in the privacy of his own apartment.

As if privacy were now possible only in public, where it could both be brought into being and verified in the eyes of passing strangers.

"And you were there when all this happened? In the car. You were driving? Oh, Saul . . ."

He feels his heart breaking for the poor man and he starts to weep. His weeping is restrained at first but then it gradually becomes unrestrained.

"What are you going to do now, Saul? I can't imagine what in the world you will do with yourself. How will you live, knowing that both Leila and Billy are dead? How in God's name will you live with yourself? I feel so sorry for you. So, very, very . . ."

He can't speak anymore for the sobbing.

# CHAPTER FOUR

Inspired, if that's not too strong a word, by his public conversation with himself, Saul returned the next day for an encore. Being a creature of habit, he made a habit out of it, and in the days to come he became an out-and-out public phone freak junkie.

A street person of sorts.

He used his apartment as a place where he could take showers and have his nightly insomnia, but other than that his life was lived in public.

Just as in the old days he used to get up in the morning, take a shower, and go to his office on West Fifty-seventh Street, he now got up, took a shower, and left his apartment at about the same time, to walk the streets of Manhattan and make imaginary calls from public phones.

Except that he now no longer paid or dialed. He just picked up the receiver and started talking.

He wandered down Broadway, down Eighth Avenue past Forty-second Street, all the way down to Penn Station, using pay phones along the way.

Sometimes he took cabs to La Guardia or the JFK airport and spent part of his day at various clusters of pay phones at these places, talking on the telephone, surrounded by travelers who were likewise engaged.

His conversations, if they can be called that, ranged far and wide. Some were local. Some long-distance. Some were with the living and some were with the dead. He still called himself from time to time, and then, as himself, he called others.

He always made sure, however, that there was somebody nearby who could not help overhearing what he was saying.

He called his dead father and tried to convince him that he had tried to love him while he was alive.

He called his mother in Chicago and apologized profusely for not having called her before.

"I've been going through hell, Mom, I really have. Have you heard? Do you know what happened? Billy died. My Billy is dead, Mom. I'm nobody's father anymore and never will be again. I hurt, Mom. I hurt. I don't know what to do with myself anymore. No, no, don't worry. I'll be fine. How are you? . . ."

He called Billy and Leila at least once a day, sometimes two or three times a day.

"Billy, it's Dad. I was just wondering how you're doing, son. No, nothing wrong, I was just calling to see . . ."

"Leila, it's Saul. When are you coming back? I miss you. I miss you so much I can hardly . . ."

Sometimes he wept. Sometimes he told jokes. Sometimes he pleaded with both Leila and Billy to forgive him.

"Please, I beg you . . ."

"Nymph," he cried out once in his call to Leila, "in your orisons be all my sins remembered."

Over and over again, he insisted in his calls to both that he had loved them with all his heart.

And although he broke down and wept on the phone, making a spectacle of himself, something in his sentimental declarations of love failed to satisfy, so that he had to call again.

"I do, I do love you, I really do, why don't you believe me?" he insisted, as if one of them or both of them were casting doubts on his assertions at the other end.

Whether he called Laurie Dohrn to seek her forgiveness or whether he called Arthur Houseman to seek his for ruining his film ("I loved your film. I adored it. It was a masterpiece"), almost all his public phone calls were designed to induce pain in him.

He welcomed guilt and pain and embraced them with open arms.

But it was only guilt and public pain that he embraced and the public remorse that went with them.

His public torment was pleasant in comparison to the torment that awaited him in the privacy of his apartment at night.

# CHAPTER FIVE

On the night of the premiere of *Prairie Schooner* in Pittsburgh, Cromwell, having been informed about Leila's death in a car accident, gave a little impromptu speech to the audience before the film began.

"Ladies and gentlemen," he told them, "it is with profound regret that I inform you about the tragic death of the star of this film. None of you here know her name, not one of you has ever seen or heard of her before, but I assure you that after you have seen this one and only film of her tragically aborted career, you will never forget her. Ladies and gentlemen, allow me to introduce you to . . . Leila Millar."

The lights went down. The movie began. When Leila's name appeared on the screen (AND INTRODUCING LEILA MILLAR), there was a smattering of applause.

It is impossible to know if Cromwell's impromptu speech had the effect of predisposing the audience toward liking the film, or if the film itself was solely responsible for their ecstatic response. A standing ovation.

There was no TV coverage of the premiere, since there were no big stars in the movie, but a local TV station ran a story about Leila on its evening news the following evening.

Helen Landau, a coanchor of the evening news, went out to the site of the accident with a small crew and shot the following segment.

Mike in hand, Helen walked along the shoulder of highway 381.

"A dream of stardom ended here yesterday," Helen said, looking right into the camera.

She talked about Leila not only playing a waitress in the movie but having been a waitress in real life. A working-class girl. She talked about this being her first film.

"And so," Helen concluded, "on what was to have been the happiest day of her life, a young woman, perhaps meant for stardom, died on this seemingly peaceful spot along state highway 381. But who knows, though stars die, their light shines on for generations, as perhaps will the light of . . . Leila Millar."

The segment ended with a publicity still of Leila's face from the movie, smiling her smile.

And so, while Saul was lying in a coma in that hospital in Pittsburgh, Leila's story began to grow.

According to Cromwell's original schedule, there were to be two more sneak previews before the film was released, but the advance word generated by Leila's death created a demand that necessitated adding more sneaks to the schedule.

Normally, a large ad was placed in the papers of the city where the preview was to play, but that was no longer needed. The story of Leila's story, along with a large picture of her, appeared in the newspapers of each city that was added to the schedule. On the night of the preview, the crowds in each city showed up in turn-away numbers.

There was just something about Leila's story, even before her so-called full story was known, that caused it to spread. Even those people who only saw a movie every two years or so wanted to see Leila's movie when they heard about her and her story.

A working-class girl. A waitress. Plucked from anonymity, where most people spend their lives, to be the star of a movie. And then to die on the day of the movie's premiere, so that she never even got to see herself on the screen. All this created a tragic poignancy that was hard to resist, and a marketing bonanza that even a marketing genius like Cromwell could not have created on his own.

What made him the genius that he was, evil or otherwise, was the way he took control of it.

Even before the extended sneak preview schedule was concluded, he was getting telephone calls from representatives of large movie theater chains, which caused him to reconsider the release pattern for the movie. It seemed possible now to postpone the opening date and instead of opening gradually, to open the film on the same day all around the country, as if he had a blockbuster hit on his hands and not a small art movie.

Having all those Leila stories in all those newspapers was fine for the time being, but his experience with stories of this kind, with stories of any kind, warned him that it could all lead to an oversaturation of the marketplace long before the film opened.

Therefore what he needed was a definitive Leila story waiting in the wings, one of those feature-length bio pieces written by a reputable journalist with impeccable credentials.

A Pulitzer Prize–winning writer currently unemployed because his newspaper had recently folded came to Cromwell's attention.

The man was getting on in years and his chances of being picked up by another paper (because of his age and his politics) did not seem very good.

He had won the Pulitzer Prize for his coverage of the civil war in Angola, but that was a long time ago and the civil war was still going on.

Cromwell called him, explained the nature of the project, and offered the kind of money that precluded needing time to think it over.

A deal was struck. Verbal at first, on the telephone, and then a formal contract was signed.

In all fairness to Cromwell, he had no idea where the story of Leila would lead. All he knew about her was what everybody knew. If he knew anything else, it was that she and Saul had been having an affair.

And because he knew this, he placed that circumspect call to Saul to see if he objected to having Leila's story made public. He wanted it to be on the record that he had Saul's approval to proceed.

And Saul, having no idea what he was agreeing to, gave it.

The same principles of investigative journalism apply whether you're writing about the civil war in Angola, insider trading on Wall Street, or the story of Leila Millar. If you're a scrupulous journalist, which this journalist was, and if you have a nose for the story, which he had, you sniff out the heartbeat of the story and then you follow it wherever it goes.

In what was supposed to be a perfunctory interview with Leila's mother in Charleston, South Carolina, one of those mother interviews you had to have for a piece of this kind, our Pulitzer Prize–winning journalist found, or had handed to him by the mother, the heartbeat of the story. The baby that Leila had when she was fourteen and that she gave up for adoption.

The rest was not necessarily easy, but neither was it as difficult as one might imagine.

People working for hospitals and for adoption lawyers tend to uphold the confidentiality they're supposed to uphold so long as they remain employed. Once they leave their jobs or are fired, they are not quite so strict with themselves.

When Cromwell was informed where the story was headed, he made only one request and that was for the journalist to leave Saul alone.

"I don't want you to bother him," Cromwell told him over the telephone. "He has suffered enough."

# CHAPTER SIX

## 1

The story, before it came out as a story, was preceded by rumors of its existence that spread from west to east via phone and fax lines. Then little excerpts from it appeared in various publications. And then the Story itself appeared in a well-known and highly reputable national magazine.

It was simply called "Leila," subtitled "An American Tragedy." Later it would be expanded and published as a book bearing the same name but a different subtitle: *Leila: A Love Story*. The Pulitzer Prize–winning author of the original story and of the book would eventually receive his second Pulitzer Prize, this time in the field of biography.

But for the time being, March 1991, it was still a magazine story called "Leila," but it was about Saul and Billy as well, and their tragic love triangle.

The story had everything in it, as one critic put it, except murder.

## 2

When the magazine story came out, Saul decided to flee town. To flee from the phone calls he was getting. From the publicity the story was generating. From the celebrity status he was acquiring. But most of all to flee from the terrible temptation to become the simplified and sanitized and slightly glorified Saul Karoo the story said he was and the public took him to be. Even Dianah, who hadn't spoken to him since Billy's death, called him on the phone and was ready to forgive him after she read the story. He fled from her forgiveness as well.

## 3

He had no destination in mind, but he had a suitcase and a passport when he arrived at Kennedy Airport.

He stared at the names of cities, domestic and foreign, for which the airplanes of airlines, domestic and foreign, were bound.

For hours, no destination presented itself to him and he hung around the airport, a vagrant in desperate need of a voyage to somewhere.

And then, a destination finally appeared to him. He would flee to the city where he was born (Chicago), to the house where he was raised, and to the woman (his mother) who had given birth to him.

### 4

The March he left in New York was not the March he encountered in Chicago. A late winter storm had blown in from the west and it took two hours by cab, through swirling snow, to get from O'Hare to Homerlee Avenue.

He recognized the neighborhood, the street, the house, but not his mother when she opened the door. Nor did she seem to recognize him. Not until he said, more as a question than a greeting, "Mother?"

"Saul?" she replied, in the same interrogative tone.

They stood there in the doorway, both bareheaded, she squinting up at him, he looking down at her. The falling, swirling snow fell on both of them in equal measure. The snow covered Saul's thinning gray hair and his mother's recently dyed and incredibly black hair.

As black, he thought to himself, as my black Remington typewriter in my office on West Fifty-seventh Street.

Finally, his mother moved back and aside, pulling the door, and Saul, changing the suitcase from one hand to the other, stepped inside.

### 5

The preliminary conversation between mother and son flowed rapidly. There was an eagerness on both sides to maintain the sounds of their voices for as long as possible without a pause. And so, in this preliminary conversation, a lot of ground got covered.

The weather was a real mess, they both agreed.

Terrible day for travel.

Did he know (he didn't) that they had closed O'Hare Airport? She had just heard it on the radio before he arrived. His must have been one of the last flights allowed to land.

Since he never came to visit her (not since college) just to see her, but stopped by on his way to somewhere else, she asked where he was going.

He considered, but not for long, telling her the truth. That he had come here to seek shelter from the world. Had, in fact, come just to see her. But he was afraid to tell her this.

And so, instead, he told her that he was on his way to Los Angeles. And as these things have a way of doing, as soon as he told her where he was going, he knew that he would go there.

"Business of some kind?" she asked.

"Yes."

"Movies?"

"Yes."

In the semipause that followed and threatened to expand into a full-fledged silence, they both turned their attention to the snowstorm outside as seen through the windows of the dining room.

"It just keeps coming down," he said.

"Shows no signs of stopping," she pitched in gamely.

But the silence, like some age-old malady for which there was still no cure, returned and settled upon them.

They tried to shake it off, but their combined efforts fell short.

"I guess I better go unpack," he said, sighing as he rose to his feet, as if unpacking were a full day's job waiting for him.

"Where do you want to sleep?" she asked, as she always did.

"In the den," he answered, as he always answered.

"The sheets are clean. They've been on the bed for some time, but they're clean. I'll get you some towels."

On his way down the stairs to the den in the basement, suitcase in one hand, towels in the other, his mother's voice followed him from the top of the landing. The farther away he went, the louder she talked so that his impression of the volume of her voice was of something constant, like the speed of light.

"I already ate. I have dinner early these days. I didn't know you were coming, otherwise I would have waited. But I'll warm up some stew for you. Or I can make you something else if you don't want stew. It's lamb stew. It's very good. But I can make you something else if you want. I have some . . ."

"Stew sounds great," he shouted back. "I'll be right up."

## 6

In the wood-paneled (knotty pine) den in the basement, which went by the name of "guest room," Saul went through the charade of unpacking.

Charade, because he never unpacked when he came here. He unzipped the long zipper of his suitcase and laid open its contents, but that was as far as he ever got.

He stared at the contents of his suitcase as if both the contents and suitcase belonged to someone else.

In his sudden decision to flee from New York, he had thrown things inside it without thinking. He had no idea what he needed because he had (at the time) no idea where he was going.

Shorts. Socks. Shirts. He fumbled with these items without removing them, taking inventory. A sweater. He had brought along a copy of the magazine with Leila's story, his thinking being that if he took it with him, it meant he wasn't really running away from it. The magazine lay inside the folded sweater.

In addition, and as a kind of counterweight to the story, he had also brought along a copy of the videocassette of the Old Man's film, the Old Man's version.

Saul had kept the cassette hidden in the closet of the spare bedroom in his apartment, so that when Leila was there she would not stumble upon it accidentally.

Why had he taken it along with him?

He had no idea. Maybe he was afraid that in his absence his apartment building might catch on fire and the videocassette would perish. For all he knew, it was the only copy left of the film as it was when it was a work of art.

The cassette lay there among his shorts and socks.

He sat down on the edge of the bed on which the wide-open suitcase lay and was suddenly tempted to lie down himself and go to sleep.

But the lamb stew was being reheated upstairs. The acoustics of the house were such that he could hear his mother's footsteps drumming a beat on the kitchen floor above his head.

He couldn't understand it. His mother had become a shriveled-up sparrow of a woman, but her feet landed like bricks when she walked. Judging from the sound, you'd think she was dropping her feet from the height of her waist. Something to do with old age, perhaps. Lack of muscular control, or something like that. Or maybe the result of living alone in a big house and wanting to hear herself passing through.

This thought and the memory of the way she looked when she opened the door, with the snow falling on her head, looking up at him, and the thought that in all probability this would be the last time he saw her alive, the last time he heard her footsteps pounding patterns on the kitchen floor, all this, and something else too, which he could not put into words, caused him to breathe a long-imprisoned sentimental sigh and to say softly, but out loud, "Oh, Mother. Oh, Mother of mine."

She called him from the landing.

"Saul. Stew's ready."

"Coming," he replied.

## 7

Saul sits at the dining room table, eating his lamb stew out of a deep soup bowl. His mother stands not far away and watches him eat.

It was still light when he arrived and now it's dark. Through the windows of the dining room, illuminated by streetlamps and the headlights of passing cars, he can see the snow falling, swirling, accumulating.

"It's really coming down," his mother says, which is what he was going to say.

"Looks like it's going to snow all night," he says instead.

"You think so?"

"Sure looks like it."

The TV, which had been on in the living room when he arrived, is still on. He knows if he weren't here, his mother would be there watching it.

The lamb stew is terrible. He can't figure out what makes it so terrible, its tastelessness, or some subtle taste that it has. But something is terribly wrong with it.

She goes back from looking out the window to watching him eat.

"How is it?"

"The lamb stew? It's wonderful."

"There's plenty more."

There was a time, Saul thinks, when his mother was a wonderful cook and an immaculate housekeeper and a woman who took great pride in her appearance.

Now she is no longer any of those things.

Saul wonders, as he eats his lamb stew, if she is aware of this decline or not.

Signs of neglect are everywhere. You don't have to look for them to see them. You have to keep looking away in order not to.

His silverware and his soup bowl contain remnants of former meals upon them.

The dishtowel his mother is now worrying with her hands as if it were a rosary is filthy. The furnace keeps coming on and each time it does, the air out of the registers blows little clumps of lint across the floor. Little lint creatures scurrying about like mice.

The House of Karoo, Saul thinks to himself.

He drains the dirty glass of water and his mother, eager for an activity, almost snatches it out of his hands and heads toward the kitchen sink to refill it.

Although he has enough unresolved problems in his life to last him several lifetimes, he casts a scholarly glance at his mother's departing feet and attempts yet again to figure out how it is possible for this wisp of an old woman to make such a racket when she walks. And on slippered feet.

The closest he can come to an explanation is that his mother snaps her feet downward at the last split second prior to contact with the floor, the way a baseball slugger snaps his wrists to crush a grand slam home run. Impossible to see with the naked human eye.

She stands by the sink, glass in hand, and lets the water run, feeling it with her finger.

Saul looks at her, at his mother, in profile.

At the dirty bathrobe she is wearing. Bought in some tourist shop in Santa Fe during a trip she and his father took over a decade ago. Geometric Indian pattern on it. The patterns and the colors were once distinct. Now they are a smudge. It fit her once. Way too big now.

Her hair, dyed black, has no discernible style but is instead a collection of several different hairdos on a single head. Parts of it were Afro. Part looks like a black beret.

And still she stands there, letting the water run. Has probably forgotten what she came there to do. Mesmerized by the sound of the running water. Thinking her thoughts, the nature of which he will never know.

The sounds of the house go on around them. The furnace comes on, first the whoosh of the flame, then the whine of the fan. The fridge kicks in. The sump pump in the basement comes on. The TV set in the living room drones, the water in the kitchen sink drips.

And then, suddenly, his mother comes back to herself. Shudders a little as if waking up from a daydream and recollects what it was she came to the sink to accomplish.

She fills the glass with water, turns off the tap, and heads back toward him.

Maybe it's the gesture, leading with the glass of water and holding it out toward him long before he's in position to take it, that brings back the memory.

The memory of the finger she carried toward him with a splinter inside it.

The way she looked.

The way he responded.

It all comes back.

"Thank you," he tells her and takes the glass of water from her hand. "Thanks, Mom."

He uses the word "Mom" cautiously, mumbling it, as if testing the waters of its meaning, if any, for him.

In a surprise move, having stood while he ate, she now sits down at the table next to him. It's as if she forgot herself, as if she sat down by mistake, but having done so feels she had to remain there for some obligatory minimum amount of time.

He eats his lamb stew and wonders if she's looking at him. Since his arrival, the longest sustained eye contact between them was out there in the falling snow when they both failed to recognize each other.

He washes his lamb stew down with the water she brought him and feels both the temptation and the terror to look at her.

Her proximity is paralyzing.

With the proximity of her body, he detects the scent of her old unwashed flesh, but it's not disgust he feels at the nearness of her, it's terror.

The cause of which is?

He doesn't know. Who knows what he would see in her wrinkle-wrapped eyes if he dared to take a really good look at them?

The temptation to look persists, like some physical pain that the proximity of her body brings into being. But he conquers the temptation, though not the terror, and does not look.

He finishes his lamb stew.

"Would you like some more?"

"No, no, thank you," he says, puffing out his cheeks and patting his stomach. "I'm stuffed. It was great."

She snatches up his soup bowl and his silverware and his empty glass and goes to the kitchen sink to wash them.

## 8

He remains seated in his chair. His mother, having washed the dishes, is now standing next to the kitchen countertop, her hands upon it, her fingers softly drumming.

They talk, making brief eye contact every now and then, because at this distance they're safely out of the range of each other's eyes.

The talk, initiated by his mother, is of teeth. Hers. His. His father's.

"I just can't get used to my dentures. I've had new ones made several times. The ones I have now were adjusted by experts, but they still don't feel right."

He's afraid she plans to take them out and show them to him, but she doesn't.

"Some people are lucky," she goes on. "Your father, for example. The first pair he got was all he needed. That was that. Forgot he was wearing them half the time. I had to remind him to take them out at night, or else he would have slept with them. I know of plenty others like that. But not me."

She shakes her head, defiantly proud of her trouble, as if, in her opinion, the better class of people never gets used to wearing dentures.

"They just don't feel right. Never did. And never will. I'm wearing horseshoes in my mouth. That's what it feels like."

They both smile.

"What happened to you?" she asks him.

He's puzzled by the question.

"To your teeth," she asks, alluding to his broken teeth by running a finger over her own.

"Oh." He nods, understanding now. "These here. I chipped them while eating something." Then shrugs, as if to minimize the importance of the event.

She seems to know nothing about the fatal car crash. The story from which he's fleeing doesn't seem to be a story she has heard, and he's not about to tell it to her.

"They have bonding now," she tells him. "I hear it's real simple and easy and doesn't hurt. You should get your teeth bonded."

"I will."

"Got to take care of your teeth while you have them."

"I know. I will."

In the ensuing silence, he sees a tense alertness taking hold of his mother's entire little body. She hears something. Some signal. Some call. And, as if in response to it, she starts to lean forward, poised for departure.

He quickly comprehends the nature of the call.

Theme music is playing on the TV in the living room, for a show she wants to watch. She has probably been looking forward to it for hours.

The least he can do is to let her watch it in peace, he thinks.

"I better turn in. I'm tired," he says and heads toward the door leading down to the basement. His mother heads toward the living room and the TV set. They pass each other.

"Good night, Mom."

"Sleep well."

He catches a look in his mother's eyes as she goes past him. The TV show is pulling her toward it, as if it were an irresistible lover, and her old eyes seem to shine brighter in anticipation of the tryst.

## 9

He took a shower in the basement, using the same little surfboard-shaped piece of soap that was in the soap dish the last time he was here . . . almost three years ago. The soap was hard as a little river rock and he had to work a lot to get it to lather.

No brilliant thoughts came to him in the shower except for the vague realization that he should have been further along by now.

Further along in what?

In his life? In his dealing with his mother? In something? In everything?

All of the above.

Further along in general.

Standing totally naked in the half-finished basement, he dried himself with the towel his mother had given him.

He observed the various pieces of furniture and the appliances that had once been upstairs and were moved down over the years.

The old upstairs fridge and the old gas range were down here now. As were the old upstairs dining room table and chairs. Along with the old upstairs living room rug.

Like some government in exile, he thought, walking barefoot to the den, carrying his shoes and socks in one hand, his clothes in the other.

There was a small bookcase in the den (made of knotty pine, like the paneling) with about thirty old hardback volumes in it. Sinclair Lewis. Upton Sinclair. Booth Tarkington. Carl Sandburg. Others. The Great Books of the Midwestern World, his father had called this collection in a moment of rare humor.

Saul considered doing a little reading in bed, but he couldn't think of what he wanted to read, so he turned off the lights and felt his way in the darkness toward the bed.

No, the darkness of the den was not haunted by the ghost of his father. The den, the whole house, in fact, was haunted by an absence of ghosts.

The queen-size bed with the too-soft mattress had once been the upstairs bed of his parents. He crawled under the covers only to realize that he had left his suitcase on the bed. It stayed there like the presence of another body next to his.

The layout of the basement was such that the living room where his mother now sat watching TV was right above his head. He could hear the laugh track of the show she was watching.

In the darkness of the den, the sound of that laugh track acquired the quality of some deity, or a chorus of deities, responding in an aloof but uproarious fashion to the private thoughts he was thinking.

His thoughts were about stories. Stories in the plural. And stories in the singular. Stories in general. Specific stories.

The story of Leila and Billy and him.

(Laugh, laugh, laugh, the soundtrack laughed above his head.)

Leila's whole life was there. In the magazine in the suitcase next to him.

The Pulitzer Prize–winning author had interviewed not just her mother but her old friends and relatives in Charleston and her friends in Venice. Saul, who knew her, knew none of these people. The writer who didn't know her and had never seen her knew more about her than he did.

The same seemed true of Billy. The writer had gone to Harvard and talked to Billy's friends (Saul knew none of them) and the resulting profile of Billy was more coherent and detailed than the Billy Saul had known.

And although the writer had never met Saul, the character of Saul that emerged in the story, supported by opinions and quotes from numerous sources, was far more satisfying and made much more sense than the character he knew.

(Laugh, laugh, laugh.)

The story of the three of them (right there in the magazine in the suitcase next to him) was a marvel of simplicity and grace and was made to seem somehow inevitable, as all good tragedies are.

A girl of fourteen gives up her child for adoption. Almost twenty years later, the man who adopted her child, now separated from his wife, meets her in Venice. The man is an almost legendary rewriter of flawed screenplays and fixer of flawed films. He has come to Hollywood to work on a film directed by Arthur Houseman who, because of ill health, was unable to finish the job himself. Leila, after years of struggling to make it as an actress, is the star of the film Saul has come to fix. He falls in love with her. Eventually, he introduces her to his adopted son Billy, a freshman at Harvard. Neither the woman nor the boy, nor Saul himself, know that they are mother and son. Leila and Billy fall in love. They have an affair that they keep secret from Saul. On their way to the premiere of her movie in Pittsburgh . . .

(Laugh, laugh, laugh.)

What Saul loved about this story of their story, as written by the Pulitzer Prize–winning writer, was the absence of any unresolved mess in either the story line or in the principal characters the story portrayed. An almost architectural sense of proportion permeated the entire magazine piece, everything balanced by something else and nothing left hanging in midair.

The story never bogged down. It had a beginning, a middle, and a tragic but satisfying end. At the conclusion of the story was the sense that the story was over.

It was so well written and so well constructed, it made much more sense to Saul than the story he had lived through.

The public story put his private experience of it to shame. It made him wonder if he shouldn't adopt it as the authoritative version of the events and the people in question.

He had fled from New York precisely because the temptation to do this was so great, but he now wondered (in the darkness of the den) if his flight from the temptation was just a brief postponement of the inevitable.

The thought of acknowledging and being acknowledged as the person in the magazine story seemed like the answer to the problem of living his life. Even his own mother, he was sure, were she to read that magazine story in his suitcase, would have a much better idea of who he was than she did now.

With just a minimum of practice he could become in private, in his own eyes, the person he was now reputed to be in public. The contradictions of his existence would vanish along with the pain of privacy.

(Laugh, laugh, laugh.)

In the living room above his head, the sitcom his mother was watching segued smoothly into another.

If only some Pulitzer Prize–winning journalist could be found to do a profile of his mother, he might be able to discover who this woman was who had given birth to him so many years ago. With his whole heart he wished to read that profile.

Oh, Mother, he thought.

Oh, mother of mine.

(Laugh, laugh, laugh.)

He could not even tell, as he started drifting off to sleep, what he meant by that flowery invocation of his mother.

Did the invocation mean to convey pity for her, or was it a plea of some kind, for help of some kind, from a son who was afraid of dying a death of some kind?

(Laugh, laugh, laugh.)

## 10

He woke up early the next morning, it wasn't yet seven o'clock, and he meant to get out of bed when he heard the rolling thunder of his mother's footsteps above his head.

Whatever little delight he may have experienced in being, for once, an early riser, was stomped to death by the sound of his mother's feet. Judging by the rhythm of those stomping feet, she had been up for quite some time.

So he stayed in bed, bemoaning the demise of the good deeds he'd had in mind upon waking. He had intended to sneak upstairs to the kitchen and make coffee. To have a cup or two alone, and then, when his mother stumbled out of her bedroom, he was going to tell her: "Good morning, Mother. Coffee's ready."

The thought of going up there now and having her say, "Good morning, Saul. Coffee's ready," was too much for him.

He stayed in bed. He tried to go back to sleep but couldn't. His mother started getting telephone calls. (At this hour, he thought.)

There was an extension in the den, not far from his bed, not far from his head, so that each time she got a call the whole den reverberated with ringing. In addition, there was the gallop of her feet as she ran (or so he imagined) to answer the phone.

He almost screamed the next time the phone rang. He jumped out of bed.

His mother was on the telephone when he snuck out the back door. She must have been talking to some hard-of-hearing old crony of hers, because she was shouting at the top of her lungs.

"I'm a tough old broad," she was shouting and laughing as he shut the door behind him.

## I I

It was still morning, not exactly the crack of dawn to be sure but well before noon, and Saul Karoo was out in front of his mother's house shoveling snow with an old snow shovel he had found in the garage.

It was getting warmer. A bright sun was shining on last night's snowfall, and in the reflected heat and glare Saul, squinting and sweating, was shoveling away for all he was worth.

It was, as late March snows tend to be, wet and heavy, one of those snowfalls much beloved by agronomists who love to translate them into acre-feet of water.

It was hard work shoveling this stuff, but hard work was what Saul sought. He was desperate to disengage his mind, and the only way he could think of doing that was to put as much stress on his body as he could.

He attacked the snow in his mother's front lawn with an almost vengeful fury, but without any discernible pattern. He shoveled away in one spot. And then he spun around and shoveled away in another spot. At times, he seemed to be trying to kill something with his shovel. At other times, it looked as if he were digging for a lost set of car keys buried in the snow.

Hopping from spot to spot, resembling occasionally a man involved in hand-to-hand combat with himself, he didn't so much clear away the snow as leave behind numerous craters in it.

His hands on the long wooden handle were so close together that the grip he was using was far more appropriate for a large stick used to whack a snake to death than for shoveling of any kind. But he didn't seem to notice or care. He simply didn't want to think about anything. Not his life. Not his mother's life. Not the story in the den. Nothing.

This stunning display of a man devoid of any physical grace or dexterity but wielding a snow shovel with fury offered an illuminating glimpse into the paradox of modern life. Here he was, this modern man, this Saul Karoo, trying to get away from his highly developed mind and lose himself in a body that had been a lost cause for decades.

His old mother, watching through the large picture window in the living room, was perplexed, to say the least, by the image of her son in the throes of frantic shoveling.

Being an old woman, she had become over the years an expert of sorts on the ways to avoid lower back problems. Observing the manner in which her son shoveled, all back and no legs, she feared a major lower back spasm in the making. She saw crushed disks. Cracked vertebrae. She saw her son in traction. A cripple.

So she rapped on the large picture window to get his attention. When he at last looked up at her, she mimed shoveling snow with her arms and bending at the knees while doing so.

She continued to do this for about twenty seconds while he stared at her dumbfounded.

He had no idea what the hell she was doing, what all her arm-flapping and knee-bending meant. It looked like a strange little dance she was performing for his benefit.

Not knowing how else to respond, Saul smiled at her and nodded approvingly, as if complimenting the dance recital of a five-year-old.

He changed course, however. To get out of her line of sight, he started moving backwards, shoveling alongside the house, heading toward the backyard.

The combination of physical exertion and the rising temperature began to exact its toll on his body. His armpits and crotch were damp. Sweat poured down his face, and his head steamed like a large cabbage in a pressure cooker.

He shoveled on, his arms getting weaker and heavier. With each successive scoop there was less snow in the shovel.

He didn't want to think, but as the mechanics of his body began to break down, his mind picked up the slack and began shoveling thoughts at him.

Who was she? he wondered.

Who in the world was this woman he called his mother?

This was not a rhetorical question but a genuine inquiry into the matter.

He took a couple more swipes at the snow and then, sweating, squinting, panting, came to a complete stop at a point in the backyard roughly equidistant from the house and the garage.

Who were all those people who called her on the telephone this morning?

What did she mean by saying, and to whom did she say, "I'm a tough old broad"?

And that strange, high-spirited laughter that had accompanied her statement, where did that come from and what did it mean?

Now that he thought of it, although he didn't want to think at all, but now that he thought of it, he had never heard his mother laugh like that before.

Was this laughter of hers a lifelong trait he had somehow managed to miss till now, or something she had developed in recent years?

Leaning on the handle of the snow shovel for support, he stood, totally spent.

His postmeridian shadow lengthened slowly across the unshoveled snow while he stood thinking about his mother.

The more he thought about her, although he didn't want to think about her at all, but the more he thought about her, the larger his ignorance of her seemed to grow. If someone were to put a gun to his head, he could not possibly write her story. He had known this woman longer than he had known anyone else on earth, but he had not a clue about what her story was.

The only thing he could say about her, with any degree of accuracy, was that she was old and still alive.

Could she, he wondered, say more about him than that? That he too was old and still alive?

Lost in contemplation of lifetimes and story lines and the extent to which one had nothing to do with the other, he remained standing in the fallen snow until his mother appeared in the back door and called him inside for lunch.

## 12

Saul is sitting at the dining room table, in the same chair where he sat the night before. And he's about to have the same dinner again, only now it's lunch, because the same aluminum pot of lamb stew is on the stove, being reheated yet again.

"You might as well finish it off," his mother says, her back turned to him as she stirs the stew slowly with a long wooden spoon.

"One thing about lamb stews," she says, "and stews in general, is that the more times you reheat them, the better they taste. But you want to make sure to reheat them on a low flame. The lower the better. That way it heats up just right, without burning the pot or wrecking the taste.

"I add a little water sometimes," she says, "depending on the thickness of the broth." She bends over the pot and sniffs. "Mmm, smells good."

Saul is not hungry, but even if he were ravenous, he would rather eat rocks than go through the ordeal of dumping that lamb stew into his stomach.

His mother moves around the house. She comes and she goes. She stirs the stew with a spoon and leaves. To go to the living room. To peek out of the window and see if the mailman is coming. Then all the way back, her feet hammering on the floor, back past him to the kitchen to check on the stew again. And then all the way back to her bedroom at the opposite end of the house. For what purpose he doesn't know. Maybe to peek out the window and see if the garbage trucks are moving up the alley to pick up the garbage.

It's a long house from one end to the other, with various rooms and closets running off a single corridor. When he sees his mother returning, at a distance and backlit by the daylight from her bedroom window, she looks completely wrinkle-free. Like some anorexic teenage girl with weird hair. And then, as she keeps walking toward him, time, in its time-lapse way, turns her into a wrinkled old crone.

Now there's a story, Saul thinks and looks away from her.

"Almost ready," his mother announces.

"Stews," she says, "should always be served piping hot."

The furnace comes on. The air blows out of the louvered registers. Little dustballs roll across the linoleum floor, unseen by her but seen by him.

Like tumbleweeds through a ghost town, he thinks.

The House of Karoo, he thinks.

Who will live here when she dies? he wonders.

Oh, Mother. The unspoken words speak of their own accord in his mind.

He has no nostalgia for this house, where dustballs now roll across the floor. Nor can he summon any genuine filial affection for this woman in a faded bathrobe, his mother. And yet the refrain "Oh, Mother" goes on and on in his mind.

He is old, she is old, but there is something about that "Oh, Mother" in his mind that seems eternal and ever young.

He has followed her with his eyes as she moved around the house and he is watching her now as she stirs the stew again.

She lifts up the wooden spoon to her lips and slurps some stew broth through her dentures.

"I think it's ready," she announces.

She opens a drawer and clatters out a ladle. She looks at the bowl of the ladle, blows something out of it, and then starts ladling out the stew into his dish.

Then, bearing the steaming plate of stew in both hands, she walks toward him. A little gnome of a woman, with sledgehammers for feet.

When she crosses some imaginary line and her eyes get too close to him for comfort, he looks away.

The loose sleeve of her Santa Fe bathrobe brushes his shoulder as she places the lamb stew on the table in front of him.

The scent of her old unwashed flesh mingles with the scent of the stew steaming upwards toward his nostrils.

His stomach heaves, contracts.

"Would you like some salt and pepper?" she asks him.

What he would like is a bilge pump to roll in and suck the lamb stew out of his dish, but he accepts her offer.

She totters off and then totters back, holding two identical stainless steel shakers, one in each hand. They look like chess pieces. Rooks.

"There," she says, and places them on the table.

And then she totters off again. Not far. But far enough away not to be on top of him.

She seems to know that it bothers him, the nearness of her body.

She seems to know on which side of the imaginary line she should be.

Sweating like a stevedore, he reaches for the salt and pepper shakers and sprinkles some of each on top of his stew. As it turns out, both the salt and pepper shakers have salt inside them. But he says nothing. What's there to say? Not even a sprinkling of crushed cigar butts could make the lamb stew any more inedible than it already is.

She just stands there, intent on watching him eat.

He can see her out of the corner of his left eye. He sees the fingers of one of her hands worrying the fingers of the other. He sees, or thinks he sees, the skin around the corners of her mouth move in tiny spasms. Like someone swallowing little fragments of sentences.

She is on the other side of the imaginary line, but she might as well be sitting on his lap.

He eats some lamb stew, unable to distinguish the taste and texture of overcooked vegetables and potatoes from the taste and texture of overcooked meat.

He wishes she wouldn't watch him eat.

He wishes she had to go to the bathroom.

He wishes she would get one of her phone calls.

He wonders why it is that she got all those phone calls early this morning and now nothing.

Maybe, he thinks, that is the way with old people. They check up on one another, in rotation, first thing in the morning, to make sure they are all still alive.

Something about that phrase "still alive" causes his mind to wander.

He doesn't want to think, but he's thinking and he can't tell if his thinking is leading him away from the matter at hand or toward it.

Nor can he tell what the matter at hand is.

Something is still alive.

Oh, Mother, he thinks, but his mind is a muddle of mothers. It's like water on the brain, only he's got mothers on the brain.

Not just his mother but mothers in general.

He's awash in mothers.

Mothers of all kinds. Birth mothers. Adoptive mothers. Fourteen-year-old mothers. Old mothers. Mothers, like his mother, who will never be mothers again. Mothers, like Dianah, who was a mother no more. Mothers who miscarry the life within their wombs and mothers with barren wombs. Mothers of the stillborn and mothers of the unborn.

And suddenly he, Saul Karoo, sweating over his steaming plate of lamb stew, feels overcome with kinship and something like love for them all. For all those mothers.

For he too . . .

He starts crying, averting his face from his mother's eyes so she won't see.

For he too . . .

He starts sobbing, blubbering, shoveling spoonfuls of lamb stew into his mouth in order to distract his mother from his unforeseen breakdown.

He too, wombless though he is, he too has known the motherlike yearning to give birth to something living and new.

Has known, within the limitations of his gender, that feeling of full-ness and expectation.

But never the joy of deliverance.

His life has been all gestation and no birth.

Oh, mothers, he now blubbers to himself, have mercy on me. Mothers, you life-givers of the world, have mercy on me please. I want to be a life-giver too. Sullied of soul and old and wombless though I may be, there is still something within me as yet unborn clamoring for birth.

Still alive!

This seemingly obvious fact, that he is still alive, and that his own mother is still alive, strikes him now as miraculous.

And before he can stop to think, before he can even plan his next move, he is moving.

He starts to slide off his chair, his arms flapping every which way as he lands upon his knees on the linoleum floor. There, gathering his body together into a figure of a sloppy-looking supplicant, he turns toward his mother.

Kneeling before her, his hands pressed together as if he were pleading, he starts to speak.

"Mother," he says, looking up into her eyes, "forgive me, please."

Unprepared for her son's extravagant display of emotion, she had instinctively stepped toward him when she saw him sliding off the chair, thinking God knows what was happening, thinking that he was perhaps having a heart attack like his father and wondering if her lamb stew was responsible.

Now that she sees that he's all right, that he's alive and well, but kneeling there in front of her, looking right into her eyes and pleading for forgiveness, she is positively horrified.

She would have known how to respond to his sudden death, but she does not know how to respond to this.

A dead son is still a son and she would have known what to do, but this man down on his knees in front of her does not seem like any son of hers.

Who is he and what is he doing?

Having stepped toward him when he fell out of the chair, she now steps back. The horror she feels only grows when he, sliding across the linoleum floor on his knees, comes toward her like a cripple without legs.

"Saul," she says, "what are you doing? Get up. Get up."

But he keeps creeping toward her.

She has backed up as far as she can go. He has backed her into a wall. She stands there shivering, looking trapped, the distance between them narrowing as he creeps on toward her on his knees.

"Oh, Mother," he cries again and again.

As old as she is, and as totally inexperienced in scenes of this sort with her son, she starts to understand what is happening.

Something real is creeping toward her.

The first real moment between herself and her son is heading directly toward her.

He is looking up at her. Her child. Her son. This old man, pleading with her.

And she pleads right back at him, like some helpless old woman confronted by a mugger. She pleads with him to abandon his assault. Let us not have something real now, she pleads with him with her eyes. I'm an old woman. A widow. I haven't got much longer to live. Please, spare me this moment.

He sees her eyes, he comprehends their meaning, but he can't help it. The momentum of the moment is moving him toward her.

He, down on his knees, may look like an overwrought sentimental buffoon, but there is nothing sentimental in what he sees. He sees her with brutal clarity.

The dead dentures in her mouth. The lusterless cheap black hair dye. The perm-burnt, pubiclike quality of parts of it. The anal-like wrinkles around her eyes. And the eyes themselves, small, smeared, full of cataracts.

She could be any old woman.

She could be anyone's mother.

And this is precisely what moves him so. That she could be anyone's mother, even his.

"Oh, Mother," he says.

And taking her reluctant hand, so small and cold and old, he kisses it and says:

"Mother, forgive me, please."

It is not lost on him that the hand he kissed is the very hand with the very index finger where a splinter once lodged, nor is it not lost on her.

She remembers the incident of the splinter. His repugnance of her pain.

His response hurt her. But this hurts even more. This is truly horrifying because it implies that everything could have been different between them. That this love she now sees could have been there all along.

She is too old to change. To start again. To suddenly start loving again. What is even harder to accept is that she is loved. It's too much to ask of an old woman. It's almost merciless.

He can see the horror in her eyes and the hope that this moment will pass. She wants her old son back, not this loving one who is down on his knees looking up into her eyes and holding on to her hand.

He also knows that the forgiveness he seeks is too all-encompassing to be given to a single little old woman in a faded bathrobe.

But although all does not go as he would have wished, all is not lost either.

Some little wriggling life is engendered between them.

And something else too.

Looking up into her eyes, he catches the moment.

A briefest of glimpses is all that he is granted, but it suffices.

In that one single peek through her unguarded eyes, he sees that the collected memories and moments of a single day of her life, of anyone's life, if fully explored, would surpass in volume the collected works of any author who ever lived. Whole wings of whole libraries, if not whole libraries themselves, would be needed to house a single day of anyone's life, and even then that life would surely be shortchanged.

And yet, he thinks, down there in his suitcase, among his T-shirts and shorts and socks, in that magazine is Leila's story. And Billy's. And his own as well.

Life, it seems, is not meaningless but, rather, so full of meaning that its meaning must be constantly murdered for the sake of cohesion and comprehension.

For the sake of a story line.

And then the peephole passageway to his mother's private universe vanishes from view, or she chooses to close his access to it.

Her eyes, through which he saw what he saw, are once again the eyes he knows, defiantly guarding the unknowable on the other side.

He is still holding her hand and she wants it back. He lets it go.

Her way of dealing with what has just occurred between them is this. She does not pretend that something didn't happen. She just cannot talk about it now. She will incorporate it into her life, but not now, not in front of him. These things take time. And although she probably has little time left in her life, these things still take time.

She walks past him, through the kitchen, and walks all the way back to her bedroom, shutting the door behind her.

He rises slowly, feeling little flutters of pain in his lower back.

# CHAPTER SEVEN

I

The traffic on the Hollywood Freeway had been moving slowly but steadily until he got off at Barham Boulevard. The traffic on Barham was backed up all the way from the overpass to the top of Barham Hill.

Highway construction of some kind, although he couldn't tell exactly what it was.

He crept up the hill in his rented car.

It took him almost twenty minutes to reach the hilltop overlooking Burbank. The other side of Barham Boulevard led straight down to the Burbank Studios where he had an appointment with Cromwell. The traffic on the downside of the hill was just as backed up, if not worse. By the look of things, it would take him at least another twenty minutes to make his descent.

The angle of the hill was such that when he had a chance to creep forward a few feet at a time, he just released the pressure on the brake pedal. There was no need to touch the accelerator.

His appointment with Cromwell was for three o'clock and it was almost three. He had left the Beverly Wilshire Hotel with plenty of time to spare, intending, as was his habit, to be at the Burbank Studios long before three.

The unexpected traffic delay was going to make him late for an official meeting for the first time in memory.

It pleased him that he would be late. That he would keep Cromwell waiting.

The pain in his lower back made him predisposed to be pleased about something.

Ever since the trip to Chicago, a little over three months ago, maybe it was the snow shoveling, or the way he fell down on his knees in front of her, or maybe even the way he got up from his knees, but ever since then, the pain in his lower back had become a fixture of his life.

It became especially acute when he was forced to sit in one place for too long. Long plane trips. Driving a car. Watching a movie in a theater. Things like that.

It was as if a living paw with retractable claws had been surgically implanted around the base of his spine and almost anything, from sneezing to laughing to stepping too hard on the brake, could trigger the claws to snap out of their hiding place and sink into his flesh.

He knew that he should see a doctor, but he also knew that he never would.

Just as he would never see a dentist about getting his broken teeth bonded.

It was too late for that. He was bonded with them as they were.

He would eventually bond with his backache as well.

## 2

The traffic, moving in spasms of a yard or two at a time, kept stopping and going . . . stopping and going . . . and then it stopped completely.

And then it resumed stopping and going again.

The rhythm was that of dots and dashes in Morse code.

An endless line of cars draped over a hill, sending a message in a repeated linear sequence to the cosmos.

Dot. Dot. Dot. Dash. Dash. Dash. Dot. Dot. Dot.

## 3

Maybe, he thought, maybe Elke Höhlenrauch had been right. Maybe the pain he was feeling in his lower back was simply the result of his spine contracting.

The less spine, the more pain.

Until eventually you were all pain and no spine.

He sighed. It even hurt his back to sigh freely, so it was a cramped, constricted sigh.

The thought of Elke reminded him that he still had no medical insurance.

No insurance of any kind.

It seemed to him, however, that the number of life's afflictions against which there was no insurance of any kind was growing.

There were, he thought, disasters in life that no Lloyd's of London, or Lloyd's of the World, or Lloyd's of the Universe, could ever underwrite.

No comprehensive insurance against folly and tragedy, against unreached destination and unrealized yearning.

He wished he had a policy right now to insure him against what he might agree to in Cromwell's office.

He had arrived in LA late Monday night.

Today was Wednesday.

But this particular Wednesday fell on both the end and middle of the work week.

Wednesday, the third of July, 1991.

Judging by the traffic, the start of the long weekend had already begun.

Cars creeping up Barham Hill and cars creeping down crept past each other, and the people inside those cars, those going up and those going down, looked at each other through their windshields like participants in some lonely diaspora.

Everyone was trying to get somewhere, but since they were trying to do so in both directions, it didn't take much imagination for Saul to imagine that the traffic jam he was caught in was in a loop and that those going up and those going down would pass each other again and again, but heading in reverse directions.

Life on a loop, like the water in recycled fountains, which neither flowed from somewhere nor went anywhere but looked busy and pleasing to the eye, going around and around.

There were no destinations anymore. Only turnaround points on loops of various sizes.

Even time, which was supposed to be linear, seemed to be on a loop to Saul.

He had a growing suspicion that the year 1991 was pivotal in this regard.

Pivotal to whom, he didn't know.

1991, reading as it did the same way left to right as right to left, was corroboration for his thoughts as he crept along in his rented car toward Burbank Studios.

The last year anybody will ever need.

It read the same way coming and going, and whether you came or went, there was no getting out of it.

He wasn't sure when these thoughts first began to assail him, but perhaps it had something to do with the victory parades on television after the Gulf War.

He hadn't followed the war itself. He hardly knew there had been a war because of his own problems. But he did watch some of the victory parades.

He could still recall some of the faces he had seen in them.

What he saw in the faces of people lining the parade routes, either because it coincided with what he was feeling or because he chose to impose his own disease upon the cheering multitudes, was a celebration of nothing less than the triumphant victory over privacy itself.

Something was revealed in those faces that human beings up to now had kept to themselves.

He didn't know what to call it, but it was as if some line had been crossed that could only be crossed once. Once crossed, there was no going back, but only around and around within the loop of the year 1991.

He had missed the war entirely, he knew nothing about its causes, but on the strength of seeing a few victory parades on television Saul Karoo saw himself as some latter-day Clausewitz who had a comprehensive theory about the causes of all wars to come.

And his theory was this.

All wars were now evasions of privacy. Wars, big and small, civil and otherwise, were collective evasions of private lives. Many, many wars would be needed until mankind was free of privacy altogether and the memory of its existence forgotten.

Wars on a loop.

4

He heard a car horn, several short repeated blasts, and saw somebody waving to him from an uphill-bound car on Barham Boulevard.

Squinting through his windshield, Saul recognized the smiling, almost laughing face of young Brad. Cromwell's former Brad. Cromwell had dismissed him and replaced him with his new black Brad, but the old Brad still had a job at Burbank Studios and was leaving work early like everybody else.

Saul returned the wave and the smile. But because the two cars were creeping past each other so slowly, both men kept waving and smiling, as if to suggest some close bond between them that would last no longer than it took their cars to pass each other.

Oh, Brad, Saul thought.

Brad was young enough to be Saul's son, and just as Saul could not think of his own mother, or any mother, or even the word "mother" without thinking of Leila, he could not think of any young man anymore without thinking of Billy.

And so from one name he went to the other.

Oh, Billy, he thought. My boy.

Billy was dead. Leila was dead. The Old Man, Mr. Houseman, was dead. And this death on a loop reminded him of his visit with the Old Man while he was still alive.

When he went to visit his mother in Chicago, he had had no plans of either going to LA or seeing the Old Man, but by the time he left his mother's house three days later, his plan of doing both had materialized.

He remembered, in a loop-within-a-loop kind of way, the last time he saw his mother.

Their parting.

They were in the living room when the cab arrived and honked its horn.

He was sure they were going to part right there, but she offered to walk him to the waiting cab.

And so they went out together. The snow had all melted, the sun was shining, and a warm southwesterly wind was blowing. March was going out like a lamb as the two of them walked slowly toward the yellow cab.

His memories of his mother up to then had been of a woman inside the house. He could not remember the last time he had seen her outdoors. Nor could he tell if the bright sunlight illuminating her face made her look a little older or a little younger than she was. But she did look different.

A whole series of women he had never seen peeked out of her old eyes, and each one of them seemed to remember a different sunny day from her life, with a promise of spring in the air.

They embraced like a couple trying out a new and unfamiliar dance, a bit clumsily, a little self-consciously, but with an eagerness both could feel.

Then he took his bag and his backache and got into the cab.

She stood there waving. Maybe it was because it was such a breezy, springlike day that she reminded him, despite her age, of a whole schoolyard full of schoolgirls waving goodbye to him.

He tried to figure out on the plane why he was doing what he was doing.

He knew why he was flying to LA, but he couldn't figure out how he had come to his decision.

Maybe it was that videocassette of the Old Man's film. Maybe just having it in his suitcase had caused the idea to be born. Or maybe it was knowing, from the newspapers, that the Old Man had only a handful of days left. Or maybe it was both. Or neither. All he knew was that he had to go there, had to see him, had to beg the dying old artist to forgive him for what he had done to his work.

Others had come on that Wednesday afternoon to pay their last respects to the master. Some were legendary figures in their own right, movie stars who had worked for the Old Man when all of them were young.

People were leaving when Saul came and people would be coming when Saul left. It was like an open house. There were parked cars everywhere on the huge expanse of land surrounding the house. Liveried drivers standing outside their limos, smoking. There was a large trampoline with some kids jumping up and down on it, but in complete silence.

The whole event had the feel of an occasion that had been announced, without Saul's knowing it, in the papers.

I am dying. Come say goodbye. Arthur Houseman.

He was met at the door by a young woman who told him to go upstairs, where he was met by another young woman who told him where to sit down and wait his turn.

There were others in the waiting room, waiting theirs.

Yet another woman, this one neither young nor old, was in charge of escorting the visitors to the room of the Old Man himself.

The procedure, Saul observed, was always the same. She first inquired about the identity of the visitor, then went off, probably to announce the person to the Old Man, then returned to escort him or her to his room. Several people ahead of Saul were so well-known that she escorted them to the Old Man's room without any inquiries.

Saul sat on a straight-backed wooden chair and waited his turn. On his lap was a yellow manila envelope with the videocassette of the Old Man's film. Inside the envelope was also a letter he had written to the Old Man explaining who he was and why he had come. He had written the letter just in case Mr. Houseman proved to be too sick to receive visitors.

The room, the whole house, in fact, smelled of cigar smoke. The Old Man had been, among his many legends, a legendary cigar smoker and either the house had absorbed the smell of Cuban cigars or the Old Man was smoking them on his deathbed.

People left the waiting room. Others came in. The room seemed to contain the same number of visitors at all times.

When his turn finally came, Saul gave the manila envelope to the woman and told her that the letter inside would explain everything.

He stood up while handing her the envelope and remained standing when she left.

Then he sat down to wait.

It seemed to take longer than usual for her to return, and when she finally reappeared (with the yellow manila envelope in her hands), she seemed to make a point of looking elsewhere while walking toward him.

Saul stood up as she approached.

The envelope in her hands, he saw, was perfectly flat. The videocassette had been removed. In a moment of joy, Saul imagined himself being forgiven by the Old Man and the two of them watching his masterpiece together.

"Mr. Karoo," the woman addressed him, stopping a few feet in front of him.

"Yes?"

"Mr. Houseman has instructed me to tell you that you must leave his house. He doesn't wish for you to be here," she told him and extended her hand with the envelope in it.

Saul's entire body was suddenly made of knee joints that one by one began to buckle.

He had made no contingency plan for this possibility and didn't know what to do next.

The people in the room could not help overhearing what the woman had told him and now they turned their heads and looked at him, wondering who he was and what it was that he had done.

"Please," the woman said, gesturing toward the door.

Taking the yellow manila envelope from her hand, he somehow made his way downstairs and out of the house.

Inside the envelope was the letter he had written to Mr. Houseman, pleading for forgiveness.

His need for forgiveness had been so great that it had never occurred to him that transgressions existed that were unforgivable.

The Old Man's house was located in Topanga Canyon, and Saul sped down the canyon, with drought-dry trees on both sides of the road rising high above him, their branches knitted together to form a tunnel of trees. And then suddenly, hurtling out of the tunnel, he saw the Pacific Ocean. Its vastness, reminding him of human vastness and of his inability to measure up to it as a man, caused his heart to ache and his cheeks to burn with shame.

## 5

He stopped at the gate and cracked open the window.

"Saul Karoo," he told the uniformed guard guarding the entrance to Burbank Studios. "I'm here to see Jay Cromwell."

The massive guard responded with monumental lethargy. He checked the list of names on his clipboard and, finding Saul's name there, told him where to park.

The lot was almost deserted, but he parked his car in the visitors' lot where he had been told to park.

He was in no particular hurry anymore. It was almost three thirty. Too late for haste since he was late already.

Getting out of the air-conditioned car, he was unprepared for the equatorial heat that awaited him. Heat rose up from the pavement and heat fell down from the sky. A heat-induced vertigo caused his head to spin, forcing him to hold on to the frame of the car door for support. With hands draped over the top of the door frame and his head bowed, he waited for the vertigo to pass.

He wondered if he was having a stroke or something, or if maybe it was just his blood sugar dropping like a rock.

The pain in his lower back was killing him. His lower back seemed to be located six or seven feet lower than usual. And somewhere far below his lower back was the pavement on which he stood, which spun like a pinwheel when he looked down at it.

Shutting his eyes didn't help. If anything, it made things worse. Made it seem that his mind was orbiting around him, like the earth around the sun.

The Topanga Canyon loop came back to him and looped around and around. He saw himself coming and going. Saw himself driving up toward the Old Man's house, anticipating forgiveness, and then, on the same loop, driving back down, unforgiven.

It seemed unfair to have to relive that pain at the same time that his lower back was hurting so.

One pain at a time, please, he pleaded, but there was no help for it. Both continued.

His mind continued to reel.

Instead of feeling the shame caused by the Old Man's refusal to forgive him, he now felt something much worse. He saw the smallness of his motive in seeking that forgiveness in the first place.

All he had really wanted was a convenient sense of closure to the whole episode. He had desecrated another man's masterpiece, but the dying artist would forgive him on his deathbed and that would be that. And then he would be on to something else.

It now seemed to him that seeking to be forgiven was even more vile than the crime he had committed.

He wondered if he had ever loved anything in his life. If he had ever really loved Billy or Leila. If what he had loved all along was only the motive behind loving them.

A motive that promised a personal payoff.

The grand consummation he had planned for the three of them in Pittsburgh was now revealed to him for what it really was. A cheap way of justifying all the aborted and dead-end story lines of his life by wrapping them up with a happy ending. As if there was an ending that could make up for the life he had lived.

His motive had murdered everything.

What else was love with a motive but the murder of love itself and those he had claimed to love?

The reeling slowed.

His vertigo began to fade.

One by one, the loops and reels in his mind began to wobble in their orbits and finally, like so many psychic hula hoops whose momentum was fading, to collapse in a heap somewhere in the back of his head.

There only remained the problem of the terrible ache in his lower back.

Holding on with both hands to the top of the door frame, he bent his knees to an almost full squatting position, trying to stretch the pain away.

Hanging from the car door frame seemed to have no effect on his back pain, but it did cause a sudden and completely unexpected loosening of his bowels. Before he could tighten his sphincter muscle, he felt a squirt of waste dampen his underwear.

What next? he thought.

He pulled himself up, hoping that the stain had not soaked through his trousers.

6

The building in which Cromwell's office was located was a long rectangle four stories high. The dingy yellow stuccoed walls were cracked and peeling. All along the length of the building were chips of stucco of various sizes and shapes, fallen from the walls and gathering there in the exposed earth in ever greater accumulations over the years.

The whole building brought to mind some downtown community college in a town that no longer had a downtown or a community. One of those forlorn places where night students went to learn new skills that were out of date when they began.

Judged on appearance alone, it was the last place you expected to house the headquarters of the single most powerful producer in the movie-making world.

But then, Saul thought, the buildings and the offices and the private residences at Los Alamos, where the A-bomb was made, were even more unimposing in appearance.

There were three entrances, one at each end of the rectangle and one in the middle.

Saul took the middle one.

There were two sets of doors. When Saul opened the second of the two and stepped inside, it was like going directly into a walk-in fridge.

He shuddered.

He was used to these exterior-interior extremes in temperature when he was in LA, but this felt more extreme than usual. He wondered if the bone-cold he was experiencing was the result of his own body's faulty thermostat or the building's. But how was one to tell?

The lobby floor, usually peppered with people walking in and out of offices at this time of the week and at this time of the day, was completely deserted. Perhaps the start of the long weekend had swept through the premises and carried everyone away.

Walking slowly toward the elevator (with that wad of damp waste in his shorts), he could hear the sound of telephones ringing in deserted offices being answered by the sound of answering machines.

Down at the far end of the corridor, he noticed the maintenance man mopping the floor. Moving backwards, the man swung the mop from side to side in sweeping but precise scythelike strokes. Something about the man, in the mood Saul was in, struck him as mythic.

He took the elevator to the third floor, got out, and took a left. For a split second, and for a split second only, the getting-out-of-yet-another-elevator syndrome got the better of him. He didn't know where he was or where he was going.

Then he remembered, as if the name Cromwell were an answer to all his questions.

It was almost four o'clock. He wondered if perhaps Cromwell had given up on him and gone home like everyone else.

If he was still in his office, then Saul was going to be a full hour late for their meeting. And although it had not been his idea to be so late, still he felt pleased, as if he had done it on purpose.

A full fucking hour late, he thought.

Despite his backache, despite his soiled underwear, Saul put a little rebellious swagger in his walk.

Through the opaque glass door, he saw that all the lights were still on inside Cromwell's office, putting to rest all hope that he had gone.

So what? Saul thought.

Feeling downright insurrectionary, he meant to open the door and swagger inside, but just as he was reaching for the knob, the door opened and the momentum of his inward-bound body was met and equaled by the outward-bound body of Cromwell's black Brad, resulting in an intimate collision worthy of two tango dancers.

Startled by the collision, lost momentarily in post-collision confusion, they both recovered quickly and then they both leaned back and laughed at what had happened.

"Mr. Karoo," the black Brad said.

"Brad," Saul replied.

The large and the once-beautiful eyes of the young black man, which had reminded Saul, the first time he had seen him, of the eyes of Byzantine saints, were still large, but were now lemur-like. Large and round and drained of something, as if something private and essential had been fucked out of them, which the eyes refused to acknowledge.

"Jay's still here and he'll be thrilled to see you," black Brad explained. He was very animated when he talked. "We were sure you were trapped in some nightmarish traffic jam. Jay forgot all about the start of the long weekend when he made the appointment. We tried to reach you at the hotel to tell you not to come today, but you had left already."

Saul's spirit sagged a little when he realized that if he had only not left so early, he could have avoided being here.

They traded places and stopped again, this time Saul on the inside and Brad on the outside.

"Have a nice weekend," Brad told him.

"You too," Saul replied.

Brad walked away down the corridor and Saul lingered in the doorway to watch him go.

Debating with himself whether to close the open door or leave it open, Saul resolved the issue by leaving it open, as if to assert that he didn't intend to stay long.

The door connecting Brad's antechamber to Cromwell's office was open as well, but not all the way. It was as silent in one room as in the other. He waited for Cromwell to come out and greet him or to call him inside, but neither occurred.

He considered leaving, sneaking away.

Then he reconsidered.

Another involuntary discharge from his bowels dampened further his already damp underwear.

Tightening his sphincter muscle, he pushed open the door to Cromwell's office just wide enough to peek inside.

Cromwell was on the telephone, for the moment listening to someone talk instead of talking himself. Just sitting there behind his desk and listening.

His whole face lit up when he saw Saul peeking around the door.

Great to see you, Doc, he seemed to be saying without saying a word. The wink of his eye, that little smile of his said it.

Saul acknowledged the silent greeting with a silent greeting of his own, nodding as if to say, Great to see you too, Jay.

But since Cromwell was on the telephone and since Saul didn't want to intrude on some confidential conversation, he smiled apologetically and made as if to withdraw back to Brad's side of the border.

Cromwell, the host of hosts, would not hear of it.

No, no, no. Come in. Come in. Come right in, Doc. This is nothing. Nothing at all. Just some jerk on the phone that I have to listen to. Won't take a minute. Come on in. Great to see you, Doc, it really is.

All this was said in complete silence. With little winks. Little shrugs. The raising or lowering of his eyebrows.

Gesturing with the point of his chin, he instructed Saul where to sit, and Saul did as he was told and sat down in the designated chair directly across from Cromwell.

# CHAPTER EIGHT

### I

Legs crossed, back straight, arms tightly folded across his chest, he sits in his chair and waits for Cromwell to get off the phone.

He has assumed as tight-assed a sitting position as possible in order to prevent any further leakage of waste into his underwear.

Contracting his sphincter for all he's worth.

His back is killing him, but the ache is the least of his problems now.

Cromwell is still on the telephone. Still listening for the most part. Every now and then he says, "Mmm," or, "I see, I do, but . . ." or, "I know, I know, but . . ." and then he listens again to someone pleading with him for something.

The whole time that he's listening, he's keeping up a silent but lively banter with Saul. Chatting him up. Conveying what he wants to convey to him with an endless variety of winks and looks and facial semaphores.

It's so damn good to see you, Doc, he tells him.

It's been a while, that's for sure.

I'm glad to see that you've recovered from that terrible tragedy, he tells him.

I was really worried about you. I mean, for a while there, you really had me worried. I didn't think you were going to pull out of it.

Some people never do, you know.

But you're looking good, Doc. You really are. Lost a little weight, didn't you?

"I know, I know, but . . ." he says with sympathy to whoever he's talking to on the telephone.

What a fucking bore this guy is, he conveys to Saul with a simple little roll of his eyes. He looks at his watch and mimes a sigh of someone desperate for the call to end.

But it's clear to Saul that Cromwell is having a wonderful time.

Such a good time, in fact, that he's letting the man on the other end of the line continue, as if the chance exists that whatever desperate plea the man is making to Cromwell might meet with success. Cromwell's silence (while the man talks) only encourages this interpretation. Makes it seem (to the man on the other end of the line) that his words are swaying Cromwell. That Cromwell's silence is one of rapt attention and serious reconsideration.

Saul knows all this because he knows Cromwell.

He feels that he's known Cromwell all his life.

He has no idea who the man or woman is on the other end of the line, but he knows that whoever it is, man or woman, black or white, young or old, that Cromwell is fucking the person on the phone. Fucking them out of something. Or fucking them into something.

That's why Cromwell was so eager to have Saul come inside.

To observe.

Saul also knows that he's the next in line. He doesn't know the details of Cromwell's agenda, but he knows that as soon as Cromwell gets off the phone, he will fuck him into or out of something.

## 2

To help pass the time while he sits and waits for Cromwell to conclude, Saul tries to figure out how long it has been since the last time he saw Cromwell in person.

Last November, Saul manages to nail down the month if not the date.

Over breakfast.

In Pittsburgh.

In that hotel restaurant.

Cromwell and his young black friend.

It was a Saturday.

The same Saturday in November when Leila and Billy died.

His mind starts to reel. Oh, Billy. Oh, Leila. Oh, Mother. To keep it from reeling, he counts the intervening months.

Starting in mid-November of last year and ending in July of this.

November, December, January, February . . .

He can't do the arithmetic in his head and has to start again. This time he resorts to counting on his fingers, which are tucked inside the armpits of the opposing arms folded across his chest.

Five months in one armpit. Three in the other. Maybe not quite three, since it was mid-November.

But over seven months, in any case.

Seven months is a long time, Saul thinks.

A very long time.

Until he entered this office and sat down in this chair, it seemed like a very long time since the last time he saw Cromwell.

But it no longer seems that way.

In a matter of minutes, Cromwell has managed to reduce that seven-month interval of separation between them to next to nothing.

To make him feel, as he is feeling now, that he was never really away from him at all.

Cromwell winks at him, raising one finger in the air to indicate that he's getting off any second. He smiles. He mimes some messages his way. Saul counters with a mime of his own. No rush, Jay, I'm fine. Or something to that effect.

But the smiling monster he's looking at, whom he thought he knew so well, appears to him now in a new, even more monstrous shape.

Behind that vast, monolithic forehead Saul sees the maw of a mind of such power that it can break the bones of time at will.

Not bend time, as has been theorized to occur in deep space, but actually break it and compress it into nothingness.

What Saul sees are the eyes of the Millennium Man winking back at him.

Maybe, Saul thinks, it's here already.

The Millennium.

Maybe, he thinks, the Millennium came earlier than expected.

In 1991. The last year you'll ever need to know.

3

He's off the phone and up on his feet. The conversation begun with Saul in pantomime now ratchets into speech.

"Damn, Doc," he says, "it's so good to see you, you old bastard. It really is. Don't ask me to explain why I'm so damn fond of you, but . . .

"I can't tell you how sorry I am," he says, "for dragging you out here in all that traffic. It completely slipped my mind what day it was.

"And I'm truly sorry," he says, "for having to stay on the phone so long. I'll tell you honestly, Doc, sometimes I wish I could be the merciless sonovabitch everyone says I am. It would be a lot easier on me if I could.

"How are you?" he asks Saul. "Sorry if I seem a little tired. Listening to that guy simply wore me out."

He's not just lying to Saul. He wants Saul to know he's lying to him. It becomes a truth of sorts, this manner of lying. A Cromwellian truth.

A countertruth.

"I'm almost afraid to tell you," he tells Saul, "why I had you fly out here all the way from New York in the first place. I hope you won't get mad at me for saying this, but the number one reason I had you come out here was because I missed you. I really did. I know a lot of people in LA, it's true, but all the people I know here are so . . ."

He is lying through his teeth, with his teeth, with his eyes, his gestures.

All become lies.

In its own way, it's a spectacular show.

A constant Darwinian devouring of deeds by counterdeeds that are themselves devoured.

This perpetual nullification provides the endless supply of energy for his dynamic personality.

So Saul thinks, looking at Cromwell.

From Modern Man to Postmodern Man.

From Postmodern Man to this.

The Millennium Man.

The last man you'll ever need to know.


# 4

The banter goes on.

Cromwell tells him this. He tells him that. Saul banters back as best as he can.

Each, according to the other, is looking good. Not just good but great.

They touch on various topics in no particular order. On politics. On the changing demographic landscape. The unusual changes in the weather worldwide. On trends in theater. There is a new Canadian ballet company that Cromwell can't say enough about.

"Astonishing," he calls it.

"They're reinventing the vocabulary of dance," he says.

"The situation in the Balkans seems unstable," one of them says.

The other concurs.

It's hard to know who's saying what when nothing at all is being said over and over again. Zerospeak.

The temperature in Cromwell's office seems to be dropping as they banter on.

Not plummeting or anything like that but definitely going down.

Or so it seems to Saul.

Or maybe it's just me, he thinks.

It's hard to tell if he's feeling what he's feeling or if he just seems to be feeling it.

The distinction between the two is blurred.

He crosses and recrosses his legs, folds, unfolds, and refolds his arms across his chest as a way of keeping his circulation going.

His armpits are clammy with sweat, and his fingers, when he tucks them inside those armpits, feel or seem to feel icy cold.

The metronomic ritual of his zerospeak banter with Cromwell is so mindless, so effortless, that he's free, while they banter on, to think his own thoughts.

Saul thinks. He ponders. He wonders why he has come to LA to see Cromwell.

He didn't have to come. It wasn't even Cromwell who called him to fly out to LA for a meeting. It was his new black Brad who called.

Saul could have said no.

But he didn't.

Curiosity got the better of him.

If Cromwell wanted him to fly out to LA, it could mean only one thing. That in Cromwell's opinion there was still something left in Saul worth fucking.

And it was this possibility, Saul now thinks, that brought him out here.

By his own reckoning, Saul had come to the conclusion that he had been fucked out of everything already.

Cromwell's invitation gave him hope that he was wrong in his self-assessment. That there was still something left inside him unfucked and intact.

Saul came here to find out what it was.

So in a way, he thinks, my presence here is an act of faith.

If the good can no longer see any good in me, if I can no longer see any good in myself, then the only thing left is to see what good the evil see in me.

## 5

And on it goes, the banter.

It doesn't matter who says what, since there is no point in any of it except to pick up your cue when it's your turn.

One says one thing.

The other says something else.

It could just as easily be the other way around.

At some arbitrary point, Cromwell reaches inside one of his desk drawers and pulls out a large yellow manila envelope and places it casually on top of the desk.

Here we go, Saul thinks.

The yellow manila envelope is larger than standard size. Longer, wider. And judging by its thickness, Saul, a connoisseur of yellow manila envelopes, figures that it contains between three hundred and fifty and four hundred pages.

Whatever is inside it is meant for him, but he doesn't know what it could be.

It's too thick for a screenplay.

Just the sight of the yellow manila envelope causes Saul's mind to reel, it triggers a yellow manila envelope loop inside his mind.

The many, many yellow manila envelopes of his life.

He has to blink rapidly several times to keep from getting dizzy. To make the loop stop.

Cromwell in the meantime is telling him things he already knows. About *Prairie Schooner*:

"We open this weekend," Cromwell is telling him.

"We're going to be on almost two thousand screens," he tells him.

This is all common knowledge. Old news. Saul knows all about the distribution pattern for *Prairie Schooner*.

Cromwell knows he knows. The only reason he's telling Saul something he already knows is to numb him before he fucks him.

Saul is wise to Cromwell, which is no defense.

"I think we're going to be a huge hit," Cromwell tells him. "A huge, huge hit."

(His prediction will prove to be accurate. *Prairie Schooner* will turn out to be the biggest commercial hit of 1991.)

"And not just in terms of box office, either," Cromwell says. "No. I think we have a huge artistic hit on our hands as well. The critics are going to love it."

(This prediction will also prove to be accurate. *Prairie Schooner* will turn out to be the biggest critical hit of 1991 as well.)

"Speaking of critics," Cromwell says, and lifts up some photocopied pages from the desktop. The pages are stapled together at the top, and Saul can see portions of the printed matter on the pages highlighted with a yellow marker.

"These are some advance reviews from the weekly magazines. They're not out yet, but they will be soon. Here." He hands them to Saul. "These are for you. You can take them with you and read them at your leisure back in your hotel, but check out the first few pages. The highlighted portions."

Saul obeys.

He reads the highlighted portions while Cromwell reads him.

He is called a genius. On page after page, in paragraph after highlighted paragraph, he reads the word "genius" attached to his name.

"Only a film-savvy genius like Saul Karoo could have taken . . ."

He is neither surprised nor pleased, nor displeased, nor proud, nor ashamed, that he is anointed a genius for what he did to the Old Man's work.

For reasons he can't explain and has no time to dwell upon, it simply seems inevitable that he should be considered a genius.

Everyone has become sick and tired of authentic geniuses. But a hack being an artist is fresh and new.

He looks up to see Cromwell looking back at him.

6

"Speaking of movies," Cromwell says in an apologetic way, as if admitting to a failure on his part to come up with a smoother transition to the business before them.

His apologetic intonation is totally countermanded by the little smile he's smiling, which says: Sometimes it's fun to be smooth and subtle in my transitions, at other times it's fun to be brutal. I feel like being brutal just now. I hope you don't mind, Doc.

He is sitting on top of the desk, his feet are off the floor, his hands are gripping the desktop. One of his hands, Saul observes, seems to be gripping the desktop harder than the other, causing one of his shoulders to dip lower than the other, creating a sense of distortion in the whole room.

"Speaking of movies," he says to Saul, and without looking, as if he knows the exact location of the yellow manila envelope behind him, he reaches back and brings it forward.

The smile he is smiling now spreads, causing the dimples in the corner of his mouth to deepen and curve.

Saul is so focused on every detail he sees that he is becoming disoriented by the details themselves. By the shape of Cromwell's fingers curled around the manila envelope. He never noticed before what long fingers Cromwell has. Long and soft and supple and seemingly boneless, like half-erect sexual organs.

"Speaking of movies," Cromwell says, holding up the yellow manila envelope, "have I got something here for you."

He puts the envelope down next to him and places his hand upon it. He pats it a couple of times, as if to indicate there is something of great meaning for Saul inside it.

And then he starts to speak.

## 7

"What's different about this project from all the others on which we've collaborated," Cromwell, perched atop his desk, goes on to say, "is that you'll be involved in it from the word go. You won't be called in to rewrite somebody else's script, because this time you will be the one who writes it.

"I know, I know." Cromwell gestures with his hands, as if deflecting Saul's objections in advance. "I know the role you like to play. Know it well. You like to pretend that you're nothing more than a high-priced hack who's happy the way he is. Who neither wants to write nor thinks he's capable of ever writing something of his own. It's a good act and you've done it well, but it's not worthy of you, and it hasn't fooled me for a second.

"Nor," he says, winking at Saul, "is it likely to ever fool anyone else again.

"Those reviews"—he gestures to the pages in Saul's lap—"that's just the beginning. When our movie opens this weekend, there are going to be many more reviews just like those. Even better. You're in for it in the next couple of weeks. You're going to be publicly exposed all around the country for being the brilliant artist that you are."

Saul knows that he's not an artist, brilliant or otherwise, but a part of him says, What do I know?

It's not that Cromwell's flattery is convincing him, but it's because there is an absence of all conviction in Saul himself.

Saul knows everything except what to do with what he knows.

## 8

"I have here a manuscript of a book," Cromwell tells him, lifting up his hand and then letting it fall on the yellow manila envelope next to him.

"A wonderful book," he says.

"It's a love story," he says.

"I think this book will be a national bestseller as soon as it comes out."

(He would be proven correct yet again. This book would sell over five hundred thousand copies in the first six months alone.)

"It's being rushed into print. It should be out in the fall of this year. The publishers are very high on it. Very high indeed.

"It's mine," he says. "I own it. I bought the movie rights to it with you in mind.

"It's a great story," he says.

"Not just a great love story, but a great story, period.

"I suppose," he says, letting his hand glide over the envelope, "you could call it a tragedy. A love tragedy. But then all the great love stories are. Or at least all the great love stories I've loved are tragedies.

"What it is," he says, "is an in-depth, book-length expansion of a magazine story . . ."

## 9

Saul felt the sickening shock of what Cromwell was talking about. What the story was and what the book was.

A grimace, as of pain, appeared on Saul's face.

Ignoring him completely, Cromwell went on.

"It's a great story," he said. "I couldn't put it down. Even though I knew ahead of time how it was all going to turn out in the end, I was still hooked. I really was."

Pausing, as if impressed that he had been so enraptured by something he had read, Cromwell then went on to tell Saul a little about the story itself.

The nature of the plot.

The characters who are caught up in it.

"It's a love triangle, is what it is," Cromwell told him.

He used all the real names (Leila, Billy, and Saul) and when he pronounced them, he did it in the proprietary way of someone who had read the book and was now talking to someone who hadn't.

Telling Saul all about Leila and Billy and Saul.

Sitting on top of his desk, his demeanor both businesslike and congenial, his legs dangling, the shoe of one foot rubbing against the shoe of the other as he talked, Cromwell went on to tell Saul all about it, as if Saul himself had not experienced a single moment of the events described.

Saul sat there, trying to summon some appropriate response to what Cromwell was doing to his life.

What he needed was outrage. But he seemed to be out of outrage. Most of it had been used up, spent here and there as the price of passage through his portion of the twentieth century.

The little he had left was so diluted that he ran the risk of appearing ridiculous if he tried to use it.

Even the shock he had experienced when he realized the kind of book they were discussing was slowly slipping away from him and giving way to the numbness normally associated with postshock syndrome.

From shock to postshock in a matter of minutes.

What efficiency, Saul thought. What economy. One on the heels of the other.

They formed a loop, shock and postshock, and the loop started spinning around in his mind. The faster it spun, the less distinction he could detect between the two.

It wasn't long before he was looking back at the moment he was in, as if it were in the past already.

As if time itself were on a loop, spinning around within the enclosed space and time of the year 1991.

## 10

Cromwell went on with the telling of the story of Leila and Billy and Saul.

He analyzed the relationships between Billy and Leila, Saul and Billy, Leila and Saul.

He delved into the nuances of character of each one of them.

He seemed to be saying that Saul might have a personal connection to the story being discussed but hadn't written the book that Cromwell had bought. Cromwell was therefore talking about something he owned to somebody who didn't.

Saul sat listening and not listening to Cromwell's enthusiastic exegesis of Billy and Leila and Saul.

His hands and feet were growing numb with cold.

His lower back hurt as if something there was breaking in half.

And, despite all his efforts at holding it in, something fluid and warm was escaping through his anus.

The incontinence of his aging body shamed him.

I'll be wearing diapers soon, he thought. A motherless old man wearing diapers.

The story that Cromwell was telling him (of Leila, Billy, and Saul) reminded him at times of events from his own life, stirred memories of Billy and Leila and himself.

The story he had lived and the story to which he was now listening were two different versions, but the fact that Saul had personally experienced one of them did not make that version the authoritative one.

In the atmosphere of Cromwell's office, it was becoming more and more unimportant which version of the two was authentic.

At some point, the whole point became which one worked better as a story.

In the book version, Leila was a brilliantly gifted actress just needing a big break.

Saul remembered a Leila with an enormous talent for living and none for acting.

The Old Man's film, in the book version, was a mess. Saul remembered a masterpiece.

By the end of the book, Saul was redeemed by the pain he suffered from the loss of the two people he had loved.

The real Saul, however, wasn't sure that he had ever loved anyone and therefore he saw no possibility of redemption for himself.

And yet he could not deny that he was slowly but surely coming to prefer the Cromwell version of the story. The Cromwell version hung together better, so much better, than the version he had lived.

Does the story work? That was the question.

His didn't. Cromwell's did.

In the book the redemption of Saul was banal, but Saul had to admit that he was not immune to the beauty of banality. Especially not if it eased the pain of being who he was.

Every now and then it occurred to him as he listened to Cromwell that Cromwell was fucking him out of something precious and irreplaceable.

A kind of colossal Oneness was slowly conflating everything in Saul's weary mind, and Cromwell seemed to be saying that the Oneness was the way to go.

"I'm the One," he seemed to be telling Saul.

"You'll have to admit," he seemed to be telling him, "that you no longer work as a human being. What counts is what works."

The monolithic Oneness in Cromwell, Saul had to admit, not only worked but gave every indication of working better than anything else on earth.

And the name of the Oneness was Nothingness.

Like a long-sought solution to a puzzle that had been so obvious that any child could have figured it out long ago, Saul finally realized who it was he was dealing with in the person of Jay Cromwell.

It was Nothingness.

Nothingness itself.

It was Nothingness he saw looking at him through Cromwell's hazel-blue eyes.

It had been there all along. Cromwell was not a man who hid anything. He left it to others to hide, to make what they wished of the Nothingness they saw.

The time, Saul thought, all that time I wasted trying to figure out the motives of this man. Who he was. Why he did what he did. What his purpose was in fucking people out of what was left of their short lives on this planet.

For nothing, that was why.

For nothing at all.

And what did Cromwell get out of it? Nothing.

Saul was sitting in a modest office in Burbank Studios, but sitting on top of a desk across from him was no longer a man but a process. It was like watching countercreation in the process of turning events, lives, stories, language itself, into Nothingness. It was like witnessing the Big Bang in reverse.

No, it was not death that Saul saw in Cromwell, for even death was an event. This was the beginning of the death of events themselves. This was a process that nullified both life and death and the distinction between the two.

The Nothingness smiled at Saul like an old friend.

The Hollywood hack in Saul recognized in the Nothingness before him the ultimate rewriter, the Doc of docs.

"I can fix you up," Dr. Nothingness said, smiling at him. "I can make you whole. I can take all the loose ends of your messy life and pull them together into a satisfying story line."

Cromwell, smiling his smile, hopped off the desk. Limber and loose and light of foot, he took a couple of steps and stopped. Closing his hand into a fist, he threw a straight, lightning-fast jab and then snapped back his arm to inspect the wristwatch on his wrist.

"Damn," he cursed cheerfully. "Always having to run. The traffic is probably still a nightmare, but I don't have a choice. There's a man I gotta see. I don't want to see him but see him I must.

"Ah-h," he sighed, full of despair, but delighting in the despair, "this is no way to live."

## I I

They took a right outside Cromwell's office and, walking side by side, set out down the long deserted corridor.

The yellow manila envelope that had been on top of Cromwell's desk was now in Saul's left hand. He had no idea when Cromwell had given it to him, nor did he remember taking it.

But it didn't bother Saul in the least to be carrying that manuscript.

He knew, he didn't know how he knew, but he knew, that he would not be involved in this project. It was a certainty so private that even he wasn't privy to its particulars.

Saul's number one priority at the moment was to get to a bathroom as quickly as possible and to hold back the torrent from gushing into his underwear until he got there.

There was a men's room at the opposite end of the corridor, on the other side of the elevator, but although he wanted to rush there, he was prevented from rushing by his very distress.

It had not been easy keeping his sphincter tight while sitting in the chair, but it was much harder to keep it tight while he walked and at the same time tried to preserve some semblance of dignity so that Cromwell would not suspect his disgraceful condition. And so he had to take small, mincing steps.

Cromwell talked as they left his office.

"There isn't an actress in Hollywood," he was telling Saul, "who doesn't want to play Leila. The agent of every superstar has called me already to relay his client's desire to be considered for the part. And this frenzy is happening before there is any screenplay, before the book has even been published. It's happening on the strength of the word that's out on the book. Can you imagine what . . ."

He went on.

Saul was listening and not listening. Although he knew that he would not be involved in this project, the thought of Leila's life being reduced to one more part in the career of some actress struck him as the final robbery of a woman who had been robbed of everything else in her life.

Oh, Leila, he thought.

When they reached the elevator, Cromwell thrust out his arm and jabbed the down button with his index finger. Saul, his sphincter weakening, excused himself and said that he had to go to the men's room.

Cromwell apologized for being unable to wait. He had to get going. He was in such a rush that he couldn't even wait for the elevator to arrive. He took the adjacent stairway instead.

"Call me when you've read the book and we'll talk," he shouted to Saul as he rushed down the stairway, relishing the rush that he was in.

## 12

Released by Cromwell's departure, Saul broke into an inelegant, tight-assed trot toward the men's room.

Trotting, running, skipping, hopping. The roots of his teeth, broken and unbroken, hurt from having to go so badly. Tears of agony welled in his eyes.

He could see by the sign on the door that he had made a mistake and was entering a ladies' room instead of a men's room, but it was too late to change course now. Some biological countdown had been triggered by his entrance and there was no aborting it.

What does it matter? he thought. There's nobody left in the building anyway.

He was in such a panic to sit on a toilet that the door of the stall confounded him when he tried to open it. Blinded by his distress, he couldn't figure out which way the door opened, in or out.

Needing both hands for the job, he tossed the yellow manila envelope over his head (it missed falling into the sink by an inch) and pushed and pulled and banged on the door until it opened. He hurled himself inside, pulling down his trousers and his underwear with the urgency of a man whose clothes are on fire.

He sat down panting, completely out of breath.

There was nothing left for him to do but let go. He let go.

The bliss of discharge caused his eyelids to flutter, and then he shut his eyes completely.

That was close, he thought. That was real close.

Whatever had been tense inside him was loosening, whatever had been tight was letting go, becoming easy and open. His shoulders sagged. The vertebrae in his neck, in his spinal column, which had felt welded together in Cromwell's office, now lengthened and stretched like Spandex. Eyes shut in bliss, he let his head roll forward.

That was close all right, he thought.

The fluid nature of his discharge, which he could both feel and hear, continued.

Must have been all those oat bran muffins I had for breakfast, he thought. And then a fruit salad for lunch. Too much roughage.

He yawned, feeling good, and then he yawned again, feeling even better.

One thing's for sure, he thought to himself. I'll sleep like a lamb tonight.

The toilet seat on which he was sitting was the most comfortable toilet seat he had ever sat on.

Its shape, or its proportions, he didn't know what it was, but there was just something about it.

This is what I've needed all along, he thought to himself. One of these toilet seats. And then during those long nights in my apartment, when I can't sleep, all I'll have to do is sit down on the toilet for a while and it'll be goodbye insomnia.

He made a mental note to get the brand name of the toilet seat before leaving the bathroom. If it turned out that it was manufactured only in Burbank and distributed locally, he could have one FedExed to New York. Or better yet, he could pick up one and take it back with him on the plane. Probably came in a discreet cardboard box. Fit it in the overhead bin.

He yawned again and opened his eyes.

The sight of all the blood in his underwear around his ankles puzzled him rather than galvanized him into any urgent action.

He looked at it in drowsy detachment.

Thank God it's blood and not crap, he thought, as if soiling his underclothes with blood were somehow a nobler category of incontinence.

He considered panicking. Under the circumstances (all that blood) he thought he had every right, if not a duty, to panic. But the problem with panicking was twofold. In the first place, it was as if he had used up whatever panic he had just getting to the bathroom in time. For the moment at least, he felt completely out of panic.

In the second place, and this was even more germane to the whole question, he was feeling good. He was feeling so good about something. And since it was such a rare thing to be feeling this good about anything, he considered it his right, if not his duty, to just go on and feel good for a while longer.

As if making a deal with himself, he thought, I'll panic later, in a few minutes.

Half-rising from the seat, elevating his rear and lowering his head, he peeked through the opening of his parted thighs and saw that the toilet bowl was full of blood. In addition to what was there already, he saw a thin but ongoing stream of blood issuing out of his anus and into the bowl.

He sat down again and flushed the toilet.

He hoped, but in a passive way, that the next time he looked into the bowl the water would not be nearly as bloody and that his anal bleeding, thanks to some hemostatic agent in his body, would be stopped.

But the next time he looked, the bowl was full of blood again and the thin flow of blood was still falling from his bottom into the bowl.

He decided not to look at the contents of the bowl anymore.

I could become compulsive about this if I don't stop, he admonished himself, yawning.

It felt so damn good to yawn.

Simply to breathe was a joy.

When he inhaled, he felt his whole chest expanding with ease. It was hard to tell which was more enjoyable, inhaling or exhaling.

I could just go on breathing, he thought.

## 13

He was feeling so good, good and sad, good and tired, but basically good, that he could consider the problem of his bleeding without the risk of ruining how he felt.

The way he saw it, although he was certainly not a doctor, was that he had sprung a leak somehow.

Some little blood vessel somewhere had ruptured.

A little vessel that he had been carrying inside his body was now carrying him away.

The image pleased him. The vessel and the voyager. The taking of turns of being one and then the other.

## 14

Out there, at the very edge of the horizon of his uncluttered mind, he saw a single sail.

He recognized it, as one does a memory, long before it was close enough to be recognized with the naked eye.

It was like seeing a distant rider on the plains in a western. Although he's far away, you can tell it's him, it's Shane, he's coming back. And the heart both constricts and expands at the prospect of this much longed-for but unanticipated reunion.

That was how it was with Saul as he watched the little sail coming toward him. It was as small as a cherry blossom petal, but growing larger.

Sailing toward him.

The image of the solar schooner had at one time inspired him to consider writing something of his own and, as such, it was a happy memory.

But at the same time it was the vessel of his unrealized longing, a reminder that he had not accomplished his task and, as such, it broke his heart, for it seemed to him now that his longing was destined to remain forever a longing.

A wave of weepy sentimentality for his (and everyone's) unrealized dreams swept over him.

He had a good cry over it and it made him feel better. Made him feel good again. Good and heartbroken. Good and scared. But basically good. He was feeling good about something again.

Something profound but simple seemed to be happening to him without, for once, any effort on his part. All that was required of him was to not get in the way.

New ideas for his Ulysses movie came to him. He had not a clue where all these wonderful new ideas were coming from.

He wished he had one of those little portable Olivetti typewriters and some paper, so that he could record the ideas for future use.

Even one of those stupid laptop things which he had never learned to use would have been nice to have right now.

But he didn't even have a ballpoint pen on him.

As a last resort, he hit upon an old device, used by men in ancient times. He would remember. He would remember it all.

"That's what I'll do," he said to himself. "And then I'll put it all down on paper first thing in the morning."

It felt so good finally to rid himself of all excuses for not getting down to work.

And so he began.

## 15

He started with the image of the solar schooner somewhere in space. Since there were no other objects around it in relation to which its speed could be gauged, the schooner seemed to be standing still, whereas, in fact, blown along by solar winds, it was hurtling through the space-time continuum at speeds approaching the speed of light.

On board the solar vessel was Ulysses.

He looked not so much like the Ulysses of old but like a Ulysses who had grown old. The mid-thigh tunic he was wearing, although made of royal cloth and trimmed with gold, was no longer flattering to his aged figure.

There was now a noticeable and unheroic paunch in his tunic.

Gone soft were his once well-shaped thighs. Gone the spring from his step.

His thinning hair was dry and brittle and streaked with gray. A scraggly, gray-streaked beard covered his wrinkled face.

The lonely look in his eyes was of a middle-aged wanderer who had lost much that he had loved and found very little to make up for it.

His teeth were still all his, but they were not all there. Some missing. Some chipped and broken.

When he peed, as he was doing now, it hurt to pee and the once powerful bull-like torrent was reduced to a series of intermittent dribbles.

Nor did it give him any pleasure, as it once had, to hold his prick in his hand. It was as if the thing he was holding and the hand that was holding it had both outlived their days.

His sleep, when he slept, was fretful, his dreams shallow, his nightmares full of regret. When he woke up, he did not feel refreshed, nor did he know for what purpose he was waking up.

It was as if the same wearisome day awaited the same old Ulysses.

When he paced his ship, as he was doing now, after peeing, a pain in his lower back hampered his movement. There was something lonely about the way he reached back to rub his nagging pain, as if there was no one left to rub it for him.

As indeed there wasn't.

The single most striking thing about seeing Ulysses pacing the deck of his solar schooner was that he was alone, passenger, captain, and crew all in one.

The once-famous warrior, wanderer, philanderer, the hero of the Achaeans, Ulysses, the king of Ithaca, could just as easily have been some King Lear of the cosmos without even a fool for company or the blessings of madness to take his mind away from the wrongs he had done.

Wrongs that could never be righted.

"Wherefore was I born?" he howled.

With nobody on board his ship to address this question to, he hurled it out into the space he was sailing through, with that combination of pathos and rage that sometimes accompanies the laments of old men and undermines their grandeur.

A close-up of Ulysses, the features of his face forming a mask of anguish and regret.

He remembered it all.

His wife Penelope, his son Telemachus, his home in Ithaca. It seemed only yesterday that he had been a happy man who could look forward to a peaceful old age in the bosom of his beloved family.

He remembered his return home after more than a decade of wandering. Dressed as an impostor, a homeless beggar. Seeing his son, a strapping young man now, whose growing-up years he had missed. How tall he was. How handsome. What shoulders he had. His beloved Telemachus.

The courage of his son, as they fought together side by side against the suitors, was all that any father could have asked for in a son.

The faithfulness of his lovely wife Penelope, in rejecting all those suitors for all those years, was all that any husband could have asked for in a wife.

He remembered their reunion. The three of them. The embraces. The kisses. The tears of joy of being together again.

But in the days that followed, something seemed not quite right to Ulysses.

Home again in Ithaca, he found himself feeling not so much unhappy as not as happy as he thought he would be to be back home again with his wife and son.

Something in the manner of Penelope and Telemachus cast a shadow on Ulysses' joy as a family man.

It was not a question of love. He loved them both with all his heart, and felt loved by both of them.

The problem was that he had loved them and longed for them both for so long that this loving in absentia had become a way of life, and a way of loving for him.

During all those years of absence, he had thought about them, dreamed and imagined scenes among the three of them. The level of intimacy he achieved in his imagination with his son and wife was astonishing for one so busy and absent from home for so long. But as often happens to family men, it seemed to Ulysses that the longer he stayed away from home, the closer he grew to his beloved family.

It was this closeness that was now the heart of the problem.

The closeness, the level of intimacy he experienced with his wife and son could not match the closeness he had imagined with them prior to his return.

At times he felt superfluous in their company.

He knew that they both loved him, but he could not help noticing that they loved each other more. That the intimacy between them was of a special kind.

What Ulysses wanted was what they had.

He knew, of course, that the love bond between a mother and her child was a special one, accepted as such by men and gods alike. He knew that he could not expect to achieve the same kind of effortless intimacy with either of them in a matter of weeks. It was wrong of him to demand, as he sometimes felt like doing, "I am back, so love me as if I had never been gone." He could not just drop in unannounced and expect to resume immediately where he had left off. He knew this. If he would just be patient . . .

But he lacked patience, as kings often do.

He wanted to hurry a process that could not be hurried.

He refused to accept the fact that he could not make up lost time. And so Ulysses, a crafty and daring king, came up with a crafty and daring plan.

There was, at the edge of their galaxy, a legendary confluence of the three mighty rivers of time where the past and the present flowed into and formed the future. If one sailed through the wormholes in space, it was neither a dangerous nor an overly taxing journey from Ithaca.

The confluence was a resort, a galactic spa of sorts, where those who could afford it went to discover the life they could have had if they had chosen a different course of action. The road not taken could be experienced there and incorporated alongside the road taken. It was the ultimate luxury of the superaffluent elite. Many became addicted to making this pilgrimage, spending their entire fortunes to live out every possible variation of their lives. Some visitors went mad due to the presence of so many parallel lives in their minds. Others, upon their return home, could not shake off a certain listlessness, a chronic disinclination toward action that stayed with them until their deaths.

Not all the side effects were extreme, but there was always some price to be paid after a trip to the confluence.

Ulysses, however, was undaunted. He had outwitted the Trojans, the

Cyclops, and even the gods themselves. He had heard the sirens singing and lived to tell about it.

An acute case of hubris was goading him on, telling him that he could outwit time as well without paying any price at all. Where lesser men had failed, he would triumph.

He would take his family to the confluence and there, in one fell swoop, he would rewrite his absent years. He would not just rewrite his own life but the life of his wife and son and make it appear that their lengthy separation had never taken place.

Despite Penelope's foreboding about the journey, despite the Delphic oracle's warnings, despite forecasts and reports of unprecedented galactic disturbances, Ulysses left Ithaca and set sail for the confluence with his wife and son and a crew of forty men.

Initially, they made steady progress. The solar winds were favorable, the sail full. Even when a storm hit, nothing about it seemed particularly alarming except its suddenness. It was as if the storm came from nowhere. And then, just as suddenly and inexplicably, it was gone.

The winds died down and then died out completely. The solar sail expired and hung limp from the long mast like a wedding veil. Everything was calm and serene while they waited for the winds to resume.

There was no warning. Nobody on board the ship heard it or saw it coming, because when it came, it came at a velocity exceeding, by an unimaginable factor of 18.6, the speed of light itself.

A tidal wave of time, ripped loose and set into motion by some incalculable force, was streaking across the universe. Ulysses' schooner was directly in its path.

The rest would have been history had not this tsunami of time traveled at such an apocalyptic speed that it precluded the possibility of any historical record being left behind.

Only Ulysses was left behind. All the others, his whole crew, his wife, his son, were swept away.

The wave moved at a speed exceeding the ability of the human mind even to record the memory of the event.

Only the calamitous inventory of consequences gave any indication that an event had occurred.

One nanosecond Penelope was, Telemachus was, and then they were no more. One nanosecond Ulysses was a king, a family man who was going to have it all, and then all was gone.

Grief-stricken, he howls. His grief becomes a rage. He claws at his face until it is covered with blood and scraps of skin hang in tatters from his fingernails.

But grieve as he might, he lacks the resources to find an expression for a grief that is commensurate with all that he has lost.

If madness could be had for the asking, he would plead for it.

Alone, all alone for the first time in his life, he sails back toward Ithaca, but, within eyesight of his kingdom, he realizes that there is no longer a home there for him. Not there, not anywhere else.

Homeless now, he sails on through space and time with only one aim in mind.

To find the gods.

To seek a reckoning with the gods themselves. To demand an answer from them: Did all this have to happen? Was it necessary that Penelope and Telemachus should die? Was it all a part of some divine plan? Or was it just chance in a random universe and the result of his own human pride and folly? He had to know.

"Wherefore?"

He sails on, looking for a passageway to Olympus, the abode of the gods, where no mortal has ever been. He wants a reckoning with Zeus himself.

He seeks information from the captains of the passing solar schooners he encounters and from the kings of the various kingdoms he passes in his journey. But none are of any help. They either do not know the way to Olympus or they refuse to provide him with the coordinates for the destination he seeks. His desire for a reckoning with the gods is seen by them all as the desire of a deranged apostate.

The word spreads about this homeless wanderer and soon no kingdom will even allow him to dock in its port for fear of retribution by the gods.

So he sails on alone. In the continual present of his mind the pain of loss lives on and the unanswered "Wherefore?" lives on and demands to be answered.

He encounters and traverses strange landscapes, mountain ranges of lapsed time, his schooner skipping from peak to peak, covering whole lifetimes in a matter of seconds, like a well-thrown rock skipping across a placid pond.

He skips across centuries and sees in passing the demise of the world he has known.

Gone.

Gone the kings and the kingdoms he has known. Gone Agamemnon and Menelaus. Gone the whole house of Atreus. Gone Hellas and Helen and Troy.

Gone as well are the empires that followed. Skipping across the time-lapse landscape, he no sooner sees an empire born than it's gone.

The Achaemids of Persia come and go. The last Darius falls to Alexander of Macedon and then Alexander falls. Gone Persia. Gone Macedon. Gone Roxane, the dark-eyed daughter of Darius, wife of Alexander the Great.

The great and the not-so-great and the anonymous come and go and are gone.

Rome rises, declines, and falls, and is gone.

The Age of This. The Age of That. Different ages come and go and no sooner do they come than they're gone.

And in every age, as in all the preceding ages and in all the ages that follow, it's bloodshed that brings down one age and causes another to rise. Millions die in the name of some name and then the name goes down in a sea of blood, but the butchery goes on in the name of some new name.

Countless crusades and endless corpses of the crucified.

"Why do we live like this?" Ulysses asks.

No answer comes. He scans the infinity of time and space, looking for some telltale sign of a trail to God.

It is no longer his gods of old that he seeks to answer his questions. It is God the Creator.

All the gods he knew as a boy, as a man, are now long gone.

Gone Zeus and Poseidon and Pallas Athena, the goddess of the flashing eyes who watched over him. Gone Hermes and Apollo and Artemis and Olympus itself, where the gods dwelled and charted the destinies of men.

Gone the gods and the men who believed in them.

Everything, even the immortals, comes and goes and is gone, but the butchery and the bloodshed continue.

The wine-dark seas of poetry, Ulysses now sees, are seas of blood.

Nor can he deny that a ghastly measure of that blood was spilled by him.

All those men he slaughtered beneath the walls of Troy, and for what? For Helen? For Menelaus? For Agamemnon? For the glory of Hellas? No, for nothing. It was all for nothing.

Even butchered cattle, he thinks, are put to better use than the use-less slaughtered men.

He sails on through black holes and wormholes and loopholes in space, looking for God.

He ages, and although his aging is but a pittance compared to the eons he traverses, he does age. His hair, what little wisps of it remain, is all white now. His teeth are gone. Wrinkles like dry riverbeds cover his face. His eyes have receded in their sockets as if pushed back by all the horror he has seen.

Gone now are his crafty ways and his famous nimble mind that out-witted everyone, himself included. In their place, perhaps as a recom-pense for all that he has lost, is a tiny scrap of wisdom, no bigger than a handout a beggar gets. But as tiny as that scrap of wisdom is, it suffices to illuminate the life of a fool.

"I had it all," he rages, "and I had it all just by being born. I was born alive in a world full of life. Wherefore, then, did I not cherish and love it all?"

"Oh, you fool," he says to himself. "You miserable fool, the miracle of life was wasted on you."

His wife, his son, any man, woman, or child, what he would not give for the privilege of loving them. He could now consume the rest of his days in the loving of a single living flower.

His heart aches to love, but there is nothing alive aboard his schooner except for himself. So out of desperation, Ulysses takes his right hand with his left and, clutching it to his bosom, he loves it.

Like some old grandfather cherishing an infant placed in his care, Ulysses rocks his living hand and sails on, looking for God.

He sails into vast dead-end tunnels of time and then sails out again and sails on.

There are no sea charts for the destination he seeks, nor are there stars pointing the way to God.

He starts to feel lost.

There are times when it seems to him that the space-time continuum he has been sailing through has split in two, and that he is now travel-ing through time alone, or space alone, he doesn't know which, and has no way of finding out.

His spirit, like his sinews, begins to grow slack. He is just a little old homeless man lost in the universe, clutching his own hand for company.

And then, on an unusually depressing day (or night), when his thoughts are at their gloomy worst, he hears music streaming toward him through the darkness of space (or time). The music he hears is of such sweetness that he assumes it to be a hallucination of his demented mind.

But then, peering into space with his myopic eyes, he discerns blinking lights in the distant darkness, and the blinking lights seem to be blinking to the sweet music that he hears.

Standing stoop-shouldered at the helm, Ulysses steers his schooner toward the source of the music and feels his sagging spirit rise again. The melody is streaming past him like a gentle spring breeze (he remembers those breezes coming off the Aegean Sea) while the deeper undertones are pulling him tidelike toward the blinking lights.

He is in rapture. He thinks he is hearing the music of the spheres.

The lights beckon like a cosmic oasis with living trees bearing blinking lights for fruit. The closer he gets to them, the sweeter the music he hears. He thinks he is nearing Paradise. He thinks he is hearing angels singing.

He sails into the lights and is enveloped by music from all sides.

It is only now, seeing in horror their strobe-lit smiles and the flickering outlines of their naked breasts, that Ulysses realizes that he has been tricked by the Banalities.

They seem to be everywhere, in front, back, on both sides of his vessel, their ravishing lips parting to make music and song, their ravishing arms, moving like silken scarves, trembling with desire to press him to their naked breasts.

"Oh, lonely wanderer," they sing, "wander no more . . ."

He had outwitted the Sirens by having his crewmen tie him to the mast. He alone of all men heard the Sirens sing and lived to tell about it. But he is alone now. There is nobody to help him, nor does he have his nimble wits to assist him. If he is to survive and continue his journey, it must be done by his will alone.

But his willpower is sorely taxed by the beautiful Banalities, creatures that are half bathing beauties, half nothingness, but so alluring in appearance that he cannot tell which half is which. And their voices are of such tormenting sweetness as to put the songs of the Sirens to shame.

"Homeless believer," they sing to him, "find your home . . ."

The song tugs at his heart, as only a song sung by the Banalities can tug at it. His old heart feels like an anchor that he would gladly drop then and there. But he knows it's a trap.

His willpower ebbing, desperate to escape before he succumbs, Ulysses steers wildly, looking for a way out. Whichever way he sails, the nubile Banalities sail right along with him, the beaming beauty of their eyes blinding him, the insinuating sweetness of their singing sapping his resolve.

"I must find God," he shouts at the top of his lungs, but he hears a note of doubt in his voice, as of someone who is no longer certain.

The comely Banalities detect his uncertainty and turn it into another song.

"God is dead," they sing to him. "There are no gods in the universe. There is only man and there is no man like godlike Ulysses . . ."

They sing, savoring the sibilants in his name, kissing him with its sound all over his body. Their eyes beam images of his once-youthful figure in all its glory and superimpose it on his aged form. He is made to seem and feel desirable again, a warrior king capable of satisfying many women and fathering many sons.

They sing his name as if in ravenous hunger for his sex.

In the reflection from their eyes, he sees himself mating with them all, one after another, sees his sons being born, sees himself in their midst, adored and beloved by them all.

"No," he cries out in despair, like someone tormented by an irresistible temptation that he must nevertheless find a way to resist. "It is not new sons that I need. I need to know why I did not love the living son that I had. Wherefore did I not love my one and only child? I need to know why I was born and why I lived the way I did."

"For nothing," the ravishing Banalities sing in reply. Their song is like a love song and a hymn and a lullaby. They sing it in three-part harmony and with such sweet piety that their "For nothing" seems both right and true. As if only in nothingness is the nirvana where all his questions will be answered once and for all.

"No," he cries out in his old man's voice, "a thousand times no. Man was not made for nothing. Not even I."

If resistance were a passing necessity, all would be fine, but it's not. The persistence of their temptation requires a persistence of resistance and he feels himself succumbing. They are whittling away at him with their song, telling him not only that it is foolish to resist but reminding him (in song) that there is nobody here even to admire his resistance. No witnesses of any kind to pass on the tale of his struggle. No Homer to make an epic of his deeds. It's all for nothing, they sing to him, nobody will ever know.

"In the ever-present present of my living mind there is still an I of whom I am aware, and it suffices that I will know," he tells them.

It is not exactly a crushing rebuttal, and he knows it, and sees that they are not crushed by it. They seem amused. All reason and logic are on the side of the Banalities in this argument, but Ulysses is an old man and old men sometimes feel put upon by reason and logic and become unreasonable out of pure spite, like little children.

His temper tantrum (which follows) is not worthy of the high-minded debate they're having, but he doesn't care. He screams. He cries. He stomps his feet and flails his arms. He's had enough. He's too old for this. He wants to go home.

"I am who I am and that's that," he screams at them and keeps on screaming until his face becomes purple. He will not argue with them anymore. There is nothing left to discuss. He was who he was and that was that.

Rickety-legged and shaking all over, Ulysses hurls obscenities at them and steers his vessel without regard for the direction he's taking, so long as it leads him out of there.

Which it eventually does.

He's so worked up, however, that even when the lair of the Banalities is well behind him, he keeps on hurling invectives at them and calling them names.

Gradually, despite himself, he calms down and resumes his search for God.

But with the return of calmness, loneliness also returns, which the Banalities had dispelled for a while.

He starts to miss them, as voyagers often miss the obstacles of their journeys.

He saw his last star some time ago and there are no longer any stars to be seen, or distant comets, or heavenly bodies of any kind.

In the space-time continuum through which he is traveling in search of God, there is nothing to be seen or heard anymore. There is only a void and no way of knowing if the void through which he's wandering is one of limits or limitless. It just goes on and on. There is no end in sight. There is nothing in sight. His only consolation is that it is not nothingness. It is a void, yes, but the void itself is something and he takes it on faith, as he must, that he is moving through it toward some other something, toward God.

His one and only consolation begins to wear thin, however, and then wears out completely, leaving him in the void without any consolation at all.

When it's night, the void is dark, and when it's day, the light of the day illuminates a void without boundaries or limits or anything within it to rest his eye upon.

The schooner in which he is sailing does not even cast a shadow, for there is nothing in the void to cast a shadow upon.

A single blade of grass would now seem to him like a landscape worthy of being called paradise.

He sails on, but he has no way of ascertaining if he is moving, because in the void he's in there is nothing to move past nor anything, however fleeting, to move past him.

There is only the time-space continuum, but even the certainty of that begins to wane. For all he knows, the time-space continuum was discontinued a long time ago without his noticing.

Alone in his schooner, he starts to feel like a sketch somebody made and left unfinished, of an old man in a schooner. A picture hanging in the void.

His only hope is God, but even that hope turns against him, because for all he knows, the void that he is in is God.

For all he knows, he has found Him.

He does not dare call out to God as once he did so freely, because a dread accompanies the impulse to call out to Him and makes him refrain. The dread is that God might answer and validate by His reply that He is indeed the void. Slack-jawed in terror of this possibility, Ulysses dares not even whisper His name.

What little faith he has left that God is not the void is a faith so small and fragile that Ulysses endeavors to hide his faith even from God.

He was once a mighty king with a kingdom, he was once a father and a husband, and now he is reduced to this. He is a rickety old man with little faith. But he clings to it.

He sails on, seeing nothing and feeling unseen by anyone. His loneliness grows out of all proportion to the tiny size of the human vessel called Ulysses in whom this ocean of loneliness resides.

Without convictions or scheme he sails on, on faith alone.

There is no true north in the outermost reaches of the universe, no north of any kind, or south, or east, or west. There is no up or down. No things that loom on the horizon. No horizon for that matter. There is only the void and a voyager within it.

There are no corners to turn in this void, or bends to go around that reveal a vision or a vista. Therefore it is not only next to impossible but entirely impossible to convey the manner in which Ulysses suddenly sees God the Creator.

Even "suddenly" is an inaccurate way to describe it. When Ulysses sees God, the only thing that's sudden is his own realization that he has been seeing Him for a long time.

There is no meeting as such between Ulysses and God. No kneeling, no handshakes or embraces. There is not even the dropping of the anchor, as if Ulysses, after all his wandering, has finally reached his final destination and can henceforth rest in bliss in the kingdom of God.

There is, Ulysses sees, no such kingdom. The God he sees is not a king who reigns or presides. The God he sees is a working God. He is God the Creator and Ulysses sees Him and continues to see Him in the act of creation.

He sees God hurling Himself from the outermost edge of existence into the nothingness beyond, plowing into that nothingness like a living plowshare and causing more time and space to be born. Over and over again, the Creator hurls, and keeps on hurling Himself, into nothingness. There is every reason to believe that this is an endless process.

Ulysses sails on after Him, in the wake of new worlds being born.

Sometimes it seems to him that God's joy of creation is so great, and His love for what He does so all-consuming, that He doesn't even notice Ulysses sailing along in His wake.

At other times, right now, for example, he worries that all of creation is a cosmic wheel and that all that God creates turns into nothingness and comes around again, so that God has to begin at the beginning and create time and space and life all over again. Over and over again.

When he prays, Ulysses no longer prays to God but rather for God to live on, so that nothingness will not have the final word.

The little faith Ulysses had, and to which he clung with maniacal desperation, is now completely gone. He has no need of faith anymore, be it large or small. In its place is an effortless kind of love for anything that lives. A love without motive of any kind.

He sees the living God plowing into the nothingness and pushing it back with creation. In addition to time and space being born, Ulysses sometimes sees, like an ocean of sparks from a forge, an ocean of subatomic particles streaming out of the nothingness and streaming past him on all sides. In those particles Ulysses sees the flora and the fauna of the subatomic world. Each little particle, he sees, is alive.

But all is not as Ulysses thought it would be when he set out to look for God. He was sure that finding God would be an answer to all his questions. It's not.

His question as to why he lived the way he did remains unanswered.

The great "Wherefore?" is still with him.

So is the pain for all the many crimes he committed.

He had hoped that God would make this pain go away once and for all, but now discovers that there is no such thing as once and for all.

Amends, he discovers, cannot be made.

Love as he might, and love as he does, he now knows that not a single moment of unlove can ever be made up.

Not ever.

Nor can he bridge the gap that separates him from God. He sails on through created time and space, but God the Creator is always ahead, always creating more, and the distance can never be bridged.

And so Ulysses sails on, following God, with no hope of ever catching up to Him, or ever reaching a place called home.

He doesn't know what course he's on, but he does know that he's not lost in the universe.

Every now and then he prays:

"Blessed be anything that lives. Father, mother, brothers, sisters, children of the earth, blessed be your very lives, for they are the joy of the world."

And then he sails on.

# John Dufresne

# LOVE WARPS THE MIND A LITTLE

'Powerful and moving'
Fay Weldon, *Mail on Sunday*

Love and life are trick matters for Lafayette Proulx: kicked out
by his wife of fifteen years, his mistress, Judi temporarily puts
him and his dog up while he embarks on writing the Great
American Novel. Futile marriage counselling, Judi's dysfunctional white-trash family and a steady stream of rejection letters
are starting to wear him down – but when Judi gets sick, Laf's
life gets serious and the knockabout farce becomes a dark but
redemptive tragedy.

'This is a most extraordinary novel pretending to be ordinary:
Dufresne takes mighty matters of life, death, love and redemption, then sets the book in the trailer-park land of Florida and
gives it a cutesy title. The result is powerful and moving'
Fay Weldon, *Mail on Sunday*

'If Amis's *The Information* had been written by a Southern red-
neck, the result might read something like this. The book's
comedy is one of delicious self-loathing, a saga of petty malice
and everyday misanthropy that celebrates the farcical nature
of failure'
*Arena*

VINTAGE

# Kurt Vonnegut

# TIMEQUAKE

'Utterly original...capable of moving from irony to lament within a sentence'
*Guardian*

Kilgore Trout, science fiction writer and Vonnegut's alter ego, predicts a global timequake will occur in New York City on 13 February, 2001. It is the moment when the universe suffers a crisis of conscience. Should it expand or make a great big bang? For whatever cosmic reason, it decides to back up a decade to 1991, making everyone in the world endure ten years of *déjà-vu* and a total loss of free will – not to mention reliving every nanosecond of one of the tawdriest and most hollow decades.

In 1996, dead centre of the 'rerun', Vonnegut is wrestling again with *Timequake 1*, a book he couldn't write the first time and won't be able to now. As he struggles, he addresses, with his trademark wicked wit, the relationship between memory and *déjà-vu,* humanism, suicide, the Great Depression and World War Two as the last generational character builders, the loss of American eloquence, the obsolescent thrill of reading books, and what 'extended family' really means.

'Fascinating digressions, epidemics, and memories, vitalised by Vonnegut's irrepressible intelligence and comic imagination, creating a movingly intimate work'
Jason Thompson, *Harpers & Queen*

VINTAGE

## A SELECTED LIST OF CONTEMPORARY FICTION
## AVAILABLE IN VINTAGE

| | | | |
|---|---|---|---|
| ☐ | THE DUMB HOUSE | John Burnside | £5.99 |
| ☐ | CANDY | Luke Davies | £5.99 |
| ☐ | LOVE WARPS THE MIND A LITTLE | John Dufresne | £6.99 |
| ☐ | A SKIN DIARY | John Fuller | £5.99 |
| ☐ | THE FOLDING STAR | Alan Hollinghurst | £6.99 |
| ☐ | THE CONVERSATIONS AT CURLOW CREEK | David Malouf | £5.99 |
| ☐ | THE GIANT'S HOUSE | Elizabeth McCracken | £5.99 |
| ☐ | ENDURING LOVE | Ian McEwan | £6.99 |
| ☐ | BELOVED | Toni Morrison | £6.99 |
| ☐ | TAR BABY | Toni Morrison | £6.99 |
| ☐ | TIMEQUAKE | Kurt Vonnegut | £5.99 |
| ☐ | THESE DEMENTED LANDS | Alan Warner | £6.99 |

---

- All Vintage books are available through mail order or from your local bookshop.

- Please send cheque/eurocheque/postal order (sterling only), Access, Visa, Mastercard, Diners Card, Switch or Amex:

☐☐☐☐☐☐☐☐☐☐☐☐☐☐☐☐

Expiry Date:_____Signature:_____

Please allow 75 pence per book for post and packing U.K.
Overseas customers please allow £1.00 per copy for post and packing.

**ALL ORDERS TO:**
Vintage Books, Books by Post, TBS Limited, The Book Service,
Colchester Road, Frating Green, Colchester, Essex CO7 7DW

NAME:_____

ADDRESS:_____

_____

_____

---

Please allow 28 days for delivery. Please tick box if you do not          ☐
wish to receive any additional information

Prices and availability subject to change without notice.